Thelvyn warned the others to be ready for anything, and they proceeded more slowly. At almost that very moment, a wind as cold as ice rushed down the steep pass into their faces. The black clouds swirled, and a face larger and more terrifying than any they had yet seen appeared before them. The horses screamed and reared in terror. Thelvyn dared not even look at that monstrous face directly, for only the briefest glance was immensely unsettling, leaving him with confused visions of a gaping mouth filled with dripping fangs, sur-rounded by writhing tentacles, and great bulging eyes that slowly wept a sickly green fluid.

THE DRAGONLORD CHRONICLES

Thorarinn Gunnarsson

Dragonlord of Mystara

Dragonking of Mystara
July 1995

Great One of Mystara
Summer 1996

Mystara™ BOOKS

**BOOK ONE:
THE DRAGONLORD
CHRONICLES**

Dragonlord
of Mystara

Thorarinn Gunnarsson

To the memory of Ayrton Senna da Silva
1960-1994

To the heroes who prove, by the events of their lives
and sometimes their deaths,
that some dreams are worthy of any price
and bring adventure back to a world
without knights in armor.

PROLOGUE

There indeed was a tale, told in words to inspire the adventurous heart to overflowing with the glories and the sorrows of the mighty deeds of those elder days. These were the events that echo through the long corridors of history to shake the silent tombs of honored kings and the very foundations of nations, as familiar in the memories of some as their waking lives, to others all but lost and forgotten in the dust of ages. Here began the Age of Dragons, when that most ancient of races awoke from its long dream of death to find that it was wise and strong.

It all began on a night when the mountains and valleys of the Highlands slept beneath the first snow of winter. Winter was long and came early to this northern land. The nights themselves were deep and deathly cold.

On the evening our tale began, the sun set early behind the ridges and peaks to the west, spreading a false twilight as the mountains cast their long shadows across the valleys and the hills beyond. To the north stood the dark, silent shapes of greater mountains yet, beyond the farthest settlement, where no men dwelled nor indeed often ventured. These were wild lands that still belonged to themselves and to the dark and fearful creatures that were rumored to haunt them. From the north that evening came a wind of bitter cold, sometimes shaking a light cascade of snow from the laden branches of the pines.

None would journey in the wild at such time by choice, but that evening there were four travelers in the heights. The snow had come unexpectedly early that year, and so the forester, Kaarstel, had gone up that day to the mines in the lower slopes of the mountains to fetch the miner and his sons back to the village, for fear that they might become trapped if the snows closed the steep trails. Although the night was clear and bitterly cold, snow could come again at any time.

As it happened, the miner and his two sons had been hard at work in the depths of their longest shaft, living and working in the darkness, with no thought of the weather outside. They had been quite surprised when Kaarstel had turned up to rescue them, unaware that they were in need of being rescued. And so they closed up their mine and their cabin and followed the forester down the trails from the heights, even though they would not be getting back to the village until after dark.

They were of the Flaem, an ancient race with a glorious past, now living in exile in a strange land, a quiet and hard-working folk desperate to build their future into the likeness of their past—which explained the dedication of the miner and his sons to their task. The Flaem had first come into the northern frontiers of the Highlands only eighty years or so earlier, when the forester had been a young man. It remained a wild and unfamiliar land even to those who had lived here all their lives.

They were generally a very cautious folk, for they were very much on their own, with little protection. The duke's army in this region was measured not in companies but in small garrisons, and such wizards as they had were mostly self-taught. Goblins were known to be in the mountains to the north, and dragons were often seen as they soared above the mountain heights like immense eagles riding the winds. But the settlers had so far been left mostly alone, and for that they considered themselves lucky.

The travelers did not care to find themselves out in the wild by night if they could help it. The forester's job was mostly to keep folk from straying into the woods and to fetch them back out again when they did. The people of the village held him in respect and a certain awe because he had been going into the woods for many years and he always returned safely, which was less remarkable than they seemed to think. But on that particular evening, he was not especially concerned. While it was a long way down to the village from the mines, this land was less wild than it seemed, with the farms and pastures just below. The various evil creatures, which were rare enough, would be kept confined to their lairs by the snow.

A sudden crack of thunder broke somewhere in the heights just behind the travelers, echoing through the hills and ridges. Kaarstel stopped where he was, there on a steep and rough portion of the trail, and he indicated for his companions to keep absolutely still while he quickly looked around. The evening sky was growing dark, and the first stars had appeared, but there was not a cloud to be seen except for a few windswept banks hugging the mountains to the north. Nor was there any sustained rumble or plume of white in any of the higher valleys to suggest an avalanche. The forester thought that perhaps it had been a small rockslide somewhere just above, hardly more than a shift of massive boulders. Then they all saw a flash, like golden light, in one of the wide ravines above, not two miles from where they stood.

In the next moment, the form of a dragon, black against the evening sky, came hurtling down from the ravine. They wondered briefly if they were about to die. Then the dragon lifted, rising in a wide circle with the slow beat of his wings, and dived back into the ravine. Almost immediately there followed another flash of golden light and a rumble of thunder.

"A dragon," one of the miner's sons said in fearful wonder.

"No concern of ours," Kaarstel said matter-of-factly. "That old fellow is just out hunting. He won't bother us.

Dragons aren't animals, you know. Actually they're quite intelligent. They don't eat raw meat if they can help it. The ones that have flame use it to hunt, which not only brings down their prey but cooks it at the same time. They prefer elk."

"You seem to know a good deal about dragons," the miner observed.

"I lived in the south when I was young, near the settlements of the elves," he said. "They taught me much of what I know."

"Elves?" the miner's eldest son said disdainfully. "What do elves know?"

"They know a good deal about this land," the forester told him. The Flaemish settlers got along well enough with the elves who shared the same land, but most folk didn't know the elves well and thought them pale, fragile creatures. They never suspected that the elves held an equally low opinion of them.

However, not one dragon but an entire pack hunted the heights that night. This fact became fearfully obvious as the flashes of dragonfire continued, often in rapid succession, while the thunder of the attack echoed like a summer storm through the range. The dragons circled the ravine, sometimes four or five together. The forester began to think that perhaps the dragons were fighting, apparently not among themselves but with something on the ground, or else they were looking for something and desperate enough to use any means to find it. Moreover, their attack seemed to be moving along the ravine. Soon it would be out on the open mountainside. If the dragons were that desperate, they might attack anything that moved in the rapidly diminishing light.

"I'm not greatly worried, since they are still a long way off, but I think we should get down from this mountain with all due haste," Kaarstel told the others.

"Should we head straight down the slope?" the miner asked. "If we follow the trail, it will be taking us closer to the ravine. If we go straight down, at least we would be hidden among the boulders."

The forester shook his head. "They seem to be looking

for something, and I don't want that to include us. We will make far better time on the trail under any circumstances. With any luck, we can be well down the slope before they come near."

They hurried along, all but running when the trail was flat enough to permit it, but all too often they were clambering between great boulders. This was no road, although it was the only trail leading up to the mines in the lower slopes. As such, it had to provide reasonable passage to horses with heavy packs when traders came up from the village. For that reason, the trail switched back on itself and circled wide around the more formidable obstacles.

They all felt somewhat safer when they left the open hillside and reached the trees. The dragons were no longer attacking as often as they had, and the blasts of golden flame and reports like thunder had lessened, but they hadn't ceased. Now the great beasts could be seen searching the outside faces of the upper slopes, circling back and forth hardly a mile above the travelers. Sometimes, when one of the dragons made an especially wide turn, it would come directly over the trail, and all they could do was stay hidden beneath the trees until it had passed.

Now that the dragons were moving out in the open, it was daunting to see just how many there were. There were at least a dozen. Often one of them would come in low to aim a jet of flame into some deep, hidden place among the stones, and in the flash of the flames, the forester could see that they were red dragons, a breed with a fearful reputation. Reds, greens, and blacks were the marauders, the dragons most given to violent ways, although that didn't mean that they were necessarily evil. The elves had told the forester that the gold dragons were noble and wise, and the whites and blues were peaceful unless crossed, although all dragons could be fierce, haughty, and dangerous if provoked. But he couldn't imagine what they could be looking for with such determination.

Kaarstel paused, for he had seen something moving in the rocks above them, suddenly illuminated in a flash of flame. He stopped and stared hard. He wasn't entirely sure what he had seen, and he wondered if perhaps it had only been some wild animal fleeing the destruction above. Then he happened to be looking in just the right place at the next flicker of light, and he saw her standing there in the shadows, clinging to the snow-covered boulders perhaps a hundred yards above them. She was a tall, slender woman, perhaps elven, judging by her dress, although any lean figure in a hooded cloak might have been mistaken for an elf in this light.

And yet it seemed inconceivable—a lone woman coming down from the mountain wilderness in winter, pursued by dragons. The forester paused. His first inclination was to rush to her assistance, but this was checked by caution. She was the object of a determined hunt by a dozen dragons apparently seeking to slay her, and he couldn't take such a danger back to the village. He glanced briefly over his shoulder, where the lights of Graez glittered in the cold air not five miles away. The dragons were searching well up the slope, apparently in the belief that she was still several hundred yards higher. Perhaps he could get her down to the trail without being seen.

"You stay here. Don't move," he told his companions. "I'm going to get her down from there."

He knew that it would take some time, for this was a steep part of the slope, rising almost like a wall above the trail and piled high with huge boulders. The strange woman had stopped near the top of the steep slope, seemingly at a loss to find a way down, although she may also have been injured or weary. The forester knew in a moment that he could find a way up that slope, and he felt certain he could get her back down again easily enough. The boulders offered hiding places in deep shadows, and that was most welcome, for there were few trees.

Moving stealthfully, he almost startled her as he came upon her out of the darkness, and she turned toward him sharply, in a way that made him keep his distance. Her leather clothing and her cloak argued against her being an elf. Also, she was of no elven breed that he had ever heard of, for she was taller than he. Nor did she seem especially pale, although her black hair and dark eyes suggested that she wasn't of the Flaemish race either. There was a great sense of native nobility about her, bolder and more hearty than he would have associated with elves. Her clothes were singed from the dragonflame, although she seemed otherwise unharmed.

Still, she bore herself as if she were indeed injured or perhaps at the end of her strength, either of which seemed likely enough. Then the forester saw that she was indeed pregnant. She spoke to him briefly, her voice clear and noble, but in words that he couldn't begin to understand.

He shook his head. "I don't know your language."

She shook her own head, obviously not recognizing his language in turn. He took her hand to begin helping her down through the snow-covered boulders, and she seemed willing to go with him. Perhaps she had found some new reserve of strength now that she knew help was at hand, for she made her way down the treacherous slope quickly and without complaint.

The descent seemed to sap her failing strength, however, and only her determination kept her standing once they started down the trail toward the village. Although she bore no sign of injury, there was no question that her dire condition was due to more than just exhaustion. Kaarstel came to fear for her very life if she ever stopped running long enough to realize that she was in a desperate state. Fortunately the miner's sons were big strapping lads, and they were able to take turns helping her along the forest path.

When the forester looked back some minutes later, he was encouraged to see that the dragons had given up their attack and were conducting a meticulous search of the more accessible ravines and valleys leading south along the mountains. He was greatly relieved, since his act of charity seemed unlikely to bring danger to the village.

The forester had failed to consider that the folk in the village had seen the flames and heard the thunder of the dragons' attack. When Kaarstel came to a hill where he could see the distant cluster of houses through a break in the trees, he saw that the entire village was ablaze with lights, and a line of torches was moving swiftly up the road in his direction. It had to be the small garrison from the village, and probably every stout man the mayor was able to find as well.

That was not a wise response to the presence of dragons, especially when a whole flight of the great beasts was lighting up the ridges with their fires, but the forester wasn't surprised. The Flaem were a calm, practical, and determined lot, but they could also be brave and fierce if necessary, not unlike the dwarves. Possibly just the sight of the locals turning out in force had encouraged the dragons to seek their prey farther down the range.

Once the travelers came to the road, Kaarstel had the miner's sons set the lady down to rest. She looked more weary than ever, and she was breathing hard. Suddenly the forester had the uncomfortable thought that she might be about to have her child. He saw that the villagers would be there in a minute or so, and she would no longer be his responsibility. The mysterious lady tried to rise as the villagers approached, and Kaarstel hurried to assist her.

The garrison soldiers rode up a moment later, and Mayor Aalsten was among them, wearing his stiff leather armor. He stopped before the forester and dropped down from his saddle. "We took stock and found that you were missing, so we suspected that the dragons must be after you."

"I'm not worth the effort," Kaarstel said impatiently. "This lady does not speak our language, but she is not well, and I fear that she is about to have her child. I believe that we should get her to the village at once."

"I daresay," the mayor agreed. "We will take her to my house. But I hope that we can find someone who has a language in common with her, since I would very much like to know why a band of dragons is chasing her across the mountains in the middle of winter. Aside from simple curiosity, our safety might depend upon it."

The strange lady proved too weak to ride, and the soldiers cut branches to make a litter for her. While they worked, the mayor and the forester went to the top of the hill to have a look toward the mountains. Dusk had since deepened into night, and the heights were a jagged black wall rising abov them into the darkness. If the dragons were anywhere near, they were not to be seen. At least that terrible danger had passed for now, and with any luck, the dragons would not return.

*   *   *   *   *

For Sir George Kirbey, it had been just another comfortable evening at home, mainly because he had been too involved with a book and a bottle of cherry liqueur to notice anything outside his own door. It was a shame, since he didn't get to see dragons nearly as often as he would have liked. He was actually quite fond of dragons, and he knew more about them than nearly anyone, certainly anyone in the village. There had been a time when he had known dragons very well, and he had even counted one or two among his friends, but he had been out of touch for a longer time than he cared to admit.

Of course, he kept that very much to himself. For one thing, most folks weren't likely to believe an old man who claimed to have dragons for friends. And even if they did believe him, people who were friendly with dragons tended not to be very popular with other people, most of whom spent more time worrying about dragons than they should. Sir George was full of secrets that he kept very much to himself, a fact that helped preserve his relations with his neighbors.

Sir George got along well with nearly everyone. In fact, he had made something of a business of getting along with people, for he had discovered long ago that if everyone liked him and he was generally honest and dependable, then everyone was likely to trade with him. Sir George called himself an old man, and he could, if he wished, look the part. He was large and solid and powerfully built, but he wasn't fat, and indeed he could be tremendously strong and quite spry. He had a round face and bright eyes and a great nose like the beak of hawk, so that he looked rather disarming and friendly, the sort of a character that most people couldn't help but like. Farmers and smiths and craftsmen loved and respected him, and he was quite at home sharing an ale or a wild country dance with them, but he could also be as civil and urbane as a southern lord.

Everyone called him Sir George because that was what he called himself, and it seemed to fit. When asked about his past, he would say only that he had once been Sir George Kirbey, a Knight of the Order of the Roads in Darokin, and that he had retired some years ago after being wounded in combat. Sir George was indeed missing his left hand, although he always wore a leather cuff strapped tight to his arm, to which he could attach any number of tools and weapons. These, he said, had been made for him by the master craftsmen of the dwarves of Dengar in faraway Rockhome.

People did not doubt him, although they weren't so sure when he said he was now a traveling merchant who had come north to trade on the frontier. For one thing, although he was comfortably wealthy, no one in the village actually seemed to do business with him. He was away much of the time, often with strange warriors and wizards he called his friends, and the villagers thought privately that he must be an adventurer. But he was so generally well liked and respected that the matter of his profession was politely ignored.

What the villagers did know about Sir George was that he was a wise and kindly man, and so well traveled that he seemed as knowledgeable of the world as a wizard. So it was that, when they found themselves with a matter on their hands that they didn't understand, they immediately sent for him. Someone came knocking on his door late that night. He set aside his book and downed his remaining cherry liqueur, then went to see who it was. At the door, he found the Kaarstel, the forester, looking very excited.

"Sir George, the mayor was wondering if you might come right away," the forester began to explain, even before he was asked. "You see, this evening I found a strange woman wandering the slopes up in the mountains. She was pursued by a most unfriendly band of red dragons."

"Dragons?" Sir George asked. "Now, what could she have done that got the dragons annoyed with her?"

"We don't know that," the forester said. "The problem is that we have no language in common with her. We don't even know her race. So we were wondering if you might know, seeing that you've traveled a good deal. But the mage says that you must hurry, for he fears that she will die anytime now."

"Then the dragons got her?" Sir George asked, looking dismayed.

Kaarstel nodded sadly. "The mage says she must have been whipped by a dragon's tail and that her back is broken, although her own magic must have kept her going. And she is so very weary. She has just had her child, you see."

Sir George could see that there was quite a story here, and it promised to be an interesting one at that, but he wasn't likely to get it all standing here on his doorstep. He hurried to fetch his hat and coat, and he followed the forester quickly down the dark street to the mayor's house. The walk provided only enough time for him to hear how Kaarstel had seen the dragons attacking in the mountains and had found the woman on the slopes below. Sir George knew at once that there was something alarming about this strange lady, who was apparently powerful enough to guard herself against an attack by a dozen red dragons, even though it might yet cost her her life. Unlike the forester, he knew better than to suppose she had just been lucky to evade such an attack. The mayor and the village mage came out to meet him in the front room when he arrived.

"Evening, Ryde," Sir George said to the mayor. "It seems that you have something of a problem?"

"It's the strangest thing I've ever seen, and I've been in Graez since it was settled," the mayor said. "The problem now is that this foreign lady seems likely to die and leave us with her child, and we haven't the first idea of who she is or where she came from."

"Is she really likely to die?" Sir George asked. "I'm told that her back is broken."

"That, along with other injuries," Heran Merstraan agreed. Although he was called the mage, he was in truth only a half-trained magic-user, otherwise a grocer by trade, who served the medical needs of the village for lack of any-one better. "She must be a sorceress of tremendous skill and power. She fought those dragons in a fierce battle and she won, although it may yet cost her her life."

"I had suspected as much myself," Sir George agreed.

"A skilled healer might save her yet," the mage admitted sadly. "Unfortunately I have neither the knowledge nor the experience."

"You can't be blamed for that," Sir George assured him, then turned his attention back to the mayor. "You say that you don't recognize her race?"

"That's true, although I must admit that our people are new to this area of the world," Mayor Aalsten said. "She is copper-skinned like the Flaem, but her hair and her eyes are as black as night, and that's highly uncommon for our own folk. You might be inclined to think that she is some odd breed of elf, or perhaps half-elf, on account of those eyes and her ears, which are slightly pointed. Her clothes looked elven."

"That could be," Sir George agreed. "There are elves to the south, even here in the Highlands, who are darker than the rest. But the elves that live across the mountains in Wendar are pale."

"Perhaps, but I would swear that she is no elf at any rate," Mayor Aalsten insisted. "She's tall—taller than anyone in this room including yourself, Sir George. I would say she's six feet at least, maybe more. And she might be lean, but she's also strong and muscular, like a warrior. No elf I've ever heard of was nearly that tall, nor particularly brawny."

Sir George shook his head. "There is an ancient stronghold of the elves far to the west and north of here, beyond the Hyborean Reaches, though I haven't heard that they look particularly different from other elves. She could not be of mixed breeding, a half-elf, for there is no such thing. Such a child would be either elf or human, depending upon the parents."

"And I will swear that she is not," Mayor Aalsten said. "That child of hers has the same features, as if they were the qualities of their race."

Sir George sighed loudly, as if he were expecting trouble. "I suppose the best I can do is take a look at this woman and talk with her if I can."

They led him to one of the back rooms of the house,

where the woman lay seemingly asleep in a great bed covered with a warm quilted blanket. She wore a white linen shirt, which must have been one of the mayor's own, probably the only clothing in the house large enough for her. She was exactly as they had described her—a tall, slender woman who might well have been an elf, except that she was nearly a head too tall. A more experienced eye would have seen at once that her features, although long and elegant, could not have been considered truly delicate. Her ears were slightly pointed and not entirely human in form, but neither did they belong on an elf. Her eyes were large and dark, noble and expressive. Sir George had only seen eyes like that once before in his life.

She opened her eyes and seemed startled for a moment to see him, almost as if she recognized him. She spoke to him in her strange language, unlike any they had ever heard, a language in which all words sounded ancient and noble, like some recited spell. Sir George answered her simply. She gestured to him, and he came close, pulling over a chair so that he could sit at her side. Although she seemed at the end of her strength, she spoke quickly, almost desperately, for there was obviously something she needed very much to say. Sir George listened intently, sometimes saying a word or two. The others could only wait patiently, feeling as they had from the first that this strange, remarkable lady was a mystery indeed.

At last Sir George turned to the others. "I think she wants us to bring her the child, and I believe we should be quick about it."

The mayor's wife arrived a moment later with the baby, wrapped snugly in a warm, soft blanket. Sir George stole a quick look out of curiosity. The child was awake, but quiet and seemingly content. As the others had said, he was clearly of the same race as his mother, his copper skin a dull, pale gray with black, wispy hair. He was curiously lean and rangy for a newborn, but perhaps for that same reason, he already bore much of the distinct, elegant features of his mother, including the same slightly pointed ears. His dark eyes looked even larger and more remarkable.

The mayor's wife laid the child carefully into the lady's

arms. She held him in silence for a long moment, looking happy and satisfied. Then she turned to Sir George a final time and said something in her odd language. He nodded and rose to leave, taking the mayor out of the room with him, leaving the strange woman in the care of Mage Merstraan and the mayor's wife. He closed the door quietly.

"So who is she?" Mayor Aalsten asked eagerly.

"Eh?" Sir George stirred himself from his private thoughts. "Oh, there is really very little that I can tell you."

"You talked to her long enough."

He shook his head. "I hardly understood a word she said, and I have no way to know if she understood me. But she seemed to feel a great need to talk, so I let her. Under the circumstances, it was the only favor I could do for her."

The mayor looked nearly desperate. "You do know something, I hope, even if you are only guessing. Our people are new in this part of the world, and we are not yet familiar with its people and their history, especially some of the more distant or obscure folk. At this point, I value even your suppositions."

Sir George nodded slowly. "I believe she belongs to an ancient and noble race, one little known to the world at large. You may surely consider her a lady, although I cannot tell you anything more of the titles she may have held or the power she may have once commanded."

"Will her people come looking for her?" Mayor Aalsten asked.

"No, I doubt that very much," Sir George told him. "Even if they do, you can expect only their gratitude. Your problem now is those dragons. They most likely think they killed her while she was crouched in some mountain crevice. I am not greatly concerned."

The mayor didn't seem to find that very reassuring, but dragons made for bad enemies. A flight of them could descend upon a village in the night and devastate it in moments. The little settlement couldn't fight a dozen dragons no matter how much warning they might have. The edge of the mountains was the most dangerous part of the realm but also the least defended, and the settlers were very much on their own. Sir George wasn't willing to discuss the extent of the dangers at that time for fear the solid courage of the Flaem might be overcome by their practical, even self-centered caution. The mayor might have the strange lady and her child turned back out into the wild. It was really too late now to decide not to become involved.

Too late indeed. For in the next moment, the mayor's wife came sniffing and fussing from the back room, carrying the child. Heran Merstraan followed slowly behind her, looking sad and perhaps a little angry at himself for his shortcomings. Sir George rose to take another glance at the strange child, with his large, dark eyes, feeling a little guilty himself. A child like that needed to be among his own kind and live the life meant to be his own, but there was nothing to be done about that. Taking him home would mean taking him through the ranks of enemies determined to slay him, and Sir George didn't even know where to look.

"His name is Thelvyn," the old knight said. "I can tell you that much about him, but little more. Treat him well, in honor of the courage and the determination of his mother. And now, if you will excuse me, I've done what I can here, and I am off for home."

"But what are we to do with him?" the mayor asked desperately.

Sir George put on his hat, then turned to stare at the mayor. "I think you should know that better than I. You know I've never had a child, and I can't begin to tell you about caring for one."

"But what should we do if the dragons come looking for the child or his mother?" the mayor insisted.

"Send for me," Sir George said as he stepped out the door. "Don't try to handle them yourself."

He walked away into the night, looking very unconcerned. But the truth was that he went home, settled into his favorite chair, and had three more cherry liqueurs while he sat up late thinking about dragons.

* * * * *

Sir George was up early the next morning. The mayor came knocking on his door right away, but he had expected that, and so he had risen early and made ready to receive guests. Nor was he entirely surprised to see that the mayor looked rather worried, even a little frightened, and he seemed not to have slept well. Sir George brought him straight into the den and sat him down with a warm drink and a plate of reasonably fresh pastries close at hand, calculated both to distract him and to direct him toward a calmer mood. Mayor Aalsten stared at the exotic decor of the den, the core of a large house filled with odd and remarkable things. Like all the village folk, the mayor was always amazed by that house no matter how often he came to visit.

"Ryde, what's worrying you?" Sir George began abruptly, as if launching a sudden attack against an unprepared foe. "Are you worried about that child, or the dragons, or both?"

"Well, the dragons worry me more," Mayor Aalsten admitted.

"I thought so."

"There isn't really much I can do to protect the folk in the village against a dragon attack except to retreat to the main garrison at Aalbansford, and that would mean a long journey in the snow," the mayor explained. "So I've been wondering what you might be able to tell me about dragons, and how much danger you think we're in. Will the dragons persist in seeking out their prey?"

"Oh, dragons can be very persistent," Sir George said, taking a seat on the other side of the fireplace. "They live a good long time—long enough to make even the elves seem short-lived. But unlike elves, they will not act slowly or put things off but will pursue any business at hand until it is done before they can rest easily. They can be especially single-minded if they are angry or frightened."

Mayor Aalsten looked more fearful than ever. "Then you think that they will not ignore us?"

Sir George shrugged. "Frankly, I believe that they are satisfied they have slain their enemy and have gone home. If they suspected that their prey had escaped, they would have been here long ago, this being a very obvious destination. At the very least, we would have seen them searching the mountains."

"And if they do come here?" the mayor asked, slowly beginning to look reassured. "What can we do then?"

"In that event, you do nothing except send for me as quickly as you can. I know how to talk to them."

Aalsten looked impressed. "Do you think that you can deceive them?"

"I have no intent of trying to deceive them," Sir George declared. "If they come here asking questions—and rest assured that they will inquire before they attack—then I will tell them the truth. The woman they seek died last night. That should please them, and they will go home."

"What if they ask about the child?" the mayor asked.

"Then I start lying." He dismissed the problem with a vague gesture. "If the woman is dead, what will they care about the child?"

"Can you do that?"

"Of course. As I see it, we have only three choices. Either we fight the dragons or we leave, neither option being entirely practical, or we convince the dragons to leave us alone. You don't see me packing to go, do you? If you don't mind my saying so, I expect that I am the only person in this village capable of talking the dragons into going away."

"So that was why you told me last night to send for you if the dragons turn up," the mayor said, at last beginning to look pleased. "We're lucky to have someone like you, Sir George, who can lie well enough to fool even a dragon."

Sir George elected to take that as the compliment it was intended to be. "So what are you going to do with the child?"

"I suppose we will keep him here at the village and treat him as one of our own, unless someone with a better claim should happen to come along."

"Has anyone expressed interest in adopting him yet?" Sir George asked.

"Oh, no. He is to be raised as a ward of the village," the mayor said. "Perhaps you do not know, but ancient Flaemish law forbids adoption, to protect the rights of inheritance of true children who may or may not yet exist."

"That seems a little extreme, considering a person like myself, who has no prospects of ever having a true heir."

"Well, in such a case as yours, you can will a person to become your heir and take your name upon your death, but not before."

Sir George was obviously involved in some deep struggle with himself, trying to decide whether to commit to a course of action that he either feared or detested. "Well, the child is not of Flaemish ancestry, and neither am I. You could just send him over to me and let a pair of benevolent foreigners make do together."

"George, the good folk of this village would never allow me to get away with that, and I hesitate to think what Duke Aalban or the Wizards of the Flaem would have to say about it," Mayor Aalsten said, apparently taken aback by Sir George's offer. "Our law is sacred to us. It's been with us since before our people came into this world, and it was one of the few things that we were able to bring with us. Rest assured that we will take good care of the lad and treat him as one of our own. Keep in mind that what he wishes to do with his life once he comes of age at sixteen is entirely his own affair."

"Yes . . . there is that," Sir George agreed thoughtfully. "And I do have to be away much of the time."

Actually, as he thought about it, he expected that everything would work out just as well that way after all . . . perhaps even better. He had never before remained in one place for very long, and so he hadn't expected to stay in this frontier settlement for that long. Still, he thought that perhaps he could wait. If nothing else, his curiosity was going to keep him close at hand.

CHAPTER ONE

Although Thelvyn had lived in the village of Graez all the years his short life, he didn't belong there and he knew it. The trouble was that he didn't have the faintest idea of just were he did belong, and the mayor wasn't likely to let him go there even if he did. And so he stayed right where he was and grew a little more frustrated with life every day, just as the village was becoming generally frustrated with him.

Most younger folk, by the middle of their teenage years, get the idea in their heads that they don't belong wherever they are. They imagine that they are in fact the descendants of kings or lords, or perhaps sorcerers or heroic knights or some other such nonsense. And they are very certain that they will become amazing persons in their own right, overflowing with courage and wisdom and all manner of great and admirable qualities, if older folk would only stop telling them what to do and allow them to be in control for a change.

Then they would go off and do amazing things, quite

confident that making a journey of a thousand leagues to fight an army of kobolds was less odious than their usual daily chores. But the kindly folk who had raised them hardly ever sat them down by a fire one night to admit the dark secret of their true origins, gave them a ring and a key and a secret map, and sent them out to discover their destiny. Thus they generally grew up to be farmers and merchants and smiths, just like their parents.

The difference in Thelvyn's case was that he *knew* he didn't belong where he was. He really *did* come from an unknown land somewhere far away, and he really *was* descended from a noble yet mysterious race, and everyone in the village knew it, too. Not that he derived any benefit from it. The villagers couldn't give him a map and any other odd artifact they might have on hand, tell him the secret of his birth, and send him home because they had no idea who he really was or where to send him. They hadn't asked for him, but they had taken him in nonetheless, and so, being generally decent folk, they felt responsible for him.

They were often given to say that they didn't know what to do with him, but this wasn't exactly the truth. They wanted him to be just like themselves, which they naturally assumed to be the best possible thing in the world. And all the time he was trying very hard to be the person he was supposed to be, except that he had no idea what that could be.

All in all, if Thelvyn was destined for a grand and adventurous life, he was sure that he was off to a very bad start indeed, and that soon he would be too old to begin. Perhaps because the situation was more a reality to him than fantasy, he was also more practical about it. Although he occasionally thought about it, he really didn't expect that the villagers actually knew the dark secrets of his heritage and all would be revealed when he came of age. Nor did he expect armored knights from his own lost kingdom to suddenly come upon his village and find him. His dreams didn't extend to fame or titles or great riches. He only wanted to be given a chance to make a life for himself, rather than the pointless pretense of a life that was not his.

If Thelvyn thought from time to time that the older folk

were picking on him, he was partly right. The trouble was that chance had brought him among the Flaemish settlers, who were themselves fairly new to the Highlands. If he had found himself in Darokin or distant Thyatis, being relatively old and cosmopolitan lands inhabited by folk of many different races, he would have been far less an outsider.

The Flaem had found him and they had kept him, but they couldn't allow him completely to become one of them. He was adept at magic, but they wouldn't teach him their own version, which they considered to be the right of their own race. He could have been a scholar, but among the Flaem, only wizards were allowed to open the important books. Instead, they insisted that he must learn something "practical."

There had been some speculation that he might be descended from some hearty breed of elf, and indeed that at one time had been his secret hope, since surely an elf would have a home somewhere in the world. Of course, he hadn't known at the time that elves were generally quite suspicious of foreigners, even other elves. He had long since grown too tall to be an elf anyway, and he threatened to grow taller yet and rather brawny.

He might have been taken for one of the Flaemish settlers, for, like them, he was copper-skinned, tall, and strong, if rather angular, even noble of features. But his thick hair was as black as fresh tar, while that of the Flaems was often red or brown. He was old enough to show some sign of a beard by this time if he was going to have one, but he showed no hint of facial hair. Most remarkable were his eyes, almost certainly not the eyes of any human race, being large and as dark as night and just as deep, with an intensity that could be disconcerting, and so people called him Thelvyn Fox Eyes. One aspect that most people were likely to overlook was that the parts of his eyes that should have been white were in fact as blue as the purest sapphire. People told him that he looked just like his mother, on the rare times when they said anything about that mysterious woman.

And so the folk of the village continued to try to make a

place for Thelvyn, and also to teach him a trade that would
allow him to live among them as one of their own. It was a
meaningless pretense, since everyone knew that he would
go off and do what he wanted when he came of age anyway,
but the pretense seemed important to the Flaemish settlers, with all their concern about practicality and tradition.
He could have been a mage, but that wasn't allowed. He
could have been a fighter, but that also wasn't allowed.
They had tried to make him a leather worker, only to find
very quickly that his nose was too sensitive to the dyes and
tanning agents.

One of the village jewelers had offered to take him on,
the problem there being that his vision was wrong in some
odd way. He had discovered that for himself in school. He
could read an open book from across the room, but not if it
was right under his nose where it belonged. Perhaps he
might have been a miner or a woodcutter—if it came down
to doing simple hard work, he was certainly strong
enough—but that was also dangerous, and none of those
folk wanted a orphan about.

In all, his prospects were looking rather grim, caught as
he was between the things he wasn't allowed to do, the
things nobody wanted to teach him, and the things that ran
afoul of the curious qualities of his unknown race. Perhaps
things might have been a little easier if he had really wanted
to try, but all Thelvyn could think about was that he
belonged somewhere else. So it happened that early in the
spring of his fifteenth year, he found himself between
prospects.

All work had a tendency to come to a stop during the
winter. First the farmers, miners, and woodcutters were
forced in by the snow, and later all the craftsmen who
turned their products into finished goods began to run
short of supplies. The jeweler had let him go just past midwinter when his stock of gold, silver, and jewels from the
mountains had diminished, and that had dropped Thelvyn
right back in the mayor's lap, so to speak, until something
else could be found for him. The mayor had in turn set him
to watching Sir George's house while the old knight was
away, mainly to have a place to send him for at least part of

the time.

But when the final snow had come and gone and the first warm breath of spring stirred the woods and the new green grass, then Kaarstel, the forester, had suggested that Thelvyn should accompany him as he made his rounds. The miners were going back into the mountains, and the lumbermen were back in the deep woods. All of that meant that the forester had a good deal of work to do clearing the remote paths and making certain that no evil things had come into the woods during the snows. As it happened, Kaarstel was getting a bit old, although he wasn't yet willing to admit it, and so he hadn't yet asked Duke Aalban to send an assistant. But he did find the help of a strong, hearty lad most useful, and young Thelvyn was the only one in the village to be spared.

For his own part, Thelvyn greatly enjoyed the work, for he liked being about in the wild. He delighted in the deep forest, with its great trees and shadows and quiet. But he especially loved the high mountains, where he could feel the cool wind and look down from the heights to see the fields and woods spreading out below him. When he looked down from some towering cliff or great pinnacle of stone, he almost felt that he could leap into the air and ride the winds. He quickly discovered that any discussion of his becoming a forester was politely ignored or turned aside, so he assumed that this also must be one of those careers that was closed to orphans of foreign descent.

"Were your people the first to come to this land?" Thelvyn asked one morning when he had gone high in the mountains with the old forester. He knew the answer to his question already, but that had always been a good way to get the forester talking about the olden days.

"One of the first," Kaarstel answered as he pulled himself slowly up a steep portion of the trail. "The elves have been here much longer—as long ago as two thousand years, maybe three. Something terrible happened in these lands once a long time ago, but the elves won't talk about that. When we arrived, the better part of a century ago, there were just a few bands of wanderers and wild elves here in these northern parts. They left when we came."

"Where did they go?" Thelvyn asked. Elves seldom came to the village, but he thought he liked them.

"Some went into the south of the Highlands, or even farther south, into the dark forests of Alfheim, to live with their kinsmen. Others crossed the high mountains north into Wendar, into cold, desolate lands where only elves dwell, to live the way they always had. I think there are still a few of those original elves somewhere in these woods, although I don't know that with any certainty. I haven't seen them."

They came to a place where a heavy branch had fallen from a tree, broken by the weight of winter snow. The branch had fallen across the path, but someone had cut it apart with an axe, then pulled the pieces off to the side of the trail. Chips of fresh wood still lay in the path, only now beginning to darken with age.

"The miners must have removed this themselves, probably when they were bringing up their ponies with supplies," Kaarstel said, which was obvious enough. "Folk who use the trails are good about tending them for their own convenience. Still, we must go on and make certain that there are no nasty creatures that have wandered into the woods during the winter."

"Is that likely?" Thelvyn asked as he hurried to follow. "I mean, this last winter was very hard. It seems to me that orcs and goblins are no more fond of the snow than other folk."

"That's actually quite true," the forester agreed. "We did have a few run-ins back when I was young, when we first came into these lands. Mostly we've been lucky to have been left alone, although I do see evidence of invaders from time to time. Then I fetch the garrison, and we hunt them out. Usually they're just passing through. We rarely seem to find anything."

"Do they ever attack the farms or the mines?"

"Not for almost three years now," Kaarstel explained. "Most of the farmers come into the village at night, and the miners build small strongholds at the entrances of their mines so that they can simply lock themselves inside until danger passes. The settlers in the northeastern corner of the

Highlands have a harder time of it, being near to a nastier part of the mountains. And of course they also have to deal with the Ethengar. I'll grant that the clans themselves generally mean no harm, but the young warriors will sometimes band together to go exploring, and they have a way of finding trouble even if they aren't looking for it."

They had suddenly come out of the woods onto one of the more level parts of the trail, where it cut along the side of the slope just beneath a towering cliff of bare gray stone rising above a steep pile of boulders. The forester stopped and stood for a moment, looking about, mostly up the mountainside to their right. The trail eventually wound up to a deep cut between two of the highest peaks. Thelvyn came up to look as well. He could see the ravine clearly from back in the village, although only from here did he notice that the cut wasn't just a dead-end canyon. But he would never have tried to take a horse through there, for the way was narrow and twisting and piled deep with boulders.

"This is where I found your mother fifteen years ago," Kaarstel said at last. "The dragons were hunting her up in that pass, shooting their flames down among the rocks. I imagine she came down that way, and they thought that she was still up there. That was a dangerous night. We had no way of knowing if the dragons would come after us, but they went on to the south and never came down to the village."

"Why?" Thelvyn asked. "Certainly the village would have been an obvious place to look."

"Perhaps because it *was* obvious, and those dragons were sure that she would stay hidden rather than go to a place where there were people and lights. Sir George was always sure the dragons believed they had killed her, and so they never bothered to look further. That seems reasonable enough."

"Do you think my mother traveled over the mountains?" Thelvyn asked. He knew the story well, but he hadn't heard it from someone who had actually been there.

"It would seem so," the forester agreed. "But I've always wondered if she was actually coming south along the mountains rather than over them. That could explain why the dragons didn't turn aside. The trouble is there's nothing on the other side of the mountains either west or north. Just cold, desolate lands of forests and plains, and no one there except bands of wild elves, and precious few of those. There's the Sylvan Realm, by the sea on the far side of the Hyborean Reaches, but Sir George looked into that and found that the folk there are ordinary elves. You may or you may not be human, but you're not an elf."

"In school, we learned about Blackmoor," Thelvyn said. "I know Blackmoor was supposed to have been completely destroyed and sank beneath the sea three thousand years ago, but couldn't some part of it still exist somewhere?"

"Perhaps," the forester said. "I don't know enough about it to say one way or the other. But the folk of Blackmoor had a bad reputation, and I can't imagine you or your mother being one of them. Your mother was a lady. I've never seen her like since."

All the same, Thelvyn often wondered if he was indeed a descendant of lost Blackmoor. There was a limit to how many unknown races from unknown lands there could be in the world, but if any did exist, then Blackmoor seemed most likely to have spawned them. But for all his dreams and desires, he was too practical to believe such things or attach too much importance to such fond speculations. It was just pleasant to think about it.

He was quickly becoming convinced that the forester had the best job in all the village. That excluded Sir George, of course, who resided in the village but was occupied elsewhere. It seemed to Thelvyn there could be nothing better than to spend his days wandering about the forests, hills, and mountains.

Of course, he wasn't forgetting that the forester spent many days outside in the rain and the snow and the bitter winds of autumn and winter, nor that the forester was in rather some danger when he scouted out the traces of monsters and evil folk that had come into these lands. And while he didn't speak of it, Thelvyn knew of the great risk that Kaarstel had taken getting his mother down from the heights, and he was always respectful to the old man for that reason.

They were late coming down from the heights and didn't

return to the village until just after dark. Thelvyn had a simple dinner with Kaarstel and stayed longer than he should have, listening to the old man's stories. He wasn't greatly concerned, knowing that he wasn't expected until late. He hurried by Sir George's house to make certain that it was secure, and then went on to the mayor's house where he was currently staying.

Always mindful of his chores, he paused in the yard long enough to gather up a heavy load of firewood for the morning's fire. Large and rather strong for his age, he could carry enough wood to serve the whole house in only a couple of trips.

Thelvyn stacked the wood in the boxes beside the hearths in the kitchen and the main room, then tended the fires one last time for the night. Spring was still young, and the nights could be cold, especially when the sky was clear and the wind was calm. The mayor's house was large but also rather empty now that his daughters were married and his son was away in the south. Mayor Aalsten was the wealthiest man in the village except for Sir George. Aalsten was also a successful merchant.

While the mayor didn't use his position to unfair advantage, which was beneath the dignity of Flaemish tradition, still, being mayor gave him special knowledge of the folk of his village, in both the products of their craft and also their needs. But he was wealthy only relative to the rough standards of the frontier, and while he was comfortable, he also lived in a manner that would seem rustic compared to the merchants to the south in the capital.

The mayor kept only one servant, an older girl who had been Thelvyn's classmate only a few years before, and she went home at night. Thelvyn performed such chores as tending the fires at night, for he liked being helpful and it seemed a fair return for his keep. Like forester Kaarstel, the mayor and the other people of the village had assumed a dire risk in taking in his mother and him. He was grateful for that, even though he was frustrated with them for trying to make him into something he was not. That night he found the mayor sitting alone in his study, going over his trading ledgers by the golden light of an oil lamp. Thelvyn brought in a couple pieces of wood for the small iron stove that sat in one corner of the room.

"Ah, there you are lad. So how was your day?" Mayor Aalsten asked, glancing up from his book.

"The forester showed me where he found my mother," Thelvyn said. "I always knew that he must have taken a chance in bringing her down, but he'll never admit that."

"He's a fine, brave man. A number of people in this village owe him their lives," the mayor agreed and settled back in his chair. "You know, Thelvyn, you will be coming of age later this year, and you're getting a little old to still be trying to find yourself an apprenticeship. You seem to greatly enjoy the time you've spent with the forester."

"Yes, I have," Thelvyn agreed hopefully, wondering if something was finally going to go right for him.

"Unfortunately, you aren't of Flaemish ancestry and you haven't been declared a full citizen by a lord of the land, and so, by law, you can't take a post in the duke's pay," Mayor Aalsten continued. "You can understand that, can't you?"

"Yes, of course," Thelvyn agreed. It explained why so many promising careers weren't among his options. When he was younger, he had always accepted that Flaemish law was inherently fair to everyone, or so he had always been told. Now he was coming to realize that the Flaem were a clannish lot, and their law was designed to exclude strangers like himself.

"The first shipments of ore are beginning to come down from the mountains," the mayor went on. "Dal Ferstaan says he can use some help at the forge now, and he wants you to go over in the morning and start work with him. You'd be put up there, of course. You can manage that, can't you?"

"I expect so," Thelvyn agreed, trying not to sound doubtful. "I have some experience working with the fires at the jewelers. It's the same thing on a larger scale, I suppose."

"The work of a smith seems a proper choice for someone the size and strength you promise to be." He paused, seeming to wonder whether he should say more. "To tell you the truth, I don't expect you shall make a career as a smith. Sir

George has always had his eye on you, and I daresay he has his own plans for you when you come of age. But we've all had our reasons for doing things the way we have. For our own part, we've felt obliged to try to make a normal life for you, at least as much as our law and custom permit. Also, Sir George has always been very concerned about your education, not just your schoolwork but also your apprenticeships, for whatever reason he sees fit. He has always insisted upon covering most of the cost of your schooling and your keep. He even offered to adopt you when you first came."

"He did?" Thelvyn asked, surprised.

"Of course, that was forbidden by a law that was never really designed to accommodate you," the mayor said, a rather candid admission for a defender of Flaemish tradition. "And you are his heir, should he fail to return from one of his journeys. But the fact remains that Sir George leads a rather dangerous life, whatever else he may want us to believe, and we had to consider the possibility that you would have to find a career for yourself if something happened to him."

"I have no idea what Sir George's business really is," Thelvyn had to admit.

"To be perfectly honest, neither do I. He likes to insist that he is a merchant, but many people believe that he is an adventurer, and you cannot convince them otherwise. The good folk of this village feel you ought to be taught an honest trade so that you will not be tempted to take up with that old knight. Sir George is my friend, but I am also bound to do what people want, although it would have been much easier if those same people had been willing to contribute more to your upbringing than advice. As I say, what you choose to do when you come of age is entirely your own affair. Until then, you are compelled to work at the forge until Sir George is ready for you, or until Dal Ferstaan kicks you out."

"I think I understand," Thelvyn said, still trying not to sound resentful. "It's just that sometimes I can't seem to do anything right."

"Well, you are rather different from us in many ways," Mayor Aalsten said. "Possibly your people have their own way of doing things that works best for them."

Thelvyn went to his room to pack so he could leave for
the smith's house early the next morning. He felt rather
hopeful, even excited, to think there were plans for his
future other than to be just another villager. If he just had
the patience to wait another year, he could decide his own
future. But he was also beginning to feel quite disillusioned
with the Flaem, whom he had always trusted. True, he had
reason to be grateful to them for rescuing his mother from
the dragons and taking him in. But he was also a little
angry that people who had no interest in his future were
dictating the terms of his life without really trying to discover what was best for him.

At least he would be able to console himself over the
next few months with speculation about his future.
Whether Sir George was a traveling merchant or an adventurer, Thelvyn thought he would enjoy becoming either
one. The only problem was that he knew nothing about
either occupation, and that could only mean that he had
yet another apprenticeship still ahead of him. But at least
he would finally be doing something he enjoyed.

* * * * *

Thelvyn arrived at his new home soon after dawn the
next morning, just as Dal Ferstaan was beginning to fire up
the forge. The first shipment of ore had only just come
down from the mines in the mountains. One storage bin
was already full, and the dirty burlap sacks in which the
loads had been brought had been stacked and tied off,
ready to be taken back and filled again. The smith's shop
was off to one side of the village with a few other shops.
This not only kept the smoke and noise somewhat removed
from the other houses, but it was also nearer to the main
road by which supplies arrived.

Dal Ferstaan had come to the village shortly before
Thelvyn had been born. He had been trained in the lower
Highlands, where smiths were common but metals were
scarce. While smiths were usually large, hard-tempered
men, Dal was short but stocky and strong. He was growing

bald and had a round, jolly face and bushy mustache, so that he was rather disarming in appearance. He was a fine craftsman, hardworking and friendly, and more to young Thelvyn's liking than most of the dour, suspicious Flaem.

Indeed Thelvyn's oldest and best friend was Celmar, Dal Ferstaan's only son. But Celmar had by misfortune inherited his father's short stature and also his mother's frailty, having been a small, sickly child, and he possessed his father's talent for metalwork but not his strength. So it was that Celmar had recently been apprenticed to the jeweler, which had proven to be an excellent arrangement, and now Thelvyn was to be apprenticed to the smith.

That morning, Celmar was on his way to the jeweler's even as Thelvyn was arriving. Celmar paused and turned back, feigning surprise. "So what is this? My father isn't commonly given to acts of charity."

"I've yet to meet the Flaemish gentleman who was," Thelvyn answered.

"And do you think you'll be able to focus your gaze on the anvil before you?"

"It helps that I'm tall and my arms are long," he said. When he had been younger, folks had assumed he was quite farsighted. When Mage Eddan had come to the village to assume the medical and educational responsibilities for the populace, he had tried several spells in an attempt to correct Thelvyn's vision. Unfortunately his magic had been to no effect, proving that this was a natural condition and not a failing of Thelvyn's vision.

"I think you'll do well enough," Celmar said, more serious now. "Don't be afraid of my father. You've had troubles, but you're not afraid to work. That's all he asks."

Thelvyn knew that to be true, for he had visited the Ferstaan home often while growing up, and he had even lived here briefly from time to time. He knew the house, and he knew the people there. He had always found it to be a happy household, with good people who made him feel welcome and at ease and never found reason to remind him that he was not of their own kind. He found Dal Ferstaan in the kitchen, preparing himself for a day's work.

"There you are, lad," the smith said. "Are you ready to

go at it?"

"If I can have a moment to change into proper clothes," Thelvyn agreed.

"Take your time and put away your things," Ferstaan told him. "You'll have Celmar's room. Now that his apprenticeship is to become final, he'll be living at the jeweler's home."

Dal Ferstaan was indeed a kindly man, having never made his son feel guilty or ashamed because he was too frail to do the work of a smith. It helped that Celmar was comfortable doing the work of a jeweler, and his father's new apprentice was not only a friend but also something of a misfit. Even a few minutes in this house was enough to make Thelvyn feel more charitable toward the Flaem, in spite of his previous misgivings.

Between his own brief experience with the jeweler and the time he had spent in this house when he was younger, Thelvyn knew what to expect. If the first shipments of ore had only just arrived, then there hadn't been time for any of it to be refined. The ore was bought from the miners for the value of its metal content, and better ore demanded a higher price, so the miners did what they could to remove the unwanted stone. Most of the metal from the frontier was shipped south into the Highlands to be worked there. The distance and the state of the roads being what they were, the merchants found it practical and profitable to ship ingots of the metal. This meant that the ore had to be refined there at the smith's. Graez had several smiths, but much of their work consisted of turning ore into ingots rather than finished goods.

The actual process of refining the ore varied according to the metal involved. Iron was one of the most difficult, since it was almost never found in the pure state but had to be reduced with hard work, much time, and a very hot fire. The first problem was preparing a hot enough fire, and all the village charcoalers were kept busy reducing timber to charcoal to feed the foundries. The ore itself was reduced by heating it and forcing air through it from underneath, so that the metal became liquid and flowed down through the crushed stone to be gathered below.

Dal Ferstaan and his two journeymen assistants set to work preparing the fires, their efforts a little awkward at first from lack of practice over the winter. Thelvyn, with his strength and endurance, was assigned to work one of the great bellows, forcing air through the ore and fanning the fire to greater heat. The bellows had to be worked in slow, steady strokes, directing the air at just the right intensity.

Dal Ferstaan came over for a look. He seemed to approve. "You're doing fine, Fox Eyes."

Thelvyn was pleased to be doing something useful for a change. All the same, he thought that if donkeys had arms, they could be taught to do the same work.

Parn, one of the journeyman smiths, came over after a time to give him a rest. Dal's other assistant showed him how the molds were laid out to receive the collected iron. The ingots were cast just like any other metal object. Since the ingots were only an intermediate form, to be melted later for further refinement, they were sand-cast by a simple method that took the least effort and time. The molds were prepared by forcing an impression into the sand of a large tray with a form of carved stone, producing ingots that were uniform in size and weight. There were surprisingly few ingots, especially considering Dal Ferstaan's claim that he always prepared a few extra. Their day of hard work had produced only a few crude plates of finished iron.

Thelvyn returned to working the bellows. Dal Ferstaan was called away by visitors in the middle of the morning, leaving his two young journeymen to watch the furnace. They were now in the middle of the long, uneventful process of getting the furnace and the ore itself up to heat, and so they remained unconcerned even when the smith did not return for some time. A cool, welcome wind came up late in the morning. The furnace room was separate from the forge, being a long shed attached to the rest of the house at one end. The side walls were great wooden panels, hinged to swing open and large enough to allow all the smoke and fumes to escape.

Shortly before noon, Thelvyn was taking yet another turn at the bellows when he happened to notice Mage Eddan standing at the outer door of the furnace shed. The wizard had come to the village only a few years earlier, but Thelvyn knew him well, since he served as the teacher for the older students as well as the local physician. He was young for a wizard of his standing, competent but not brilliant. He had come to the frontier to establish his professional reputation without competition from his fellow wizards. Perhaps because he was so young, he tried hard to be stern, commanding, and aloof to gain his students' respect. He combed back his fiery red hair into a lion's mane and always dressed in dark clothes in the style of the Flaemish nobility, wearing a long, elegant jacket with a flared stiff collar and a short cape.

Having noticed that Thelvyn had seen him, he seemed about to say something, but in the next moment, he was joined by the mayor and Dal Ferstaan. They spoke together briefly. Mayor Aalsten deliberately stood with his back to the door, so he wouldn't have to look inside. Then the mayor and the wizard left together and headed back into the village. The smith stood for a moment, apparently lost in his own thoughts. At last he stepped inside.

"Parn, Merron . . . can the two of you watch the furnace for a few minutes more while I have a talk with Thelvyn?" he asked.

Thelvyn gave the bellows to one of the journeymen, then hurried to follow the smith around the outside of the furnace shed to the kitchen. He knew something was wrong, for the smith seemed troubled. He thought he could guess what the problem was. The wiser minds of the village had invented more restrictions to place upon him to make his life more difficult—all in the name of doing what was best and fair for him, of course. Any charitable thoughts about the Flaem he had been entertaining immediately disappeared. He had always before assumed, perhaps in his innocence, that they were just carrying out the letter of their restrictive law as it applied to resident strangers. Now he was beginning to wonder if they were deliberately making things difficult for him in the hope that he would go away.

Dal Ferstaan took a seat at the head of the kitchen table, indicating for Thelvyn sit across from him. "I'll get right to the point, lad. Some folks in the village, Mage Eddan in particular, seem convinced that you have finally found work suited to you, and they've insisted that I take a five-year contract on your apprenticeship. I think you know what that means."

"It means that you own my services for the next five years, and I cannot leave unless I can buy out the remainder of my contract," Thelvyn said, still trying to understand why such terms had been ordered. It felt like a prison term to him, restricting him to a life he hadn't chosen until he was twenty years old. By that time, he feared, it would likely be too late for him to begin training for a new career.

"Mage Eddan is behind this if you ask me," the smith continued. "Why he should care is beyond me, seeing that you finished your required schooling more than two years ago. It might be nothing more than a well-intended plot to keep you at honest work and save you from Sir George, who is looked upon as leading a wild and mysterious life, even though everyone trusts and respects him. The mayor seemed reluctant to have a hand in this, and he arranged certain terms to make things as easy as possible for you."

"He did?" Thelvyn asked, encouraged.

"That he did. For one thing, they didn't ask me to buy your contract, but in their role as your guardians, they gave it to me. That's the only reason I went along with this. Since I have no stake in it, I can easily set my own price whenever you may wish to buy back your contract—say, perhaps, one brass penny, which would satisfy the letter of the law. For now, it seems to me that you're better off here than anywhere else in the village, except of course with Sir George."

"I agree," Thelvyn said, once again feeling slightly more charitable toward the Flaem than he had a moment before. Between their sudden acts of uncaring sternness and great generosity, they certainly knew how to keep him guessing. He decided that in the future he would rely upon the Flaem he knew to be his friends, but not the rest.

"Well, things aren't as bad as they could have been," Dal Ferstaan said, rising. "What do you say? I think we should get back to work before those ham-handed journeymen blow up the furnace."

CHAPTER TWO

The first day of spring was a date dictated by the
calendar, but it had precious little to do with the
seasons and did not bother to take the weather
into account at all. Only the year before, on the
night of the spring festival, the crowd had broken up into
small groups and moved indoors because the snow was too
deep for dancing. This year, spring was ahead of schedule
and had already been lurking temptingly for nearly a
month before the spring celebration, and thus people were
in a better mood for it.

Everyone, that is, but Thelvyn. The spring festival went
very much the way of the harvest festival and the midwinter's feast and the celebration of high summer. Thelvyn was
considered too young to drink, and no one ever wanted to
dance with him. The dances were intended to bring all the
boys and girls of the village together, under disgustingly
well-supervised conditions, for them to decide whether or
not they liked each other. But the girls never wanted to
dance with Thelvyn, since they knew that their parents

wouldn't approve of him. So, from Thelvyn's point of view, this was just another Flaemish conspiracy to keep him from having something they wanted to keep for themselves, such as their daughters and all the good trades.

He had gone to the dance with Celmar Ferstaan, who had conspired with his father to make certain that Thelvyn attended in the company of his friends for fear that he would not otherwise have gone at all. Thelvyn was tall and strong and rather good-looking, in a noble and mysterious way. The girls looked at him like frightened rabbits when they were alone, or pointed and whispered and giggled when they were together.

By Flaemish tradition, the girls asked the boys to dance, but Thelvyn hadn't been asked once. Celmar, who was skinny and pale and had rather stringy, dull red hair, had been asked no fewer than than a dozen times. In fact Celmar was doing enormously well for himself. He soon noticed that all the girls were asking him about Thelvyn, so he realized he was earning by default all his friend's dances. As the night went on, he finally decided Thelvyn should be apprised of the situation.

"You could arrange to meet one of the girls in private, you know," Celmar said. "They all want to talk with you—perhaps a little more than talk, if you know what I mean."

"Why should I bother?" Thelvyn asked. "They just want to gossip about me to their friends. If their fathers found out, I'd have to have a long talk with the mayor and that pretentious wizard. And that would be the least of my troubles."

"Not if you're careful," Celmar insisted. "Now, listen to me. Merilanda, the jeweler's daughter, has taken a liking to me. She's asked me to dance four times tonight already. She could ask around discreetly and find you a girl who is interested and whose parents aren't so worried by the prospects of having in the family a tall, clever foreigner who seems destined for good things. We're not all a bunch of insufferable snobs, you know. Only the ones you've always had to deal with."

"If you think it's worth it," Thelvyn agreed reluctantly.

"You disappear for a few minutes, and I'll do what I can," Celmar said with a wink.

Thelvyn nodded. "I'll go and check on Sir George's house."

He slipped away quietly into the shadows, so that none of the older folks would notice. Even after two weeks, Thelvyn was still in a bad mood over the circumstances of his apprenticeship to Dal Ferstaan. At least Ferstaan and his family, even his two journeyman assistants, had helped to make him feel at home, and his work at the foundry was going well. Of course, all he had done so far was to help turn out stacks of iron ingots.

He was glad he had finished his required studies well ahead of the other students his age so that he no longer had to go to school and face Mage Eddan. He had decided that the wizard, self-appointed defender of Flaemish tradition, was doing everything he could to chase young Thelvyn out of the village. It was a wasted effort, for Thelvyn fully intended to leave when he came of age later that year, or the next spring at the latest.

He remained extremely curious about what Sir George might have in mind for him, especially since he had learned that the old knight had named him his heir and had even considered adopting him. He wondered just who Sir George Kirbey really was—whether he was in fact the wealthy, mysterious adventurer he seemed to be or the traveling merchant he claimed to be. Either way, Thelvyn didn't doubt that he would be better off in the old knight's company. Sir George had been away an unusually long time, as he had warned when he had left early the previous fall, and there was no certainty about when he would return.

Thelvyn stopped short, rousing himself from his thoughts. As he came around a corner, he saw a pale yellow light in one of the back windows of Sir George's house, although the rest of the place was dark. He quickly concluded that some thief had waited until everyone was away at the dance to ransack the place. Thelvyn did not hesitate, responding to some fierce instinct he didn't know he possessed. Using his key, he carefully opened the front door, choosing that entrance because it was farthest from the room with the light at the back of the house. He reached around inside the doorway and located the hiking staff Sir George kept there.

He closed the door quietly, then paused for a moment to listen. His oddly shaped ears were unusually sensitive, and his big, dark eyes gave him the ability to see in the dark almost as well as an elf. He had always tried to keep his abilities hidden, since people found him peculiar enough as it was.

After a moment, he was sure he could hear someone moving slowly and quietly along the hall toward the doorway on the far side of the room from where he stood. Apparently his entrance hadn't been as secretive as he thought. At least the thief was now forced to come to him in the darkness, where Thelvyn had the advantage.

After a moment, the figure of a woman appeared in the opposite doorway, obviously assuming she was hidden by darkness. The woman was young but also the tallest female Thelvyn had ever seen, taller even than he himself by several inches. Although she was wearing a loose robe, she still appeared quite slender. Her height meant she couldn't be an elf, and thus she lacked his own ability to see in the dark. Still, he had to concede that she had the advantage of reach. She might also have the advantage of experience, and she most certainly had the advantage of carrying a long, slender-bladed sword. While Thelvyn was brave, he was also no fool. He knew he would have to remain calm to win this fight.

The tall woman stepped farther into the room, then stopped, apparently having come close enough to see his outline in the darkness. "Thief!" she cried loudly

Well, it was nice of the enemy to declare herself. Thelvyn swung his staff against the blade of her sword, hoping to take her by surprise and knock the weapon from her hand. The metal rang, but he had underestimated her strength. She swung the sword wide in return, missing him completely, although the move was obviously intended only to make him keep his distance. Then he realized that she probably knew she was fighting someone who didn't have a real weapon.

The battle continued in a series of fierce but awkward

swings and thrusts, a comic fencing match in the dark between her long, light sword and his staff. Thelvyn's intent was to capture his enemy, since he could image what the mayor would have to say if he actually killed someone in Sir George's house. It was a fight to the death as far as his opponent was concerned, but she was having trouble finding him in the dark. After a long moment, Thelvyn decided he needed to find some way to get that sword out of her hand.

He wondered if he could duck beneath one of her swings and come up inside her reach. A sharp rap on her head should settle the argument. Suddenly he was aware of movement behind him, and he turned to see a second figure sneaking up on him in the darkness, this one much smaller than the first. Startled and fearful of finding himself trapped, he swung the staff sharply, and with a tremendous hollow thump, the metal end of the staff connected with a helmet. The smaller figure stood for a moment as if surprised, then toppled to the wooden floor with another loud thump.

"Korinn!" the woman shouted.

Thelvyn took advantage of the woman's distraction, using the staff's handle to hook the hilt of her sword and snap it out of her hand. It flew across the room and stuck point-first in the post beside the door. Then he brought the staff around in a final quick movement and struck her in the head, somewhat more gently than the first figure, since she wasn't wearing a helmet. She went down as well. Thelvyn turned when he became aware of someone else running down the hall bearing a small lamp. He relaxed when he saw that it was Sir George. Then he thought about what that might imply, and he decided that he shouldn't relax after all.

"Thelvyn!" Sir George declared as he saw the scene of battle. Then he looked quickly about the room, holding up the lamp. "Ah, blessed be! At least nothing seems to be broken."

"Except for their skulls," Thelvyn said, although the tall woman was already starting to move. "Are . . . are these your friends?"

"Well, they used to be," Sir George said, looking closely at the woman. "You watch them a moment while I get a restorative potion. Better yet, I'll watch them while you get the potion. You know where I keep such things."

Thelvyn hurried to fetch the small dark bottle from an unused corner of the liqueur cabinet in the den. By the time he returned, the woman was sitting up with her back against the wall and glaring. Sir George took the bottle and held it under her nose, removing the cork just long enough to allow a small, icy-white cloud to escape. The tall woman stopped glaring after a moment, although she continued to rub the side of her head. Thelvyn saw that she was quite young, although older than he, and rather pretty. Her features, especially her pale complexion, light blue eyes, and long, soft hair suggested that she was a barbarian of the Northern Reaches.

Sir George hurried over to tend to the second attacker, who was indeed a dwarf. He seemed quite young and was dressed in the usual plain, sturdy clothing of his kind. A battle-axe lay beside him. A sturdy iron helmet, bound in leather, had saved him from more serious injury. Thelvyn found the helmet behind a chair, sporting a rather serious dent. The dwarf was unconscious. He responded reluctantly to the restorative potion, although he did not seem to come around entirely until after Sir George had guided him back to the den and placed a glass of wine in his hand. The tall woman sat in a large chair on the far side of the room and resumed glaring at Thelvyn over a cup of ale. Thelvyn stayed as far away from them both as he could.

"Well, now that that's over, I suppose that introductions are in order," Sir George declared. "Everyone, this is Thelvyn Fox Eyes. I've told you about him."

"The strange lad with the mean stick," the tall woman said, still glaring and rubbing her head. Her voice didn't possess the rather distinctive Northern Reaches accent as Thelvyn would have guessed. Instead, she sounded like a Thyatian. Under the circumstances, he said nothing.

"Thelvyn, this is Solveig White-Gold, otherwise known as Solveig-the-*G*-is-Silent," Sir George continued.

"George!" she said, redirecting her glare to him.

The old knight noticed that Thelvyn obviously didn't understand the jest. "Her name is spelled with a silent *g*, since in the language of the Northern Reaches, all final *g*s are silent. And that rather dazed fellow is Korinn, son of Doric, also known as Bear Slayer."

"Pleased to meet you," the dwarf said, so dryly that it was hard to know if he was being sarcastic.

"Now, what about you?" the old knight asked Thelvyn. "I didn't find you at any of your previous haunts, so assumed you were at the dance and would show up eventually. How is the dance, by the way?"

"Terrible . . . at least for me. None of the girls will dance with me."

Solveig glared at him. "They're probably all afraid of you."

"It's the old problem about being a stranger in this land," Thelvyn explained. "I've come to realize lately just how clannish and snobbish the Flaem really are."

"Well, we're all strangers here. Perhaps we can just have our own little dance." Sir George glanced at Solveig, who was still glaring. He turned back to Thelvyn. "Well, perhaps not. Are you still at the jeweler's?"

"No. That ran afoul of the same problem I had with reading," he replied. "I couldn't focus on anything that close, and I couldn't do the fine work if I moved back far enough to see it. Dal Ferstaan asked to have me as an assistant at the foundry, but Mage Eddan got the mayor to make him take a five-year contract on my apprenticeship. Since Master Ferstaan didn't have to pay for my contract, he says I can buy out anytime I need to for a penny. I keep a penny under my pillow."

Sir George had to hide a smile. "You were never meant to be a smith, my lad. But it does you good to be there for now. The hard work will build your strength, and crafting metal at the anvil will give you better dexterity with your hands. That will put you just that far ahead when the time comes to begin training with weapons."

"Begin?" Solveig declared in disbelief.

"The lad has a natural ability," Sir George told her.

"Then you do have plans for me?" Thelvyn asked

hopefully.

"Of course I have plans for you," the old knight insisted as he contemplated broaching a bottle of his favorite cherry liqueur. He handed the bottle to Thelvyn. "Open that for me, lad. The trouble is that the Flaem have a prior claim to you, according to that high and mighty law of theirs, and they won't let me have you until you come of age. I've asked to have you as my apprentice. That's not possible, they say, because you are a ward of the village and cannot leave. Well, it's not as if we don't know your birthday. Seven weeks to the day before the midwinter feast, and after that, you belong to yourself. Then you can do what you want and go where you want."

"Sometimes I think I'll be too old to do anything by then," Thelvyn said as he opened the bottle and handed it to Sir George. Solveig and Korinn held on to the drinks they already had, quietly refusing the cherry liqueur.

"Nonsense!" Sir George took his small glass over to his favorite chair and sat down heavily. For a moment, he sat and thought, tapping the wooden arm of the chair with the small hook he was wearing on his left sleeve cuff. "Lad, I'm afraid we'll have to be off again in just a few days. We've been caught up in some business that will likely keep us occupied for the rest of the year, and people are waiting for us in the south."

"What about me?" Thelvyn asked hopefully. "I know there's no point in asking to go with you, since that would place us both on the bad side of Flaemish law and ruin your chances of doing business here. But I would very much like to begin training for this future that you have in mind for me."

"As it happens, that's just what I have in mind," Sir George said. "The problem is that the good people of this village are going to insist upon putting you where they want you, so we might just as well leave you where you are for now. If things change, they'll probably just get worse. I'm going to have a little talk with Master Ferstaan to secure his cooperation in letting you continue your studies in secret. I'm going to send you home with a pile of books from my own collection, which I want you to read before the end of the year."

"Books?" Thelvyn asked, mystified but not opposed to the idea. Reading was difficult for him, but he enjoyed it.

"There are some things that I want you to know. A good deal more history, if nothing else. History and geography from books the Flaem didn't write to suit their own purposes. And if you should happen to read anything that doesn't agree with your previous education, I want you to know that my books are the ones you can trust. Hello, was that someone at the door?"

"I'll see who it is," Thelvyn offered.

He hurried off to the front door, wondering who else might have noticed the lights in the house. But when he opened the door, he found Celmar Ferstaan and Merilanda waiting on the step. Another girl stood behind them in the darkness. Celmar and Merilanda both leaned forward to look at Solveig's narrow-bladed sword, its point still buried deep in the wooden doorpost. Apparently being knocked soundly on the head had been enough of a distraction to cause her to forget about it.

"Are you entertaining yourself?" Celmar asked.

"Sir George came back," Thelvyn explained. "We were having a talk."

"You can talk tomorrow," Celmar told him softly. "We've found you a girl." He lowered his voice even more. "Perrena says that she will kiss you."

Thelvyn honestly didn't know what to do. If it had only been someone other than Perrena Talstae, he would have found it easier to say no.

* * * * *

Sir George and his odd companions stayed only a couple of days, and then they were off again. Thelvyn had the impression that they wouldn't have come back at all except that there was something here they needed, no doubt one of the many oddities in the old knight's collection, but he never found out any more about it and he didn't ask. Sir George's business was his own, no matter how much Thelvyn wanted to be a part of it.

Before they left, Thelvyn made several trips back to the
Ferstaan household with the books Sir George had selected
for him. Some of them looked quite ancient, while others
were obviously new, but they were all large and heavy. He
was eager to begin reading, since he was curious about
what knowledge he lacked of the outer world and also what
parts the Flaem had seen fit to change.

Thelvyn also made his peace, as far as he was able, with
Solveig White-Gold, who obviously took her name from
the light golden color of her hair. Thelvyn knew that the
people of the Northern Reaches took their names in the
same manner as the dwarves, but Solveig would never
mention her family name or admit to being the daughter of
anyone. He actually got along quite well with Korinn,
which was surprisingly, since dwarves were notoriously
slow to make friends. Perhaps knocking a dwarf silly in fair
combat was a quick way to earn his respect.

When they were gone again, Thelvyn's life returned
pretty much to what it had been before. Once again he
spent most of his working time tending the fires and pumping the bellows. He became quite good at this work and
could soon handle any part of the process himself. Dal Ferstaan had an arrangement with two groups of miners to
buy all the ore they produced. Twice each week a small
train of packhorses would come in with sacks of fresh ore
ready to be dumped into the bins, and once a month a
trader arrived from the south, eager to purchase all the iron
they had produced.

Whenever he had time, Master Ferstaan would take
Thelvyn over to the forge and teach him some tricks about
crafting the metal. Soon the young apprentice was making
hinges and latches and various other simple devices.

Master Ferstaan was also dutiful in his promise to Sir
George about making certain Thelvyn had some time each
day with his books. Thelvyn's higher education remained
very much a secret, for fear that others in the village, especially Mage Eddan, would take exception. At first, Thelvyn
was fearful that his reading would be much as it had been
back in school, which had been a dull, endless practice in
reading and writing and math, interspersed with the

painful memorizing of historical dates and other lists.

As it happened, these books proved to be much more interesting. Unlike stern mages, books made a point of explaining why things had happened as they did. Books written by dwarves and gnomes taught him things about metalworking and machines that Master Ferstaan could never have imagined. Soon Thelvyn suspected he knew more about the history of the world than most of the mages of the Flaem, although he privately felt that the fire wizards had no real interest in learning a great many things. They were too pleased with their own comfortable view of the world.

One thing Thelvyn noticed right away was that Sir George had provided a few books about magic, including a spellbook. That couldn't have been a mistake. Although the old knight had said nothing to him about it, he assumed he was supposed to be teaching himself any magic he could. He knew that magic-users weren't commonly self-taught, but he was determined to try. And so he did what the books told him, keeping his own book of spells close at hand so he could memorize them. He began to practice his magic in secret, more fearful than ever of what Mage Eddan would have to say.

Sir George came thundering back into the village one afternoon just past the middle of summer, together with his two new companions, each leading a packhorse. The old knight stopped by the forge briefly to tell Thelvyn that he was needed. That came as a surprise to Thelvyn, since he wasn't yet an active member of the group. He couldn't imagine what they expected of him. He hurried over as soon as he was able, pausing only long enough to wash and change his clothes after the day's work at the foundry. He was a bit nervous. He hoped that Solveig and Korinn had forgotten the circumstances of their introduction.

Thelvyn found a note waiting for him on the door, telling him to hurry along to the tavern as quickly as he could. When he arrived at the Two Pines Inn, he found that there was already quite a gathering assembled in the large private room in the back. Looking about, he saw that all the village elders were present, and a few other folk besides.

Although he was the last to enter, the business at hand had not yet begun. Mage Eddan, studiously noble as always, was only now taking his seat in the dark corner well to one side of the fireplace. The mage seemed pleased to retreat into such a secure corner, as far as he could get from the company of foreigners. Mayor Aalsten was seated in his usual place of honor, looking very ill at ease as he stared at his mug of ale, a certain sign that something was wrong.

Since all the seats were taken, Thelvyn joined Solveig and Korinn as they stood discreetly off to one side. Solveig had the grace not to wear her rather fanciful barbaric armor, but she was remarkable enough under the best of circumstances. Sir George, who was still negotiating the proper drink with the innkeeper, looked even more unusual for the company he was keeping these days. The villagers had become used to him over the years, but now they saw him as he was, an old knight wearing a hook where his left hand should be and somehow less quaint than he usually seemed.

"How have things been here at the village?" Sir George asked suddenly. Something about his tone suggested that he wasn't just making conversation.

"Quite well, actually," the mayor conceded. "Spring was early this year, the weather has been good, and it's been peaceful."

"Have you seen any dragons in the mountains?"

Mayor Aalsten nearly jumped at the mention of dragons. "Good heavens, no . . . not in some years, as you know. Should we?"

"I might as well come straight to the point," Sir George went on, seeing that he had already frightened the mayor quite enough. "We've come faster than the news itself, it seems, but word of it won't be far behind us. Bands of dragons have been attacking farms, mines, and even small villages in the far eastern frontier, up along the edge of the Wendarian Range leading into the Plains of Ethengar. So far they've stayed on the other side of Eastern Reach pass above the Colossus Mounts, so we are talking about a very remote region indeed."

He was obliged to wait for a long moment; the elders

were all too busy talking among themselves. Thelvyn was at least as frightened as the others looked. His first thought was that the dragons were looking for him.

"Are the dragons headed in this direction?" Mayor Aalsten asked.

"That I cannot say," Sir George admitted. "That depends on the reason why they have chosen to abandon their usual isolation and begin attacking settlements in organized bands. That's not normal behavior for dragons."

"What's so unusual about dragons attacking settlements?" someone asked.

Sir George shook his head. "What is unusual is dragons doing anything in organized bands. Dragons are typically loners. They'll work together only in response to what they perceive as major events, and they'll band together to fight only in response to major threats. I can't for my life imagine what could be going on in that part of this world that they would find threatening."

"Could it be a response to our own recent settlements in those lands?" the mayor asked. "I wonder if the expansion of the frontier, especially all the mining in the mountains, is encroaching upon their territory."

"No, I don't think so," Sir George answered. "The settlements are nothing new, nor the mining. There have been elves in those lands for thousands of years, and the Wendarian Range on up into the Northern Reaches was once a major branch of the nation of the gnomes, although they've mostly withdrawn into other parts of the world in the last few decades."

"Then I have to ask one question," the mayor said. "Could this be in any way related to the events of almost sixteen years ago?"

Sir George shook his head firmly. "No, I doubt that very much. At least not more than incidentally."

"I'm not so certain of that," Mage Eddan commented, speaking for the first time. "We have no previous knowledge of this remarkable race that gave us Thelvyn and his mother, but I recall the tale of how his mother came to us across the mountains. The dragons either feared or hated her so much that they banded together to hunt her down, but she possessed the magic to survive their attack. That leads me to suspect that his mother came from a race of extraordinarily powerful wizards, who might be locked in some ancient battle with the dragons."

"If you think that I come from a race of powerful wizards, why were you so reluctant to teach me magic?" Thelvyn asked.

"I never dared . . . for your own sake," Eddan insisted. "Some races have practiced a particular form of magic for so long that it has become a part of their nature. Our own people have practiced fire magic so extensively that we no longer have the ability to do other types well. Teaching you an incompatible form of magic could have been disastrous for you."

Thelvyn noticed that Sir George looked rather dubious but elected to say nothing on that subject, so he did the same.

"My point is this," Eddan continued. "The events of sixteen years ago and the present raids of dragons upon our settlements could very well be the incidental effects of an ancient war or rivalry previously unknown to this part of the world."

"That may well be," Sir George agreed disinterestedly.

"But what are we to do about it?" the mayor asked. "Have you heard of any way we can defend the village against these beasts?"

"Dragons are not beasts," Sir George said. "Now, I know that you people have had little contact with real dragons. Most of the old stories describe them as great evil beasts that eat people and guard fabulous treasures. If some hero in a story needs a treasure or a magical item or is seeking a reputation as a warrior, all he needs to do is find a dragon to kill. But you should know that dragons are the oldest race in this world, that they are overall the most intelligent species, and that very few of them are evil. It's just that dragons keep to themselves. The only ones most people are likely to run in to are the evil ones out hunting for mischief."

"That's no comfort," the mayor declared. "But what do we do about them if they come here?"

"Just get out of the way," Sir George replied. "We don't have the magic or the force of arms here to fight even one dragon, at least not without considerable loss of life. My advice is this: The dragons are still far away, so don't worry about them too much. That's a matter for the archduke of the realm and the Council of Dukes and Wizards. But if word does come that dragons are headed this way, then you need to find a safe place where the people of the village can retreat, with a good store of supplies laid aside in the event the village is destroyed."

Sir George did his best, but the villagers didn't want to hear what he was trying to tell them. They wanted to defend their homes, but the simple fact was that if the dragons did come in this direction, there was really nothing that anyone could do about it. After a time, he decided to stand back and allow them to argue the matter, since they obviously had no intention of following his advice. They were more inclined to demand that Duke Aalban do something about the defense of the frontier, or else give the archduke the authority to do something in the defense of all the Highlands. Privately Sir George told his companions that Duke Aalban, like the other dukes, would rather fight dragons himself than grant more power to the archduke.

At last Sir George suggested to his companions that they should leave, since their knowledge and advice was no longer wanted. Night was falling, even though night came especially late by the middle of summer this far north. They retired to the den in Sir George's house, the only place he knew where he was likely to find a bottle of his favorite cherry liqueur. Thelvyn noticed that Solveig and Korinn seemed to find the Flaemish settlers about as irritating as he did.

"I wonder why we even bothered," Sir George commented when he had sunk into his favorite chair with a small drink in hand, tapping the wooden arm of the chair with the tip of his hook. "For all the good it did, they might just as well have waited until the duke sees fit to tell them about the dragons."

"Will they follow your advice?" Korinn asked. Being a dwarf, perhaps he was used to hard heads.

"Oh, I imagine they will—if the dragons come any closer and they've had the time to decide that it was their own idea. The trouble is that I have no idea whether the dragons do have some purpose in mind, or if they're just attacking everything in their neighborhood."

"Are they looking for my mother or me?" Thelvyn asked. "I know you might not have wanted to admit that to the village council, knowing how suspicious of strangers the Flaem are anyway."

"You really have had your fill of them, haven't you?" Sir George asked. "No, my answer to the question was my honest one. If for whatever reason the dragons had decided to resume the hunt for you or your mother, they would have remembered where to look. The fact that they are two hundred miles away and not here suggests to me that the events are not related."

"What about Mage Eddan's theories about my race?" Thelvyn asked. "Could there be some ancient war between my people and the dragons?"

"I find that very unlikely," Sir George insisted. "As you may guess, I know a thing or two about dragons. Nearly everything most people know about dragons comes from the stories they've heard, which tell about how fierce dragons are, but the hero always kills the dragon in the end because that's the way stories work. But in real life, the dragon almost always wins. Aside from the fact that dragons are big, fast, and well armored, they are also highly intelligent, and they tend to live a very long time. That makes mature dragons the most powerful and experienced magic-users in the world. I can't imagine any other race making a specialty of fighting dragons."

"That might explain why this mysterious race of Thelvyn's is so rare," Korinn commented dryly.

"I've been told that my mother defended herself against a band of dragons and defeated them," Thelvyn pointed out.

"She didn't defeat them. She eluded them," Sir George said. "That isn't quite the same thing, although I must admit that it still showed remarkable ability on her part. Still, I wonder. I've tried to arrange for a teacher for you, a magic-user who is not of the Flaem, but things haven't yet worked out. Have you been reading those books on magic I gave you?"

"Oh, yes," Thelvyn said. "I've had a problem finding time to practice much, but I've learned five of the basic spells already."

He cast a spell of light on Sir George's hook, causing it to glow brightly. The old knight reacted with such alarm that Thelvyn was afraid he had done something wrong.

"Whoa, hold it a minute!" Sir George declared, removing his hook and burying it beneath the cushion of his chair until the spell faded. "What do you mean when you say you've learned five spells? I only gave you books on the history and general theory of magic. There couldn't have been any actual spells in those books."

"But there were . . . in the black spellbook," Thelvyn insisted.

"What spellbook?" Sir George asked. "I've never had an extra spellbook, so I'm sure that there couldn't have been one among the books I gave you. You can't just pick up someone else's spellbook and begin using it anyway."

"I've never heard of anyone being able to teach himself, either," Solveig added.

"Well, there are certain special situations, such as when either the individual or his race is strongly inclined toward the use of magic," Sir George said. Then he looked very thoughtful. He seemed to lose all inclination to argue the matter further. Thelvyn watched him for a moment, suspecting that he might have guessed where that spellbook came from.

"Whether Thelvyn's people are involved in this or not, the problem right now is the dragons," Korinn said. "Do you have any idea why they are attacking?"

Sir George shook his head. "It's too complicated to guess. Indeed I wonder if we will ever know. If it turns out to be only reds and blacks, then I'm not greatly concerned. They could be squabbling with each other or with the goblins or kobolds over the spoils of the ancient settlements of the gnomes in the mountains, although most of those settlements are either failing or already abandoned. Or they could just be in the process of putting down a renegade who has gotten completely out of hand. Renegades are insane by definition anyway."

He noticed that Thelvyn seemed to be full of questions. "Lad, dragons are a very proud race, and it is their pride as much as their loyalty to their Immortal, known to others only as the Great One, that binds them as a race and a nation. Now, within the greater Nation of Dragons are the Hidden Kingdoms of the Dragons, in which dragons of similar type will pledge their allegiance to each other under a particularly wise or capable leader, for their mutual prosperity and protection. Even the chaotic reds, greens, and blacks usually don't dare break draconic law.

"But there are always the renegades—violent, greedy dragons so swollen with self-pride that they aspire to make themselves into kings or even Immortals. They build support by subduing lesser dragons, usually those as evil and mad as themselves. But if a renegade begins attacking dragons belonging to one of the Hidden Kingdoms, then the other dragons will band together and put down the renegade and his cohorts. Of course, since most dragons keep to themselves, these renegades are about the only dragons that the rest of the world knows about. As far as most people are aware, all dragons behave like renegades."

"Are there any circumstances when a Kingdom of Dragons would make war upon other races?" Korinn asked.

"Only in self-defense, or in retaliation for an especially evil deed that has been perpetrated against them," Sir George said. "All I can think of is that the Wizards of the Flaem might have done something to provoke the dragons, something that is not yet common knowledge. They're an arrogant lot, and they can be so single-minded in their hatred of the Alphatians that they might try something especially stupid, like trying to capture dragons to use as battle mounts. I can be more certain about the situation when I know what breeds of dragons are involved."

"Meaning the golds?" Solveig asked.

Sir George nodded slowly. "If the golds are involved, this would have to be nothing short of war."

CHAPTER THREE

If the wiser minds of the village had been trying to convince themselves that Sir George had been wrong on the subject of dragons and their recent activities, the next morning found the arrival of information that was even harder to dispute. A company of Duke Aalban's own soldiers, under the lead of a young captain who was tall, handsome, and very much under the impression that he was talking to a bunch of stupid rustics rode into Graez later that morning.

Thelvyn had been running an errand for the smith and had seen their arrival at the garrison, and he found the entire scene to be vaguely amusing and satisfying. If the Flaem could act aloof and superior even to each other on the slightest pretext, then imagine the attitude of one small frontier settlement toward the populace of a slightly newer, smaller frontier settlement. What Thelvyn found most interesting of all was that Flaemish hierarchies were so well established that the mayor and his friends seemed to recognize, and even accept, their inferior lot.

The captain of the duke's company had little enough to say, and none of it was particularly reassuring. Bands of red dragons were attacking settlements, farms, and mines on the far northeastern frontier. They had also been harassing the Ethengar nomads. It didn't yet seem to be a state of open war, since the dragons could easily have done more damage than they had, so this so far this was considered to be only an incident. In spite of the villagers' expectations, the captain's company wasn't under orders to stay and reinforce the local garrison. The soldiers were needed to the northeast, where the dragons were most likely to attack first.

All citizens were advised to be cautious. The village, the farms, and the mines were to avoid calling attention to themselves, and to that end, they were advised to light no large fires during the night and to shutter their windows. All travelers were to hasten as quickly as possible through open areas and to be cautious with their own fires at night. So declared Duke Aalban, who was confident of his ability to handle the situation.

When Thelvyn brought him this news, Sir George seemed rather amused by it all. "Very much what I predicted. Duke Aalban knows that he can't handle dragons, but he also doesn't want to grant any greater powers to the archduke. The only way he can manage this 'incident' is if it does in fact go away."

"I don't understand," Thelvyn protested. "Why is Duke Aalban afraid of the archduke? Doesn't he already owe full allegiance to him?"

"You're thinking of how the matter of kingdoms usually works," Sir George told him. He was sitting in his favorite chair in his den, contemplating a bottle of cherry liqueur—not drinking it, just contemplating the unopened bottle. "This is the way things work among the Flaem, at least as far as I have been able to tell, and I'm not entirely certain that even they understand it any better. Traditionally the rule has always been a matter of balance between the king and the fire wizards.

"But the Flaem had been wandering for hundreds of years in some pretty strange places before they came into this world. During that time, they had traveled in large bands under the leadership of the men we call the dukes, in the more ancient definition of a duke as a war leader or great captain, not as a title of traditional nobility. They couldn't very well maintain a true kingdom during this age of wandering, and I suspect they were really only bound together by their tremendous hatred of the Alphatians and their desire to find and defeat their ancient enemy. But you know about that, I suppose."

"That's what they taught me in school," Thelvyn agreed. "The Flaem and the Alphatians fought a great war, so great that it destroyed their own world. Survivors from both sides escaped through gates into other worlds. The Alphatians arrived first, fifteen centuries ago, and have established a great empire in the east. The Flaem arrived only some hundred years ago. Now that they have found their ancient enemy, they will stay here until they have become strong enough to renew the war, and just as likely destroy this world in the process."

"A long, long time will pass before the Flaem are able to fight Alphatia . . . if ever," Solveig White-Gold said. "The Alphatians are an empire equal to Thyatis, while the Flaem are still a very small, rustic, impoverished band of vagabonds."

"Most likely the Alphatians will find and crush the Flaem long before that happens," Sir George added. "For one thing, however much they desire it, the Flaem themselves are not cooperating much in the plan to build their own great kingdom. The dukes were their only leaders all through the age of wandering, and they don't want to see that change. They all want to be the king, but they don't want anyone else becoming king.

"So instead of an actual king, they came up with the title of archduke as the ceremonial commander of the realm, except that he has no great power otherwise and holds no lands. In fact, most of the time he has hardly any authority at all. In a time of great crisis, he will be granted the authority to assume command of all the dukedoms of the Flaem, including the elven lands in the south. But the archduke only has the authority and the force of arms granted to him by the dukes, and under most circumstances, they would rather keep that entirely for themselves."

"But the dragon raids might change all that," Thelvyn observed.

"That's precisely the point," Sir George agreed. "The northern dukes will need the forces of the southern dukes in addition to their own to fight these dragons. And if you think the northern dukes are reluctant, consider the southern dukes, who aren't under any immediate threat. Now, in all this mess, we also have the fire wizards, who have good reason to support the archduke. First, they see a strongly unified kingdom as the best way to rebuild the past strength of their race so that they can renew their war with the Alphatians. They also have a better chance of taking power away from the archduke for themselves, since they firmly believe that they are the only rightful rulers of the Flaemish race. They've had precious little success trying to control the dukes. Too many political enemies to attempt to defeat, and the dukes are very experienced at keeping what they have."

"And whoever tries to handle the dragons will need the wizards," Korinn added.

"Exactly so, and the archduke's advantage in this is that the wizards have always been allied with him," Sir George continued. "You mark my words. The next move will be on the part of the wizards. Just how they plan to react remains to be seen. They may attempt to win more power for the archduke, and themselves, at once. Or they may sit tight and wait for things to get worse, until the dukes are frightened and contrite enough to grant powers to the archduke that they will not easily get back."

If nothing else, Thelvyn was finally beginning to understand something about politics. As far as he could tell, it was a subtle way of treating someone unfairly or taking something from him without actually breaking the law. Which was perhaps to say that he understood politics very well indeed.

As the days and then weeks passed, matters only got worse. More precise accounts of the dragon raids were carried deeper into the realm. These accounts should have been reassuring, as indeed they were to calmer and more practical heads such as Sir George's. There had been very little loss of life, for the dragons typically came upon the victims with a great deal of noise and fury but were always rather slow in their attack, giving people a chance to flee. Sometimes the damage they did was only superficial, while at other times the destruction they brought upon a settlement was complete. But if no news was indeed good news, then many people found any news concerning dragons to be alarming.

The influence of the dragons and the panic they brought was felt over a wide area of the realm, partly due to the tidings of their coming and partly because the dragons themselves seemed to be attempting to breed fear. Soon dragons had been seen flying alone or in pairs, perhaps as scouts or patrols, in almost every part of the Highlands. On the frontier, dragon scouts were spotted in the sky over the village once or twice a week. The Flaemish settlers began preparing for the worst. The mayor and Mage Eddan even adopted Sir George's plan of preparing hidden caches of supplies in the mountains once they could convince themselves that it was their own idea.

Sir George's last prediction wasn't long in proving itself correct. Barely three weeks after the first warning, a group of senior fire wizards, leading a company of soldiers, arrived from the south. They declared that they had been sent from Braejr itself, dispatched by the archduke and by the leaders of their own order to investigate the dragons. That seemed a little surprising at first, since they were headed in the wrong direction by traveling northwest from Braejr into the principality of Duke Aalban. The remote village of Graez was the most distant corner of the frontier from the site of the actual attacks.

But the wizards explained that they were in fact proceeding by the best method by following the line of mountains as they circled around the lands of Duke Aalban and across the top of the frontier, ultimately reaching the region of the known attacks. In this way, they explained, they were unlikely to miss anything. The general belief among the villagers was that the noble Wizards of the Flaem were stalling, or at least being entirely too doggedly academic when quick answers were needed.

The wizards and their guards spent the night in the village, complaining loudly about the discomforts of the wild and that a wizard's lot was always an unhappy one. Needless to say, their behavior did not engender much confidence in their ability to handle dragons. For his own part, Thelvyn was relieved that no one had brought up the subject of himself, his mother and the curious events that had occurred many years before. He couldn't escape a certain feeling of guilt, a suspicion that he was somehow at fault.

He certainly didn't want the wizards to discover that he was perhaps the descendant of some unknown race who were ancient enemies of dragons. He was practical enough to admit that he was just an apprentice smith with pretensions of being a magic-user and no idea how to fight dragons. He could easily imagine being handed over to the dragons by the nervous fire wizards, in the hope that the dragons would go away.   But the wizards departed into the wild the next day. Dragons continued to be spotted every few days, but they didn't attack. Summer deepened toward autumn, which always came early in the Highlands, and life in the village returned pretty much to normal.

Then one evening Sir George told Thelvyn that he would be going away with Korinn and Solveig soon. Thelvyn would have liked to ask where they were going and what they were doing, for it was unusual for traders to set out in the fall and not return until spring. He had been thinking lately that he was getting old enough to speak plainly with the old knight. But that seemed to betray an unspoken trust between them, and he decided that this wasn't quite yet the time. Everything would change when Sir George returned next spring, or so he thought, for he would then be of age.

"Your studies have been going well?" Sir George asked of him one afternoon while they were taking a short walk in the woods.

"Yes, they are," Thelvyn replied. "You know, it's a funny thing. When I was in school, it took me long, hard work to learn new things. My vision still makes it hard for me to read from books. But now I can sit and read for a short time, and suddenly I've learned more in a hour than I used to learn in a week."

"Perhaps learning something is easier when you know why you're learning it."

"Oh, I have no idea of that, except that you seem to think that it will be useful for me," Thelvyn insisted.

"Well, that knocks my little theory right out the door," Sir George said, amused with himself. "What about the magic? Are you still learning magic?"

"Yes, that's coming along well. And that's also been very interesting. I had always thought that magic was just a matter of memorizing and mastering spells. But that becomes much easier as you come to understand the spells by learning about the history and theory of magic. I'm coming to believe that all things in life have evolved for a reason, and that all things are in some way related to all other things. That seemed terribly complicated at first, but it makes understanding things much more manageable."

"Well, that's good to know," Sir George said as he regarded the trees. "I plan to have some other work for you when I return next spring, and I need you to be prepared. I don't mind leaving you at the forge for a while longer because it gives you time to study, time that will be harder to find in the future."

"I'm trying hard to be patient," Thelvyn said, hoping that he didn't sound as if he were complaining. "Then you really will not be back home again till spring?"

"No. This is dull, nasty business, and a long journey besides," the knight explained. "All the way to Thyatis and back. Taking Solveig home again is always a tricky proposition."

Thelvyn was startled. "But I thought Solveig came from the Northern Reaches. Of course, she does talk and act like a Thyatian sometimes."

"I didn't think you'd met enough Thyatians to know," Sir George said. "Solveig has the same problem you do, in a way. She comes from the Northern Reaches, of course. She was born there. But she was brought to Thyatis at a very early age. As a slave, in fact."

"A slave?"

"To a very real extent, yes," Sir George said. "Politics in the Northern Reaches are, shall we say, rather extreme. If Solveig herself knows the truth of the matter, she keeps that her own secret. Most likely her own family or clan was slain by their political enemies, but she was spared because of her age and then sold into slavery in Thyatis. Or she may have been kidnapped by enemies of her family as an act of revenge or provocation. Or she could have been sold secretly by her own clan because she presented some difficulty, perhaps because she was a female heir or an illegitimate one, or an inconvenient heir for any number of reasons. It isn't even unheard of that her clan sold her secretly just to be able to make a false accusation of kidnapping and murder against another clan. Such events are not only known but fairly common."

"I can't much imagine Solveig as a slave," Thelvyn admitted.

"That she never was, not really. You see, she was bought and later adopted by a very wealthy and powerful family, one that had two sons and no daughter. Appearance is everything in Thyatian social circles, where every great family must have at least one daughter of remarkable beauty to present to high society. I never did find out what they do with the ugly ones. Anyway, she was purchased to fill a specific need, like an elegant villa or a new coach, more than a toy but less than a true daughter."

Thelvyn could appreciate the situation. She had been given a life as a matter of convenience, while he had never been a convenience to anyone.

"Of course, Solveig complicated the issue herself," Sir George continued. "She continued to grow. She remained a striking beauty, but she ended up about five sizes too large to suit the bill. On top of that, she always retained the heart of a Northlands warrior. She actually learned the craft of fighting by training as a gladiator in Thyatis, one reason why she's the best. She never fought as a gladiator, of course, since that would have been a devastating humiliation to her adopted family."

"Did she really want to become a gladiator?" Thelvyn asked, remembering the stories he had heard about that.

"No, that's a terrible life," Sir George said. "She just wanted the best training. I hope to be able to convince her to train you in the advanced use of weapons soon. You do have her grudging respect in that regard, you know, since you were able to disarm her."

"Well, I did have an advantage," Thelvyn admitted. "I can see in the dark."

"Perhaps, but she had the advantage of experience, and besides, you were using only a hiking staff. Don't underestimate your abilities, lad. You have the makings of a great fighter. I just hope you don't choose to limit yourself to only that, for you also have the making of something much more."

Thelvyn felt the inclination to argue, but thought better of it and said nothing. His life in the village had left him feeling rather useless, not just because he had failed at so many things but also because the Flaemish settlers had ways of making him feel useless and out of step without even trying. There were so many things they had refused to allow him even to try, all the while making it seem that the fault was entirely his own. He had to remind himself that the fault had not been his own, and that he was probably capable of more than he suspected. Sir George obviously believed that he was capable of a great deal. And when he thought about it, he realized that Sir George's opinions were the ones he respected most.

And so the days passed while Thelvyn worked at the foundry during the day and read his books by night. He slipped away to spend time with Sir George and Solveig and the dwarf, Korinn, whenever he could. So it was that summer catapulted into autumn in that rather abrupt manner typical of the north, when a sudden cold storm came crashing down from the mountains to the north. The warmth of the sunlight ebbed, and cool winds frolicked back and forth through the forest to turn the leaves red and gold. Then Thelvyn knew that Sir George and his companions would soon be going away once again, and his life alone in the village would be far more dull and sad until the old knight returned in the spring.

Thelvyn was so occupied with his own concerns that the

world could be overrun with marauding dragons and he would hardly have noticed. But dragons did not overrun the world, or the Highlands, or even any farm or settlement within a hundred miles of the little village of Graez. One day people paused in all their preparations for the harvest and the coming winter, and suddenly they realized that they hadn't seen a dragon in the sky for at least a week.

When they also realized that there had been no word of new attacks in many days, then they began to hope that the invasion was over. Perhaps the dragons had become bored with the whole affair and had gone away somewhere to spend the winter. That was an enormously reassuring thought, since everyone knew that the best way to get rid of dragons, and really almost the only way, was if they decided to go away on their own.

Of course, there remained the question of whether or not the dragons would resume their attacks next spring or summer. Even Sir George had no opinion on that account, since he honestly had no idea why the dragons had begun their attacks in the first place. All he could say was that only extraordinary circumstances could have led the dragons into such behavior. Any motives as remarkable as that weren't likely to simply go away during the winter, which suggested that the dragons would be in no better mood next year.

But privately he reluctantly admitted that if the attacks were resumed next year, then he would most likely have to look into the matter and decide what he could do about it. To Thelvyn, that seemed to be a most remarkable thing to say, even for him, and the most alarming part was that Solveig and Korinn seemed to take him at his word.

Eventually the day came that Sir George and his companions began to make ready to depart. Thelvyn did what he could to help them prepare, hurrying with his chores at the foundry so he could be at their disposal. On that same day, news came from Aalbansford by way of the village garrison that the party of fire wizards sent to investigate the attacks by the dragons had returned, and they had announced their discoveries while passing through on their way back to Braejr.

Their conclusions were simple enough: The dragons were gone for now, so perhaps it was best to simply wait and see if they come back next year. After a long moment of amazement, Sir George considered that carefully and remained lost somewhere between amusement and disgust. Thelvyn was somewhat less surprised. He was beginning to understand the Flaem very well by this time, and he knew their preference for simple solutions.

"Well, at least I can go away for a while without worrying about you the whole time," Sir George said the next morning as he waited with his companions outside his home. Each of them was leading two packhorses. "If the dragons should return before I do, I trust that you will do the clever thing."

"Stay out of the way?" Thelvyn asked.

"You stay as far away from dragons as you can," the old knight told him. "The matter with your mother may be long forgotten as far as the dragons are concerned, or it may not. Just remember that you look like your mother, and a dragon that gets a good look at you may recognize you for what you are."

"I'll remember," Thelvyn promised. "If the dragons happen to threaten the village, is there anything in your house that I should try to save first?"

"Well, you know where the major treasures are kept," Sir George said. "But worry about yourself first. Like a dragon, I keep the better part of my horde secret."

Sir George pulled himself awkwardly into his saddle, having only one hand to keep his balance, and Thelvyn handed him the leads of his two packhorses. Solveig and Korinn lifted themselves into their own saddles, although the dwarf was required to use a mounting stirrup that hung lower than the usual stirrups, similar to those used by knights in armor. Dwarves seldom rode full-size horses, preferring sturdy little ponies, but Korinn rode with the grace of an expert once he was in the saddle.

"Look for us to return in the spring," Sir George told him. "I cannot say exactly when, but I hope to be back early. Watch out for yourself, and remember your books."

Then Thelvyn stepped back and watched as Sir George and his companions rode away into the sunrise, turning onto the main road, which led into the forest, to Aalbansford, then south into the heart of the realm and beyond. He wanted more than anything to be going with them. Even if adventures were every bit as dangerous and uncomfortable as he was told. Even if Sir George was nothing more than the doddering old trader he pretended to be, and the most exciting event in his life was haggling over the price of wool. Anything was better than staying in this place. Thelvyn thought the coming fall and winter would be the longest he had ever known. At least the next time that odd little band rode out of town, he would be with them.

* * * * *

Thelvyn thought that he had never had such a wonderful birthday. It was only modest as far as parties went, but it meant that he had turned sixteen and had finally come of age. Dal Ferstaan actually gave all his assistants the day off in celebration of the event. Not that a day off really mattered all that much, since early snows had closed the trails, and there was no new ore coming down from the mines. Without a steady supply of ore, it was only a matter of time before the foundry closed down for the winter. There would be many days without work yet to come, but most of them would be without cause to celebrate.

Even Celmar Ferstaan, who had always been Thelvyn's best friend in the whole village, came to join the celebration. Mila Ferstaan, Celmar's mother, prepared an especially fine dinner for the occasion, which was remarkable in itself. She was one of the finest metal engravers in the village but not a particularly good cook. Afterward they passed around a bottle of excellent Darokin wine and drank to Thelvyn's future. Then came the part everyone had had been waiting for, for Dal Ferstaan brought out a small bag of coins and set it on the table before Thelvyn.

"This is your pay for your last year's service, according to the terms of your contract of apprenticeship," the smith said. "I've known from the first that you had no wish to remain. You've done good work here and with little cause for regret, or so I hope. All the same, I suspect you have other plans for your future."

"I do," Thelvyn agreed. "Or at least plans have been made for me, although I'm not sure yet what they are. Just the same, whatever Sir George has to offer me, I expect that it will be the life I prefer."

"Well, we all expected as much," Dal Ferstaan agreed. "And to that end, in honor of the promise I made you when you first came here, I'll allow you to buy back your contract at the cost of one brass penny, which is more than I paid for it. Then legal custom will be satisfied, and you'll be free to go where you wish."

"I've waited a long time to be my own person," Thelvyn agreed.

"That you have," the smith said. "And it would also be for your own good, for you remain bound to the will of the village council for as long as you remain under a contract of apprenticeship."

Thelvyn paid the smith the brass penny, which he had set aside long ago for this very purpose and which he had brought with him that night. He never suspected that the contract gave the village council any authority in continuing to dictate his affairs, even now that he had come of age. As it was, buying back his contract was far more important than his sixteenth birthday. Then Dal Ferstaan gave him his contract, which had been written on heavy parchment, then rolled tight and tied with a black ribbon.

"Well, there you have it," the smith said. "You can stay here or not, as you please. I'll continue to pay you an apprentice's wages for the work you do, but there won't be much until next spring."

Thelvyn had to consider that quickly. "I think I should move into Sir George's house. He was concerned that I stay with my books, and a long winter alone there would be just the thing. But I also think I should continue to help you here, so certain people in the village don't fuss that I am unemployed."

"There's Flaemish laws against being unemployed, of course," Master Ferstaan said, looking concerned. Thelvyn was beginning to be surprised that he hadn't been tossed in prison years ago, what with so many Flaemish laws.

Thelvyn had been obliged to wait sixteen years to move into Sir George's house, but he hadn't expected to do so that very night. It hardly seemed polite, as if it meant that he could hardly wait to get away from the Ferstaan household. All the same, Celmar jumped up and insisted upon helping him pack that very moment, and the elder Ferstaans didn't object. Packing was a relatively small detail, the bulk of his possessions being the great stack of books Sir George had loaned to him. But the two journeymen helped to carry the books out to a handcart, and Thelvyn was on his way in a matter of minutes.

The streets of the village were dark and deserted by that time, for night came early in the last days of autumn. Celmar had insisted upon going with him and helping him to get settled. They both felt like a pair of inexperienced thieves trying to make off with their loot as they pushed the noisy, uncooperative cart and tried to avoid dumping its contents into the mud.

Thelvyn was certain they were making enough noise to summon the entire garrison, especially with all the concern lately about dragons. But they met no one. No eyes peered out of windows or doors to see what was happening. And that was just as well, since Thelvyn had had enough of meddlesome Flaems poking their noses into his affairs.

"So it has come at last," Celmar said. "I always knew you would be going away someday, but someday always seemed a long time off. Now here it is."

"I'm not going anywhere yet," Thelvyn insisted. "Not for weeks or even months. Nor am I going away forever, you know. As long as Sir George lives here in the village, I suppose that I will also."

"What's the true story about Sir George?" Celmar asked suddenly. "Is he really a former knight and a trader as he claims? If anyone should know, you should."

"Well, I'm sure he was once a knight," Thelvyn said. "He still has his old armor, made to his size, and the emblems of his order and such. And I've seen no evidence that he's not a trader, nor has he ever spoken to me of any adventures he has had beyond those that any traveler in the wild might have known. He may be a trader, but he certainly doesn't trade in common goods. His house is full of oddities and ancient artifacts."

"Many say he is an adventurer, he and his odd companions," Celmar said.

"Again, that's more than I know for certain," Thelvyn insisted. "Sir George says Solveig is one of the best fighters around. I could certainly believe she's an adventurer, but I don't know anything about Korinn except that he's young for a dwarf, and a quiet, clever fellow as well. They call him the Bear Slayer."

"And those are your friends?" Celmar asked skeptically. "They seem pretty strange to me."

"Celmar, I'm pretty strange myself," Thelvyn reminded him. Celmar grinned.

They had reached the front door of Sir George's house. Once inside, he claimed one of the five guest rooms—Sir George had anticipated having a good deal of company when he had built his home—and he brought his clothes and other personal belongings there. The books he brought to the den, since that seemed like the proper place for reading. It was a big house and a lonely one when there was no one about but himself, especially through a long, dark winter, but he thought that he would enjoy the adventure of being entirely on his own for the first time in his life.

"Well, here you are," Celmar observed as he stood just outside the front door, ready to depart. "Are you sure you'll be all right on your own?"

"Of course," Thelvyn insisted. "I know how to cook and care for myself. I've done it often enough for Sir George and his crew in the past. I have my wages, and I know where I can purchase anything I might need."

"Are you sure it's all right to settle into Sir George's house without him being here?"

"Certainly. He's told me that I should. I'm his heir, you know. As long as I stay away from his undergarments and his cherry liqueur, I'm welcome to anything here." Thelvyn laughed. "You worry too much, Celmar. Or are you just afraid of Sir George?"

"It's just such a big, empty house," Celmar replied.

Thelvyn stood at the open door for a moment longer

while Celmar hurried away into the night, taking the hand-cart back to the smithy. He hadn't realized at first that his friend really was concerned for him, or that Celmar found both Sir George and his great house to be vaguely frightening. Thelvyn's friends had grown up with him, and they thought of him as one of their own, unlike many of their elders. And while the Flaem were on the whole a very practical, reasonable people, their instinctive distrust of strangers was easily awakened. He wondered sometimes whether they had acquired that trait during their long Age of Wandering, fifteen centuries of moving from world to world after they had destroyed their own land in an ancient civil war. They must have seen many curious places, people, and creatures during that time.

And *they* thought *he* was strange? Thelvyn found that more disquieting than ever.

He suddenly realized that he had finally severed his ties with the Flaem and their cold, suspicious laws and their narrow, tradition-bound ways. Now that he had both come of age and bought back his contract of apprenticeship, they no longer had the means to make his decisions for him or dictate how he would live, the things he would know, or the life he would have. Freedom was such a new experience for him that he didn't yet know what he thought about it.

Thelvyn was about to step back inside when he saw that someone was watching him from around the corner of the house across the street, a tall figure in dark clothing. When he looked closer, he could see that it was Mage Eddan, dressed in his long black cloak with the stiff upright collar. Although Thelvyn kept it hidden from everyone except Sir George, his night vision served him well. Knowing that he had been seen and most likely recognized as well, the wizard elected to confront the problem head on and stepped forward.

"Changing your residence already?" Mage Eddan asked simply. "I suspected that you would."

"Is that what you came to see?" Thelvyn asked, daring to speak as his own master.

"No, other concerns brought me out tonight," the wizard said. "Being well trained in magic, I soon become aware when someone nearby is using magic. When I sensed that someone in the village had been learning magic, I didn't need long to discover that it was you."

"That is so," Thelvyn admitted, deliberately vague.

"Who is teaching you?" Eddan asked sharply. "Is it Sir George?"

"I've been teaching myself. Sir George gave me the books."

"Yourself?" Mage Eddan paused a moment, looking surprised and uncertain. "I forbade you to learn magic. I have my reasons, most of them out of concern for your own welfare. I insist that you stop."

"I have come of age today," Thelvyn reminded him. "And I have bought back my contract of apprenticeship. By Flaemish law, I am now free to make my own decisions."

"Yes, that is so," Mage Eddan agreed, pausing a moment to reconsider the matter. He seemed less hostile. "Well, perhaps it is best after all. While you were still a child, I had a responsibility to protect you from danger. A parent may allow a child to take certain risks when risk becomes necessary to learning, but the role of the guardian is more strict. As you say, the decision and the responsibility are now your own. But are you really aware of the risks?"

"I believe I am," Thelvyn said, confused by this rather sudden change in attitude.

"And yet you find the risk is a price worth paying," the wizard said, then nodded. "I can sympathize with your desires. Just be very careful. And if you have any problem, you are to come to me. I would rather teach you myself than have you experimenting on your own."

Mage Eddan turned sharply and walked away into the night. Thelvyn watched him for a moment, wondering just how much he really could trust the mage. Then he closed the door and went to his new quarters to unpack, amused to think that he could probably have frightened the wizard into giving him proper training months sooner. He did indeed know the risks he had been taking; the books had always stressed that. Where magic was concerned, a little knowledge was indeed the most dangerous thing in the world.

CHAPTER FOUR

The approach of spring proved to be a time of great anticipation. For the folk living on the northern frontier of the Highlands, spring brought with it the fear and uncertainty of not knowing whether the dragons would renew their attacks this year, perhaps sweeping their path of destruction farther into the realm. For Thelvyn, spring brought only impatience for Sir George and his companions to return from their latest travels. Then perhaps Thelvyn's own life would finally begin.

Thelvyn had expected that his life would become easier once he had come of age, that the Flaem would respect both his right and his ability to make his own decisions. He realized later that he should have known better. The Flaem were basically a good folk, and when they weren't distracted by suspicion, then they invariably tried to be helpful, at least insofar as they defined help.

The people of the village noticed right away that he had moved into Sir George's house, and that was followed at once by the unexpected news that he was and always had been the old knight's heir, which led to a great deal of interest in, and enthusiasm for, young Thelvyn and his prospects. It also led invariably to speculation about just how much wealth Sir George really had. Soon he was generally regarded to be one of the wealthiest men in all the Highlands. Although he already had the largest, most comfortable home in the village, the rumor began to circulate that this was only a place he came to for peace and solitude, to make his secret plans or to escape the attention of his rivals and his enemies. People began to say that he probably had great palaces of his own in far-off Darokin, where he had lived before, or even Thyatis, and that he was away in such places during the long months he was gone.

Into the middle of all this speculation came Thelvyn, who suddenly found that he had gone from being the village misfit to being the heir of a great trading empire and one of the wealthiest misfits in the world. He did not of course believe a word of it; he knew that George Kirbey was comfortable and even quite wealthy, at least by frontier standards, but he wasn't a merchant prince. All the same, Thelvyn suddenly couldn't go out of the house without someone having to introduce him to one of the suddenly eligible daughters of the village.

Of course, all their Flaemish prejudices remained firmly in effect. They didn't want their own daughters to marry a foreigner of uncertain origin and race no matter how much money they expected him to inherit, and so they only introduced him to the daughters of their friends and neighbors. At least, since they weren't trying to marry him to their own daughters, that might prove that their only concern was indeed his own best interests, and not that they hoped to profit from his good fortune. And so it happened that in no time at all half the people in the village weren't talking to the other half, but that didn't stop them from talking to Thelvyn.

The coming of spring sent the village back to work. Soon the shipments of ore were coming down from the mines, and the charcoalers were back at work in the forest. Dal Ferstaan asked Thelvyn if he wished to help out at the foundry. As it happened, Thelvyn was perfectly willing to help. He had spent the long winter buried in his books, having only just recently made his way through the stack that Sir George had set aside for him, and several other stacks besides. He was convinced that if he didn't get out of that big lonely house and get away from books for a while, then something very bad was going to happen to him.

He was becoming too nervous now to read anyway, between his impatience for Sir George to return and the attention the village was devoting to matrimonial affairs. The foundry seemed a very good place to spend some time. He could go there and hit things with heavy hammers until he felt better.

Whatever strange Immortal held the questionable devotion of Sir George did not intend for the old knight to miss any of this. Just when everything had reached a state of furious speculation about Thelvyn and Sir George, the knight and his companions came riding back into the village with expectations of a long-awaited and well-deserved rest. One of the most important reasons for having settled here was the simple peace and quiet of the frontier and the constant, unexcitable Flaemish settlers. He had known these people for some time and had believed that they lacked the ability to surprise him. He was still unpacking when Thelvyn arrived from the foundry, having come in a hurry.

"Sir George, you have to get me out of here before I go insane!" Thelvyn declared without so much as a how-do-you-do.

For once, the old gentleman was at a loss for words. "What?" he asked ineloquently. "Why are you worried about going insane?"

"Because it must be contagious!" Thelvyn seated himself on the end of the bed. "I moved in here after my birthday in order to have more time for my reading. Well, word got about that I am your heir, and the rumors got completely out of hand. Now everyone says that you are really a powerful and fabulously wealthy merchant from a faraway land, and they're all trying to get me to marry everyone else's daughters."

"Not their own daughters?" Sir George asked. Thelvyn

afforded him a dark look. "No, I suppose not. I'm a foreigner here also, you know. How very peculiar. The Flaem generally hate getting carried away with themselves like that, so it must be the dragons. For a group of people so utterly devoted to destroying their enemies and ruling the world, they really don't handle stress very well. Well, you've come of age now. I suppose the first step is to get you out of that foundry."

"I bought back my contract on my birthday," Thelvyn explained. "Master Ferstaan kept his word and sold it to me for one brass penny. He's been giving me busy work, but I know he needs to clear the way soon for a new apprentice."

"That's a start," Sir George said. "Why don't you run back and tell Dal Ferstaan that I'll have other work for you from now on. We'll see what we can do about it in the morning."

The others weren't in any mood to talk that night. Instead they sat quietly at the table and later in the den; that was a common enough state for Solveig White-Gold, and a perpetual one where Korinn was involved. Even Sir George sat alone, lost in his own thoughts, which was definitely *not* usual with him. But there was no sense of despair or concern, so Thelvyn felt certain they were simply tired after a long journey. He did what he could for them, but otherwise he was satisfied to wait.

They had not returned alone, however, although Thelvyn hadn't been on hand for their arrival and hadn't known of George's new guest. The new member of their company was a curious little man who was introduced as Mage Perrantin, although he was obviously not of Flaemish descent and did not belong to the fellowship of fire wizards. In spite of Thelvyn's apprehensions, he wasn't at all like the suspicious, self-satisfied Flaemish magic-users. Rather, he was a very pleasant fellow, and they got along well from the first. Perrantin was rather short and unremarkable, looking more like a timid merchant than the master wizard Sir George claimed he was. His hair was gray and balding, but he was neither as old nor as plump as he appeared at first sight. He had known Sir George for a great many years, from the time when the knight had resided in Darokin, although Perrantin hadn't visited in the north for as long as Thelvyn could recall.

Indeed the mage was the only one up and about that evening, for he was going through Sir George's collection of artifacts and oddities with great enthusiasm. He happened to see a small glass case tucked in a dark corner of the room, and he peered at the wide, jeweled collar inside. "I say, this is new!"

"Funny you should say that," Sir George commented. "As a matter of fact, it's really quite old."

"Alphatian, and one of the early dynasties, judging by the quality of the work," the mage continued blissfully, ignoring Sir George. Thelvyn was familiar with the piece, and he had always thought the work crude, the jewels large but badly cut.

"It was made for a certain would-be great emperor, Demases the Fourth," the old knight explained. "The odd shape of the stones has a purpose. Each of the forty-two larger green stones possesses an individual ward against each of the forty-two legendary poisons used by the ancient Alphatians for political assassinations. It worked quite well, and Demases soon grew secure in his belief that he couldn't be poisoned. That being the case, his enemies eventually circumvented the thing and poisoned his bathwater, that being the only time he was known to remove the collar."

"Very clever!" Perrantin exclaimed, seeming to approve. "But how did you come by it?"

"Well, his successor had an improved version, a periapt against poison made in the form of a ring he never had to remove. I suppose this other one, being superfluous, was given as a gift to some barbarian king or chief, and it eventually ended up in the hands of the Ethengar, who had no idea what it was. Neither did I until I researched it."

"Have you ever tried it out?"

"Certainly not!" Sir George declared. "After fifteen centuries or so, I don't trust those wards to still be effective."

Perrantin made some vague noise, perhaps of agreement. Thelvyn knew Sir George made the collection of historical objects something of a hobby. But he had never imagined that the old knight and his friend were so avid on the subject, nor that anything in his collection, which Thelvyn had always assumed were just trinkets and oddities, was really rare and valuable. Perrantin continued his hasty inspection, peering first at one thing and then another.

At last the mage returned to his chair by the fire, apparently having decided to postpone further examination until the light of day. Thelvyn was sitting at the bar so the others could have the chairs and sofa. He noticed Perrantin looking at him, almost as if he were just another item in Sir George's collection of oddities.

"So you are George Kirbey's young protégé," the mage remarked.

"I'm not sure I would use that word," Thelvyn said. He wasn't quite certain what it meant, but he had an idea. "The villagers have always had their own ideas of what was best for me, and they would never let Sir George exercise full control over me."

"I'm told that you've been teaching yourself magic," Perrantin continued briskly.

"Yes, I have," Thelvyn admitted. "When I found the books on magic among those Sir George had given me, I thought I was supposed to."

"No one is supposed to be able to teach himself magic," the mage said, his brow wrinkled in thought. "Have you been having any problems?"

"No, not really." He hesitated timidly. "Mage Eddan became aware of what I was doing. He tried to stop me at first, then finally said that I was to go to him if I had any trouble. I never needed to, and I don't think I would have wanted to."

"No, I think not. These fire wizards are a sneaky lot, desperate as they are for anything that gives them an advantage in rebuilding their ancient kingdom." The mage paused, watching Thelvyn shrewdly. "Do you understand what you have been doing, or are you simply practicing the spells?"

"Oh, I've been reading all the books about magic," Thelvyn said.

Perrantin turned to Sir George. "You've brought me all this way to teach magic to a boy who needs no teacher? What do you expect me to do for him, anyway?"

Sir George shrugged. "I was hoping that your instruction might bring him along even more quickly. And with less risk, if you don't mind my saying so. I don't have to tell you that the lad will benefit from having a proper teacher, no matter what the circumstances. My intent in giving him those books was simply to introduce him to magic."

Perrantin sighed and looked over at Thelvyn. "You no doubt still have a great deal of work to do. I can see already that you do not have a primary interest in being a magic-user, but that doesn't mean you won't be good at it. I don't consider myself primarily a magic-user either, but I'm very good at it and people call me a wizard. George says you're eager to work."

Thelvyn shrugged. "I'd rather be doing something than not. Perhaps I've been among the Flaem too long."

* * * * *

Thelvyn rose early the next morning to prepare breakfast. Sir George had no servants, and Thelvyn was still uncertain of his own position. He felt the need to earn his keep somehow, and he didn't yet consider himself one of Sir George's companions. Nor was he certain just what part he would play in the group, since he still had no definite idea of what they did. Solveig and the dwarf were obviously warriors, while Perrantin was both a wizard and a historian. These were useful roles whether they were traders in exotic items and antiquities, which they seemed to be, or adventurers, which they were reputed to be.

Sir George arrived at the table early and waited patiently for Solveig to appear. He didn't have to wait long. When Solveig entered the kitchen and immediately went to the stove to investigate the toast, Sir George gestured for Thelvyn to take a seat at the table. The young recruit did as he was instructed, sensing that something was about to happen.

"You know, I was just telling young Thelvyn about your

remarkable talent as a warrior," Sir George said as Solveig took a seat opposite the knight.

"Yes—a fascinating story," Thelvyn agreed, sounding eager.

Solveig paused and looked up slowly, glaring at the old knight. She looked like someone who had arisen too early, her long hair unbraided and unkempt. She wore only a heavy robe of white cotton never intended for someone her height, so that she appeared to have extraordinarily long legs. Thelvyn noticed that her legs were as pale as the belly of a dead fish. Northland girls were obviously slow to tan.

"Anyway, we were thinking that you would make the perfect tutor for Thelvyn, since you are both rather tall and strong," Sir George continued.

Solveig glared even harder; Thelvyn had forgotten just how good she was at that. "George, you might be able to talk a dwarf out of his beard, and I've always admired your talent. But I also know your tricks, and right now I find you about as obvious as a band of orcs trying to sneak through a lingerie shop. I have no interest in teaching this rangy young man to fight."

"I want him to learn from the best," Sir George insisted. "He has a talent for it, you know."

"No, I don't know."

"You've seen him fight," Sir George reminded her. "I was thinking of the circumstances of your first meeting."

Solveig scowled. Thelvyn remembered being told that she had been impressed by that. "Well, he is a quick and clever lad, and he keeps his head in a fight."

"And you know that I've never had a son of my own. . . ."

"So you say, at least," she snapped.

"But the lad is my heir. I want him to be prepared."

"Then you teach him to fight," she pronounced. "You used to be a knight."

"Well, perhaps I will!" Sir George declared defiantly.

"You?" Solveig said incredulously. "You haven't the patience of a yak in heat. You don't even fight in a normal manner, now that you've taught yourself to use those gadgets you attach to your wrist cuff."

"I'll teach him the way I was taught. I'll make a proper

knight out of him," Sir George said, raking his hook over the table like a cat sharpening its claws. "Don't worry, child. I knew all there was about fighting before you were even born."

Solveig glared at him again; she obviously disliked being called a child. "Very well, then. I'll do it. But it has to be done right. Do you expect him to be both a wizard and a warrior?"

"The lad has great potential, and I want him trained properly," Sir George said and made a hopeless gesture. "Oh, very well, I'll let you try. But only because I know how good you are."

"Only too true," Solveig agreed smugly.

Thelvyn sat and stared in disbelief. Solveig had been right about one thing; Sir George really could talk a dwarf out of his beard. Fortunately for the knight, it must have been too early in the morning for her to heed her own warning. Sir George had obviously known she wasn't at her best then, and he had timed his attack with the cunning of a wild animal on the hunt.

Immediately after breakfast, Sir George declared that the first objective was to get Thelvyn a proper sword. To Thelvyn's great surprise, Sir George took him back to Dal Ferstaan. When he thought about it a bit, he realized he shouldn't have been surprised. The master smith looked enormously pleased when they arrived, like someone who had an interesting secret.

"Sir George talked with me last fall about your coming of age," he said. "He told me you would be going off with him, and he asked me to make you the finest sword I could."

"I'm grateful for all you've done, Dal Ferstaan, seeing I was never allowed to raise the lad myself," Sir George said sincerely.

"I've done the best I could," Master Ferstaan said. He unwrapped the sword from its protective cloth and offered the hilt to Thelvyn. "I could never have made steel so fine myself. The metal was bought from a trader in the south. I've worked on it throughout the winter."

Thelvyn marveled at the weapon. Although the blade

was long, the balance was perfect. The hilt guard was massive, a flattened bar of metal that was bent downward slightly and formed in the shape of an arrowhead. The hilt itself was just long enough to be held easily in two hands, but not so long that it felt awkward when held in one hand. The metal was as bright and shiny as polished silver. The blade was engraved on both sides with the figure of a dragon stretched out full length.

"I've made the blade larger than usual," the smith explained after a moment. "I knew that, with your height, you could use the added length and weight. And of course your time at the bellows and the forge left you stronger than ever, so that you can hcft a heavier sword."

"It's . . . beautiful," Thelvyn said in wonder.

The sword was so long that Thelvyn couldn't wear it at his belt and had to strap it across his back. He had always expected wearing a real sword would feel quite adventurous, but to his surprise, he felt rather self-conscious with the monstrous blade strapped to his back. The people of the village had never treated him like anything but a child, and a rather dull child at that. Wearing the sword made him feel like a pretentious child playing with something he shouldn't be.

Of course, he wouldn't be taught to fight with a real sword. For that purpose, Sir George took him to the lumber mill for a couple of small boards to cut into a pair of wooden practice swords, and several thin planks that could be made into simple shields. These weren't crude toys, no matter how they looked. Sir George kept in mind not only Thelvyn's but Solveig's considerable size and strength, but also the fact that they would be going at each other for all they were worth.

Sir George felt confident that he could have taught Thelvyn all the lad needed to know, for he had indeed been a knight. But he had many other matters to attend in the short time that he expected to be home, and it suited his purposes to give Solveig and Thelvyn something to do. For one thing, if Solveig was involved in Thelvyn's training, then Korinn would feel obliged to teach the lad a few things about dwarvish fighting with short sword, axe, and mace.

"You've had some training with weapons before, I trust," Sir George said.

"The usual," Thelvyn answered. "Learning to use a weapon is a part of the regular schooling here. I was better than anyone else, but they wouldn't allow me to learn anything beyond the rudiments."

Suddenly a cry rang out. "Sir George!"

He stopped as he saw a middle-aged woman hurrying across the street to join them. "Sir George, I just heard that you had returned home."

"Only last evening," Sir George replied. He was obviously talking to someone he could not for his life recall.

"And there you are, living all alone in that big house!"

"Not entirely alone," Sir George said, beginning to look rather uncomfortable. He declined to point out that he always had a group of adventurers in residence these days.

"Well, if you get too lonely, please keep the Widow Varsteel in mind," the woman said. "She's a wonderful cook, and she has three strong boys besides, although she's not so old that she wouldn't mind another lad or two of her own. You do know where she lives, don't you."

"Yes, of course. Thank you." Sir George turned away abruptly, looking frightened and bewildered. After a moment, he glanced at Thelvyn. "You warned me that the villagers have been trying to marry you off to other people's daughters. It seems they've now turned their attentions toward me. Life was a good deal simpler when they assumed I was a bold rascal."

"Are you going to call on the Widow Varsteel?" Thelvyn asked innocently.

"Most certainly not!" Sir George declared.

"Good. I was beginning to worry about my fabulous inheritance."

* * * * *

Thelvyn's first lesson with a sword came that very afternoon, beginning just after lunch and continuing well into early evening. In spite of her reluctance that morning, Solveig approached the task with patience and determination, and she proved herself to be an excellent teacher. Not wishing to provide entertainment for the entire village, she insisted upon practicing a short distance into the forest. She chose a small clearing, and Korinn found a seat upon a large stone.

It wasn't long before Thelvyn felt frustrated. He could hold his own when he was free to follow his instincts or to improvise his own strategy. He was no match for Solveig in a fair fight, but she didn't find it easy to defeat him. Owing to her experience and her training as a gladiator, she could disarm an average swordsman in moments, but Thelvyn was nearly her own height and strong and quick as well. What proved difficult for him was mastering the standard movements and strategies, the drills and exercises of military or gladiatorial training. When it came time to prove what he had learned, he began to second-guess his ability and lose confidence.

"Let's take a rest," Solveig said after about an hour. She seated herself on one of the stones scattered about the clearing.

"I hope Perrantin has better luck making a wizard out of me," Thelvyn said, discouraged. "I don't know if I'll ever get the hang of this."

"Nonsense," Solveig replied sternly. "Do you really think you should learn everything in one afternoon? I'm giving you the same training I had, and I trained for months."

"I wasn't under the impression that I have months," Thelvyn said.

"Don't worry so much about it," she told him. "Fighting with a sword is very much like magic in one respect: you will only do as well as you believe you can. Have these people really given you so little reason to expect that you can do anything right?"

Thelvyn was surprised to hear her say that, and also rather embarrassed. "Is it that obvious?"

"Perhaps I shouldn't say this," Solveig told him. "A sterner master might say I was spoiling you. But in all my life, I've only known one other person who showed as much natural talent with a sword as you do, and that was myself."

Thelvyn accepted that for what it was worth, keeping in mind that he was probably the only student she'd ever had.

Under the circumstances, Thelvyn hoped Sir George and his companions would be home long enough to give him adequate time with his lessons. He hadn't needed for Solveig to remind him that he needed many weeks, perhaps months, of practice to become an experienced fighter. Thelvyn had suspected from the first that he wouldn't have long before they'd be gone again, and he wasn't certain if he'd be going with them. He could imagine himself left behind once more to watch the house, with another stack of books to read and firm admonitions to practice his spells and exercises with his sword.

As it happened, he was right about one thing. Something did come up, just as he expected it would. Only a couple of weeks after Sir George had returned, the dragons were back.

There had been no word of actual attacks yet, but dragons were being seen regularly in the northeastern Highlands, flying slowly over farms and villages much as they had the year before. If there were no reports of attacks yet, no one doubted that the first strikes would come at any time. And the earlier the attacks commenced, the more likely the dragons were to reach the village before autumn brought their assaults to an end. So it was that the people of the village stopped for a time in their spring chores to lay aside stores of supplies in hiding places in the mountains.

Thelvyn noticed that Sir George obviously seemed quite concerned, and he wasn't inclined to be fearful or excitable like the villagers. The old knight called a meeting of his companions in his den the same evening news of the dragons arrived. He selected a bottle of his best cherry liqueur, which he had Thelvyn open and pass around. That in itself was an ominous sign, which everyone recognized. It happened only when Sir George had a very serious matter on his mind, since that was the only time he was likely to forget that no one else cared for the stuff.

"Dragons," Sir George grunted.

"Well, George, you always did have a way of cutting straight to the heart of the matter," Perrantin said, watching his glass as he turned it slowly in his hand. "Do you really expect us to do something about them, or are you just complaining?"

"That's the trouble," Solveig interjected. "Everybody complains about the dragons, but no one ever does anything about them."

"Oh, very funny," Sir George declared. "To tell you the truth, I'm inclined to think that we really should look into the matter. The only things protecting the Highlands are a bunch of dukes, who hope the dragons will go away, and those foolish fire wizards. There's more competence in this room than there is in the rest of the Highlands put together."

"True enough," Perrantin agreed. "But there are also a good many dragons, and you aren't a young man anymore. Do you have even the slightest idea of what to do about them?"

Sir George shook his head helplessly. "I'd have to learn more about the situation—how many dragons are involved, what their intentions are, and what set them off in the first place. But to tell you the truth, I was thinking about business."

"Ah, that's more like it," Korinn remarked, perking up.

"Actually, I was thinking that we could combine business with more business, as it were," the old knight continued. "What we know of the situation is that the dragons come down along the mountains from the northeast, attacking clans of the Ethengar in the far northern steppes before moving into the remote settlements of the Highlands. For all we know, these dragons could be attacking settlements along the Wendarian Ranges all the way up into the Heldannic Lands and beyond."

"If they were, I think we would have heard some word of that when we were in Thyatis or Rockhome last fall," Solveig pointed out. "News of something like that tends to get around."

"I'm not so certain," Sir George commented. "Those are some very wild lands. The point, at any rate, is that the attacks are obviously moving along the mountains. And Torkyn Fall is right at the front of the line of known attacks."

"If Torkyn Fall still exists," Perrantin said dubiously. "The cities of the gnomes have been failing for some time."

"Solveig, Korinn, and I were at Torkyn Fall just a little over two years ago," Sir George said. "There was still too much going on for it to have simply blown away by this time. But I was also thinking that if Torkyn Fall has been under attack, the gnomes may be trying to evacuate the city in the little time they have between the opening of the roads after winter and the return of the dragons in spring."

"But Torkyn Fall is one of the greatest underground cities of the gnomes," Thelvyn protested. "What could dragons do against a city inside a mountain? Korinn, how would the dwarves respond to such an attack?"

"Ordinarily we would simply close the gates and remain inside," Korinn replied. "A solitary dragon, or a small group, would go away soon enough. However, a larger group of dragons might be determined enough to keep up their attack until they get inside. Even then, dwarves can usually fight them fairly successfully, since they are at a disadvantage in tight spaces."

"This situation is somewhat different," Sir George said. "Torkyn Fall is rather more vulnerable than the gnomes anticipated, there are a good many dragons in this case, and gnomes aren't known to be particularly good fighters. Their usual response to a prolonged assault is to withdraw and escape. They also have a tendency to spend too much time trying to evacuate their treasures and then have to get away however they can when things turn against them. The gnomes of Torkyn Fall might be very grateful if someone they knew and trusted happened to show up to help them get their treasures to safety. That's one piece of business I had in mind. And we might just learn more about the dragons at the same time. That's the other item of business."

"Well, I for one would welcome having a close look at some of those gnomish treasures, even if we have to give them back," Perrantin remarked. "When were you planning to leave?"

"We should have left a week ago," Sir George said. "As it is, I would very much like to leave tomorrow if we can. I wonder if it is already too late tonight to see about a horse for Thelvyn."

"Your wish is our command," Solveig said as she rose. "Korinn and I will hurry over to the stables to have a look."

Thelvyn had mixed feelings. Even though he had eagerly awaited his first journey with Sir George, he realized now that he was more afraid of dragons than he thought possible. Dragons had been his greatest danger all his life, but they had always remained a distant threat. He had never anticipated dragons being a part of his first adventure, and his fear of them fought with his excitement.

He collected all the glasses of cherry liqueur, planning to pour their contents back in the bottle when Sir George wasn't looking. Solveig and Korinn left at once to see about a horse, for the evening was early enough that the stablemaster might still be about, waiting for any late travelers in need of a fresh mount. Thelvyn hurried to his room to pack.

As an orphan and a ward of the village, he possessed few clothes, for the Flaem tended to be forgetful in matters of charity. But Sir George had always made an effort to keep him in reasonably good clothes. He was able to find three sturdy shirts and two pairs of rugged pants for everyday use. Shoes were quite another matter. Like most of the village children, he had gone barefoot most of his life, and he hadn't been inclined to change that habit when he had come of age. As it was, he had only one pair of worn-out shoes to wear in the winter. He certainly couldn't arrange for a cobbler to make new shores by morning. Fortunately Solveig had a pair of sturdy riding boots she had never worn, and by chance the boots were only slightly large.

Solveig brought him leather travel bags and gave him advice on the best way to pack. Later he found Sir George sitting alone in the den, deep in thought. Thelvyn found it hard to say just why, but he thought the dragons concerned the old knight more than he let on.

"You've waited a long time for this," Sir George remarked.

"I suppose I have," Thelvyn agreed. "I just hadn't expected it would be something so dangerous. I hope I won't be a bother."

"We'll be doing our best to stay out of trouble."

"Are you really a trader?" Thelvyn blurted out suddenly.

"A trader?" Sir George asked. "That seems entirely too pedestrian a description of the work we do. We are dealers in antiquities . . . errant knights under the banner of ancient history. But that's an unusual business, which sometimes requires unusual talents. That explains the need for business associates such as Solveig and Korinn."

"Then you aren't really a band of adventurers?"

Sir George laughed. "I suppose that all depends on how you look at it. You might say that we fall in that uncertain area between simple traders and common adventurers. We're professionals. You're not disappointed, are you?"

"No . . . not in the least," Thelvyn said thoughtfully. "It's reassuring to know that if I've fallen in with a band of adventurers, at least you seem to be fairly respectable professionals."

CHAPTER FIVE

The next morning was brisk, with the promise of a clear, cool day to follow. Thelvyn rose well before sunrise, excited about his first adventure and eager to be under way. He dressed and was ready to go before the others were out of bed. He made a hot breakfast while the others were getting ready, and he even had time to straighten up the house. Then he helped carry out their gear. Unaccustomed to wearing boots, he fell down the front steps.

Solveig and Sir George brought out the packhorses first for the others to load, then went back to the stables behind the house to saddle the riding horses. Solveig did most of the work, since it was difficult for the old knight to buckle the straps one-handed. Sir George seemed quite pleased with himself, his concerns of the previous night forgotten, as if he preferred traveling to the comforts of home. Solveig was quiet and seemed to be moving a bit slowly. She was never at her best in the morning. Korinn appeared and began to pack busily. Mage Perrantin shuffled out of the house last, blinking like an owl with a hangover.

Sir George and Solveig emerged from the stables at last, leading their horses and Thelvyn's. Thelvyn's mount was in most ways very ordinary: dark brown, with big, black eyes and rather nervous ears. But to Thelvyn, it was beautiful, graceful and powerful and surely one of the most exceptional horses he had ever seen.

"He certainly is a beauty," Thelvyn commented as he accepted the reins. "What's his name?"

"*Her* name is Cadence," Solveig told him sharply. She handed Korinn the reins of his horse and turned back toward the stables, then turned once more and looked at Thelvyn. "Are you familiar with horses?"

"Well, not as familiar as I should be," Thelvyn admitted. "There aren't many horses here in the village. The Flaemish settlers don't have much use for them, and they never saw the need for me to be an experienced rider."

Solveig began to look concerned. "Do you even know how to ride?"

"I . . . I haven't actually ridden before," he said with great reluctance. "But I do know how it's done. I've read quite a lot on the subject, so I know the theory."

"Oh, my word," Sir George said to himself softly. He turned to Mage Perrantin, who was leaning against the wall with his eyes closed. "You've had some training in medicinal magic. What do you have for a first-time rider?"

"Pity," Perrantin said.

Thelvyn was beginning to get the idea that he was in real trouble, and he suspected the form it would take. Sir George addressed the problem as well as he could, hurrying into the house to return shortly with an old soft towel, which he folded and laid across the saddle. Solveig found the solution highly amusing. Thelvyn climbed into the saddle, determined to salvage his wounded pride. He did well enough for his first time. The only problem was that Cadence, who had been busy making nervous ears, decided she wanted nothing more to do with him. She didn't quite succeed in bucking him off; he elected to come back down to the ground voluntarily before it became an issue.

"That's odd," Solveig commented. "She had no objection

to letting me ride her last night."

"Let me talk with her a moment," Sir George said, leading the horse off to one side. They did indeed seem to have a little talk; Thelvyn watched closely, curious about the secrets of dealing with horses.

Whatever was said, Cadence made no further objection to her new rider. When Thelvyn returned to the saddle, she made a few more nervous ears and looked at him once over her shoulder before deciding to make the best of the situation. The others climbed into their own saddles, each grabbing the lead rope of a packhorse, and they were on their way a few moments later. That was when Thelvyn began to discover the difference between the theory and the practice of riding a horse. Cadence greatly simplified the problem by ignoring him as much as possible and simply following the others.

Half a mile down the road, Sir George remembered to send Solveig back to lock the front door of his house.

*　*　*　*　*

Thelvyn had always thought he knew the geography of the Highlands fairly well, between what he had learned in school and conversations he had overheard between travelers. Geography was a matter of pride with the Flaemish settlers, who knew the names and locations of all the towns and villages in the realm. Aalbansford was the seat of the territories held by Duke Aalban and one of the very first settlements occupied when the Flaem first came into this land. That supposedly made it one of the major cities of the Highlands.

Thelvyn usually rode near the center of the group beside Perrantin, and their travel provided hours each day, day after day, for the mage to provide his young student with intense and largely uninterrupted training. Thelvyn had no plans to become a wizard. A professional magic-user had time for little else but study, and Thelvyn lacked the inclination to give magic his undivided attention. But he had always been good at magic, he learned very quickly, and he could expect to be competent enough that magic would always be a useful skill to him.

They made the ride all the way to Aalbansford that first day, for they were traveling fairly light and fast. Thelvyn was impressed with the miles of farmland they passed as they approached, all freshly plowed fields bordered by neat walls of stone with rows of well-tended orchards between to break the spring and autumn winds.

Aalbansford was three or four times as large as Graez, which made it just large enough to be considered a real town but much less than Thelvyn had expected of so important a place. What he did not yet know, of course, was that most of the farmers had their homes on their own lands and did not come into town at night as they did in his own village. This was a more civilized land and less subject to the dangers of the mountains and the forest. There was even a castle, the residence of Duke Aalban, perched on the hill above the town. Even Thelvyn recognized that it wasn't much of a castle, hardly more than a simple fort of dark stone, but it did have a couple of spires topped with pennants that rippled in the cool night wind and windows that shown with yellow lights.

Few towns in the Highlands were much larger than this place. In a sense, all of the Highlands was a frontier, with no part of it older than a hundred years. That was when the Flaem had first come into this land, bands of exiles from a world they had helped to destroy. They had first arrived in the area of Braastar, the oldest and still largest city, but soon afterward the dukes who had led the seven bands of Flaemish exiles in their wandering had gone out into the wilderness to establish holdings and towns of their own. The area held by Duke Aalban was as large as any, filling the pocket between the mountains in the northwest corner of the Highlands, yet there were only three real towns in that area, if Graez could be considered a town, and perhaps a score of small villages.

The Highlands were growing slowly, partly because the Flaem were determined to keep their lands to themselves and thus restricted the number of strangers who settled. Thelvyn hadn't realized it before, but he was beginning to understand that the hold the realm held over this land was still so new and fragile that the recent attacks of the dragons could easily destroy everything.

All the shops were closed and locked up by the time they rode into town at dusk, but there were warm lights in all the windows of the homes. On the whole, Thelvyn believed that the people here lived very much as they did in his own village, although they might have been slightly wealthier. Sir George led them through the dark streets to the inn, a large building with two stories and many windows and a large stable for the horses. The others knew this place well and led their horses immediately to the stables; Cadence followed the others without hesitation.

Thelvyn tried to jump down as soon as they entered the yard, intending to help the others unsaddle and tend the horses. He discovered to his great surprise that his legs were reluctant to move, and even when they finally did, they protested mightily. This wasn't his first time out of the saddle that day, of course. They had stopped to rest the horses three times, and he had felt the soreness in his legs more each time. When he finally did get himself out of the saddle, he found that he could hardly stand.

Now he understood perfectly what everyone had been so concerned about that morning. As it was, he was no use to anyone that night. His companions had to help him into the inn, where they left him sitting at a table while they tended the horses. The inn was large and comfortable, with a dining room separate from the tavern.

Thelvyn didn't rest well that night. He felt even worse the next morning. Indeed the only way they were able to get him back in the saddle was to have Perrantin apply his knowledge of magic to the problem. He had a potion that he carefully rubbed into Thelvyn's lower back, deadening the nerves from his waist down, although the mage explained that it would take away not only the pain but also all other sensation. At the moment, Thelvyn didn't regard that as a liability.

They continued east that day to the small town of Traagen, which was slightly out of their way. Traagen was the seat of Duke Veerbyn's holding, and like Aalbansford, it was located on a river with a bridge crossing it. The next day they journeyed almost due north, through a very hilly, wooded land, which led them quickly away from the older parts of the realm and back again toward the frontier.

That same afternoon they saw the first dragons. With his sharp eyes, Thelvyn spotted them first, a group of three red dragons flying close together far to the east. Sir George saw them, too, once he was told where to look. The dragons were coming steadily in their direction, so that the others soon could see them as well. Sir George suggested they stay well within the cover of the woods, since dragons could see at least as well as Thelvyn.

Fortunately these remote lands were heavily wooded, so they were able to continue riding as the dragons drew near. They brought their horses into hiding beneath some larger trees as the huge creatures passed overhead barely a mile to the north. At that distance, Thelvyn could see the dragons clearly, moving their broad wings in long, slow sweeps while they turned their heads back and forth, scouting the land. They were by no means horrible to behold, but rather graceful and even quite noble.

Suddenly the dragons turned and began swooping low, heading directly toward the place where the companions were hidden beneath the trees. Sir George gestured urgently for them to lead the horses farther back beneath the trees. Thelvyn felt himself go pale with fear, knowing only too well that there was no way they could hope to defend themselves against three dragons.

The dragons separated, landing in open spaces among the trees, where they could surround the travelers and cut off their escape. The companions remained hidden in the most dense portion of the woods. The horses shifted and nickered fearfully, and Thelvyn held tightly to Cadence's reins to keep her from bolting. Suddenly he turned sharply when he saw one of the red dragons hardly a hundred yards behind him, crouching down to peer at him beneath the lower branches of a tree.

Almost sick with fear, Thelvyn pulled Cadence deeper into the brush so the dragon couldn't see him. He recalled only too well the story of how the dragons had hunted his mother to her death. If this dragon were to see him clearly and recognize his race, Thelvyn would almost surely meet the same fate. But after a long, terror-filled moment, the dragon withdrew, spreading its broad wings and leaping into the sky, followed quickly by the others.

"What was that all about?" Solveig asked. "Intimidation? That's not like a dragon, at least from what I know about them."

"They seemed interested only in giving us a good scare," Sir George said thoughtfully. "Either that or they decided we weren't worth the trouble."

They waited a few minutes to let the horses recover from their fright before they continued on. Thelvyn tried to keep the others from noticing that he was still shaking from terror. He felt ashamed, but he had definite reason to believe that his presence made their situation all the more dangerous. The dragons might ignore their party otherwise, but not if they recognized Thelvyn.

A long day of riding brought them at last to Nordeen, a small frontier village similar to Graez. Nordeen was the largest of the settlements that had been attacked the previous year, although the town had hardly been devastated by the raids. Just outside the village, they passed through an area where some farms been burned by dragons, although most were inhabited and seemed untouched. In the village itself, the burnt remains of houses and shops stood alone or in small groups, while other buildings remained intact. As Sir George had said, the dragons seemed to have interests other than blatant destruction.

They located the only inn, and Sir George got his companions settled quickly, arranging for a warm dinner once they had tended the horses and taken their packs to their rooms. Before he sat down, he set out to discover what he could about dragons and their involvement in local affairs. He didn't have to go far to seek it. The innkeeper had a great deal to say on the subject of dragons, some of it quite loudly. Sir George had all the information he needed and returned to their table before dinner was served.

"Well, that was all very interesting," he said as he joined the others. "Our good innkeeper reports that his business could hardly be worse. He is quite dependent upon the merchants who come up from the south every year to trade their goods in exchange for metals and woods and furs, just as they do back home. But the traders aren't coming this year. Too many of them were accosted upon the road, their goods destroyed or appropriated by dragons, and several never reached their destinations."

"I can hardly blame them for staying away," Korinn observed.

"Quite," Sir George agreed. "Of course, so many of the mines and smaller settlements were ravaged last year that there are fewer goods coming into town from this region anyway. Apparently Duke Ardelan is doing all he can to keep open the newest settlements on the other side of the Eastern Reach, which mostly involves sending more soldiers than he can spare. The innkeeper believes that the eastern settlements would have been abandoned last year except for an early snow that closed the pass before that could happen."

"And now that the pass is open?" Solveig asked.

"I suppose that the eastern settlements must have calmed down somewhat during the winter," Sir George said. "That should change soon enough now that the dragons are back. There has been no word of actual attacks, but I doubt that anyone is really encouraged by that. More likely the duke's soldiers are keeping the settlers from fleeing."

"That is possible," Perrantin agreed. "Of course, if the dragons were attacking anything that moved on the road last year, the settlers might be as reluctant to flee as they are to stay. Two or three dragons at either end of the pass would effectively cut off the Eastern Reaches."

"I certainly hope that's not the case," Sir George said. "I plan to be on the other side of the pass by tomorrow night, and that's a long, hard ride."

Solveig, who had been this way before, seemed rather doubtful, although she said nothing. By the next morning, Sir George didn't seem so certain himself, although he had them all up and on the road early. At least Thelvyn was beginning to feel his old self again. This was the first time in several days that he was able to get into the saddle without the benefit of the potion.

They came down from the hilly region almost at once, and then they rode for two or three hours through a deep, dense forest of tall, ancient trees very much like Thelvyn had known at home. The mountains drew steadily nearer, standing tall and dark as the morning sun rose slowly behind them. Thelvyn soon observed that the road was leading them directly toward a deep break in the line of mountains where the ridges and peaks to their right almost touched the northern mountains on their left.

As they came nearer, he could see that the break between the two ranges of mountains, as narrow as it seemed, was not the deep pass he had expected but a valley. The land between the mountains was rolling, with deep folds and great piles of boulders that had tumbled down from the heights through the ages. The valley was deeply forested, never more than eight miles across nor less than five. Even more curious, it ran straight for as far as he could see, a forty-mile swath leading right between the mountains and out the other side. This was the Eastern Reach, the narrow valley that connected the Highlands to the northern borders of the Steppes of Ethengar.

They paused to rest at the entrance to the pass. Now that Thelvyn was able to move about freely again, Solveig had him practice with his sword whenever they stopped for a time. Thelvyn wasn't inclined to complain. Not only was he impatient to improve, but he also found it a quick way to loosen up after hours in the saddle.

They were on their way again soon, since Sir George was anxious for them to get through the pass that day. Thelvyn watched with interest as they moved slowly between the two great walls of mountains. The lower slopes began to climb steeply from the valley floor, sometimes in grassy inclines that spread out like fans onto the plains, yet so steep that Thelvyn would not have wanted to climb them. Nevertheless, they offerred the easiest access into the mountains, for in other places. the valley was framed by towering peaks and ridges or by great walls of stone almost as sheer as cliffs. The valley rose gradually to a point somewhere near the middle. Thelvyn guessed it must descend again on the other side.

"The ice made all of this, I suppose," Mage Perrantin remarked as they rode along.

"Ice?" Thelvyn asked. The mage's words made no sense to him.

"The Highlands were at one time a frozen wasteland," Perrantin explained. "At one time, great rivers of ice came down from the mountains, cutting all the cliffs and deep valleys into the distinctive shapes you see before you. In this case, the ice formed from heavy snowfalls in the mountains on either side and moved down into this valley in the form of two glaciers, one moving east into the plains and the other west into the Highlands. They must have originally cut the valley somewhat deeper than it is now, but it has since been filled in a bit with debris washed down from mountain streams."

"All caused by ice?" Thelvyn asked, still surprised by the thought. "But rock is so much harder than ice."

"Well, you have to consider a river of ice is the weight of a small mountain. There are places in the world, such as northern Norwold, where you can still see these same processes in operation. Of course, the fall of Blackmoor and the Rain of Fire changed the shape of the whole world forever, and the Highlands slowly grew warmer and the ice receded over a period of eight centuries. At that time, elves migrated into these lands, and they lived in peace and seclusion for perhaps five hundred years. How it happened is unknown, for of course no one survived the incident, but the elves somehow found an ancient Blackmoor device and activated it."

"What does a Blackmoor device do?" Thelvyn asked.

"The wizards of Blackmoor built many different devices, which did a great many different things," Perrantin explained. "The most notorious were their devices of war, which exploded with almost incomprehensible force. The explosion could spread fire scores of miles away, and then the smoke and dust would spread sickness and death for years to come. The effects of the device activated by the elves were carried eastward by the winds into the Colossus Mounts and far out into the Steppes of Ethengar to World Mountain, making that a fearful place even to this day."

"Yes. Well, Perry has a Blackmoor device of his own," Sir George said, sounding rather nervous. Even Korinn looked a little fearful at being reminded of that.

"I know what it is," Perrantin said defensively. "I do not consider it dangerous."

The valley slowly rose to a high point, then descended gradually down the other side. They reached the midpoint early in the afternoon, which came as a surprise to both Sir George and Solveig when they realized they had come so far already. They both admitted that the road was somewhat different than it had been the last time they had traveled it. The way had been widened and improved, and it cut a straighter path through the forest. Many boulders and other obstacles had been moved aside, and bridges of sturdy timbers had been built over streams leading down from the heights. It was no wonder Duke Ardelan was so fearful of losing the eastern holdings to the dragons, after he had done so much to open up the new territory.

In spite of their original doubts, they made the passage of the Eastern Reach that same day, although night was falling quickly when they came out from between the two great expanses of mountains. The mountains to their left, a spur of the Wendarian Ranges, made a sudden turn northward, while the Colossus Mounts to their right continued on for several more miles. The land before them was in the shape of a large pocket almost completely surrounded by mountains, opening to the southeast into the Plains of Ethengar.

Although the horses were tired, Sir George urged them on for several miles beyond the pass. Because this land was in the shadow of the mountains, darkness came early. Even now only a hint of daylight lingered in the western sky above the black barrier of the heights. And when they came into the forest beyond the Reach, the shadows were as deep as darkest night. The horses slowed to a shuffle as they attempted to find their way in the dark. It seemed pointless to go any farther that day.

When they came to a small clearing where they could look up and see the gathering stars, even Sir George was ready to make camp for the night. Thelvyn could see his breath, white and frosty against the night sky when he looked up. So far he had enjoyed a warm bed every night. Then something caught his eye in the distance.

"Fires," he warned. "There in the mountains. Are there any settlements or garrisons there?"

Sir George moved to where he could see the fires in the high slopes on either side of the opening of the pass. He swore briefly in some foreign language. "I don't believe it! Dragons lit those fires, you can be sure of that. No one else in these lands would dare light so much as a candle at night. The dragons are keeping sentinel above the opening of the pass. Now we know why no one has tried to withdraw through the Reach."

"We must have passed just beneath them in the gathering darkness," Solveig remarked. "We passed within a quarter-mile of one of those fires, but they weren't burning at the time. This will make going home rather tricky."

"Can you see the dragons themselves?" Sir George asked.

Thelvyn stared for a moment. "No. They must be staying out of the light of the fires."

"I don't see them either," Korinn offered.

"Thelvyn can see in the dark as well as any dwarf, but I doubt that anyone but a dragon has his distance vision," Sir George said. "If he can't see them, then they probably can't see us. That is exactly why I wanted us to get through the Reach as quickly as possible. Life is going to be considerably more dangerous for us now. We'll have to be more careful, even if it means taking more time. Lad, it's going to be up to you to watch the sky and the high places around us."

Thelvyn wasn't certain he wanted to be responsible for the safety of the group. He was only an apprentice, along for the experience. But he had to agree that he if was best able to give them warning, then he had to do all that he could. Discovering dragons just behind them was a great inducement to keep going a little farther that night. Thelvyn and Korinn took the lead to act as guides, since they could see best in the darkness. At least the road continued to be good, a tribute to Duke Ardelan's determined and possibly wasted efforts to open the eastern lands.

As they traveled on throughout the next two days, Thelvyn found that he didn't miss the comforts of an inn as much as he expected. He was young and of a strong and hearty breed, whatever it was. And that was just as well, for they had to swing wide around the few small settlements they came upon. No matter where they went, he always found a dragon watching somewhere. Often they circled slowly in the cool mountain winds in the distance. Flights of dragons passed low over the woods several times each day. Often he would see a dragon watching from hiding, either crouched on some lofty slope or else in the cover of the woods atop some high hill. There was no indication yet that the dragons were attacking; the settlements showed signs of previous damage, but none showed signs of recent attack. All the same, it seemed best not to tempt them. The travelers stayed within the forest as much as they could, even when it meant having to leave the road.

Thelvyn had to admit that he rather enjoyed the sight of dragons, as long as they kept their distance. He found that there was something vaguely familiar about them, even nostalgic, and gazing upon them made him feel excited and sad at the same time. He expected that might be because of some unknown association between dragons and his own race. Of course, he also had to admit any ties he felt to dragons were most likely of his own making, since he knew they also had the capacity to awaken in him a very deep, unreasoning fear. There remained the very real possibility that the dragons would be just as eager to roast him or rip him apart as they had been to destroy his mother. That was all the encouragement he needed to keep his distance. All the same, he was tremendously frustrated to think that his mortal enemies were also the only ones who could tell him about himself.

In spite of all the precautions they were forced to take, they were able to cross the wide valley of the eastern frontier in a couple of days. This brought them to the edge of the great Wendarian Range, which now began to run slightly north of due east for some two hundred miles before it began to fragment into a series of ranges that included the Mengul and, farther north, the forbidding Wyrmsteeth Mountains. Sir George's intent was to stay in the lower slopes of the mountains, above the steppes and any possible distraction from tribes of the Ethengar. He intended to turn north into the mountains once they found the old road that led directly to Torkyn Fall.

The last of the frontier settlements behind them, they entered a completely wild region. Anyone they met from now on would most likely be someone they would prefer not to meet. Sir George didn't fear the Ethengar. He traded with them regularly and was known and trusted among them, a rare honor. However, meeting one of the tribes would demand various time-consuming calls of courtesy and ceremony. The greater danger now would be bands of humanoids, orcs or goblins, and as they traveled east, they would also be likely to find kobolds or even trolls. Their one hope, curiously enough, was that the rampaging dragons had been threat enough to drive all the other dangerous things out of the mountains. Beyond the Highland frontier, the dragons themselves actually became less of a danger. They were still seen regularly, coming and going through these mountains, always on the wing, but their attentions were focused farther west.

There were no trails to follow. At other times, Sir George would have most likely headed south through the steppes, taking advantage of his good standing with the Ethengar. But according to reports, the dragons had also harassed the tribes during the previous year, suggesting that the plains were not an entirely safe place to be this year as well. Their progress was slowed greatly by the rugged, steep land, and so they didn't find the road into the mountains until nearly the middle of the fifth day since leaving the frontier. Sir George had them stop for a moment while he and Solveig dismounted to have a look at the road.

"Definite signs of recent traffic," Solveig observed. "Some wagon and cart tracks. Some horses. Even more people walking . . . mostly gnomes. All of this within the last two weeks, possibly longer. This has been a dry spring."

"Then Torkyn Fall is still inhabited," Sir George concluded. "All of this traffic could be taken as a sign of evacuation, although it could be the first rush of traders after the passes opened. Considering that these mountains are crawling with dragons, I don't expect that all this traffic represents normal spring trade."

"However, it does indicate that someone is making it in and out of Torkyn Fall on a regular basis," Perrantin said. "That would seem to suggest something encouraging about our own chances."

Sir George stood for a moment, staring into the mountains to the north. At the moment, there were no dragons to be seen, but they were coming and going regularly. "This is going to be the tricky part. We won't have the forest to hide us much longer, and we have every reason to expect that the dragons will be watching Torkyn Fall closely. They may even have it besieged. Perhaps we'll meet someone coming down from the city who can tell us the situation, but if we do not, that in itself will tell us to expect the worst."

"What if the dragons have closed the city?" Korinn asked.

"Then we do the best we can. We got past them once in the darkness, and we might be able to do it again."

They didn't have far to go, no more than thirty-five miles, but in these mountains, that would be slow, hard travel despite a decent road. Sir George didn't expect them to arrive at Torkyn Fall much before nightfall of the next day. There were dragons about, all of them flying past quickly, mostly in the distance, but fortunately there were also a good many places to hide. Many of the high slopes were long, gentle slopes, meadows of deep green grass in a warmer time of year, but others were covered with a scattering of tall, lean pines, hardly the protection of the dense lowland forests but good enough. And while travel was slow in the steep, rugged slopes, there were always deep shadows they could slip into until danger had passed.

The peaks and high ridges were still white with heavy winter snowfalls, and pockets of snow remained in sheltered places among the boulders. The next morning began with a scattering of dull gray clouds, and the clouds continued to gather until, by early afternoon, the sky was almost completely dark and overcast, cutting off the tops of the higher ridges and summits. As the afternoon continued, the clouds dropped steadily lower. Thelvyn was disappointed, since he had been waiting for days for his first sight of the triple cones of the Three Fires Volcanoes as they rose just behind Torkyn Peak. His consolation was that the low, heavy clouds kept them hidden from dragons.

"If I had to guess, I'd say we'll have snow by nightfall," Sir George said.

"We could try going faster," Solveig offered. "That will tire the horses faster, but they'll have time to rest before we start back."

"Oh, I don't mind the snow," the old knight insisted. "It might not be comfortable, but it should help us get to the main gate without being seen. Unless the dragons are sitting right in front of the gate."

Perrantin made a face. "George, you think of everything, don't you?"

As Sir George had predicted, the clouds sank lower and lower. Night and snow began to fall at almost the same moment. Thelvyn was tempted to ride with his head down against the icy wind, but he knew he should be watching for danger, especially after Sir George put him in the lead. Even his remarkable vision couldn't penetrate much more than a few dozen yards ahead. The clouds had settled over the top of the mountain, so that they were riding in a deep, misty fog while the snow fell, slow and heavy.

Thelvyn was unable to escape the feeling that danger waited hidden in the night only yards away. He couldn't know until it was too late whether there were dragons lurking beside the gate of Torkyn Fall or if there might be none within a hundred miles. He feared losing the road in the darkness, condemning his companions to wait out the storm in any shelter they could find, and the threat of the horses taking a misstep that might plunge them down a treacherous slope.

Thelvyn never asked Sir George whether they should stop or turn back, for he soon realized that it was already too late. The storm was too harsh, and it was doubtful they could survive unless they reached the shelter of the hidden city of the gnomes. Sir George reckoned that Torkyn Fall had been no more than five miles away when the snow had first begun. Cadence walked with her head low to the ground, but she kept up her slow, dogged pace. Thelvyn had long since come to the opinion that she was an exceptional horse, but his experience with horses was of course limited. He did his own part, peering into the misty, snow-filled darkness ahead, alert to the slightest danger.

The dark shapes of boulders loomed suddenly out of the darkness. Thelvyn slowed Cadence even more, seeing signs that this was the broken rubble of a recent rockfall carefully cleared away from the road just enough to allow the passage of a wagon. A moment later, Cadence stopped of her own accord as the darkness ahead became a wall of stone, although the road itself disappeared into the blackness of the mouth of a wide cave or tunnel.

When he looked closer, Thelvyn could see that the tunnel continued only a few yards before ending in a massive door of metal. The door and surrounding rock had all been blackened by flames, just as the debris of stone had been ripped or blasted from the face of the cliff itself. He didn't see it until he dismounted and stepped closer, but the door had been dented and rent. Dragons had obviously tried to break into this place. Thelvyn used his spell for a magical light to provide a better look at the door.

"Torkyn Fall," Sir George said.

At that same moment, the great metal door began to slide slowly to one side. A golden light flooded out from the small opening, blinding Thelvyn's sensitive eyes. A moment later, a gnome peered cautiously around the edge of the door, staring at them in great surprise.

"Sir George Kirbey! By my father's whiskers!" the gnome exclaimed.

"Parkon?" Sir George asked.

"Merciful heavens! Come inside at once," Parkon exclaimed, gesturing for the door to be opened wider. "This is no night for an old knight like you to be out in, I must say."

The massive door rolled back slowly, and the companions led their horses inside. After a passage of a couple of dozen yards, they entered a chamber of immense size. By both appearance and smell, this had to be the stableyard, for there were rows of stalls along both walls as well as piles of straw and bins of grain. A few carts and wagons were drawn up out of the way in the corners. Another party was preparing to set out, a group of a dozen gnomes dressed for cold weather and bearing large packs, together with seven carts filled almost to overflowing, pulled by sturdy ponies.

Thelvyn had never seen gnomes before. They looked a good deal like dwarves, only less stocky. Most had great, long noses, and most of the older ones had short, bristly white beards. He thought he recalled that the two races were in fact related. Parkon led them quickly to one side of the empty stables, where young gnomes helped the companions with their horses and gear.

"How did you know we were out there?" Sir George asked, puzzled.

"I didn't," Parkon insisted. "As you can see, we were trying to get a caravan out the main gate under the cover of the storm. We have other, safer exits, but this is the only one we can get our wagons and carts through."

"Then the dragons are after you?"

"They have been relentless," the gnome said. "But I can tell you more about that later. What brings you here at such a time?"

"We've come to find out about the dragons, and to see what we can do to help you," Sir George said.

"Then you've come just in time."

As he unsaddled Cadence, Thelvyn paused to watch the caravan of gnomes file out through the gate into the darkness. They'd have a long, hard night ahead of them, not daring to stop until the snow ended or they were safely down from the heights. But their chances were better with the storm than with the dragons.

CHAPTER SIX

Torkyn Fall was unlike anything Thelvyn had known from his sheltered life on the frontier. He had been aware that his Highland village had been rather remote and backward, but now he was beginning to suspect that the Flaem were in fact an altogether primitive folk. The underground city of the gnomes wasn't a series of natural caverns as he had expected from stories he had heard. If the halls and chambers of brownish-gray stone had originally been natural caverns, the gnomes had long since mined and expanded the passages, which ran far more straight and true than ordinary caves. The floors were smooth, and the high ceilings were supported by columns of brown stone. He had no idea where the light was coming from, for there were no lamps, torches, or fires. He assumed that it must be magical.

The younger gnomes in the stable insisted that they would care for the horses properly, so the companions collected their packs and followed Parkon into the inner chambers. Thelvyn was quick to notice signs of considerable damage.

Many of the walls and ceilings had been cracked and broken, and piles of crumbled stone had been neatly swept aside.

Torkyn Fall had obviously been under attack and apparently getting the worst of it. At first he couldn't imagine what even such formidable creatures as dragons could do against an underground city, except possibly by a magical assault. As they went deeper into the caverns, he began to realize that the city was strangely vacant. The few chambers he saw appeared to have been abandoned and stripped of their contents, although he could still hear the sounds of machines and industry echoing through the passages.

If Torkyn Fall was indeed well advanced in the stages of evacuation, there was at least no shortage of furnished rooms for guests. Parkon led them to a suite of chambers, where each claimed a comfortable, well-appointed room of his own. Thelvyn washed and changed, taking advantage of their brief rest to unpack and hang up his clothes for the first time in many days. When he emerged from his room, he found that the gnomes had laid out a generous meal in the large common room in the center of the group of apartments. Solveig and Korinn were already at the table with Parkon, while Sir George and the mage joined them only moments later.

"Parkon, you remember Solveig White-Gold and Korinn Bear Slayer, Son of Doric," Sir George said as he took his place at the table. "And I've probably told you about Mage Perrantin, my old associate in the business of history and antiquities. And finally my heir, Thelvyn Fox Eyes."

"Yes, I remember you spoke of him last time," Parkon said, studying Thelvyn closely. "The lad of uncertain race and origin."

"I may be a descendant of the lost race of Blackmoor, but that's only a guess," Thelvyn explained.

"If so, you are an antiquity in yourself," the old gnome said, smiling. "I am Parkon Lighthammer. In the advanced state of evacuation you find us in, I am presently the leader here at Torkyn Fall."

"Then your people have decided to abandon the city?" Sir George asked.

"The dragons have left us little choice," Parkon replied

wearily. "Our position here was weak enough, as you know. We were afraid they could cut off our trade with the outside, but now they seem likely to bring our own tunnels down upon our heads."

"I noticed the damage," Korinn agreed. "I was dismayed to see what damage dragons are able to inflict against a city built inside a mountain of stone. In the past, we dwarves have always found our own strongholds to be secure against attack, but now I fear how Rockhome would fare if the dragons bring their attacks to our lands."

"I daresay your people will fare as well as you ever have," Parkon assured him. "Your cities are built in hard, ancient stone. As you can see, Torkyn Fall is built inside stone that has its origins in deep flows of lava from the volcanoes of this region. We've found it easy to mine, since it is a very soft, crumbly stone, and that allowed us to build a city of chambers and passages unlike any other gnomish or dwarven city in the world. Our excavating devices have been able to eat their way through the stone as if it were cake. But the stone is also quite fragile and unstable. The blasts of fire and lightning from the dragons are shaking apart our entire mountain."

"Could your city still be saved if the dragons should abandon their attack?" Sir George asked.

Parkon shook his head slowly. "We dare not dwell here, for we realize now that we have been as fortunate as we have been shortsighted. This is indeed a volcanic region, and very unstable. If the dragons do not themselves destroy Torkyn Fall, then the inevitable earthquakes associated with volcanic activity would make this place unsafe."

"Do you know why the dragons are attacking?"

"No, we have no idea. We had assumed that they were after our treasures, until we learned that they are raiding from the Heldannic lands all the way to the Highlands." Parkon hesitated a moment, seeming to consider something important. "Sir George, there are certain of our most ancient treasures here that we have not dared attempt to remove ourselves. You and your companions have experience in such things. Would you consider removing our ancient treasures to safety?"

"Well, yes, I suppose we might be persuaded," Sir George agreed cautiously. "If you can trust us with your treasures, that is."

"That goes without saying," the gnome assured him.

Thelvyn wasn't entirely sure just what treasures the gnomes wanted to have taken away. Considering the stories he had heard about gnomes and their inclination to invent useless or extremely complicated devices, he was uncertain just what they would consider a treasure. They loved gold, silver, and jewels as avidly as any dwarf, which seemed to suggest that their most valuable and ancient treasures probably were of a conventional sort. The trouble was that dragons were also especially fond of such treasure, and legend held that a dragon could smell gold from miles away. If that was true, then running about the dragon-infested wilderness with their treasure wasn't a particularly wise thing to do. Of course, it was never a particularly wise thing to do under any circumstances, so their situation probably wasn't that much worse.

Perrantin and Sir George went away with the gnomes the next morning to look into the matter of selecting and packing the treasures, and probably to discuss the price of such a service. Torkyn Fall was short on inhabitants but not in goods, since there was a great deal that the gnomes simply couldn't take as they evacuated. They could afford to be extremely generous under the circumstances, since the alternative was simply to leave it to the dragons.

While the elders of their band were thus occupied, Thelvyn was left to view the city of Torkyn Fall in the company of Solveig and Korinn. For the first time since he had met Korinn, the dwarf was not only exceedingly friendly but also quite talkative. Perhaps being in his own element, as it were, felt comfortable to him. He insisted upon leading Thelvyn on a tour of the city, as if this were an important lesson that he alone could conduct properly.

"As Master Parkon said last night, the design of this place is different from most of the cities of either the gnomes or the dwarves," he explained as he led them through the corridors. "Most often both dwarves and gnomes will find natural caverns of great size and build houses and mansions inside them very much like what you would find aboveground. Carving out chambers and passages of such size as these would be a task of overwhelming scope, even with the use of excavating devices. But this volcanic rock mines very easily, and so the gnomes have been able to transform the natural tunnels into halls and chambers of great size, all finely cut and smoothed.

"The advantage of this design, of course, is that so much space is available for habitation, and usable underground space is always limited. This is an interesting and unique place, and I regret seeing it destroyed. But I'm not certain that I would wish for another place like it."

He brought them into one of the larger chambers and looked about for a moment, then pointed upward. "There, you see? The gnomes knew from the first that the natural stone could not be trusted to support itself in these larger chambers, so they had to build supporting columns, beams, and rafters to take some of the weight. In some places, they imported columns and beams cut from granite from other mountains in this area, but then they found something easier. Do you notice the shape of the beams and rafters?"

"They were carved to look like wood," Thelvyn said.

"They were wood," Korinn told him. "The beams and rafters, even the supporting columns, were real timbers. Once the timbers were set in place, the gnomes employed magic to convert the wood to stone."

"That was clever, if you know how," Thelvyn observed. "But I suppose that none of this is likely to save the city now."

"No, I've checked that. The attacks of the dragons are opening up long, deep cracks in the stone, some of them going right through the mountain."

Korinn led his companions through the passage with certainty, although Thelvyn knew he had visited it only once before. Apparently some things were a matter of instinct for dwarves. For his own part, Thelvyn was almost sad to see how large and grand Torkyn Fall actually was and how much had already been abandoned, not to mention how much had been damaged or destroyed. One of the saddest and at the same time one of the most amusing things he discovered was that the gnomes were driven by certain odd, relentless instincts of their own. Although they could hope to evacuate only some of their possessions before their city fell about their heads, their smiths and craftsmen were still hard at work making more.

Most remarkable, at least to Thelvyn, was the fact that Torkyn Fall was larger than any aboveground town he had ever seen. There were eight complete levels and parts of three more above that, plus several more below. Each level consisted of corridors and chambers wandering through the great plateau formed by the ancient lava flows. If all the tunnels and chambers were laid out flat together, they would have covered the area of a large city.

Of course, many of the passages had started as natural tunnels, so the gnomes had hardly been required to excavate it all. There were even two remote sections of long, gently winding tunnels of black obsidian, as dark as pitch and as smooth as glass. Deep in the very heart of the city were the tunnels leading away into the surrounding mountains, sometimes miles away, where the gnomes had mined veins of the purest metals, especially gold, silver and other metals that were rare in most parts of the world.

Last of all, Korinn brought them to the largest chambers, which formerly had been the heart of the underground city. These chambers were in an almost straight line from the main gate, following a series of natural caves that had formed through the center the plateau, shaped and enlarged through the years by the gnomes. The innermost chamber was also the largest, the great Chamber of the Fall. While the front of this chamber had been cut into a series of ledges, terraces, and long, massive ramps and bridges of stone, the back was a natural cavern of tremendous size, over three hundred feet high in the center. An underground stream emerged near the top, tumbling in a long, misty stream into a small, deep pool, which drained by some unseen tunnel below. This was Torkyn Fall itself, from which the city of the gnomes had derived its name.

"The back half of the chamber and the fall itself are natural," Korinn explained. "The underground stream passes through a chamber, where it drives a waterwheel to turn the machines of the gnomes. There is another waterwheel turning more machines below, where the pool drains through a narrow tube. The fall serves as more than just a source of wonder and beauty, for the falling water cools and refreshes the air of the city, which would otherwise be stale and foul from the fumes of all the work done here."

"Then the pool is drained at exactly the rate needed to keep it from overflowing?" Thelvyn asked.

"That is correct. Of course, there is an overflow pipe somewhere along the side, which would drain off any excess water before an overflow could occur."

Korinn climbed up on one of the walkways, where he could face the center of the chamber. The mist of the fall felt cool and damp, but the sound of that long, narrow curtain of water plunging into the pool was only a fraction of what Thelvyn would have expected, perhaps because the water was more like a heavy rain than a thundering stream by the time it reached the surface of the pool. Then Korinn lifted his hands to the sides of his mouth and made a sound unlike anything Thelvyn had ever heard, although he supposed that it must be singing.

"The fine dwarvish art of yodeling," Korinn explained, noticing his companion's obvious surprise. "Surely you've heard of it."

"Well, I've heard *of* it," Thelvyn admitted, "but I've never actually heard anyone yodel before."

"You have to hear it from a dwarf to hear it done right," Korinn said. "I thought I might give it a try, seeing this part of the city is more or less deserted. You don't mind, do you?"

"Mind? I was wondering if you might teach me how to do it."

The dwarf looked as if he couldn't have been more pleased.

* * * * *

Sir George concluded his business with the gnomes fairly quickly, but they were delayed a few days in departing because of the weather. Thelvyn was sure that in the lower lands, only fifty miles away, there had been only a long, slow, cold rain. Back at home in the Highlands, folk would be making ready for the spring planting, and the first shipments of ore would be coming down from the mines and charcoal from the forest to feed the foundries. But here in the mountains, matters were decidedly different. The snow had fallen steadily all though the night of their arrival and the next day, then returned the day after that. Even then they could not depart, for such a heavy snow would have closed the road. They were obliged to wait three more days for the clouds to break, and another two days after that for the sun to melt enough snow for them to get through.

Fortunately Thelvyn had enough to keep him busy. Perrantin continued to help him pursue his studies in magic, and Solveig insisted that he join her in daily practice with the sword. Although he hadn't expected that the dwarf was serious, Korinn was more than willing to teach him to yodel. Thelvyn had a good, strong voice and he learned quickly. Dwarves chose their friends carefully and were slow to make them, so Thelvyn was grateful for the opportunity.

Still, they had to be careful not to remain too long or the dragons might return in force. The gnomes would be able to lead them through the passages to one of several small, hidden entrances to Torkyn Fall. Even so, their best hope of evading the dragons would be to leave as soon as possible, since the only hidden entrances where they could bring the horses were all within two or three miles of the main gate. After they departed, the gnomes intended to sit tight and bide their time. Some of the tunnels to their mines led for miles into other parts of the surrounding mountains, and the mine tunnels themselves were fairly extensive after centuries of work. They had discovered another fairly soft area of rock and intended to spend the next few weeks bringing their excavating devices to bear on the task, with the hope of opening a new entrance more than twenty-five miles away where they could evacuate their city right from under the long noses of the dragons.

Sir George wasn't so certain the dragons could be held off for much longer. They didn't have to destroy the city from the outside; the stone was so soft that, between their magic and their strength, they could tear out the main gate any time they pleased. He advised the gnomes to evacuate their goods and treasures into the area of the mines where they would be working and then bring the tunnel down behind them, abandoning Torkyn Fall altogether. But Sir George and his companions were removing the last of their most ancient and valuable treasures, so the gnomes were content for now.

"You will get our treasures into the hands of our agents in Braejr as quickly as you can?" Parkon asked one last time as they prepared to leave.

"I promise you I will," Sir George insisted. "You can trust me, if for no other reason than that I don't want the entire race of gnomes after my head."

"Oh, your honesty was never in question," Parkon insisted. "I don't know if we will ever meet again. This land has not been kind to us these past few years, with our cities falling one after another. We have strongholds in other lands, places were our race is flourishing. I think you know the place I mean."

"I might even visit you in your new home someday," the old knight said. "Just keep in mind what I've told you about the dragons. You'll need to protect yourselves better after this."

The gnomes released the large locks and latches on the hidden gate, then pushed open the massive portal. Thelvyn was sent through the passage for a quick look outside, since he was most likely to see any hidden danger. They had elected to leave at night, having successfully evaded the dragons once in the darkness. The hidden gate opened up on a short passage like a natural cave, barely half a dozen yards deep, which in turn came out upon a small ledge near the bottom of a deep, narrow ravine, where a half-frozen stream bubbled beneath the snow-laden branches of a stand of pines. Because this place was shielded from the sun for most of the day, the snow here was still very deep. Even so, Thelvyn could see clearly where the trail must run hidden under the snow along the side of the stream. The night was frosty cold, but the sky was clear and filled with stars.

Since he saw no obvious dangers, he went back to call the others. The dragons involved in the siege were large and glaringly obvious in the light of day. But on a moonless night, all dragons were black and considerably harder to see. Still, there had been no attacks during all their stay at Torkyn Fall, so there was some reason to hope the dragons had turned their attentions elsewhere. There would almost certainly be scouts watching the main gate, but that might be all.

"The gnomes said to follow this stream down through the valley for the first five miles," Sir George said.

"The sun should be close to rising by the time we reach the end," Thelvyn said. "The snow is going to be deepest down inside the valleys. I'm afraid we'll have to walk the horses."

"That's probably best," Sir George agreed, then glanced back as the massive gate of the hidden entrance swung closed. "If we had to come back, do you suppose any of them will hear us if we knock?"

Thelvyn was sent ahead to scout, while the others followed, leading the packhorses. To transport the treasure, they had three more packhorses now than they did when they arrived at Torkyn Fall. Neither Sir George nor Solveig were especially happy to have horses that had been spending a large part of their lives underground. The new horses carried nothing but fodder, intended to last until they returned to the Highlands. In all the old stories Thelvyn had read, there had never been any mention of the fact that horses ate a lot and that much of their food had to be packed along with them in lands where grazing was difficult.

As flattering as it was, Thelvyn wasn't pleased to find himself once again responsible for the safety of the group. Solveig was their best scout, but he could see much better, especially in the dark. He was also inclined to wonder if he was the most expendable. The valley was deep and narrow, and he often had trouble finding the path buried deep beneath the drifted snow. Some of the drifts were quite deep, so he had to force his way through. The trail he left was well defined by the time Cadence followed in his steps.

The valley was beautiful in the moonlight, with the little stream bubbling beneath broken sheets of ice, and the snow piled deep in the limbs of the trees, making strange shadows on the boulders.

It was slow travel in the darkness and the snow. Thelvyn guessed that he was making no better than a mile in an hour's time, but he had anticipated that. He had grown up in the mountains and the wilderness, and he knew what to expect. From the instructions the gnomes had given them, he knew they should be approaching the place where the main road followed a wide ledge about halfway up a steep slope directly above them. As he rounded a narrow path between the stream and the cliff, he looked up to see just such a ledge about thirty yards above him.

Then he stopped short and leaned back into the shadows of the cliff. There was a dragon on the ledge, straddling the road. His heart recoiled in cold fear as he recalled his terror when the dragon had looked at him beneath the trees. From this distance, he couldn't hope that the dragon would fail to recognize him.

The trail was too narrow for his horse to turn around. He urged Cadence gently backward. Once they were under the cover of the nearest tree, Thelvyn risked a second look. His sight was too keen for him to have been mistaken; there was indeed a dragon on the road above. All he could see was its massive haunches, back, and tail. The dragon lay facing up the road, its tail curled around so that he could see only a part of it. He wondered if it was asleep.

"Back," he told Cadence softly. "Don't make a sound."

Somehow he managed to get the horse turned around, and they made a slow, quiet retreat back up the valley. There was no indication yet that the dragon was aware of him. Dragons were said to be enormously clever and tricky, although he had found that most of the stories he'd heard differed from the real world on many points. He came upon the others on the trail about a hundred yards back. He gestured for them to remain silent.

"There's a dragon on the main road above the valley," he explained softly.

"A big one?" Solveig asked.

Thelvyn looked surprised. "They come in different sizes?"

"Any size is bad news for us," Sir George said. "Is there any other way around him?"

"No, the only way down is through this valley," Thelvyn said. "But I think we might be able to get past it one horse at a time. The dragon is on the road about thirty yards above the valley floor, and we'd only have to be out in the open about twice that distance before we reach the trees on the other side. I think the dragon might be asleep."

"That assumption has gotten a number of adventurers killed in the past," Perrantin pointed out.

"Cadence and I made a fair amount of noise before I saw it. Can dragons hear any better than I can?"

"Well, I'm not entirely certain about your hearing," Sir George admitted. "Offhand, I would say no. Like hawks and eagles, dragons have tremendous vision for distant objects. It helps them to hunt from the air. They don't have the same need for keen hearing, since it would hardly help them over the noise of their wings flapping."

"Lucky for us, or the beast would be upon us by now," Korinn said impatiently.

"Dragons are not beasts," the old knight corrected him sternly, then looked thoughtful. "Frankly, we have no choice but to give the lad's plan a try. Even if we went back, I doubt we could make enough noise for the gnomes to hear us without bringing the dragons down upon us. Besides, the gnomes would never dare open the gate, fearing a trap. Perry, do you have any spells that might keep the horses quiet for a while?"

"As a matter of fact, yes. I decided to bring along a sleepwalker's potion after the last time we found ourselves in a similar mess," Perrantin said, checking his pack. "It's not actual sleep, mind you, but rather a form of hypnosis. The horses will have no will or conscious awareness of anything except doing as they are directed. They'll make no noise whatsoever, but they'll have to be led very carefully, since they won't be watching out for themselves."

Since the effects of the potion lasted for nearly an hour, they elected to go ahead and put the horses under the spell, since horses tended to be rather noisy animals when they became nervous. Besides their five riding horses, they had seven packhorses, and each had to be led across separately. Thelvyn still wasn't very experienced with horses, and he wouldn't have wanted to attempt it under the best of circumstances. Nevertheless, he was elected to go across first, since he was best qualified to stand watch.

Perrantin gave him the small dark bottle that contained the sleepwalking potion. "If the horses start to come around, give them some more. It hardly matters how long they stay under. As tractable as they'll be, they can be ridden fairly normally. If the dragon starts toward you, give him some as well."

"How?"

"Just loosen the lid and throw it at him," the mage explained. "If he tastes or even smells any of this, he'll lose interest in everything else for a while."

Cadence was standing as still as a statue, her head held low, although she responded quickly enough when Thelvyn took her reins. Her eyes were wide open, but she didn't seem to see where she was stepping as he started onto the trail. That wasn't encouraging, since he didn't know the condition of the trail below the cliff and it was hidden beneath the snow. If any of the horses should stumble on a hidden stone or step into a hole, it would be curtains.

Thelvyn led Cadence to the very edge of the woods, stopping under the last tree to take a careful look about. The dragon was still in exactly the same position as before, so he decided to lead Cadence out onto the narrow, snow-buried ledge that ran between the bottom of the cliff and the stream. He could make out the shapes of several large stones beneath the snow, and he had no doubt there were others he couldn't see. He walked almost in a shuffling fashion, feeling his way with his feet. Then he was careful to lead Cadence exactly where he wanted her to step so that she would leave a clear groove in the snow for the others to follow.

He dared not take too much time, for fear that the others would soon be coming up behind him. The open portion of the trail was only about sixty yards long, but it seemed to take almost half an hour to walk a distance that normally would have taken no more than a few minutes. Worse yet, he could no longer see the dragon as he came through the long, gentle curve along the middle of the cliff. Finally he led Cadence beneath the trees on the far side and tied her reins to a branch. Then he hurried back to the edge of the clearing to stand watch.

Someone else was coming through the open part of the trail, already past the midpoint. Now that he was looking back, the distance didn't seem nearly as great. He looked up to where the dragon lay on the road above, still motionless and seemingly asleep. He could see more of the dragon's broad back and even some of the shoulders from this angle. There was just enough light from the stars to see that this was indeed one of the reds, although he could still see nothing of its head or neck. When he looked back at the lower trail, he saw that it was Solveig.

"I'll take your horse with me on down the trail a ways," she whispered when she was beside him. "Sir George will stay behind to watch the packhorses. Korinn will be along next. As soon as the mage is across, you'll need to go back for another horse."

The dwarf was already leading his horse across, having started as soon as he saw Solveig reach the trees on the other side. Like Thelvyn, he had the ability to see well in the dark, although his short stature made dealing with the horses difficult for him. Then Perrantin brought across his horse. Although he didn't seem a particularly adventurous type, he seemed to be calm and composed. Thelvyn suspected that he wouldn't have hesitated to fight the dragon himself to protect the ancient artifacts of the gnomes. When the mage arrived safely, the three of them took their horses a short distance down the trail and left Perrantin to watch them. Then Thelvyn returned to begin collecting the packhorses. There were seven packhorses in all, including the three provided to them by the gnomes. It would take some time to get them all across safely.

At least each trip across went quicker now that the trail had been established. They had to hurry just the same, since the potion that kept the horses quiet would be wearing off soon and they wanted to avoid administering another dose. While the horses could be ridden in their present state, it wasn't wise. The horses needed to see and feel where they were stepping, and they needed to be able to react to the unexpected.

Thelvyn was making his second trip across with a pack-horse when he was startled by a sudden flash of light behind him, bright enough to briefly cast long shadows on the stones and trees. He turned quickly, afraid he would see the dragon, breathing flames.

Yet he saw nothing. A moment later, a deep, rumbling boom seemed to ripple like a wave through the stone of the mountain itself, a sound not unlike distant thunder. As he waited, there was a second flash of light, then another, not at his back but four or five miles away, lighting the sky above the deep, narrow valley. The dragons were once again attacking Torkyn Fall.

On the road above him, the dragon sat up and brought its great head around to face to the north. Perhaps from the creature's height, it could see others of its kind circling over the plateau, cracking the stone with blasts of their flame. Thelvyn drew the horse he was leading as far into the shadows against the face of the cliff as he could, hardly daring to hope that the dragon would be too distracted by the distant attack to glance down into the ravine. After a moment, the dragon rose and spread its broad wings, then leapt straight out from the ledge of the road, passing directly over Thelvyn's head. It brought itself about with long, powerful sweeps of its dark wings, climbing slowly as it moved away toward the north. In a moment, it was gone.

In spite of his terror, Thelvyn thought he had never seen anything more majestic in his life. He was also more grateful than ever for the mage's potion, knowing how a horse would normally have reacted to such a sight. He lead the pack-horse quickly to the trees, less mindful of the danger now that the dragon was gone. If the dragons remained occupied with the attack on Torkyn Fall several miles to the north, their best plan now would be to get themselves as far away as possible while they still had the cover of night. He left the packhorse with the others, pausing for a brief moment to assure Perrantin that everyone wasn't dead. He met Solveig on the way back, with Korinn close behind her.

"There's only one more packhorse, plus Sir George still has his own horse," he told her quickly. "Have everyone ready to continue on as soon as we get back. We have to get away from here while we can."

Sir George didn't have to be told how things stood. The need for quiet had gone with the dragon, so he had attached the lead of the remaining packhorse to his saddle and was already on his way. At the narrow part of the trail along the edge of the stream, the slack in the lead failed to keep the second horse directly behind the first. The packhorse kept stepping into the water. Thelvyn hurried to take the lead of the packhorse before it came to grief on the wet, icy stones. Distant flashes continued to illuminate the night sky, and the mountains shook with dim echoes of thunder.

Thelvyn and Sir George found their companions waiting beneath a small stand of snow-laden pines several hundred yards beyond the clearing. All the horses, still under the effects of the potion, stood as still and silent as statues. Perrantin and Solveig stood close by their own mounts, waiting nearly as motionlessly as their horses. Thelvyn realized they probably had seen very little in the moonless darkness beneath the trees.

"Torkyn Fall won't last much longer," Sir George said. "The dragons are losing their patience, or else their game has served its purpose."

"I'm not familiar with dragons, I must admit," Solveig said. "But I do get the impression that those blasts are much more powerful than normal dragonfire."

"Dragons possess a magic that is almost entirely their own," Perrantin explained. "Like elves, nearly all of them are magic-users to some degree, and they have spells to direct or augment their natural weapons. I don't speak from personal experience, of course, but that is what I'm told."

"And I can guess who told you," Solveig remarked.

"Very well, then, sagacious one," Sir George said. "Just how much longer will the horses be like this?"

"Oh, they should be coming around any time now," Perrantin said.

"Well, we really cannot afford to wait any longer. We'll have to lead the horses until they recover. Unless I am mistaken, we should come to the road any time now."

Thelvyn was placed in the lead to find the way in the darkness, but this time they were less concerned. They believed that the dragons were completely occupied with their attack on Torkyn Fall, although that might have been a false assumption. Thelvyn kept that very much in mind, and he continued to watch carefully for any hidden signs of danger. The trail followed the side of the little stream for another quarter of a mile, then turned suddenly and climbed steeply up the side of the ravine before coming out onto the main road at last. As soon as he was certain that there was no immediate danger, he went back to help lead the packhorses up the path. Fortunately they were all recovering from the effects of the potion now, or it would have been a difficult climb.

A pale light was beginning to illuminate the morning sky when they gathered on the road, although the sun wouldn't rise above the high mountains to the east for some time yet. The flashes of dragonfire were beginning to fade, although the thunder of the blasts continued to echo through the mountains. In the dim light, Thelvyn could see the dark forms of dragons soaring above the ridges only a few short miles to the north.

"The dragons are probably fairly certain they have everyone trapped inside the city for now," Sir George said. "Just the same, we must get away from here as quickly as we can and be ready to seek shelter if the dragons should begin sweeping over a larger area. We won't rest safely tonight until we reach the forests of the lower slopes, and they're still many miles away."

At least Thelvyn was no longer expected to take the lead. He now brought up the rear, watching the sky behind them. The horses were still fairly fresh, since they had kept a slow pace and hadn't been ridden. They left the heaviest snow and ice behind deep in the sheltered valley. The road itself was almost completely clear, especially by midmorning, after they had descended several miles from the greater heights.

If the horses were able to keep the pace, they might even make it down into the lower slopes by nightfall as Sir George had hoped. Thelvyn was pleased to be leaving the heights behind, not only to get away from the dragons but also to escape the cold. His greatest comfort was that they would be down from the mountains by the next day, back to lands where it was already spring and there were forests in which to hide from passing dragons.

CHAPTER SEVEN

Thelvyn was glad to be home again. He would never
have believed such a thing possible, and under the
circumstances, it proved to be a hard thing for him
to accept. Adventures had a way of doing that to a
person, especially when the adventures turned sour.

Of course, it helped to know that he probably would not
be there long. Sir George had possession of the ancient
treasures of the gnomes, and he was understandably nervous about that. He wanted to be rid of it before anyone
discovered they had it. If Duke Aalban, the archduke, or
the Wizards of the Flaem discovered what he had been
carting about in their lands, he would be in serious trouble.
At the very least, they would demand a tariff. Sir George
hadn't made any arrangements for paying tariffs with the
gnomes. He was worried about what Flaemish law might
have to say on the subject of the possession of such treasure, since he apparently didn't trust their laws any more
than Thelvyn did.

As it happened, Sir George was concerned about more

than the treasure. He was even more concerned about the dragons. They had been able to get back through the Eastern Reach the same way they got through the first time, by sneaking past when the dragons weren't watching. Although there had been no attacks west of the Reach yet this year, dragons were frequently spotted throughout the northern half of the Highlands. The first assaults might be only days away.

The presence of the dragons redoubled Sir George's concern about the treasure of the gnomes. He was determined that the dragons weren't going to discover the treasure was in his possession and come looking for it. He had assured Thelvyn that, contrary to legend, dragons could not smell gold from miles away. All the same, he had to transport the treasure into the south very soon now, and he would prefer to do it before he had to contend with the dragons.

On their first night back, Sir George called the others together to discuss the matter and decide on a course of action. Thelvyn took care to bring everyone his or her favorite drink before Sir George served the cherry liqueur. Thelvyn was beginning to earn everyone's respect in many small ways, as well as some larger ones.

"George, I can tell these dragons have you worried," Perrantin observed. "And that, in turn, makes me worried, considering you know more about dragons than anyone else in the world. What in particular is troubling you?"

"Well, the more I discover about this situation, the more worried I become," the old knight admitted. "Dragons simply don't make war without very good reason. I can think of no possible reason for their present actions, meaning that this could very well be the result of something going on among the dragons themselves."

"Any guesses what that might be?" Perrantin asked.

"How could I begin to guess? I was never privy to draconic politics. In theory, I know how they conduct their business, but I don't know anything specific about their leaders or what their policies might be. For centuries, even thousands of years, they have gone their own way and had their own concerns, but they have had little contact with the realms of men, elves, and dwarves. The only contact the outside world has had has been with the renegades, mad dragons who have broken with draconic law for purposes of their own."

"The only contact in this part of the world, at least," Thelvyn pointed out.

"Are you referring to your unknown race?" Sir George asked. "If your people do still exist, they don't live anywhere in this part of the world. And I simply cannot see how events in another part of the world could cause dragons to begin attacking unimportant settlements out in the middle of nowhere. Consider this: Dragons have been attacking in the mountains of the Heldannic lands, at Torkyn Fall, along the northern edge of the Plains of Ethengar, and here on the frontier of the Highlands. All of these places are on the edge of the wilderness. Beyond the mountains of the Wendarian Range, civilization simply doesn't exist."

"Do you think the dragons are fighting to maintain those lands as their own?" Perrantin asked. "Civilization has been pushing north toward those mountains lately."

"Only here in the Highlands," Sir George pointed out. "Torkyn Fall was first begun almost a thousand years ago, and the Ethengar have held the plains even longer. Granted, that might be the issue here, if the dragons have come to think of the mountains and the lands beyond as their own and are now willing to fight to prove the point. But whatever the cause, I suspect that it is not yet their official one. All anyone has reported seeing so far are reds and a few blacks and greens. No one has seen any white or blue dragons, and certainly no golds. I admit that the others might simply be sitting back and letting the more contentious breeds do the dirty work, but the fact that these breeds are not involved tells me that the Nation of Dragons has not yet decided to go to war."

"You've spoken of the Nation of Dragons and the Hidden Kingdoms of the Dragons before," Thelvyn said. "Where are they? Or does anyone know that?"

"Well, they are not 'hidden' in the usual sense of the word," Sir George explained. "Dragons are not territorial as other races are, settling themselves on a piece of land and drawing borders on a map and calling it their own. Their kingdoms exist in their alliances, and dragons of the same alliance don't necessarily live together in one place but may be spread over a large portion of the world. Thus their kingdoms encompass portions of other nations, places like Rockhome or Darokin, where people may not even know of their presence, but their kingdoms may also overlap each other. In some of their favorite places, you will find as many as six or eight kingdoms existing over the same piece of land, but that isn't usually a problem for them. Their kingdoms are said to be hidden because you cannot find them on maps and may indeed exist in the very place you yourself call home, but you would never know it."

"Then the Highlands could be a part of several of the kingdoms of the dragons," Thelvyn asked.

"That goes without saying," Sir George agreed. "The area encompassed by any one kingdom depends upon whether or not there are any dragons allied with that kingdom living in the area, and that changes fairly often. Dragons move about more than most people think, so the shapes of their kingdoms are changing all the time. Now, if you are still wondering if recent settlement in these lands has upset the dragons, I should think not. If anything, lands occupied by people are generally more interesting."

"Dragons are fond of livestock," Korinn said.

"That they are *not*," Sir George insisted. "They prefer elk and deer; they will eat cattle and horses only in times of need. And they do not care to eat people at all, which is against draconic law. Only renegade dragons have been known to snap someone down, mostly as a gesture to infuriate his companions. But as I say, the renegades are all mad."

"Then the dragons presently raiding are not renegades?" Perrantin asked.

"No. Renegades would be killing and destroying purely for the sake of death and destruction. There is something very calculated, even restrained in these attacks. They have something in mind, some goal or policy that has yet to become apparent to us."

"But that suggests that the Nation of Dragons is behind this," Perrantin said.

"Not necessarily," Sir George insisted. "Dragons aren't like people. Dragons have long childhoods and typically continue to grow slowly during their entire lives, which can be as long as several thousand years. Although they do have something of a natural limit, beyond which additional size seems more a function of magic, since only the wisest and most powerful magic-users of the dragons will continue to grow. At any rate, the dragons I've seen so far in the present troubles have been fairly young, judging by their size."

"Those were *small* dragons?" Thelvyn asked, amazed.

"Mature, but rather young," he explained. "There seem to be no older dragons nor gold dragons of any size. That seems to suggest that these are rogue dragons, young ones who are full of themselves and impatient with the dictates of their elders. They will sometimes act out policies that may be popular among the dragons but that the parliament has not yet approved. Of course, at times the parliament is pleased to allow the younger dragons to act upon policies that their elders would not wish to make official."

"Is that the situation here?" Solveig asked.

Sir George took a quick swallow from his glass and nodded. "That would explain why the younger dragons are attacking with the appearance of some plan, although the goal itself is not yet apparent."

"Oh, that's just fine," Solveig complained. "Even dragons play politics. Destroy all my delusions that in some odd corner of the world there exists a place free of duplicity."

"Draconic politics tend to move very slowly, because there is not much in the world that dragons want," Sir George said. "That's the part that really worries me. These dragons want something, and I can't imagine what. I just don't see any hope for it. The only way to discover what is going on is to ask a dragon. Perry, what's the best way to do that?"

Perrantin shrugged. "Ask *very* politely? Honestly, now, how am I supposed to know that?"

"The usual method is to try to subdue the dragon by defeating it in battle. With all due respect to our most worthy companions, I don't see that we have a ghost of a chance of doing that. I was wondering if we could accomplish the same thing with magic. Any suggestions?"

"Well, I can't think of any right off the top of my head," the mage said. "I suppose that I could research the matter."

Perrantin disappeared into the pages of all the books of magic he could find in Sir George's rather extensive collection. Whether or not he was particularly enthusiastic about the prospect of hunting dragons, he was irresistibly drawn to a problem, especially if it involved some obscure or remarkable aspect of magic. This matter required both. He really didn't hold much hope of finding what he wanted here, even if Sir George's library consisted of rare and unusual books collected during his years of extensive travel. But he had a couple days to look while the others made the necessary arrangements for their journey south to find the gnomes to deliver the treasure of Torkyn Fall. That was all the time Perrantin needed to know whether or not he was likely to find anything here.

Solveig and Korinn were somewhat less enthusiastic about the prospect of hunting dragons, and understandably so. Although they were both intelligent, well educated, and could be quite urbane, they were still basically nothing more than adventurers, mercenaries in the service of the old knight. As such, they were willing to assume risks, even great risks, but the risk had to be within reason and promise a reward worthy of the risk. They had been willing enough to undertake the journey to Torkyn Fall, even as dangerous as it had been, because it had been extremely profitable. Taking on a dragon to discover what it might have to say was not only dangerous but also seemed unprofitable.

Thelvyn wasn't certain how to predict the resolution of this difference of opinion. Under other circumstances, he would have expected that Solveig and Korinn, as adventurers in the pay of Sir George, would yield to his wishes. But their arrangement seemed more of a partnership, with each offering his opinion and sharing equally in the final decision. He wondered if the rule of the majority would hold, and Sir George would surrender to the wishes of the others if the vote went against him. And if Sir George was prepared to insist, whether the others would refuse to go.

Thelvyn was also extremely uncertain of his own position. He might be Sir George's heir, but he had no idea whether that made him a partner, an apprentice, or just hired help. Sir George had never spoken with him on that matter. He was treated like any other member of their group, although there had been no discussion of what payment or percentage of profits he might receive from their business with the gnomes.

Nor did he know what to think about Sir George's most recent proposal. His first impression was that he should continue to stay as far away from dragons as possible, considering the fury they had shown his mother. Then he realized that if they could indeed subdue and question a dragon, he might have a chance to question the creature about his mother and his race. On the other hand, perhaps he was better advised to keep his secrets to himself.

He used what little time he had by immersing himself in his lessons. Since Perrantin was preoccupied with his research, Thelvyn was on his own with his studies in magic, although he had enough to keep him busy. Solveig also kept him occupied with lessons in the use of his sword, especially now that she seemed to feel more certain her teaching would be to good effect. Thelvyn hadn't actually used his sword in battle yet, but he had handled himself well in some dangerous situations. Indeed, he hadn't been in a position to realize just how well he had conducted himself on the journey to Torkyn Fall. He had been aware only of what he perceived to be his mistakes, most of which had been entirely of his own imagination.

* * * * *

Mayor Aalsten arrived in the middle of the morning, and it was immediately obvious that he was upset about something. Sir George led him into the den, and Thelvyn fetched him a fresh pastry and a glass of cordial. One reason the mayor and Sir George had always gotten along so well was that they both enjoyed cherry liqueur. Thelvyn wondered if they were the only ones who did.

"Sir George, the dragons are back," the mayor declared.

"I've noticed," the old knight said. "Are you trying to tell me that there have been new attacks?"

"Oh, indeed there have. More houses have been burned in the countryside around Nordeen, and a few inside the village itself. And now Duke Ardelan has said that the dragons have closed the pass into the Eastern Reach."

"Yes, I was aware of that more than two weeks ago," Sir George said, unconcerned. "I was there."

"Then perhaps there is no great cause for concern," Mayor Aalsten said, already looking less worried. "Duke Aalban has sent word that, although the dragons have returned and the attacks have resumed, they do not seem as determinedly aggressive this year."

This time Sir George looked surprised. "The duke said that? I wonder where he got that idea. Indeed, the closing of the Eastern Reach suggests to me that the dragons are more determined than ever."

"But the wizards have also said that the dragons appear less aggressive this year." The mayor looked confused. "They wouldn't have said that if it weren't true, would they? I assume they've looked into the problem."

"I suspect they are simply trying to protect people from panic," Sir George said succinctly, not to mention charitably. "It might be best for you to keep this to yourself, Mayor, but you really ought to be prepared to evacuate the city, with shelter and supplies hidden in the mountains, as you did last year. We were in Torkyn Fall, one of the great underground cities of the gnomes beyond the Eastern Reach, only days ago. The city was half in ruins. As we were leaving, we saw the dragons tearing into the mountain as if it were an anthill."

"But that's terrible!" the mayor insisted. "I've heard of Torkyn Fall, but our people had always assumed the city was deserted."

"It probably is by now. We went there to learn what we could about the dragons and their attacks, and what we discovered was most disquieting. Dragons are attacking from the Highlands to the Heldannic lands, and possibly beyond. The dragons have been laying siege to Torkyn Fall since long before their appearance in the Highlands last year. My concern is that when Torkyn Fall is destroyed, the dragons are going to be turning their attention in this direction."

"But surely the wizards will do something about it."

Sir George looked vaguely uncomfortable. "Your people are still fairly new to this world, and your wizards have no familiarity with dragons. That's why I've been looking into this myself."

Mayor Aalsten went away looking no happier than when he had arrived. At least he was now determined to see that all proper precautions would be taken, although Sir George was less certain that he would remain so once the dukes and the wizards began issuing more promises of security. Sir George still possessed certain knightly instincts that required him to do what he could to protect the weak, even when he knew they would probably disregard his advice.

"Will the dragons come this far?" Thelvyn asked after they had seen the mayor to the door.

"That depends on how quickly the dragons move on their plans," Sir George replied as they returned to the den. "I won't know that until I know what their plan is. The point is that, once they decide to make serious war, they could easily devastate the Highlands in a matter of days. You can fight a dragon, or even two or three of them, but no force in this world can fight their entire race. Perhaps if they demonstrate their powers sufficiently to make their point, they might just tell us what they want."

"That would probably be the best solution," Mage Perrantin said. He was sitting in a corner of the den, reading a large book written in some obscure language. "It would be easier to give them what they want than try to fight them for it."

"If we could get them to start talking a little sooner, we might be able to arrive at a less violent solution," Sir George said. "The trouble is that I expect the dragons will be much more reasonable than anyone else is likely to be."

"True enough," Perrantin agreed and returned to his reading.

"Should you have told the mayor that you are trying to do something about the problem?" Thelvyn asked. "He might tell Mage Eddan, and word could get back to the duke or the Wizards of the Flaem. I don't think they like anyone interfering in their affairs, no matter how incompetent they are."

"Yes, that may well be true," Sir George admitted. "However, I'm not particularly concerned. We will be leaving very soon now."

Sir George had said once that he would probably have to do something about the dragons, and it seemed that he certainly meant to try. Of course, Thelvyn knew him well enough by now to be sure that the old knight wasn't about to do anything foolish or unduly risky. If Perrantin couldn't find a fairly reasonable way to subdue a dragon with magic, George would give up the attempt. That same awareness was perhaps the only thing that kept Solveig and Korinn from flatly refusing Sir George's proposal for a dragon hunt. They would at least wait to see what plan was offered, if any, and weigh its risks against its chances of success. But they remained unenthusiastic about the idea.

At dinner that night, Sir George approached Perrantin with a very important question. It seemed unlikely that the mage had discovered a way to deal with dragons, or he would have said something about it. But Perrantin had said nothing, and he was running out of books. He sat at the table squinting, looking very much like someone who had been reading too much.

"Perry, I really must put it to you," Sir George said. "Time is passing, and we must deliver that treasure as soon as we can. We can delay another day or two if we must, but I need to ask if you are anywhere near finding an answer."

"Then you might just as well start packing," the mage said. "I've done the best I can. I've looked through every book you have, and I've yet to find a hint of what we want."

Solveig and Korinn looked happier immediately, although Sir George frowned and seemed defeated. "Then there really is no way to subdue a dragon by magic?"

"On the contrary, I would guess there almost certainly is some way," Perrantin explained. "I'm just saying that your library, as remarkable as it is, isn't extensive enough for such obscure research. Dragons have kept to themselves for so long that there has been little need to use magic to confront them. As far as I can tell, dragons have been making themselves fairly scarce since perhaps five hundred years after the fall of Blackmoor and the Rain of Fire. At least."

"Rather longer than that, I must admit," Sir George said. "I don't know the ancient history of dragons that well myself, but something very nasty happened during the age of Blackmoor, some two hundred years or so before its fall. The wizards of Blackmoor made war upon the dragons and defeated them. That's frankly about all I know, except that the wizards gave the dragons some valuable token of peace, and the dragons have kept to themselves ever since."

"Well, you could have told me that before," Perrantin said impatiently. "Not that it would have made any difference, I must admit. They knew how to fight dragons, but their secrets were lost with them. The fall of Blackmoor nearly destroyed the world, so you can imagine such a force left behind a scarcity of books. Of course, some of that magic could have been rediscovered, or other spells or magical artifacts might have been found that are useful against dragons. I need a more extensive library, a library dedicated to the study of magic."

"We simply don't have the time to go all the way back to Darokin," Sir George declared.

"Well, there's one alternative," Perrantin said. "As it happens, perhaps the third or fourth greatest library of magic in this part of the world is only a few days away in Braejr. That's where we're taking the treasures of the gnomes anyway."

"In Braejr?" Korinn asked, surprised and rather dubious. "How can that be? The Flaem have been in this world barely a hundred years."

"The fire wizards have been busy," the mage explained. "It's that Alphatian thing again. The Flaem hate the Alphatians so much that all the wizards and the archduke can think about is finding a way to fight them. The really funny part is that the Alphatians don't even know the Flaem are here, or they'd have raided the Highlands with such fury that the present attacks of the dragons would have seemed insignificant."

"Actually, I daresay the Alphatians already know of their presence," Solveig said. "You don't keep the existence of an entire nation secret at the same time you're trying to do business with that part of the world. I consider it more likely that the Alphatians just don't care enough to make an issue of it. The Flaem have been wandering through various worlds for centuries, nursing their hatred, but the Alphatians settled fifteen hundred years ago, and they've mostly been devoted to their own affairs. I suspect that their ancient rivalry with the Flaem is mostly a matter of legend."

"That seems likely," Sir George agreed.

"The Thyatians and the Alphatians have been rivals from some time now," Solveig added. "The Thyatians know them as well as anyone. Now, I don't doubt that they'd like to crush the Flaem, but perhaps no more than they want to subjugate the rest of the world. And fighting the Flaem right now would require going through Darokin or Alfheim, which they wouldn't be prepared to do."

"Whatever the case, dragons are our immediate problem," Perrantin reminded them. "The fire wizards have some rather ambitious schemes of their own, but to put them into action any time soon they need power. To that end, they've been assembling one of the largest libraries in existence. Their agents have been looting the schools of magic and the workshops of every major magician in this part of the world."

"Will they allow you inside?" Thelvyn asked. "The Flaem are unbelievably protective of their secrets."

"Well, they've always let me in before."

Ever since Perrantin had brought them back to the point, Solveig had been sitting in her chair brooding, as if her mercurial Northland temperament had taken a drastic swing. Now she looked up at Sir George, a hint of one of her classic glares flashing in her eyes. "Why is this our concern? For all of our grand professional pretensions, we're really only a group of glorified antique collectors. This seems like a tremendous risk, with no promise of profit."

"Aren't you concerned about this situation?" Sir George asked.

"Of course I am. I might be a professional, but I am hardly a complete mercenary. If there were something we could reasonably hope to accomplish, I'd be glad to help. But you seem to be suggesting that the five of us should walk right into the middle of an invasion of dragons, not to mention Flaemish wizards."

"I'm not suggesting we take any unreasonable risks," the old knight insisted. "I can't tell you how much risk this would involve until our good wizard discovers the magic we need. When he offers us the best information he can find, we'll know exactly how the matter stands and we can decide then. I'm not asking you to commit yourself to this quest now. My own hope is that Perry can find us something that gives a high probability of success with the least risk. If he can't, I have no intention of pursuing it any further."

"That sounds reasonable," Korinn said rather cautiously.

"Yes, but the Wizards of the Flaem should be doing the same thing themselves," Solveig pointed out. "That happens to be their duty to the realm. Our resources are limited, and no one is going to pay us for this. Where's our profit?"

"Rampaging dragons aren't good for business," Sir George said. "If they begin to make travel impossible, we will all have to find new careers."

"I have alternate career choices," Solveig shot back.

"And dragons are notoriously wealthy," Sir George continued.

Korinn looked up, immediately interested. Dwarves dreamed at night about the fabulous hoards of dragons. Of course, dragons dreamed at night about the treasuries of the dwarves, so things were pretty even.

"As you say, we can wait to see what Perry can find for us," Solveig finally agreed guardedly. "George, I'm still curious about your own motivations in this. You don't really expect to acquire dragon treasure or other rewards. The fact is, you are obsessed about the subject of dragons, and we both know why. Do you expect to learn the deepest secrets of the dragons from this quest of yours?"

"I have a great many expectations, I must admit," Sir George said candidly. "My most basic motivation comes down to this: You've said yourself that I know more about dragons than anyone, which leaves me best qualified to try to negotiate with them or handle the problem they pose by some means other than war. And I must also admit to being rather intrigued by the prospect of the greatest and most challenging quest of my career, a quest that might as well have been made for my talents."

Solveig nodded slowly, her reluctance still obvious. "I suppose I can understand your reasons well enough, as long as you can promise that you won't allow them to interfere with your judgment. And as you say, we still don't know whether or not we are going to find a reasonable plan. We can decide this matter in Braejr a week or two from now, when Perry has done his best at the library of the Flaem."

"That is all I've been asking," Sir George insisted. "Then if everyone can get ready, I do believe that it would be in our best interests to leave for Braejr in the morning."

Thelvyn hurried to pack as soon as he had cleaned up after dinner. Preparing for the trip on such short notice wouldn't be too difficult, since they had known they would be leaving soon and they had nearly everything ready. The ancient treasures of the gnomes were still safely packed for travel. The gear for the horses was all laid out in the stables, and packs containing extra fodder and various other necessities were already prepared. Except for packing their clothes, they had little to do except saddle the horses, load the packs, and ride off.

Regarding the nature of Sir George and his company, however, Thelvyn hardly knew what to think. Just when he had finally reconciled himself to the fact that Sir George and his companions were extraordinary traders in antiquities and not a band of bold adventurers, that was exactly what they proposed to become. The journey to Torkyn Fall had been dangerous and adventuresome, but taking on dragons was quite another matter. He didn't feel ready to do his part in such a quest, although he had to admit that his remarkable vision made him an asset to the group.

Yet he was still fearful of dragons. He had often wondered if he were a descendant of the ancient race of Blackmoor, although he couldn't comprehend why that made his people the special enemies of the dragons. Since Sir George had spoken of the vague legends of the war between Blackmoor and the dragons, he thought he understood a great deal more than he had. A war three thousand years past would still be quite fresh in the memories of dragons, who lived for hundreds or even thousands of years.

There was so much about himself that only the dragons could tell him, whether to confirm or deny his suspicions about himself and his own people. The only problem was he had to make himself known to a dragon before he could ask any questions. He couldn't help but remember how relentlessly they had hunted his mother.

He was in the stables checking their supplies when Solveig entered. She paused when she saw him, then took a second look. "What's the problem, lad? Does the prospect of meeting a dragon face-to-face make you nervous?"

"I have reason to be."

She nodded. "I probably know about as much about your past as you do, so I understand your concern. Still, if you ever want to find out about your past, this is the only way. I can't blame you for being afraid of dragons. They scare me. Neither one of us is a coward, but we have sense enough to know what we should be afraid of."

"I suppose so," Thelvyn agreed. "We have something in common, I suppose. We both grew up in places we did not belong."

"I don't know about not belonging," Solveig said. "I have to admit that you seem nothing like the Flaem, and I doubt you ever could be. But Thyatis was home for me. I understand those people, and I understand the way things work there. The adventurer in me needed some time away from their politics and all the complexities and the duplicity of that life, but I can play the game as well as any of them. Compared to the real thing, I'm really not much of a barbarian."

"Have you ever thought about going back to the Northern Reaches?" Thelvyn asked.

"Yes," she told him as she prepared her packs. "I've thought about it, but I doubt I ever will. You see, that's where we are very different. I look like a Northlander, and I may enjoy playing the part by taking one of their names and wearing a form of their armor, but I do so to hide who I really am. I know my own people are boorish, violent barbarians, and we really have little in common. When I am done with adventuring, I will almost certainly go back to Thyatis and return to being Valeria Dorani. Your situation is different. Sir George was quite impressed with your mother, and he has always insisted she was a great sorceress and a true lady. That suggests that your own people must be worthy."

"That really doesn't worry me," Thelvyn said. "I'm not afraid to go home again, but I can only find out where home might be from the dragons, if even they can tell me. I don't know if I want Perrantin to find what we need or not."

"Then you should probably get yourself ready to face the dragons," Solveig replied. "I have no doubt that Perry will find exactly what we need. In my experience, those two are infallible at finding trouble."

CHAPTER EIGHT

The first day began very much as their journey east to Torkyn Fall. They left early and traveled well into the evening before they came to Aalbansford. They spent the night at the same inn, and in the morning, they checked to be certain that their packs were well stocked with fodder. But this time they didn't follow the main road to the east. Instead, they crossed the bridge back over the river and headed south into the wilderness, toward the very tail of the line of mountains as they curved back around to the east.

They found a trail leading south through the forest, clear and well defined so that it made for fairly easy, quick travel, although it wasn't wide enough for wagons or carts. The others in the party had journeyed this way before, and they knew it well. Sir George explained to Thelvyn that there were several advantages to choosing this route. For one thing, it was more direct than following the main road, and they expected to save at least a day of travel. It also kept them on the same side of the river as their destination. The only bridge farther south was still under construction.

The route also kept them well away from dragons and inquisitive dukes who might want to inspect the contents of their packs. Of all the dangers they might face, Sir George was still most concerned about being required to pay a tariff on the gnomes' treasure. Of course, they couldn't begin to pay a real tariff on such riches; most likely a portion of the treasure would be seized as payment, unless the entire load was confiscated as contraband. At the least, they'd lose part of the treasure, and the group would find their professional reputation and the trust they enjoyed greatly tarnished. At the worst, they could find themselves imprisoned as smugglers and thieves.

After a couple of hours, they came to a narrow place between the end of the mountains and the Aalban River, and they were slowed down a great deal while they made their way through some rough country in the ridges above the river. They didn't come down from this region until well after noon, even though the distance was hardly five miles, but the horses had tired quickly over the rugged ground. That afternoon they entered a hilly, heavily wooded land, although the character of these woods differed from the dark pine forests to the north. The horses needed rest after the rough passage above the river, and they didn't go much farther that day. They stopped for the night when they reached the deep woods to the south.

When they continued on the next day, Thelvyn expected they would come down out of the hills once they began to move away from the mountains, but that wasn't the case. Sir George informed him they would travel through hilly country all that day and the next, coming down into the plains only for the final day of their ride to Braejr. Travel was slower in this rugged land, but Thelvyn noticed that they seemed to have left the dragons behind. He realized only that evening that he hadn't seen them making their usual patrols for the entire day.

That wasn't necessarily remarkable in itself, but he had been seeing dragons at least once a day for the last several weeks. The dragons had restricted their attacks to the northern Highlands the previous year, although their

patrols had ranged freely throughout the realm. Apparently
the dragons weren't patrolling the uninhabited central
region of the Highlands at all.

Perhaps the weather helped keep the dragons away. Early
in the afternoon, the sky turned cloudy, beginning with
high, pale clouds that steadily sank lower until rain threatened at any time. The rain began in the form of a cool,
heavy mist late that afternoon, just as they came within
sight of the fields beyond the small village of Beraan. This
village was even smaller than Thelvyn's home in the north.
On that dark, rainy afternoon, it also seemed a quiet and
sad-looking place. They were all glad to see it all the same,
since it meant that they could spend a cold, wet night in a
warm, dry bed at the inn.

The rain lasted most of the night, but at least it wasn't
heavy, so the road wasn't much the worse for it in the
morning. Even more accommodating, the rains ended
before dawn, and the clouds began to break up and blow
away. They came down out of the hills that day, camping at
night at the edge of the woods before leaving the forests
behind for gently rolling plains of short green grass. They
were apprehensive about riding the better part of a day
completely in the open, for there were only occasional
stands of trees, hardly large enough to be called woods.
Perhaps the dragons were indeed staying to the north, for
this was now the third day since they had seen any.

They left the plains behind late that afternoon and
entered a land that was even less hilly but more wooded,
although the scattered woods often separated sprawling
farmlands. There were farmhouses at the ends of long
lanes, with barns and stables, the fields all neatly divided
by hedgerows and fences of wood and stone. Thelvyn
could see that these were older homesteads than he knew
in the north, for everything looked comfortably arranged
and settled rather than newly carved from the wilderness.
He was becoming quietly excited, thinking that he was
finally going to see civilization.

He didn't have long to wait. They rode at a fair pace for
over an hour through the fields that stretched outward from
the city of Braejr. To Thelvyn, it seemed interminable. Folk

of the outlying farms couldn't easily retreat to the safety of
the city walls if danger threatened. He failed to consider
that in the more civilized regions, there were few dangers
the farms would face, short of invading armies or an attack
from dragons. At last they came out from behind a small
cluster of trees, and he could see the walls of the city only a
couple of miles beyond.

Now Thelvyn could see that the city of Braejr was in no
way like the many wondrous places in faraway lands he had
heard described. The walls and towers and the tops of
buildings were made of a dull gray stone, solid and stout,
all very functional but not very esthetic. The city lay at the
very junction of the Aalban River and the Areste River,
which began in the heights of the far western reaches of the
Highlands before cascading down through the plains.

Some two-thirds of the city was encircled by a high,
strong wall of that same gray stone, running in a wide loop
from the bank of the Areste on the west to the bank of the
Aalban on the east. Two of the most impressive structures
in the Highlands, the archduke's palace and the Academy,
were located in Braejr. That wasn't saying much, however.
Both were long, sprawling structures, built specifically so
that their fortified outer surfaces formed a part of the walls
of the city. Both, like the outer wall, were simply and
solidly built from massive blocks of stone and looked very
utilitarian, not at all like the drawings Thelvyn had seen in
books of the palaces and great mansions of Darokin and
Thyatis.

The only entrance into the city by land was through the
gate fort, which was a rather formidable structure in itself.
Of course, the entire southern part of the city faced the
northern bank of the juncture of the two rivers, although
even parts of that approach were fortified to a fair extent.
None of the original bank remained. Most of the city's
warehouses and other large buildings had their backs to the
river, with massive outer walls of the same gray stone
descending straight into the water, just like the outer walls
of the Academy and the archduke's palace, offering no
landing for boats. Stone quays where boats could be
docked occupied the only open spaces between buildings,

and even these places could be easily defended if need be. The city wall encircled a large open space to allow room for expansion, including some empty areas within the city that had a tendency to revert to swamps.

Indeed, as they rode through the empty streets, they passed several areas that were still open land. There were two such regions, one on either side of the north gate, just beyond the market and the smaller shops on the streets just inside the gate. The largest such area was in the very heart of Braejr, which was rather optimistically called the city park. These areas were dark and wooded, and none of them seemed to be particularly safe, not only because they looked wild enough to harbor thieves and natural predators, but also because the ground in these places was mostly wet and marshy, the original state of the entire area between the two rivers. If not for the vigilance of the wizards and their stock of vermin-killing potions, Braejr would have most likely been hopelessly plague-infested.

Thelvyn's first impressions of the city were mixed. He was used to the cool, fresh mountain air of the north and the smaller settlements of the frontier. Granted that his sense of smell was slightly more keen than that of human folk, he thought Braejr smelled of entirely too many people living all together, with too many animals and too much cooking and the smoke of too many fires. He also understood, as his companions could have told him, that Braejr was only a small, simple town compared to some of the large cities of the world. Perhaps it was just as well that his introduction to civilization on a grand scale was a gradual one. They crossed to the eastern quarter of the city to an inn the others knew of, in the area of the shops and the quaint, comfortable homes of the middle-class merchants and master craftsmen.

They could bring the ancient treasures of the gnomes into such a place as this, which provided the best security they would find in Braejr, at least without advertising the fact that they carried goods of great worth. The inn had the second advantage of being only a minute's walk from the Academy, where Perrantin would be spending the next few days searching the great library of the Wizards of the

Flaem. It was late in the afternoon by the time they had settled themselves in their rooms, too late for Sir George to attempt to make contact with the agents of the gnomes who would take charge of the treasure. Once darkness fell, they moved the packs containing the treasure to their rooms as discreetly as they could manage. As always, Thelvyn shared a large room with Korinn and Solveig, the younger members of their company staying together so that Sir George and Perrantin could sit up half the night, if they wished, locked in obscure discussions and professional debates.

The various members of the group went their separate ways early the next morning. Mage Perrantin dressed himself to look his most wizardly and hurried off to spend the day in the library of the Wizard's Academy. He even took his lunch with him, which served to indicate just how serious he was. Sir George went off into the merchant's quarter to search for the gnomish agents who would take the treasures of Torkyn Fall off their hands. That would be a relatively quick and simple business once he found them, since all negotiations and payment for services had already been made. They would all be relieved to get those valuable artifacts off their hands. The others, of course, were left behind at the inn to guard the treasure.

Thelvyn was aware that Braejr was not a particularly cosmopolitan city by most standards. The Flaem wanted to keep the Highlands to themselves. While they wanted to encourage trade, they didn't care to have too many foreigners coming to stay in the lands they considered their own. Korinn, Solveig, and even Thelvyn were, by their appearance, obviously foreigners. The local folk weren't hostile and probably never would be, but they still had a way of making strangers feel unwelcome and uncomfortable. So it was that no one in their company was especially eager to go out and see the city, which didn't have all that much to see in the first place. That made staying in the inn much easier to bear.

Sir George returned just before noon and quietly informed the others that the arrangements for the transfer of the treasure had been made. In the next day or two, a group of gnomes and their bodyguards, who had been in the north Highlands purchasing metals, would stay the night at the inn. That same evening, they would take the appropriate packs down to the stables as they went to tend their horses. The next day, the gnomes would leave with several packs apparently full of fodder, which they had not had when they arrived. Since they had already been met by the customs officials when they entered the city, their packs wouldn't be checked on the way out.

Perrantin returned late that evening, apparently only after he had been expelled from the library at closing. While he had not yet found what they needed, he was very encouraged.

"The wizards have been very busy since the last time I was here," he explained. "The library is more extensive than ever. And while they are said to have stolen most of their books from other collections, they've at least had the decency to catalog everything in great detail."

"Well, of course they have," Sir George insisted. "They only stole those books in the first place so they could search through them for anything useful. They want to know exactly what they have."

"That's going to make looking much easier and faster than I had anticipated," Perrantin said. "If I haven't found what we want in three days, then we can safely assume that it isn't there."

"Three days?" the old knight repeated thoughtfully. "You can bet that agents of either the archduke or the wizards are watching us. Well, not actually spying upon us perhaps, but at least keeping track of our business. They might begin to take an active interest if we spend too much time doing nothing. I really should be giving them something to look at besides the fact that you are ransacking their pilfered library."

"They've noticed that already, I'm sure," the mage said.

"Perhaps, but I want them to have the impression that you're doing nothing more than indulging yourself while you're waiting for me. I suppose I might distract them by going about to all the usual shops we haunt, looking at antiquities and talking to our old friends and acquaintances. Very much what I would otherwise be doing."

"I'd hate to have you make such a sacrifice on my account," the mage remarked dryly.

"It really is for the good of the cause."

The next day was uneventful. Perrantin went back to the library to continue his research, and Sir George went out on the town to give the appearance of attending to business of his own. The others were once more required to stay behind at the inn, since they still had the treasures of Torkyn Fall to guard. As they had been promised, a small group of gnomes and their four warrior guards arrived at the inn later that afternoon. That evening, when they went down to tend their horses a final time, Thelvyn helped Solveig and Korinn take down the packs that contained the treasures. The gnomes arrived to tend their own horses soon afterward, and in the process, the packs were discreetly moved from one side of the stables to the other.

They all felt much better about the situation at once, considering the trouble that might have been involved if they had been discovered in possession of such valuable artifacts. Still, they wouldn't be entirely out of danger until the gnomes had made a safe departure from Braejr with their treasure and were well on their way without discovery. Perrantin was nearly heartbroken when he returned late from the library, wishing he could have taken the time to play with the artifacts one last time. With the fall of the last of the great cities of the gnomes, such a treasure might never again be seen in that part of the world. And they had been riding about with it all stuffed inside packs of fodder.

At least the next day they were no longer required to keep watch at the inn, and Thelvyn had the chance for his first real look about Braejr. They went out dressed as discreetly as possible, although there was nothing much they could do to disguise the fact that they were foreigners. Thelvyn's one consolation was that everyone was so busy staring at Solveig and Korinn that most failed to see anything very unusual about him.

They were dressed well enough that they were able to visit the wealthier shops without attracting the annoyance of either the shop owners or the city constables. They were, after all, the companions of Sir George Kirbey, dealer in antiquities and treasures. Perhaps to show that he was indeed the true heir of the old knight, Thelvyn had lately begun to develop an appreciation for jewels, antiquities, and other treasures. His rather brief apprenticeship to the jeweler in his home village had taught him a basic appreciation for the art of jewelry, and his subsequent education at the hands of Sir George had developed it further.

Thelvyn also wanted to see the foundries, for he had heard that in Braejr, where there was an abundance of wizards, the smiths used magic rather than wood and charcoal to heat their furnaces. His interest in both jewelry and smithying endeared him greatly to Korinn, as indeed it would to all honest dwarves, and Solveig was tolerant enough about their desires to pay a visit to the smithies. In Braejr, all the dirty shops, foundries, smiths, tanners, and others known for the smoke, smells, and messes associated with their work were grouped together in the southern part of the city, on the broad point of land where the two rivers came together.

Rumor for once proved true. The furnaces of the forges and foundries were indeed heated by some magical means, which of course produced a great deal less smoke than the usual method. The Wizards of the Flaem were experts in many forms of fire magic, and they had created a process so simple and effective that a trained magic-user didn't have to be in attendance to make it work. The trouble was that Thelvyn couldn't see how it was done, and the smiths were not about to reveal their secrets to a group of foreigners. Korinn wasn't greatly impressed. He explained later that the dwarves had long had their own ways of accomplishing the same thing.

Sir George was waiting at the inn when they returned that afternoon. His day of pretending to attend to his usual business had been frustratingly successful. The Flaem had brought their ancient designs and techniques in jewelry with them from their own world, and the new generation of Flaemish jewelers were finally coming into their own. Their forms and styles were the only new thing the world had seen in some time, and Sir George could have sold all he could pack away to wealthy patrons of Darokin and Thyatis. But he didn't want to make any purchases until he knew whether or not they would be having other business with dragons.

Perrantin returned some time later, in a considerably better mood. He could hardly contain himself until they had gathered in a private parlor of the inn for dinner. He had brought a small pile of papers with him.

"I finally found what I was looking for, and in the most obvious place," he explained eagerly. "Remember my telling you that the fire wizards have been thoroughly cataloging their books? Well, all I had to do was to look under *d* for dragons. Quite simple."

"Fancy that," Sir George muttered, half amused and half annoyed.

"Nothing is ever that obvious in a library of arcane studies, as a matter of tradition," the mage said defensively. "The Flaem just don't know any better. It certainly is much more efficient, but I'm still not certain I would care to see it become a trend."

The old knight nodded. "If wizards knew what they were doing, it would put half of them out of work."

Perrantin glared for a moment, but his enthusiasm got the better of him. "Anyway, this afternoon I came across a second-generation copy of an ancient elven text on the subject of dragons. This is one of the legendary forty-eight volumes assembled by Ilsundal himself during the elven Age of Wandering, in his attempt to collect and re-create the ancient lore and magic of the elves of Evergrun from the time before their alliance with the men of Blackmoor."

"The elves remember Blackmoor?" Thelvyn asked excitedly.

"Not very well," Perrantin explained. "Granted, most of what we do know about Blackmoor comes from the writings and the legends of the elves. The trouble is, they chose to forget most of what they had known. You see, the elves of that time lived in the southern continent, at the far end of the world from Blackmoor, and contact between the two came late. That brought the elves to a bitter debate concerning their future. Many welcomed the sciences of Blackmoor, while others denounced the ruin that the misuse of that knowledge brought to their own ancient lands. That contention remained even after the fall of Blackmoor, for some elves wished to use their recently aquired knowledge to build a new realm for the elves. But by that time most elves held a bitter opinion of Blackmoor and its teachings."

"Which is why, for pity's sake, you must never tell an elf you might be descended from the race of Blackmoor," Sir George said to Thelvyn. "Now, the chief of the elves, who believed that their only hope lay in a return to the old ways, was Ilsundal, who led the faithful elves into the north to found a new homeland built in the image of Evergrun."

"Alfheim?" Korinn asked.

"Their first kingdom was the Sylvan Realm, in the far northwest," the mage told him. "You dwarves try hard to ignore the elves and everything about them."

Korinn shrugged but said nothing.

"But why did they leave at all?" Thelvyn asked.

"Because there was nothing left of Evergrun," Perrantin explained. "The Rain of Fire destroyed almost everything, and then the land itself was lost beneath the ice after the shape of the world was changed. Of course, Ilsundal and many of his followers remembered the time before the fall of Blackmoor, since elves live so long, and they had known in their youth old wizards and scholars who remembered Evergrun as it had been before the coming of the men of Blackmoor. Naturally they realized that if they wanted to return to the old ways, then the first thing they had to do was to put their heads together and assemble all the lore and magic they had ever heard, before more of it was forgotten. They knew that their great migration would be long and difficult, and also that the greatest danger along the way would be to their elders and to the knowledge they held. Thus they assembled the forty-eight volumes of the *Heimsleidh*, the Way of the Land."

"Did you find all forty-eight volumes in the library here?" Sir George asked.

"Indeed I did. I can't imagine how the fire wizards managed to steal a complete set from the elves of Alfheim. Even the sight of copies of the *Heimsleidh* is forbidden to non-elves."

"You could make a fortune selling copies to the wizards and scholars of the world," Sir George mused. "I doubt that the Flaem have the slightest idea of the value of what they have. Perry, we are going to have to make a trip back to that library some day very soon."

"But if the wizards of Blackmoor were giving so much lore and science to the elves, then much of what was known in Blackmoor about dragons might also have been made known to the elves," Thelvyn said, bringing them back to the matter at hand. "Would such knowledge be included in these books?"

"Well, one volume of the *Heimsleidh* contains a long chapter devoted entirely to dragons," Perrantin replied. "The elves who wrote that volume probably no longer knew whether that lore had been elven or from the wizards of Blackmoor, and it probably didn't matter. The dragons were the enemies of Blackmoor, which didn't necessarily make them allies of the elves. Still, elves and dragons have always left each other very much alone."

"Never mind that," Solveig said impatiently. "What does the chapter have to say about dragons?"

Perrantin looked uncomfortable. "I have no idea, to tell you the truth. I don't speak High Elvish."

Sir George uttered some dire-sounding words of an uncertain nature. "Then how, by the beard of Beranthesis, do you know that you found the chapter about dragons?"

"Because it had lots of illustrations of dragons. That just stands to reason, doesn't it?"

"Did you by any chance make any copies of the text?"

Perrantin handed him the stack of papers, enough to comprise every page of a large chapter. Thelvyn looked over the old knight's shoulder and saw that the pages were perfect copies, including the illustrations, as if the mage had pulled the pages themselves out of the book.

"How do you do that?" he asked.

"A simple spell," the mage explained. "You just lay a blank sheet on the page you want to copy and say the magic words. I have it on a magic scroll so I don't have to relearn the spell between each use. I can make you a copy of it when we get home."

"Well, this is indeed about dragons," Sir George observed. "It says here that the dragons first came into this world ages ago from one of the outer planes. That confirms something I've always suspected."

"And what is that?" Perrantin asked.

"That Ilsundal was an absolute crackpot who was incapable of knowing the difference between fact and mystical nonsense," the old knight declared, looking rather disgusted. "Granted, perhaps he never heard, or did not like, the story the dragons tell about their own origin."

"He could have just been repeating what nonsense he had been told," Solveig pointed out.

"Oh, that's likely enough," Sir George admitted. "Elves make a habit of taking nonsense and beating it until it works, and Ilsundal elevated that to an art. He was determined to make that Trees of Life business work, even if he had to become an Immortal to pull it off. Well, after such an auspicious beginning, I wonder if we can trust anything the *Heimsleidh* has to say about dragons."

"I suppose we can at least look through the material and see," Mage Perrantin suggested, looking disappointed. He had been so hopeful after finding the *Heimsleidh*, the legendary source of all learning—legendary among wizards at least.

Sir George and Perrantin went through the chapter on dragons thoroughly that evening. At first their efforts didn't seem very encouraging. As Sir George had said, elven history was almost remarkably lacking in incidents involving dragons, not so much because elves knew how to deal with dragons but rather that dragons had little reason to deal with elves.

As it happened, the key to what they needed was to be found in more recent elven history. Alfheim was a land of magic, created by the elves to suit their own needs, and as such, contained several places of dangerous, uncontrolled magic. Most of these were gateways through time and space. At times, without warning, strange creatures would emerge suddenly from other times, other places, even other planes of existence, creatures both magical and mundane.

Worse yet, many of these creatures were hybrid forms, a terrible fusion between two or more greatly different beasts and monsters, and some of the most deadly of these fantastical creatures were of vaguely draconic forms.

When such creatures appeared suddenly and escaped into the forests of Alfheim, the elves were forced to deal with them as best they could. Some were fought in conventional manner, hunted down and destroyed with spear, bow, and sword. Others could only be fought with magic. That suggested the strong possibility that the elves of Alfheim did indeed have the magical means to subdue or even destroy creatures of comparable size and strength of dragons. And if the Wizards of the Flaem had managed to make off with a complete copy of the *Heimsleidh*, they probably had other, more recent books of lore and magic taken from the elves that might tell how to deal with dragons by some means other than fighting. If that failed, Perrantin could still continue to follow other references. As he had said, the wizards had cataloged everything thoroughly.

Thelvyn was learning a good deal, but he also realized that he was only slowing things down by asking for explanations. When Solveig and Korinn were ready to retire to their room, he elected to go with them.

Solveig sighed heavily. "I thought for a while there that we might be on our way to Alfheim. I suspect watching Sir George trying to talk the elves into parting with some of their deepest secrets would be like the meeting of two insidious and unrelenting forces."

"Have you ever been to Alfheim?" Korinn asked as he seated himself on the end of his bed.

"Once, just before you joined us," she said, stretching her long back. "That was quite an experience. I wouldn't mind going back, but I'm not in the mood for it just now. You have to be in the mood, to deal with elves on their own ground. I don't suppose dwarves are ever quite in the mood for elves, are they?"

Korinn shrugged. "I've never had much problem with elves, at least the few I've met. I'm a Syrklist dwarf, remember. Live and let trade, that's our family motto. I was worried we might have to go to Alfheim myself for a while, I must admit. But my reasons are a little more obvious."

"You wouldn't have any trouble from the elves, if that's what worries you," she told him. "You might not have much luck going by yourself, however. But the elves know and trust Sir George. His business requires him to know people's secrets and see their treasures, so he works hard at earning everyone's trust. As one of his companions, you would be included in that trust."

"But what about me?" Thelvyn asked. "I have to worry about dragons recognizing me for what I am. Would the elves?"

"I doubt that very much," Solveig insisted. "You don't know for certain yourself that you are descended from the people of Blackmoor, so I doubt that the elves would recognize that. Whatever complaint the dragons had with your mother might have been something entirely different."

"Do you think we're likely to be on our way to Alfheim?" Korinn asked. "Our two elders seem to believe they might find what they need here."

"I have no idea," Solveig admitted. "But I believe that we will be on our way somewhere in another couple of days or so. Those two are as good at finding trouble as they are at getting out of it. The part I don't care for is waiting to find out if we really are going to get back out of the trouble they've found."

* * * * *

Perrantin returned to the inn toward the middle of the next morning, insisting that Sir George and the others follow him back to the library at once. The Academy was a sprawling structure, consisting of a large central building, the wizards' residence, and two slightly smaller buildings joined by wings. The north building was the library, linked to the wizards' residence by the wing that contained the student dormitory, while the south building and its adjoining wing was the actual School of Magic.

They entered through the main doors of the Academy, into the great hall of the wizards' residence. Much of the interior of the Academy suggested a grandeur and grace anticipated but yet to come. The main halls and chambers were massive but looked unfinished, as if the simple bare gray stone awaited completion with a veneer of polished marble or some other elegant dressing. The library itself was clad in richly carved panels and beams made from the hardwoods of the Highland forests, a commodity that was plentiful and very inexpensive locally.

Thelvyn had never seen so many books in all his life. There were several large chambers on the first level alone, each rising through the first two stories of the building, with the second level in the form of a railed walkway, open in the center. Row upon row of massive shelves of dark wood stood ten feet high throughout the middle section of each chamber. He noticed that the shelves were only half filled, with entire sections standing completely empty. Apparently the Wizards of the Flaem were still plotting their acquisitions.

The outer walls all had tall, narrow windows, with individual desks located before each window where they would best receive the light. Two bookstands accompanied each desk, one straight ahead and the other on the right-hand side, with a shelf overhead. However the wizards had come by their books, at least they encouraged serious study. They found Perrantin seated at a desk in a corner by himself. He didn't seem annoyed by the delay in Sir George's arrival; he was so involved with his reading that he hadn't noticed.

"George, we were following the right path after all," he declared with some restraint when he saw them approach. "The elves have indeed been dealing with the monsters by adapting existing magic to a different, sometimes larger scale. I believe I am beginning to discover the original spells. There seem to be any number of ways to frighten a dragon."

Thelvyn declined to ask if that was a wise thing to attempt, as much as that seemed obvious to him.

"Do you think you can find a spell that will suit our purposes?" Sir George asked.

"Well, I'm not so certain about that," Perrantin admitted. "Frankly, it seems that the one thing the wizards of

Alfheim always have to do is to expand the scale of the spells involved, at least when dealing with some of the larger, more powerful monsters that sometimes pop out of their sites of bad magic, a situation that more or less describes a dragon."

"Then we might still need to go in search of someone who actually has such a spell?" Sir George asked. "You know, I might be able to talk the elves into parting with such spells if we explain why we need them."

"Perhaps, but I hope not. I might be experienced enough to know how to expand the scale of such a spell myself. We're talking about the creation of a magical artifact, you know."

They paused, waiting in silence as a party of soldiers in the bright, fresh uniforms of the Guard of the Palace of the Archduke marched across the room, their high boots echoing across the stone floor. All of the travelers looked up at the same time, suspicious that the archduke's soldiers had come to discuss the matter of the ancient treasures of the gnomes. Thelvyn swallowed, wondering if his brief career as an adventurer would end prematurely in prison. The captain of the guard walked boldly up to Sir George and stood at attention, saluting smartly.

"Do I address Sir George Kirbey, former knight of Darokin, now a resident of good standing of the realm, and his company?" he inquired.

"You do," Sir George agreed.

"Then I present you with this official summons," the young soldier said, handing Sir George a scroll tied with a black ribbon. "I am instructed to take you at once for an audience with Archduke Maarsten."

"The archduke himself?" Sir George asked apprehensively. If Maarsten was prepared to handle this personally, they were probably in a great deal of trouble indeed.

CHAPTER NINE

Sir George wasn't encouraged that the archduke had sent such a polite summons. That was simply the way these things worked; uncommon criminals were granted uncommon courtesy. As a former knight and a merchant of quality goods, he would be treated with proper respect as long as he continued to deserve it. He knew they would be saying "please" and "thank you" even as they marched him away to prison, or possibly the gallows. The only advantage in his position was that those of authority in this matter should be willing to listen to his arguments in his own defense.

Of course, the fact that this was a summons and not a warrant was encouraging. The archduke might have decided that his best move would be to maintain the goodwill of the gnomes and their allies, the dwarves, by being magnanimous. If he, the wizards, or the dukes confiscated a portion of the ancient treasure of Torkyn Fall, the Highland trade in raw metals would suffer greatly. He might even have sent the gnomes on their way with his blessing, and all he wanted now from Sir George were the answers to a few difficult questions.

They were taken at once to the archduke's palace on the other side of the city, an even more cavernous structure than the Academy, and were asked to wait for their audience with the archduke. After a fairly brief wait, they were escorted to the private audience chamber of the archduke, which seemed to suggest that the meeting was not to be a matter for public attention. The audience chamber was a rather large room, richly paneled in dark hardwood and decorated with solid furnishings, with shelves for an extensive library as well as various lesser artifacts of Flaemish history.

Archduke Maarsten was younger than they had expected, probably no older than Solveig. He possessed the striking, even dashing features of the Flaemish nobility, quite unlike the lean, hawkish appearance common to the wizards, who were frequently from the lesser aristocracy or older merchant families. He had the fiery red hair characteristic of his race, in his case worn regally in a full lion's mane, accented by a jacket with a stiffened collar of Flaemish tradition. He knew how to bear himself well, so that he seemed larger and more regal than his rather modest height would have suggested. Thelvyn realized after a moment that Mage Eddan of his own village was a pale imitation of him.

The archduke was seated behind his massive desk, but he wasn't alone. In a large chair beside him sat a taller man, in all ways a typical Flaemish wizard in appearance, bearing, and dress. Thelvyn felt nervous at once to find himself in such company, remembering the vague but consistent injustices he had always suffered from the restrictions of Flaemish law, and also the suspicion that Eddan had shown him. Worse yet, the wizard noticed him almost at once and watched him closely.

"I am Archduke Jherridan Maarsten," he said, then indicated the wizard. "Mage Byen Kalestraan, Senior Wizard of the Academy of the Realm."

Sir George bowed his head. "I am Sir George Kirbey, a former Knight of the Order of the Roads of Darokin. My companion, Mage Perrantin of Darokin, my partner in business. Our associates, Solveig White-Gold and Korinn Bear Slayer, Son of Doric."

"Solveig White-Gold?" Maarsten mused. "That seems more a title than a proper name, although I can see how you came by it. Are you of the Northern Reaches?"

"I am descended from those people," she answered. "I am in truth Valeria of the House of Doranius, first family of Thyatis. Perhaps you can appreciate why I choose to keep that identity to myself when I travel abroad."

"You must give your father gray hairs," he said, smiling. For a moment, he seemed very young. Then he glanced at Thelvyn. "You seem to have not been anticipated."

"Thelvyn Fox Eyes, my young apprentice and heir," Sir George explained quickly.

"Another remarkable name. You're not of Flaemish descent, are you, lad?"

"No, sir," Thelvyn replied, remembering the warning to be discreet about his origin. "I'm an orphan of some unknown race, but I was born in the Highlands and I've lived here all my life."

"Well, have a seat, all of you," Maarsten said, indicating various chairs scattered about the room. "Sir George, if you and the mage don't mind sitting here by the desk, my discussion will be with the two of you."

They seated themselves, Sir George and Perrantin taking the chairs in front of the desk that had been indicated to them. Thelvyn sat as far from Mage Kalestraan as he could, off in a dark corner by himself.

"I suppose I should get right to the point," Maarsten said. "I've been told that you people have been doing a little reading in our library on the subject of dragons."

Sir George was so surprised he almost fell off his chair. He had come expecting to answer some very difficult questions about the ancient treasures of the gnomes, and he was unprepared for this.

"Of course, our library is open to all scholars, especially wizards," the archduke continued. "You have not committed a crime, and it is by no means our intent to treat you as criminals. Sir George, you live in the north, and you knew as well as anyone the threat the dragons represent to the people of this land. I even commend your desire to do something about the problem. No doubt you trust in your own abilities to deal with this dilemma, but you must also understand our position. We do not have any assurances that you are equal to such a task, and we must be certain that you do not make the situation worse by your actions."

"Yes, I can appreciate that," Sir George admitted. "But how did you know we have been researching dragons?"

"We keep track of what the people who use our library are reading so that we may better serve their needs with new acquisitions," Mage Kalestraan explained. "Our librarians, when they reshelve the books you have been reading, use a simple spell that causes a book to return to the last page read. Therefore they determined a rather alarming trend in the areas you have been researching."

Thelvyn kept his comments to himself, but he thought it was just like the Flaem to have some grand excuse to justify their sneakiness. Under the circumstances, however, he could hardly blame them for being nervous.

"So I think that we should get right to the point," Archduke Maarsten said. "What have you learned? Surely you are aware that our wizards have been searching those same texts for the past year."

"We were looking for exactly what you must expect," Sir George admitted freely. "We've been seeking some way to subdue a dragon by magic, so that we could talk to him and discover just what really is going on. We can speculate all we want, but the dragons want something that is not apparent from their actions, and only they know what it is."

Maarsten considered that thoughtfully. "Yes, there is some wisdom in what you say. It hadn't occurred to us, I must admit, that we might in fact be able to negotiate with the dragons."

"Your people are fairly new to this world," Sir George added. "You don't have much experience with dragons, and you don't have the experience to know that most of what your books are telling you about them is legend, rumor, and misconception. Dragons have always been my particular field of study, and I know more about them than most of the greatest wizards and scholars because my information is from the source. I can tell you that if you haven't had much luck in dealing with the dragons yourselves, it's probably because you are being misled by those you reasonably expect to be authorities."

"I must admit that, for all the stories and legends there seem to be about dragons, actual historical accounts of real dragons seem to be rather limited," Kalestraan conceded. "But why do you feel concerned enough about this matter to become involved?"

"Well, on the practical side, I must admit that dragons are bad for my business. But I was formerly a knight errant, and I suppose I still possess certain dutiful instincts. Knowing a good deal about dragons, I'm in a better position to be able to do something about them. Therefore I feel that I have something of a duty to try."

"Commendable, I suppose," Archduke Maarsten agreed guardedly. "Assuming that your primary concern is not the legendary hoards of the dragons. Or is that only just a legend?"

"No, dragons are quite wealthy," Sir George admitted. "However, subduing a dragon doesn't mean that you have won the right to his hoard. The only way to get a dragon to part with his treasure is to slay him, and that is indeed far more often a matter of legend than actual occurrence. I am not prepared to be foolish on this account. Slaying a dragon and getting him to talk are two entirely different matters. Unless we could find a very reliable way to force a dragon to speak to us, we weren't going to go off hunting for one."

"Well, you seem like intelligent, knowledgeable, and reasonable people," the archduke said. "I think that we could benefit from your advice. At the same time, I can't allow you to go running off after dragons until we've had a chance to sort this matter out and decide what is best. Until then, I see no reason why you can't just stay here. We could provide rooms for you right here in the palace."

"If it's not a bother," Sir George said guardedly.

"No, no bother at all," Maarsten insisted. "You and your friend can work together with our own wizards sorting fact from fantasy and try to arrive at some magical or diplomatic means of dealing with the dragons."

Maarsten's plan seemed to please no one but the archduke himself. Sir George recognized that they were essentially under house arrest, to keep them from attempting any unauthorized activities, but he wasn't in a position to protest since the alternative was full-fledged arrest. Kalestraan obviously didn't like it, although he also chose not to protest. Even so, he apparently thought they were nothing more than a band of adventurers who should be tossed out on their ears. Archduke Maarsten may have been thinking exactly the same thing, but he recognized that they did had some very useful advice, and he was not about to toss them out into the streets until he knew what it was.

They went at once to move their belongings from the inn to the archduke's palace. At least they were spared the indignity of an armed escort. Indeed, it seemed they were free to come and go as they pleased, as long as they didn't attempt to leave altogether. They were moved into a group of rooms in the diplomatic wing of the palace, a large well-appointed area reserved for visiting dignitaries. Thelvyn had a room to himself, more luxurious than he had ever known in his life.

It was a good thing they weren't being watched every minute, since Sir George would have gotten himself in trouble right away. He was of the opinion that there was more going on here than was apparent. The fire wizards had indeed been searching the same texts for the past year, and there was no indication that they had found anything. They hadn't made an attempt to control even a single dragon, at least as far as anyone knew. Sir George was curious to learn just what they were doing. He also wanted to know why the archduke seemed to be leaving the matter entirely in their hands, although his decision to detain Sir George's company for any advice they might offer suggested that he was becoming impatient with the whole affair.

The only problem was that Sir George's own research wasn't getting very far. He had never developed many contacts among the Flaem. The reason he had settled in this land was that it was too new, too remote, and too poor for very much to be happening here, making it one of the few places he could go with expectations of staying completely out of trouble for lack of trouble to get into. Of course, that hadn't turned out particularly well. Perrantin spent his days at the Academy, comparing notes and searching texts with the local wizards, but he admitted that they were making little progress, due to the rather lukewarm interest on the part of the wizards. As Sir George had observed, the fire wizards had a serious problem, but very little desire to solve it.

As it happened, Korinn was able to find some answers to that particular problem. Dwarves were slow to make friends, even among their own kind, and they could be suspicious and antagonistic of each other. But that situation changed very quickly in foreign lands, and two dwarves traveling abroad, even if they belonged to rival clans, could immediately become like two brothers in the face of hostile strangers. All he had to do was seek out the ambassador from Rockhome on the pretext of wishing to have a letter sent home with the next diplomatic courier. While he was at it, he made a few vague comments expressing his general exasperation with the Flaem. In no time at all, the ambassador had brought out a bottle, two glasses, and a tray of pastries, and they spent the afternoon discussing politics and various other shortcoming of strangers.

That evening, after dinner had been served and the archduke's palace was dark and quiet, they all gathered in Sir George's room to discuss the events of the day. Korinn had a great deal to tell.

"It's all very interesting, if you happen to like politics," he said, glancing at Solveig. "I suspect the problem with dragons couldn't have come at a worse time as far as the wizards are concerned. The rumor is that they were just about to make some major bid for power, with command firmly established here in Braejr with the archduke and themselves. The attacks of the dragons wrecked all their schemes and caught them so completely by surprise that they haven't yet recovered."

"Could that simply be the dwarvish ambassador's clever theory?" Sir George asked. "Archduke Maarsten would have to be aware of that."

"He was," Korinn insisted. "He was in favor of the plan, because the bid for power would have placed most of it squarely in his own hands, where the wizards want it. You've told us before that the wizards want the Highlands to become a wealthy, influential nation to advance their own goals, and Maarsten is in complete agreement with that. The ambassador said Maarsten is a fair and honest man in his own way, but you have to share his goals. He doesn't want power for himself, but he does believe that the Highlands needs a king, and his personal goal is to make the Highlands a true kingdom in his lifetime.

"But that isn't directly relevant to our present problem, although you have to know that to understand the matter fully," he continued. "The ambassador says something was about to happen that would have turned the Highlands upside down, but the dragons managed to do that first. The wizards didn't do anything about the dragon raids last year because they concluded that the dragons were merely unsettled. They advised that the dragons would forget about their complaints over the winter, and that any action taken against them would only provoke them into open war. Now the dragons have returned, but the wizards seem either unwilling or unable to take any steps against them."

"Did the ambassador suggest why that might be?" Solveig asked. "Or what excuses they might be giving the archduke?"

"No. That's the factor in this affair that remains a complete mystery," Korinn answered. "The most popular assumption among the people, the dukes, and even the various foreign concerns is that the wizards are trying their desperate best to find an answer, and they simply cannot."

"Well, we can be certain Archduke Maarsten wants to find an answer," Perrantin mused. "I suspect matters have reached the point that Maarsten could simply request whatever authority he wants, and the dukes would have to pledge it. If he is indeed such a conscientious man about the welfare of the Highlands, then he'll want to act now and spare his people any more damage to their lands."

"Unless he feels he needs to salvage the reputation of the wizards to complete his own bid to make himself king," Sir

George added. "Frankly, the wizards are the only major allies he has. Except for the people of Braejr and Braastar, the only two free cities outside the control of the dukes, the people of the Highlands owe their primary allegiance to their own duke."

"And that's precisely the point," Korinn said, becoming a little impatient. "It seems that Kalestraan descended upon Maarsten in righteous fury the night before last, spouting complaints about what we were doing. Apparently he made quite an issue of why we should be compelled to stop our activities at once."

"Why?" Solveig asked. "If we can save their reputations for them, why should they care?"

"For fear that we might succeed, believe it or not," Korinn said. "The wizards need to do something to save their reputations, but they need to do it themselves. If a band of antique merchants can step in and do what the mighty Academy cannot, they won't look very good."

"Ah, I see," Sir George declared, scratching his head with his hook. "The archduke needs to prod the wizards into doing something. He called us in, hoping to use us to do some prodding, perhaps even hoping that we might actually contribute something useful. By ordering us to help the wizards, he was able to order the wizards to discuss solutions whether they liked it or not."

Solveig nodded. "And by involving the wizards, rather than just ordering them to make their books available for our research, he gives them the opportunity to take a share of the credit if we are successful."

"And avoid the blame if we are not," Sir George added. "Well, now I know exactly how to handle this situation."

"The dwarvish ambassador says it is well known in diplomatic circles that the wizards believe they control Archduke Maarsten," Korinn said. "Apparently they do control Maarsten in some matters, but only to the extent that they can talk him into something he already wants. Yet we've seen for ourselves that *he* controls *them* very well."

By the next morning, Sir George was more certain than ever that he knew just what to do. When Perrantin was ready to go back to the Academy to continue his research, Sir

George decided to go with him. That seemed reasonable, since he was in fact the expert on the subject of dragons, *but* he was going for purposes of his own. He insisted upon taking Thelvyn with him, which wasn't at all to the liking of his young heir. Thelvyn preferred to keep his distance from the fire wizards, especially Kalestraan.

As it happened, Sir George nearly found himself outguessed a second time. Kalestraan wanted to compare notes on dragons and had already sent for him, although the old knight had left before the message arrived. Even before Sir George could ask, he was directed to Kalestraan in his private chamber in the main building of the School of Magic.

The Flaem seemed to build everything along the same lines. Kalestraan's private chamber looked very much like that of Archduke Maarsten. Like the archduke's it was large and wood paneled, the main difference being that the mage's chamber had more books and objects of historical and arcane value piled onto every shelf, table, and odd surface. Sir George seemed to think he could easily like such a place, although Thelvyn thought that it looked spooky. Kalestraan was seated at his desk, looking mysterious and menacing in his black jacket with its stiff high collar.

"Your friend has been telling us some rather remarkable things about dragons, which he claims to have learned from you," the wizard said. "I was wondering how you came to be in possession of such knowledge."

"Well, I used to be a knight," Sir George said, as if that were a reasonable answer. "Knights have a professional interest in dragons."

"True enough," Kalestraan agreed, "but your information about dragons goes beyond common or even professional knowledge. I don't want to give you the impression I doubt your honesty and integrity, but before I can completely trust the accuracy of your information, I have to know why you should have knowledge of dragons that even the experts do not possess."

"Well, that's reasonable," Sir George admitted. "You see, I received information from as close to the source as I could. Have you ever heard of the dragon-kin?"

"Do you mean *wyverns*?"

"Actually, I'm speaking of the drakes."

Kalestraan looked surprised. "I've heard about such things, but nothing more than rumors of their existence."

"Well, they do exist," Sir George insisted. "I daresay you don't see them in this land for two reasons, the first being that you hardly ever see them in their native form at all. They're shapechangers, able to take the form of men, dwarves, or elves. The Flaem are human, but they also have certain traits all their own, and drakes cannot take that form. They stay among people they look most like, to remain hidden. They are seldom actually evil, but they are always rather amoral, even mischievous, and many become professional thieves. They are unusually clever."

"And you know how to find them?" Kalestraan asked.

"You have to know what to look for. Now, there are three types of drakes that are actual dragon-kin. The most common in civilized parts are the mandrakes, which have the ability to take human form. Wooddrakes can take elven form and usually live in the elven woodlands. And, of course, there are the colddrakes, or icedrakes, who dwell underground because they cannot easily tolerate the light of day. They take the forms of dwarves and gnomes."

"Rare, solitary creatures, I should imagine," the wizard said.

"Rare indeed, but hardly solitary," Sir George explained. "They are dragons, and they belong to the greater Nation of Dragons, but they feel uncomfortable in the company of their draconic cousins. Being very sociable, they will most often assume their alternate forms and dwell secretly among their adopted races. They usually lead quiet, even furtive lives, fearing discovery. As I said, many become professional petty thieves, or they find work at taverns, or pretend to be adventurers. And mandrakes will often work at stables, for they have a great affinity for horses."

"That's all very interesting," Kalestraan mused. "Have you happened to discover a drake?"

Sir George looked uncomfortable. "You must appreciate, of course, that I cannot betray any trusts."

"Of course. The identity of this drake is not important to

the issue."

He nodded. "Many years ago, there was a worthy knight of Darokin who was secretly a drake. He was, you might even say, an exceptional drake, for he did not merely live on the fringes of the world of men but actually became a part of that world. The fact that he was a mandrake in no way diminished his abilities or his honor as a knight, and you could have trusted him as you would any other knight."

"Well, the word of a drake is as close as you can come to that of a dragon himself," Kalestraan agreed. "I don't want to seem hostile, but frankly, we haven't been having much success in finding magic that is effective against a dragon."

"I find that surprising," Sir George said. "I've lived in this land long enough to know that your people are specialists in fire magic, which one would naturally assume to be the most obvious and effective weapon against a dragon. Am I correct in assuming your wizards actually attempted to confront a dragon last year?"

Kalestraan looked unhappy about that. "Yes . . . we did. We were fearful about the effectiveness of our magic, and so we didn't commonly advertise the fact we would be attempting to fight a dragon—only that we were gathering information on the matter. We didn't wish to create expectations that we might not be able to fulfill. The best thing that I can say about the situation is that the dragon allowed our wizards to withdraw. That was, I must suppose, more a gesture of superiority than generosity."

"It was, in part," Sir George agreed. "But such a gesture was also within the bounds of draconic law. Dragons fight, when they fight, to decide some important issue when reasoning has failed. They value their lives highly and will not often fight to the death. But what you say is very interesting. It seems to be an indication that these dragons are following draconic law, which means they might be rogues but not complete renegades, which is quite encouraging. It means they can be reasoned with."

"Bringing us back to the reason why you wish to subdue a dragon in the first place," Kalestraan concluded. "That would now seem more promising than ever."

"Perhaps. You said your wizards were not successful?"

Kalestraan looked displeased at having that particular matter brought up again. "I do not want this discussed outside this room."

"Of course not."

The wizard frowned bitterly. "To be perfectly frank, we've been having some trouble adapting our fire magic to this world. The various spells and magical artifacts from our home world aren't as effective here. We've done what we can by establishing Braejr as the center of our power, and we can do very much as we please here. But our powers diminish as we move away from the center of our magic. The northern frontier is too distant, and our spells lose effectiveness quickly as we go north. We cannot fight the dragons where they are, and yet we cannot afford to wait for them to come to us. That is why we seem unable to act."

"Oh, I see," Sir George commented pensively. "Does this affect only your fire magic, or any magic you attempt?"

"It is with our own fire magic, of course," the wizard said defensively. "We give our fullest attention to perfecting our native magic, and that doesn't allow much time to study other magical forms."

"Well, I can't believe you've assembled one of the greatest libraries in the known world entirely because you just happen to like books," Sir George declared. "You have a tremendous amount of knowledge right here. And, I might add, a most capable wizard to help you. Perrantin isn't the greatest of wizards, but he's cracking good, especially at problem-solving in magical matters, mostly because he has tremendous versatility as a master of various disciplines, while most wizards concentrate their efforts only on their own special type of magic."

Mage Kalestraan frowned and sat in silence.

"Come on now, old boy!" Sir George declared. "I can fully appreciate your position. You need to do something soon to keep your reputation with the people of the Highlands intact and to repair the damage already done. Of course you also want to pressure the territories you've been working so hard all these years to build, which the dragons are taking apart piece by piece. Speaking frankly now, just between you and me, isn't that the truth?"

Kalestraan nodded slowly. "I regret to admit that it is."

"Well, now, it's not as bad as all that," the old knight assured him. "All you need is to have your best wizards work with Perry at finding a good way to subdue a dragon, and then you can send us on our way. If we succeed, you get to claim a large measure of the credit, and that leaves your reputation in a considerably better state than it is now. If we fail, most likely no one will ever hear of us again, but no harm comes to you."

Kalestraan considered that carefully for a moment, then glanced at the old knight shrewdly. "I think I should accept your offer, since it seems I have nothing to lose and the possibility of much to gain. But I would still like to know what you seek to gain from this. You were prepared to do this thing yourselves, without making any bargain with us."

"The answer I gave the archduke was the true one," Sir George insisted. "I may be a fool by risking so much, and twice a fool for leading my friends into such danger. They know that they can go with me or not as they like, and I won't be going anywhere until we have a plan with a reasonable chance of success. You can certainly understand such a sense of duty. It is, I am sure, your own sense of duty that now forces you to set aside your justifiable pride in your own abilities and those of your order and accept the help of strangers. I cannot imagine a dwarf or an elf putting his duty above his pride, nor even many men."

Kalestraan somehow managed to look flattered and uncomfortable at the same time, only too aware that his motives were hardly so noble. But whatever his motives, Sir George had convinced the wizard of the value of his own plan. Things began to improve quite rapidly after that. The complete resources of the Academy were thrown into the task of finding an answer to the problem at hand, and the best among the Flaemish wizards and scholars were consulted. Perrantin found himself the slightly bewildered captain of a friendly, eager crew, and they set to work with a vengeance.

They were already beginning to make solid progress on the problem by the following afternoon. When Perrantin returned to the palace of the archduke that night to have dinner with his companions, he was still blinking from hours of staring at ancient texts. It was hard to say whether or not he was pleased, since he was almost always thinking about something else.

"You know, I really must find a spell for tired eyes," he said when he joined the other in Sir George's room.

"I think you should worry more about failing vision," Korinn remarked.

"Oh, I have a spell for that," the mage replied. "The way I go at it, I have to employ it about every three years."

"Would it be too soon to ask if you are making any progress?" Sir George inquired.

"No, it is not too soon at all," Perrantin answered, blinking twice more. "In fact, I suggest we make ready to depart the day after tomorrow. When we began asking ourselves what manner of magical device would frighten a dragon, the possible answers led us back to what the elves of Alfheim use to fight a monster that would otherwise be invulnerable. The answer became obvious once we knew what we were looking for. The elves use artifacts that are instruments of entropy, which is about the only thing that would frighten a dragon."

"It frightens me as well," Sir George remarked. Solveig and Korinn seemed to agree with him, and Thelvyn could understand why. A sphere of entropy was the ultimate force of destruction, existing expressly for the purpose of destroying everything else. For that reason, entropy was the most dangerous of all forces to attempt to control, since its capacity for destruction could easily turn against the one using it. A magic-user generally had to be both utterly evil and completely mad to study and use magic devoted to the forces of entropy, although the results of such study could sometimes be used to good effect, but only with the greatest care.

"Well, I don't much like it myself," Perrantin replied. "I've never worked with the forces of entropy before. The best advice is to leave such things alone, unless you simply don't have any choice. In this case, we don't. So there it is. I'm willing to try it, since I have every reason to believe that it works. As I say, the elves do it from time to time."

"Then I am also willing to try," Sir George added. "But

what about the rest of you? You are invited to be part of this and I wish you would, but I can understand why you might have reservations about being involved either with dragons or instruments of entropy, much less the two of them together."

Solveig frowned. "If Perry thinks his device will work, then I'm willing to trust it. No offense, George, but in this matter, his opinion has to count most with me. I can see that, for all their bold talk about defeating ancient enemies, the Flaem don't have enough courage to do anything for themselves. And no one else is going to care enough until it's too late, since their own lands aren't yet immediately threatened. Frankly, if this does subdue a dragon, I wouldn't want to miss it for the world."

Korinn only nodded.

Thelvyn was surprised when Sir George turned to him. "I had just assumed that I would go where you go," he said.

"You have your own reasons to be worried about meeting up with a dragon," the old knight reminded him.

"I know," he agreed. "But I still have to go."

"What about the archduke?" Solveig asked suddenly. "Kalestraan talked him into detaining us for fear of what might happen."

"And Kalestraan will talk him into letting us try it," Sir George said. "The same reasons that worked on the mage will work on his master. You have to remember that he is as desperate as anyone to have something done about the dragons. Right now, we're all he's got."

"He could order his own wizards to do the job," Solveig pointed out. "The Flaem are notoriously suspicious and contemptuous of strangers. My guess is that he'd rather have his own people do this."

"Well if he does, then they're welcome to it," Sir George declared. "My interest is in seeing that the job gets done, not doing it myself. My concern is that we'd get blamed if these incompetent fire wizards make a mess of things."

"Do you have any other concerns?" Korinn asked.

"Yes . . . that the archduke might insist upon sending some of his own wizards with us. This is going to be difficult enough as it is."

CHAPTER TEN

uriously, the fire wizards had the ability to put together a weapon in a hurry when they were properly motivated. Indeed, Perrantin was left feeling a little suspicious about the whole affair. All the while he had been directing the research to find a magical artifact, he was certain they could have done the same thing without him. Even admitting that they had been frustrated because their own fire magic failed to function properly as they traveled beyond their own lands, it was easy enough to find other magic that did work described in the books. Perrantin had to agree with Sir George that the Wizards of the Flaem were either the most cowardly lot in existence, or else they had reasons of their own why they could not, or would not, fight the dragons. Wizards weren't generally known for their courage in the first place, but they were known for attracting secrets as well as keeping them.

It wasn't the best situation, but it seemed as good as anything they were likely to put together on their own. Of course, once the necessary magic had been discovered and adapted to their purposes, the magical artifact itself still had to be constructed. And that proved to be the next problem. Although the artifact could be constructed before they left, its final preparation could not be accomplished at Braejr. As an instrument of entropy, it could only be infused with its specific properties at a place where the forces of entropy were manifested in the physical world. The good news was that the nearest such place wasn't far away, at World Mountain, in the middle of the Steppes of Ethengar. The bad news was World Mountain itself.

"Oh, my," Sir George remarked. "Just what is this weapon, and why do we have to take it there of all places?"

"Actually it's just a staff with an artifact of power at the top, in this case a dragon cast from magical metal," Perrantin explained. "When the head of the staff is placed through a gateway into the void between the realms of existence, then the metal will contain and channel the forces of entropy."

"And that will scare a dragon?" Sir George asked. "Aside from the obvious fact that it scares me enough already."

"Dragons are especially vulnerable to the powers of entropy," the mage went on. "While dragons are mortal, they are also creatures of magic. At other times, the fusion of different natures isn't a disadvantage but a source of strength. However, the forces of entropy cause a separation between their mortal and magical natures, leaving them weak and ineffective."

Solveig frowned. "I'm not sure, but I think you just told us that your staff of entropy causes a dragon to be both physically and magically weak."

"Extremely weak," Perrantin agreed. "Given enough power, the staff could even force the dragon's magical and physical aspects completely apart and kill it. This artifact would be useful against any magical being, or indeed anyone using magic."

Once everything else was ready, they still had one final problem to face before they could depart. Sir George had to convince Archduke Maarsten to let them leave. In effect, they were still under house arrest to prevent them from doing this very sort of thing. But Sir George wasn't concerned. He had put together a convincing argument, and Byen Kalestraan would be there to lend his support. Once again they were all brought together into the archduke's private chamber, although the others merely listened while Sir George and Kalestraan explained the plan and how the artifact itself was supposed to work. Maarsten didn't look particularly impressed.

"You know I kept you people here to do this very work," he said when they had concluded their explanations. "You also know I had you detained to prevent you from doing something that would bring the wrath of the dragons down upon this land. Can you assure me that your plan will in fact succeed?"

"Well, there can be no absolute promise of success," Sir George replied. "But I'm still confident about this. I wouldn't go hunting for a dragon unless I was quite certain the device would work."

Kalestraan nodded slowly. "I, too, believe the artifact has the power to subdue a dragon, and I believe these people are both experienced and resourceful enough to use it properly."

"As that may be," Maarsten agreed cautiously. "But my concern is that you will earn us the wrath of the dragons whether you succeed or fail. I must believe that if you demonstrate to the dragons that you possess the means to defeat them, then their own best policy would be to move against us immediately in great force. That would be my own response."

"The fact is, no weapon in the world is going to defeat every dragon all at the same time," Sir George responded. "If you continue to take no action against them for fear of offending them, they will destroy you. Things really can't get worse for you."

"But is it possible to go to war with dragons and hope to win?"

"No, you cannot win," the old knight declared flatly. "As you might recall, the entire reason for trying to subdue a dragon is to get him to talk to us, to tell us what this is all about. It's the only way I can think of to open negotiations. If you prefer to admit defeat, I can just as easily offer them your surrender. That might work as well for you as anything, since draconic law recognizes capitulation as a means to reestablish negotiations."

"I do *not* wish to surrender," the archduke insisted.

"Well as it happens, I believe I can offer you something better," Sir George said. "Obviously, none of us is of the Flaemish race. We can do this, and the dragons never need know of your involvement. If we fail, we bear the responsibility and the consequences. But if we succeed, you enjoy the benefits and can claim a large portion of the credit for having supported us."

Maarsten frowned. "It seems to me that in agreeing to your plan, I must also in effect agree to allow you to negotiate peace with the dragons on the part of the Highlands."

"Not only the Highlands, but also the tribes of the Ethengar, the gnomes, the baronies of the Heldannic lands, and everyone else suffering from the attacks of the dragons," Sir George reminded him. "You can trust me not to promise them anything you would not be willing to support."

"Oh, very well, then!" the archduke declared, more amused than annoyed. "I'm beginning to believe you could talk the entire race of dragons out of their hoards, their horns, and their hallowed homes. Just keep in mind the responsibility that you bear. This will likely be our only chance for a peaceful settlement with the dragons. If you fail, we will have no choice left other than to fight them."

Thelvyn knew that gathering the support of strong allies would be difficult. Darokin and Thyatis were far removed from the attacks and would not see the need. The clans of Ethengar and Ylaruam were fragmented and would be more trouble than help as allies. The dwarves and elves were unlikely to enter into an alliance with anyone else, especially with the Flaem, even if they were having trouble with the dragons themselves, which they were not. Archduke Maarsten had to face the fact that the Highlands would have to be nearly in ruins before anyone would be inclined to help.

Now that Maarsten had given them his blessing, they were sent on their way with all the assistance they required, plus some for good measure. Several of their horses were replaced with hardier steeds, including Thelvyn's own Cadence. That wasn't entirely to his liking, since he had gotten used to Cadence and considered her an especially competent beast, even if Solveig continued to insist that she was mediocre at best. His new horse was also a brown mare, very much like Cadence in appearance, but larger and sturdier. And quite possibly younger as well.

Thelvyn was also given new clothes, including a vest of chain mail made of fine, sturdy mesh. He thought he looked rather impressive in it. To his disappointment, he found it rather heavy and difficult to wear, although he thought that he would become used to it. It puzzled him that this was called light armor. Solveig wore her own somewhat heavier armor with ease, although she made a point of not wearing it unless she anticipated the need. Korinn also had his own, but Sir George and Perrantin were both given light armor. They weren't in the habit of wearing it, but they agreed it would be a good idea to have it for this occasion. While Sir George carried all the weapons he required, most of which attached to his wrist cuff, Thelvyn and Perrantin were both given long, thin-bladed knives, and they were all supplied with metal shields.

Under the circumstances of their agreement with Archduke Maarsten, they would not set off with great fanfare. Instead, they slipped quietly out of town very early one frosty, misty morning. Few even took notice of their leaving, and few beyond the staff of the archduke's palace and the inner circles of the Academy would even know they had been here, or that they had received help from the Flaem. They would be entirely on their own. But they were going to be very much alone in any event.

They headed east from Braejr, crossing the river by means of a large ferry that substituted for the bridge the Flaem seemed to find so difficult to complete. After that, they rode across gently hilly country of glades and woods, lands held by elves who were new to the Highlands. Many of them had fled south to escape the expansion of the frontier. There were no actual roads, but the paths were solid and riding was easy and swift, although Thelvyn never saw an elf. Sir George harbored his own reservations about going this way, passing south of the massive Colossus Mounts through the pass above the dangerous Broken Lands. This would bring them into the southwestern corner of the Steppes of Ethengar, with many long miles of the great, open expanses of grassy plains to cross before they came to World Mountain.

Sir George's concern in crossing the plains wasn't for dragons or other dangers, but for the clans of the Ethengar themselves. He was actually on very good terms with the Ethengar and traded with them regularly, although he also insisted that he preferred to have to deal with them only when he had business with them. Their hospitality was a time-consuming affair, and passing through the steppes would require making peace, with appropriate ceremony, with each clan they encountered. The approach across the steppes to World Mountain would have been shorter and simpler from the north, but that would have meant passing through the Eastern Reach, as they had on the way to Torkyn Fall, and that way was under control of the dragons.

Thelvyn spent the first day making peace with his new horse. Because his experience with horses was so limited, he hadn't been in a good position to appreciate that Solveig's judgment of his first mount had been correct. His new horse was restless, and she seemed to have serious reservations of her own concerning her new rider, so that she fussed and made nervous ears when he tried to handle her. Fortunately, Sir George had a way with horses. He took her aside to calm her, and that seemed to improve both her temper and her opinion of Thelvyn. She settled down to business once they were on the road, and Thelvyn could finally see her advantages over his previous horse for himself. Since no one had told him her name, he decided to call her Cadence. It seemed easier to remember.

Because the elven trails were so well defined, they made good time and were alongside the Colossus Mounts by the end of the first day. This brought them beyond the elven lands into rough and hilly country, which slowed them down considerably. They were approaching the northern bounds of the Broken Lands, territories held by orcs and hobgoblins, and Sir George had no trouble convincing the company to move very quietly now. They found a secluded camp for the night in a low place between the hills, surrounded by trees and boulders, but even then he wouldn't let them light a fire. The risk of the light being seen in the darkness was great enough, but the smell of smoke was equally dangerous.

Most of the next day was spent making their way through the wild, rugged land along the southeastern edge of the mountains, after the last of the well-kept elven trails had joined the primitive trade road. There was no trade between the Highlands and the Ethengar; this road existed to serve the limited traffic to Rockhome. Most travelers preferred the much safer route farther south through Darokin, passing north of the borders of Alfheim into Rockhome from the south. The archduke had vague plans to establish forts along the edge of the mountains to keep the road open, but the dukes seemed unlikely to grant him that authority any time soon. And so the road remained wild and dangerous, so that only occasional merchants used it in the usually correct assumption that intermittent traffic would take the orcs by surprise.

By the middle of the next morning, once the sun was up and the day was turning warm, they began to come out of the rugged woods. Then, as they gained the tops of a hill, they could see the Steppes of Ethengar stretching out before them in the distance. The plains began quite abruptly, like a great sea of grass that washed up to the edge of the stony, wooded hills to the west. While Thelvyn had been told to expect gently rolling hills, these slopes were so long and so gradual that half a mile or more might pass between the top of one and the next, so that the land was really more like a series of gradual rises and depressions. His first thought was to wonder how anything so flat could be called a steppe.

Sir George had difficulty plotting their best course across the steppes, despite his familiarity with the region. Although he never stated it, he certainly seemed to believe the quickest way across the steppes was not necessarily the most direct but the most discreet. His first plan was to travel somewhat north. Their destination was in the northern steppes, but much farther east. The rivers would already be swelling with the spring melt from the mountains. Thelvyn recalled that those same rivers had been dry, rocky beds during their journey to Torkyn Fall.

Still, they couldn't journey too far north, or they would find themselves presented by other problems. The most immediate danger to the northwest would be the Gostai goblins, a small, hostile folk, while various bands of hobgoblins and orcs ranged to the south, along the border with the Broken Lands. These scattered humanoid bands looked and lived much like the clans of Ethengar, riding upon great wolves and other fierce creatures rather than horses, and they were all the more dangerous for their habits. On the whole, they tended to be more clever and patient than their cruder brethren in other parts of the world.

There were also several areas of bad magic, to be avoided at all cost. In such places, strange, evil creatures were likely to appear entirely by chance. Even Sir George wasn't sure of the range of dangers such places presented, but he had learned from the Ethengar where they were to be found, and he knew they must be avoided by any means.

Late on the second day since entering the steppes, they paused for a moment to gaze into the sky at a pair of distant shapes, which looked vaguely like horses. Thelvyn thought they might be the legendary winged horses, for the open, grassy steppes were well adapted to such creatures. He watched them for a long time, forgetting that his vision was much better than that of his companions. After a time, the two remarkable forms turned and drifted nearer, although not directly toward them.

Soon he could make out that they had the wings and heads of great eagles, with hooked beaks, but the bodies of mighty lions. He decided they must be griffons. He also decided it was time to warn his companions.

"Griffons indeed," Sir George agreed. His distance vision was also good. "A rare beast in most lands, but they're not uncommon here. Their favorite prey is horses and there are more wild horses here in the steppes than there are anywhere in the world."

"I've heard that griffons will attack horses on sight," Solveig said nervously. "Are we in any danger?"

"I think not," the old knight replied. "They must have seen us some time ago. Their vision is legendary. And while I admit that they are getting rather close, they haven't changed their course. If they've fed recently, they're not likely to attack mounted horses."

"I wish we had our artifact of entropy ready," Perrantin added, noticing that Solveig was stringing her bow. "Not much else is likely to discourage a pair of griffons. A band of those things are said to be able to bring down a dragon."

Sir George sniffed disdainfully. "Not likely. Griffons are faster than all but the swiftest dragons, but they don't have good mobility. A dragon can strike from a distance with its breath, while a griffon has to be in contact with its enemy to use its beak and claws. They wouldn't be very effective against a dragon's armor anyway."

For whatever reason, the griffons decided to leave them alone, gradually soaring off to the northeast.

"Are we likely to see any dragons?" Solveig asked.

"That was one good reason for not going too far north, although I'm glad you brought it up," Sir George said. "We know dragons have raided the clans and their herds, but I wonder if they were merely coming down from the mountains to the north looking for food. Given a choice, they don't seem particularly fond of horses or yaks. Since there's not much else in the steppes, they don't generally come here."

No one felt the need to point out that if a dragon did appear, there wasn't much they could do about it. There was no place to hide; the grass was still short this early in the year, unlike later in the summer, when it often grew higher than a man's head. Despite Sir George's reassuring words, they watched the sky and the low hilltops carefully. Nevertheless, two days later something else saw them first— or rather someone. Thelvyn saw them before the others did. They were approaching quickly from the north but still so

distant that even he could see only the dark outlines of
small, lean horses. Considering his remarkable vision, there
was reason to hope the riders hadn't yet seen them. Sir
George led them quickly into one of the low places between
the hills, although that offered little protection unless the
band passed them some distance away.

"Could you tell who they were?" Perrantin asked.

Sir George shook his head. "I couldn't make out their
clothes or gear, much less their features. I'm not even sure
they were men. Lad?"

"They were riding horses," Thelvyn said. "From what I
understand, that suggests men rather than goblins or orcs.
I'd guess it's the Ethengar."

"Are we in any danger?" Korinn asked.

Sir George made a face. "That depends on how fast I
can talk our way out of trouble."

The dwarf brightened, then grinned broadly. "In that
case, we have nothing to worry about."

Thelvyn waited quietly with the others. Although the
surrounding hills were quite low, he could no longer see the
approaching riders. There had been fewer than a dozen in
all, but that was enough to make trouble for their group.
The Ethengar were known for their skill with bow and
arrow, even from a galloping horse.

The riders swept over the top of a hill barely a quarter of
a mile away, and there was no longer any question of where
they were headed. As they rode, they made great gestures
of delight, waving their arms and standing in their saddles.
Some displayed their riding abilities with daring tricks. Of
course, such gestures upon meeting strangers weren't necessarily friendly signs, not with a people like the Ethengar.
Thelvyn noticed that none of the riders had drawn a
weapon. His companions made a point of keeping their
hands well away from their own weapons, although they
obviously weren't pleased with the situation.

Only Sir George dared to move, gesturing to suggest that
he had business here as a friend, but it seemed unneces-
sary. As the riders came nearer, they recognized him and
shouted his name. They seemed even more delighted when
they recognized Solveig. The Ethengar were small and

lean, with fine black hair and deceptively delicate features. There was something oddly intriguing about the shapes of their dark eyes, something Thelvyn couldn't define, unlike any folk he had ever seen before. They were quite young, probably not much older than he, and the men had intriguing mustaches, which hung in long, narrow strands on either side of their mouths.

After their initial display of exuberance, the riders became quiet and brought their horses to a halt in a loose cluster facing the travelers. They bowed their heads, and then one of their group, acting as leader, dropped down from his saddle and led his horse forward a few steps. Sir George and Solveig did the same. Speaking the language of the steppes slowly and imperfectly, the two of them conferred briefly with the leader. Solveig returned to her horse after a few moments, leaving Sir George to conclude the negotiations.

"Well, we seem to be in reasonably good luck," she reported quietly to the others. "Sir George and I visited the clan of these people only three years ago, and they remember us well. The Ethengar tend to find Sir George a rather remarkable and delightful character, and they love him like a favorite uncle. I hesitate to admit they also find me a rather remarkable character."

"Everyone does," Korinn assured her.

Solveig made a face. "The unfortunate fact remains that we are each and every one rather odd and unusual characters. At any rate, we have been invited to their camp for a small celebration in our honor and a warm place to spend the night. Their clan is camped a short distance to the northeast, not far out of our way."

"Is Sir George going to accept their invitation?" Perrantin inquired. He didn't seem pleased by the prospect, but at least he seemed resigned to it.

"I suspect he will," Solveig replied. "There are certain advantages in doing so. One is that we can restock our supply of fodder for the horses. I also suspect that Sir George is hoping to be offered a totem of safe conduct. Once such a totem is bestowed upon a traveler, other clans will honor the bearer and his companions."

Sir George returned a moment later, wearing a look of
stoic resignation. The expression seemed to be common
among people who met the Ethengar. "We seem to be
expected for dinner. Well, I suppose that it might be worth-
while. We can at least get fodder, a few other supplies, and
some good advice."

"Is there something I should know about Ethengar hospitality?" Thelvyn asked, feeling uneasy from the way the
others were reacting.

"No. They make fierce enemies, but they can be the
most honorable and generous people in the world," the old
knight explained as he returned to his horse. "However,
their cooking, including what they choose to cook, sometimes leaves something to be desired. I've eaten yak before,
and I can assure you that the beasts are appropriately
named."

They returned to their saddles and were led quickly over
the grassy hills, the young warriors serving as a playful
escort. They seemed to find endless delight in showing off
their riding abilities, which were admittedly impressive.
Watching them, Thelvyn was inclined to feel somewhat
embarrassed by his own lack of experience. His embarrassment turned to distress when they directed their attention
to him and began to gesture grandly and shout. At first he
thought they noticed something about his appearance.
Then he became convinced they were more interested in
the fact that he was the youngest member of the company,
much closer to their own age.

"They want you to ride with them," Sir George told him.

"Do they realize I'm not very good at it?" Thelvyn
asked.

"Some things are self-evident," the old knight said in a
way calculated to be teasing. "I think you should oblige
them. They won't judge you by your ability so much as by
your willingness to try. They enjoy showing off, but they're
tremendously flattered when someone is willing to play
their games with them."

Still feeling self-conscious, Thelvyn urged his horse gently forward to join the young warriors. He had forgotten
that Cadence wasn't the same sedate horse he had ridden

to Torkyn Fall, and she had already become excited by the frolicsome behavior of these strange, shaggy horses of the steppes. Responding to the slightest encouragement, she shifted immediately into a swift trot, playfully springing forward so that she seemed to almost fly over the ground.

The young Ethengar responded with great delight, giving chase, which only inspired Cadence to even more speed. Step by step, the chase evolved quickly into a race as Cadence stretched out her long legs into a gallop. Perhaps she sensed that she was larger and more graceful and longer of leg than the shaggy little mounts of the steppes, and she meant to show these puny horses what she could do. She was just about to leave the others behind when suddenly she began to slow quickly of her own volition. Thelvyn sensed that he was only along for the ride.

Just as suddenly, his ride came to an abrupt end. Although he had no idea how he got there, he found himself hanging upside down in midair. He had just long enough to realize that he was falling, and he found himself lost between the desire to have it end and the fear of how it would. At that moment, he came down heavily onto the middle of his back. The air was knocked out of his chest, and for a long time he found himself sliding upside down across the grass. The last few yards ended in a brief, violent tumble, although his mount had already slowed enough that he wasn't seriously injured.

Cadence appeared a moment later, standing over him, looking vaguely concerned down the length of her nose. Then she began kissing him wetly, as if she were checking him for broken bones. The Ethengar arrived a moment later. They shooed away the horse and began checking him over for injuries. It quickly became apparent that he was neither harmed nor even particularly shaken by the incident. The young spring grass, still damp from the morning dew, had absorbed the worst of the impact. They helped him to his feet, their concern already turning to amusement.

Solveig turned up a moment later. "Are you all right?"

"I'm fine," he insisted, becoming more embarrassed by his lack of riding skill than ever. "What happened?"

"Your horse sneezed," she explained. "The sneeze loosened her belly strap enough that the saddle turned."

As his mind formed a picture of what had happened, he began to appreciate why the Ethengar were so amused. As he thought more about it, he realized he had managed to impress the Ethengar in about the only way he could have, with a highly unusual turn of bad luck. The grinning Ethengar quickly readjusted the strap and helped him back into his saddle. Then they were on their way again, more sedately than before.

The camp of the clan was only a couple of miles farther. Thelvyn knew the Ethengar did not make permanent settlements but followed the half-wild herds across the steppes, setting up their camps for a few days to several weeks at a time. When the camp came into view, Thelvyn noticed their great circular tents, with roofs like low, flat domes, although these structures were much sturdier than simple tents. A latticework of slender poles was mounted in a circle, then crowned with poles hung from a center post to form the foundation of each structure. The outside was then covered with a thick wall of heavy, crude hides and mats of rough felt or canvas. Called yurts, the huts were arranged in a loose cluster, with pens for the horses scattered about. A group of empty wagons stood around the outside of the camp.

The camp itself was not easily defensible. It stood half-hidden in one of the deeper depressions between the low hills. Several warriors stood watch atop the surrounding hills at all times. Bands of young warriors patrolled the steppes for miles around; indeed, it was such a group that had encountered Sir George's party. It was the responsibility of these outriders to spot an approaching enemy early enough to summon other warriors of the tribe or else handle the problem themselves.

With the announcement of visitors, the entire tribe turned out for an immediate celebration. Thelvyn was beginning to get the mistaken impression that the Ethengar were about the most friendly people in the world. The truth was that they saved their delight for the few visitors they trusted. Generally they didn't get along well with anyone, especially each other. In the steppes, it was almost easier for the tribes and clans to trust a stranger, since foreigners weren't in competition with them for the best grazing lands and sources of water.

After a lifetime among the suspicious Flaem, Thelvyn wasn't entirely comfortable to see such affection lavished upon complete strangers. As soon as he and his companions rode into the camp, eager hands were waiting to take his horse and to carry his packs. A woman in warrior dress emerged from one of the central yurts and flung her arms wide with a cry of delight, aimed obviously at Sir George himself. She was short and rather stocky, even for one of her compact race.

Sir George sighed. "Now I know where we are."

"Deordge, you old wolf!" she exclaimed, her accent giving her trouble with his name. "What are you doing here?"

"I've come to visit you, of course," Sir George insisted, forcing himself to be gracious. "Well, everyone, this is Sirontai, the tribal war chief."

"A remarkable woman," Perrantin muttered under his breath so that only Sir George could hear.

"Still traveling about with your tall, pale daughter, I see," Sirontai remarked.

Solveig turned briefly to the others and flashed a smile. Had she been a wolf, it would have been called baring her fangs. Her message was that no one was ever to mention this again.

"And this lad is my heir, Thelvyn Fox Eyes," Sir George added, noticing that Sirontai was staring.

"Fox Eyes?" she repeated, then turned to the others and translated the name for them. The Ethengar seemed to find it an excellent name, nodding and muttering their approval. Thelvyn tried hard not to blush.

"Allow me to introduce the other members of my party," Sir George continued, wanting to bring this to a conclusion. "Korinn Bear Slayer, a valiant warrior. And finally Mage Perrantin, my oldest friend and business associate, a wizard and scholar of noble purpose."

Sirontai relayed his introductions to her people, then turned back to Sir George. "You must, of course, feast with us this night. There will be such good food as we have, for we do not have time enough to prepare a proper feast in your honor. But there will be much music and song."

"That will be quite sufficient, I assure you," Sir George said. "I must admit, we are only passing through on dire and pressing business. But I will speak more of that later. We must be away again with the morning."

"Then you will be taken where you may spend the night in peace and comfort. Your horses will be tended," Sirontai said.

The others were led away by the people of the tribe, each eager to have one of the stranges spend the night in his own yurt. Much to Thelvyn's surprise, Sirontai waited a moment and then discreetly joined him, even though he had already been claimed by the younger members of the tribe to join them in the yurt set aside for the unattached warriors.

"Sir Deordge is such an old dear," she said softly. "That is why we cannot resist teasing him."

"Teasing him?" Thelvyn asked.

"I follow him about like a love-happy bride," she explained. "You can see for yourself how it worries him. It is most amusing."

Thelvyn was inclined to agree. And judging by Perrantin's comments and Solveig's rather sly expression, Sir George was probably the only one who wasn't aware that it was only a game. He was too preoccupied with his fearful evasions to realize it.

CHAPTER ELEVEN

The Ethengar built a great fire in the center of the village, since there was no single yurt large enough to hold everyone. They prepared furiously for the feast all that afternoon and on into the evening. When everything was ready, they hurried to their yurts and put on their finest clothes and jewelry, so that they emerged looking even stranger and more gaudy then ever. The warriors, young and old alike, put on their armor of hardened leather and their round iron hats trimmed with collars of fur, while the others wore heavy robes with bright, intricate patterns or shirts and jackets worn with loose, full pants made of pressed felt. Sir George had explained to Thelvyn that each clan had its own patterns and designs made in its own colors, so that they would always recognize a clan member on sight.

Finally they all sat down to a feast that did justice to Sir George's worst fears. It was entirely possible that the only thing worse than yak was the previous night's yak, which seemed to be what they got for their dinner. Thelvyn tried to be charitable in his judgment, realizing that there wasn't much variety of food available in the steppes, and the Ethengar were forced to do their best with what they had. Part of the problem might have been that they seemed willing to cook just about anything they could find. He supposed he would find it palatable enough if he had eaten such things all his life. He had also heard that elven cooking was something to be missed.

Once the feasting had ended, the members of the tribe seemed to take turns partying, which was to say that they never all got up and did it all at the same time. A small group of musicians sat off to one side, playing intricate, vaguely comprehensible music on strange instruments. Often one of the young girls would sing in a high, clear voice, or a small group of girls would rise to perform some gentle dance. Then two or three young warriors would leap up and perform some wild dance of their own, dances that were fast and complex enough to show off their strength and dexterity, not unlike the antics they delighted to perform in the saddle.

As the night progressed, some of the dances could best be described as cavorting, since the performers were having a little more to drink than was necessarily good for them. The Ethengar were especially fond of a clear drink that tasted even more vile than it smelled. It was kept in half-cured leather flasks, apparently so that the hide could impart a certain flavor all its own. Sir George had warned Thelvyn about the drink earlier, expressing his personal theory that it was fermented from the cold sweat of pregnant mares. The old knight had also passed out small flasks that could be hidden inside their clothes, to act as a place to discreetly transfer their share of the drink.

"Whatever you do, don't drink more than a small amount," he explained. "If you're not used to it, this stuff will leave you unable to eat for as long as three days. I once considered marketing it to the courtiers of Darokin as a diet aid."

As the night deepened, the Ethengar began to mellow somewhat and become quietly happy, responding to the effects of drink and song. Thelvyn had been watching

Sirontai, remembering her admission to him that she entertained herself and her tribesmen by teasing the old knight. She was sitting rather circumspectly to one side of Sir George, while to the other side sat the frail and wizened elder shaman Yagatu. Now that everyone was feeling quite friendly, Sir George decided it was time to talk a little business.

"Things are getting a bit nasty in the outside world," he began. "Dragons have been raiding the northern settlements of the Highlands. They haven't been waging outright war yet, just harassing an occasional farmhouse or barn or a portion of a town. They've apparently been attacking travelers on the open road, which is not at all good for business. Recently I've heard that dragons have been striking in the Heldannic lands as well."

"Good!" Yagatu declared with great satisfaction. The Ethengar had never been on good terms with the Heldannic folk.

"That made me worry somewhat about crossing the steppes," Sir George continued. "The mountains and forests of other lands offer some protection, but the steppes leave a person no place to hide."

"There has been trouble," Sirontai admitted, reluctantly at first. "There have been attacks in the northern steppes, usually within sight of the great mountains of the north. Yurts and wagons have been destroyed. But mostly they come to feed upon the herds. They often frighten the horses, but there are no reports they have killed any. In that, at least, they show that they are civilized."

"That is what I keep trying to tell people," Sir George remarked.

"Few tribesmen will go now into the far north," she continued. "We know of the attacks in other lands, and that other people are having a harder time than we are. We hope the dragons will not bring their war upon us. We have little they desire. But mostly we know better than to hope too much.

"When I was young, the Gostai had grown great in numbers and attempted to move south into the steppes," Yagatu said. His words seemed unrelated at first, although the others waited patiently for him to continue. "Now the goblins are between us and the northern mountains, and the dragons attack them. We could have used a dragon or two in the old days."

"As much as I respect dragons, I admit that they serve only themselves," Sir George said. "I've traveled around, and I know quite a good deal about dragons. I know dragons don't usually do anything without a reason, and there certainly has to be a reason behind what is happening now. I was thinking that if I could just get a dragon to talk to me and tell me what they're after, we might be able to find a way to stop these attacks."

"You must have great faith in your ability to talk if you expect to be able to chat with a dragon," Sirontai said. The others nearby had stopped to listen, and they seemed quite impressed.

"Well, it's not quite as easy as all that," Sir George admitted. "I don't expect a dragon to just tell me what I want to know. But dragons do live by their own rules, and they are very strict about abiding by their rules, even when they have been defeated. If you are able to subdue a dragon in combat, it will usually do its best to serve you, as long as you aren't being unreasonable in what you ask. Of course, it will still be trying to figure a way to get back at you."

"Ah, then I do begin to understand you," Sirontai declared. "I would have asked next if it is your intention to find a dragon and make war upon him. With all due respect to your companions, that would not be wise. Your intention, I suspect, is to find some other means to disadvantage a dragon so that you may ask of him what you seek."

"You do understand," Sir George agreed. "My companion, Perrantin, is a scholar of great ability. He searched all the most ancient books, and he consulted the greatest wizards, and he was able to discover the means to make a magical artifact with power enough to frighten a dragon into submission."

"Then you are traveling in the wrong direction," she said. "If you have such a thing, you will find a dragon quickest by heading north."

"We have such a thing, but it isn't ready yet. Spells of

great power must be cast upon this device, and the only place where the final spells may be cast is upon World Mountain, in the Land of Black Sand."

His words left every single Ethengar speechless. For a moment, even Sirontai looked so completely frightened that Thelvyn was frightened in turn. He reminded himself that these were a simple folk and probably very superstitious. He had lived all his life among the Flaem, who were too practical to allow themselves to be ruled by their fears, so he wasn't used to being in the company of superstitious folk. Sir George had once told him that there were too many real monsters in the world to waste time being afraid of monsters that didn't exist. From what little he actually knew of it, he could understand how World Mountain could be a source of their fears.

"Sir Deordge, we have always thought of you as a master trader," Sirontai said slowly, finding her voice at last. "We know that you are among the most clever of men, yet honest and generous and also a great scholar in your own right. But we had never considered that you and your companions were among the greatest of heroes, that you would dare to make such a dangerous journey."

When he heard that, Thelvyn was sure he had even more to worry about than he thought.

"Then you consider our journey too dangerous?" Sir George asked.

She thought hard for several moments before she answered. "The shamans of our people journey there from time to time, and the bodies of our great khans are laid to rest in the white palace near the summit of World Mountain. But these are journeys of specific purpose, part of an understanding that has long existed between our people and the spirits of that place. I confess that I would not go there without cause. But I suppose that you have sufficient cause, for your quest will benefit our people if the attacks by the dragons are ended. For this reason, you may very well find favor with the spirits."

"I believe I understand the dangers," Sir George said. "To reach World Mountain, we must first cross the Land of Black Sand, a dangerous land where we cannot expect to find food or drink for man or beast. The Land of Black Sand is a place of madness and restless spirits, but it can be crossed if you know the means. Then we must ascend the mountain itself, but only if our purpose finds favor with the spirits."

"Yes, that is so," Sirontai agreed. "It will be a difficult and possibly a dangerous journey under any circumstance, but I believe that you will succeed."

The companions rested well that night, each one a guest in a different yurt. While such accommodations hardly rivaled a soft bed in a fine inn, it was still much better than camping in the wild. The next morning they were awakened at dawn and given more small gifts of food and other supplies. The horses were led out, already saddled, their packs filled with fresh fodder. Then, as all the folk of the camp stood about to watch them depart, Sirontai brought forth a curious standard, a group of four small triangular flags, like pendants, each made in a different design and color. These were attached to a short crosspiece at the top of a long, slender shaft of wood.

"This shall be our final gift of parting, Deordge, in recognition of your need to travel quickly and safely over the steppes," she explained. "Such a totem as this may be seen perhaps once or twice in a lifetime. It tells all the other clans and tribes that we have declared you to be upon a great and holy quest, and you must not be disturbed. There are many totems of safe conduct, but this one is our most sacred, and no one will dare defy it, for it states that the importance of your quest is beyond challenge."

"Will they recognize this totem even if it's carried by strangers?" Sir George asked.

"That will not be questioned," Sirontai insisted. "Totems of safe conduct have been given to foreigners who have need to cross the steppes swiftly and in peace if their purpose is of great importance. Although I do not wish to seem to question your trust, you must not use the totem without just need. If later you return upon common business but you use the totem lightly to insure your safety or speed, then the wrath of the Ethengar will be fierce."

"I will not abuse it," Sir George assured her. "If things

go well for us, then someday soon I will return it to you."

"We would be grateful for that. The totem has been in the keeping of our tribe for all the years of our history, more years than we can now recall."

The companions returned to the steppes, somewhat refreshed from having spent a night in relative comfort. From that time on, anyone who rode in the front of their group would carry the totem of safe passage, holding it high so it could be seen clearly from miles away. Sir George wasn't particularly worried about meeting other tribes of the Ethengar; he knew the customs of this land and how to proceed safely. But those same customs would have required them to share the hospitality of any tribes they encountered, which might not have been as convenient as their first brief, overnight stop. None of the Ethengar would approach them while they carried the totem.

After their afternoon and night with Sirontai's tribe, they needed only three more days to reach the edge of the Land of Black Sand. One day in the steppes looked very much like the next, always with the same swells and dips of low hills, or else land so utterly flat that even Thelvyn's sight was uninterrupted until the horizon disappeared into the distant haze. The only striking change came when they had to cross the Streel River, a difficult undertaking, since the river ran swift and high from the melting snows of the northern mountains. Soon after that, they descended almost imperceptibly into the ring of hills bordering the great depression known as the Sea of Flowers, camping that night on the edge of Lake Talkai. The lake was a poor affair, only just beginning to fill with the waters of the spring rains, and it would disappear again in the dry heat of midsummer.

The next morning they skirted the edge of the lake to the north, then rode on across the Sea of Flowers. There were no flowers yet so early in the year, but the grass was deeper and greener here than any they had crossed so far. Thelvyn was sure he could see the summit of a great, dark mountain rising above the hills straight ahead in the east. They camped that night in a sheltered place in the hills of the eastern border of the depression.

At dawn the following morning, even Perrantin could see the dark shape of World Mountain as the sun rose behind it. By that time, Thelvyn had become aware of a small mystery. When they camped in the wild, Solveig was up as early as anyone, eager to pack and be on the way again. He remembered how slow to waken she had been in the morning when they were at home, and he wondered what made the difference. That morning he found himself riding beside her. To protect herself from the bright sun, she was wearing the floppy, broad-brimmed straw hat she usually carried rolled up in her pack. He decided to ask her about what was puzzling him.

"I'm always in a hurry to get up in the morning," she explained. "When your back is as long as mine, you never sleep comfortably on the ground."

Thelvyn frowned, considering that. "But you don't have any more length of back than I have. You just have longer legs."

He realized too late that he was possibly a little too familiar in showing how well he was aware of her proportions, but she found his concern amusing. She glanced at Sir George, who was riding in the lead, and dropped her voice. "When we are at home, Sir George tends to keep us all up a little too late with his need to talk and drink that vile cherry stuff of his. On the road, you go to bed very soon after you stop for the night."

"True enough," he agreed.

"Also, the fact is that we both have long backs, and mine does bother me," she added. "I broke my back in a bad fall from a horse four years ago, and it has never quite been the same."

Thelvyn looked fearful, remembering his own fall from Cadence a few days before. "You broke your back falling from a horse?"

"That was very soon after I met Sir George," she explained. "We had been attacked, and I was knocked from my saddle. I woke several hours later to find that the battle was over, and Sir George had packed me away safe and sound in a shepherd's cabin he had found in the woods. He had me put back together again fairly quickly, although he would never admit how he managed that. Repairing a broken back, especially so quickly, requires a fair amount of skill with healing spells. Sir George always insisted that there was no injury to the nerve, only the bones, but I have never been certain whether or not I believe him. Although he will usually stand back and allow Perrantin to handle all matters related to magic, I know that he is a magic-user of some experience himself."

"That would explain why he had all the books necessary to get me started on my education in magic," Thelvyn said.

"The story I told you happened at the time of my first meeting with Sir George," she added. "He had been with Sir David Southworth. I suppose you never met him."

"Sir George has spoken of him, but I never knew what became of him."

"None of us know," Solveig said. "He went away on business of his own and never returned. At the time I first met Sir George and Sir David, they needed a warrior and guide to help them recover certain artifacts they had discovered, and I had come highly recommended to them. We never got there, at least not that time. Sir George took me to the townhouse he maintains in the merchants' quarter at Darokin until I recovered."

"That was exceedingly kind of him."

"Actually, he left me the key to his house and went away on business for four weeks," she said, smiling. "Would you leave a fashionable townhouse in the most elegant city in the world in the care of the tallest barbarian warrior woman you ever met? I assumed that anyone that insane and trusting needed me."

"It sounds like Sir George," Thelvyn said. "The thing I wonder about is this old friend of Sir George's who didn't come back."

"Sir David Southworth was also a former knight of Darokin, but a younger man who had developed a taste for adventure and wealth. He preferred the life of a true adventurer, so he would travel with Sir George only occasionally. I suppose he was also a little too sure of his abilities. He would plunge ahead into dangerous situations without proper planning or the help he needed. But the life of a trader is always dangerous."

Thelvyn thought it was also fair to say that traveling in the wilds was always dangerous. Because the goal of their quest was so tremendously dangerous, he had a tendency to forget that the rest of the journey was risky as well. He had been feeling rather secure the last few days, since it had been a long time since they had seen a dragon. But that didn't mean they were safe. There were many nasty creatures in the steppes—griffons, orcs, goblins. He also realized he had no idea what to expect when they came to World Mountain, although the thought of going there had obviously impressed the Ethengar.

They rode that morning through the last of the hills bordering the depression of the Sea of Flowers. When they came out of the hills into the steppes above, they were able to see World Mountain more clearly than ever, a single peak like the cone of a volcano rising almost directly ahead of them. The Land of Black Sand lay hardly more than twenty miles ahead. Thelvyn was sure he could see the land turn dark and barren in the distance. It seemed to shimmer with heat, even though the spring morning was quite cool. The mountain itself stood another thirty-five or forty miles beyond. Sir George, still riding in the lead and bearing the totem, was turning their course somewhat south.

"We don't want to cross any more of the Black Sand than we have to," he explained when they paused at midmorning. "The Land of Black Sand is much wider east to west, and we'd have to cross some forty miles or so of it if we approached from that direction. We can shave that to less than twenty by coming up from the south, even though it will take us an extra day of riding just to get there."

"Is it that important?" Korinn asked. "What can we expect to find there? My own home is to the south of the steppes, and we have heard many tales of these lands. I have heard the Land of Black Sand is a place of great magic and evil, but nothing specific."

"I think we will find it less dangerous than legend has it," Sir George answered. "That is often so with matters of legend. I really have no idea what to expect, because I've never been here before. But the Ethengar come here, especially their shamans. They all seem to agree that the dangers are manageable if your purpose is good, and if you keep your head."

"Is the distance any less from the north?" Perrantin asked.

"About the same. The problem with that is that the lands north of the Black Sands are held by orcs. There are also several areas of bad magic we'd have to avoid."

When they rode on again, Sir George angled their course even farther southward. The indistinct region of darkness that marked the Land of Black Sand came slowly closer for a time, but Sir George adjusted their path to keep it always at about the same distance, at some five miles to their left. He seemed reluctant to travel any closer, even though they were still well out in the green grass of the steppes. Thelvyn found himself staring in that direction, perhaps in the irresistible need to watch for danger. His remarkable vision was sharp enough to see anything as large as a person from miles away. But as long as he watched, he never saw anything moving among the dark boulders and low dunes, for the misty haze tried to frustrate his sight.

Sir George allowed the horses to keep an easy pace so they'd be rested for the ride across the Land of Black Sand. As they rode along quietly, the dark form of World Mountain began to move slowly around to their left. They camped that night in a deep place between the hills, where they were somewhat hidden from sight, although the steppes were too flat even here to offer much protection. Having that strange land only a few miles to the north left them more fearful than usual, and none of them but the dwarf rested well. Korinn seemed able to sleep through anything. The fact that the horses were nervous seemed to suggest there was some reason for their restlessness besides their own imaginations.

The next day was much the same as the one before, except that they awoke with the threat of the Land of Black Sands near at hand, the great, dark form of World Mountain standing tall and brooding over the strange land. As they rode on through the day, the mountain moved slowly around to their left until it stood directly north. By late that afternoon, the great mountain was slightly behind them. Their course had swung steadily northward during the day, and the mountain was closer than ever, perhaps twenty miles away. They were only four or five miles from the edge of the Black Sand.

The terrain was somewhat hillier here, so that they were able to make a camp in a deep depression between the hills, and for once they were reasonably well hidden from view. Nevertheless, they didn't dare light a fire. The Land of Black Sand seemed more forbidding than ever, leaving them with the uncomfortable sense that something was patiently waiting for them, even daring them to enter. They all hurried to tend the horses before making camp.

"It makes me nervous to lie down in the middle of a place like this," Thelvyn complained.

"You've spent your entire life in the northern forests," Solveig told him. "You miss the trees."

"I also miss having a place where it's safe to make a fire," he said. "What I don't understand is how the Ethengar ever find enough wood to build a fire."

Solveig looked at him and seemed about to say something, but decided otherwise. She probably decided he didn't want to know.

When they sat down to have their cold dinner, Thelvyn decided it was time to talk about the Land of Black Sand. They should be entering it in the morning, and he wanted to know what to expect. He would have asked sooner, but his respect for his elders had prevented it until now. Actually, the question had already come up, but Sir George had been vague in his answers except to say that he expected it to be less dangerous than legend allowed. Sir George wasn't in the habit of being deliberately evasive with his friends, but he was very good at changing the subject.

This time, Korinn was also prepared to insist upon some direct answers. As he had said before, he had grown up near the lands of the Ethengar, and their history and legends were very much a part of his childhood. He was more fearful of the Land of Black Sand than he wanted anyone to know.

"Frankly, I don't know what to say," Sir George admitted.

"It is said there are strange beasts and monsters haunting the dunes and boulders of the Black Sand, not to mention spirits in the form of monsters. I don't know if that's true, but I intend to be cautious for the sake of our safety. That's why I insisted upon crossing at the most narrow point."

"You've said that shamans have made the journey to World Mountain," Korinn said. "Do they have some special means for getting through unharmed?"

"Not that I know of," Sir George admitted, and glanced at Perrantin.

The mage shrugged. "All I know for certain is that World Mountain is the site of a gateway to the realm of the spirits aligned to the Ethengar. Early in their history, the Ethengar were guided by benevolent spirits, which taught them most of their customs, laws, and crafts. Because of the proximity of World Mountain, the Land of Black Sand is fairly crawling with spirits."

"Spirits?" Thelvyn asked uncertainly. "What do you mean by spirits? Are we talking about ghosts?"

"Good heavens, no!" Perrantin declared. "These spirits are magical beings that had their origin in one of the outer planes of existence, to use the more technical term. The gateway at World Mountain has brought their realm in close contact with our own, and many have crossed over into this land. Some of the original spirits have since merged their being with the land itself, or so the Ethengar believe, and the greater ones are quite similar to Immortals. But many lesser spirits have since crossed into this world as well."

"And the lesser spirits are the dangerous ones?" Thelvyn asked.

"Some of them are extremely dangerous," the mage agreed. "They are said to be utterly evil, even insane or mindless. But the influence of the greater spirits keeps them confined to this region, at least for the most part."

"However, the shamans are able to make their holy journeys here in relative peace," Sir George added. "It might be that benevolent spirits act as their guardians and fend off the evil spirits. That's why I hope they might find favor with our own purpose and protect us, especially if we enter with the totem of safe conduct in plain sight. I wanted it as much to impress the spirits as other clans of the Ethengar."

"And if we do not impress these spirits?" Korinn asked.

"I still don't believe that we have anything to worry about," the old knight insisted. "The Ethengar take the bodies of their great khans to rest near the bridge to the spirit world on World Mountain, so they are able to make the journey here and return unharmed. It could be the evil spirits don't care to take on a large party."

"A large party?" Solveig asked, looking about as if expecting to find other companions in their camp. "Are we a large party?"

"Getting there will be the hard part," Sir George insisted. "On the way back, we'll have the artifact of entropy to protect us. Anything capable of frightening a dragon should be sufficient to send a spirit running."

"I can't help but think these spirits must be tremendously powerful," Thelvyn said. "Their presence seems to have devastated this land."

"The spirits didn't do that," Sir George said. "They might be confined to the Land of Black Sand, but they didn't create it. Strangely enough, the elves were responsible for that. As you have probably heard by now, the elves of the ancient Highlands found and activated a Blackmoor device."

"Yes, I know about that," Thelvyn said quickly. "The explosion devastated the Highlands, which was why it was mostly uninhabited until the arrival of the Flaem a hundred years ago."

"The Highlands were actually rather fortunate," Sir George explained. "The smoke and wind carried away the worst of the magical influences, which spread eastward across the Highland Mountains into the steppes. Then the dust of the explosion settled here in the northern steppes, and its raw magical influence created the Land of Black Sand."

They arose early the next morning and set out again, this time directly toward World Mountain and the Land of Black Sand, only a few miles ahead, with no better idea of what to expect than before. They would have preferred being better supplied for a journey into such a dead and desolate land, especially with more water and fodder for the horses. They were unlikely to find any water fit to drink there or any suitable grazing for the horses, which would be dependant entirely upon the grain they were packing. Sir George assured them they shouldn't be in the land for more than a couple of days, three at the most. The supplies they had should last more than long enough.

Thelvyn rode in front with Sir George, putting his remarkable vision to the task of watching the Black Sand ahead for dangers. There was little to be seen, however. The shimmering haze that hung over the Land of Black Sand was heavier than ever, so he was able to see only a mile or so into that region. World Mountain, now less than twenty miles distant, looked farther away than it had two days ago. He didn't need for Sir George to tell him that something was different today. He hoped it was nothing more than a change in the weather, perhaps a hint of the inevitable spring rains, for the sun seemed less bright and the color of the sky was dull and pale.

Thelvyn noticed that no one was speaking. The horses were nervous and fitful, and also unusually silent. A cool, almost damp wind was stirring, moving through the short spring grass in waves, although the sound of it seemed dull and remote. Increasingly he was beginning to feel as if the world itself was waiting for something to happen. Perhaps it was indeed only the weather; he hoped that was all, as unpleasant as a storm might be in the deadly land ahead. But he couldn't escape the uncomfortable feeling that they were anticipated, that something evil was waiting for them to enter its dominion.

Then, without warning, great branches of lightning leapt out from the dark form of World Mountain, seeming to flash right out of a clear sky. Vast, spreading arms and claws of streaking light arced out for miles in every direction at once, across that dark, hazy land, reaching down to flicker and dance over the boulders and black dunes. Thelvyn, who had been looking right at the lightning when it struck, was left blinking by the flash, his sensitive vision blurred. He listened as he tried to force his reluctant eyes to open, waiting for the roll of thunder that never came. When he was finally able to focus his eyes once again, he saw dark, rolling clouds as black as night itself spreading out from World Mountain in all directions, like an inky flood flowing across the sky.

"How remarkable," Sir George said almost to himself.

"Do you know what this is?" Solveig asked, bringing her horse up beside his.

"It's what the Ethengar call the Wind of Black Madness," he explained as he recovered from his amazement. "The winds are said to cause madness, but the effect is unpredictable. People are affected to varying degrees, and some not at all. It only happens once or twice a year, and it's always preceded by brilliant flashes of lightning over the Land of Black Sand. This one seems to be an especially violent episode."

Perrantin was looking troubled. "You say it only happens once or twice a year, and yet it just happened to wait until the morning we arrived?"

"Yes . . . that does seem rather suspicious, doesn't it? I suppose there must be certain factions among the spirits who do not wish us well."

"What do you suggest?" Korinn asked.

Sir George shrugged. "I suppose we should turn around and run like the dickens. That's what the Ethengar do when they see lightning over the Land of Black Sand. The problem is that the effects of the winds aren't confined only to that region. They can be carried well out into the steppes. At least the danger is lessened as it moves farther away."

They couldn't afford to run the horses that hard and that far, in spite of their desperation, or they might find themselves without horses altogether. The best alternative was to settle the horses into a steady trot that the sturdy beasts could maintain for miles. Even at that, they knew they couldn't escape the winds altogether. This manifestation was simply too strong, and the winds were moving too quickly. Their best hope was to get themselves as far away as possible so the effect was diminished. Thelvyn kept looking behind as they rode, watching the wall of black clouds as it expanded outward from World Mountain like a ring of waves in a pool. The dark, heavy clouds roiled and surged. Chain lightning flashed along the underside of the storm, sometimes leaping to the ground below.

Soon, Thelvyn could see the winds moving beneath the black ceiling of clouds, lifting a dull, dark-gray blanket of dust as it moved through the rocks and dunes. The shimmering haze that always hung over the land was being transformed into a dark fog. He swallowed nervously, knowing it was only a matter of minutes before the winds were upon them, but he elected not to warn his companions just yet. There was really nothing they could have done anyway. Perrantin was bent over in his saddle, trying desperately to read one of his books of magic in the hope of finding some spell that might protect them.

Now, Thelvyn could see the leading edge of the wind pass beyond the Black Sands onto the steppes. The swirling blast of dust suddenly became sheets of wind driving violently through the grass over the tops of low hills. He decided it was time to warn the others. If they were going to do anything to protect themselves, it had to be done at once.

"The winds are just behind us!" he warned. "They'll be upon us in a few minutes."

"We'll just have to take our chances," Sir George said, although he sounded pessimistic. "Perry, would that potion we used on the horses back at Torkyn Fall work on us?"

"I am certain it would," the mage replied. "I'm just not sure how much good it would do. The effect only lasts for an hour, and repeating the magic could be deadly."

"I was only thinking of using it on any of us who show signs of madness," Sir George explained. "The Ethengar say the winds affect only a small portion of any company, and not all at once."

"Sir George!" Thelvyn shouted suddenly.

The others jumped at his sharp warning, for they had all been staring back apprehensively at the winds sweeping across the steppes. They had just come over the top of a low rise, and three large, rather remarkable forms waited directly in their path only a few hundred yards ahead.

Thelvyn wondered at first if the madness was beginning to affect him already, so he could no longer trust his eyes. He could swear that he saw three forms, like tall, massively built men, or perhaps one of the giant breeds of orcs, taller even than Solveig by more than a head, except that they were covered with thick, shaggy hair and had the great, impressively ugly heads of yaks, complete with a pair of wide upturned horns. He blinked, wondering if the vision would go away, and then he took an even closer look to be certain they were indeed not giant orcs or some other evil creature.

They wore the stiffened leather and simple plate armor similar to that of the Ethengar, with the same loose pants of dark felt, but their eyes blinked wildly and the nostrils of their broad noses flared when they breathed. Thelvyn's vision was too good even from this distance to miss such details. The larger two of the yak-men bore stout pikes with heads of bright steel, one side bearing a long, curved blade shaped like a scimitar, while the other had a heavier head like that of a battle-axe. The smallest of the three carried a bow and wore a scimitar as big as a broadsword.

Sir George saw this remarkable band as well, and he brought the company to a quick stop.

"You see them, too?" Sir George asked, seemingly relieved. "Well, now, this is unexpected."

"Are we in any danger?" Solveig asked, watching the strange warriors. They waited patiently, entirely unconcerned and showing no signs of hostility.

"Actually, I don't think so," Sir George said at last. "I've heard stories that, in times of great need, the shamans of the Ethengar will summon the three Yak Brothers to protect their clan. The only reason they could be here is to help us."

"Are they spirits?" Thelvyn asked.

"Indeed they are," Sir George said.

They rode forward again, this time more slowly and cautiously than before. As they came closer, Thelvyn saw that the Yak Brothers were even taller and more massive than he had thought. The tallest of the group stepped forward to greet the approaching travelers.

"Sir George Kirbey and company?" he said in a voice like a deep bovine grumble.

"At your service," Sir George said politely.

"That is very much the other way around," the yak-man replied. "You may call me Hornhead. My brothers are Clovefoot, the small one with the bow, and Wobblebelly. As you may have guessed, we take this form when we walk in the world of mortal folk because the people of this land expect it of us."

"Then you have come to help us?" Sir George asked.

"We have been sent to help you," Hornhead answered. "There are many, many spirits in this land, some greater and some lesser, some evil and some not. Your quest has importance to the future of the people of this land, for they cannot easily endure the wrath of the dragons. Some who are evil would like to see destruction brought to the lands of grass, and they prefer that you fail. Some who are good are determined that you should not fail."

"Do you know why the dragons are attacking?" Sir George asked, seeing a chance to get an answer to this whole mystery.

"No, none among us know that. The spirits of this land are tied to the land, and so we cannot see the things that happen in other lands. That is why your quest is important."

Thelvyn frowned. That precluded the chance to put in any questions of his own.

"Then you can get us to World Mountain safely?" Sir George asked.

"That is why we were sent," Hornhead replied. "While your people are in our presence, they have no need to fear the Wind of Black Madness. The lands of grass belong to the spirits of good, and our will is supreme here. The Land of Black Sand is the place where the spirits of evil are strong. Things will not be so easy there, but we will get through."

And with that, the Yak Brothers put their weapons on their shoulders and stalked away, back toward the north and the great storm of black clouds, wind, and lightning that hung ominously over the Land of Black Sand. Sir George and his companions sat in their saddles for a long moment and stared. The abruptness of these events left them feeling uncertain about whether they could trust these large, solemn creatures.

"You know, lad," Sir George said to Thelvyn at last, "my adventures have gotten a whole lot stranger and more complicated since I started bringing you along."

"Don't blame me for any of this!" Thelvyn insisted. "So what do we do now? Are we going to follow them?"

"I don't see why not," the old knight replied. "Don't look a gift yak in the mouth, I always say, especially when the gift is from the spirits."

They had only just turned back toward the Land of Black Sand when the first blast of the wind struck. It was fierce, cold, and damp, like the leading wind at the front of a storm, and Sir George stood for a moment in his stirrups, leaning against the wind until it settled into cold, fitful gusts. He looked up to see that the black clouds would soon be passing above them as well.

CHAPTER TWELVE

The winds seemed as if they would never end. Thelvyn rode in silence at the end of the line of horses, often almost standing in his saddle to stare ahead at the Land of Black Sands. The great canopy of black, furious clouds had spread out to cover the land for as far as he could see, hiding World Mountain entirely from sight. The clouds did not seem to extend beyond the bounds of that region, nor did they threaten to roll out across the surrounding steppes in the way a true storm might. They just hung over that desolate land, brooding or perhaps even challenging, seeming almost to dare them to stop. Lightning flickered across the surface of the clouds, leaping down with quick, sudden flashes in the darkness to strike among the black hills and boulders of the hidden lands below.

Thelvyn still was uncertain about trusting the Yak Brothers, and he could see that Sir George had reservations of his own. But the simple fact remained that they go with them or not at all, since they couldn't hope to fight the evil spirits of this land on their own. The cold, damp wind continued to blow against them, and the sky roiled dark with the great mass of black clouds brooding just before them, although they were not yet beneath the clouds and still rode in the light of a pleasant spring morning.

Perrantin had been silently seething with frustration from the start at his inability to ask the hundreds of questions on his mind. Like his friends, he didn't dare to approach the Yak Brothers lightly. The three spirit warriors were tall and powerful, and their coldly emotionless, silent manner made them intimidating company. Their presence frightened Thelvyn in spite of himself, although he was far less afraid of their true enemies for having them at hand.

An hour's ride, at a less hurried pace than before, brought them back to where they had been when the lightning warning of the winds had first begun. In yet another hour, they came for the first time to the edge of the Land of Black Sand itself. The grass of the steppes slowly became shorter and more pale and withered as they approached, as if some terrible influence was choking the very life out of anything that dared approach its domain. The Yak Brothers, who had been picking handfuls of grass and any stray flowers they might find to eat, disdained such grazing altogether. Almost abruptly, in the space of less than a hundred yards, the grass gave way to areas of dull, gray-black sand. When they left the last yellowed clump of grass behind, they never again saw even the slightest sign of any growing thing.

"Twelve miles to the base of the mountain. We will not go up the mountain tonight," Hornhead declared. He was the only one of the three who ever spoke. "We will wait until morning. Going up the mountain and back again will take all day, and you must not be there at night."

As they entered the Land of Black Sand, they came beneath a fierce cover of black clouds, which hung dark and threatening above them. It was a colorless place, with jagged boulders of great size rising like dark islands from a sea of black sand and dust beneath a black sky. Lightning continued to flash across the surface of the clouds or strike the ground, sometimes close around them, but the Yak

Brothers remained unconcerned, as if their influence were all the protection anyone needed. Thelvyn noticed with some interest that no matter how close the lightning came, he never heard more than a low grumble. The cold, damp wind continued to blow, chasing the sand and dust across the dunes.

At least the Black Sand was fairly firm, which made for relatively easy footing for the horses. The first time they stopped to rest their mounts, Thelvyn discovered that the sand was extremely loose, dry, and treacherous when he moved more than a few yards away from their group. Clearly the Yak Brothers were exerting some magical influence to make their journey as quick and easy and possible.

At first they had passed only through low hills of dark sand. Soon boulders began to appear. Initially they came upon small, jagged stones that poked their heads only a short distance above the sand, but over the next couple of miles these grew to great boulders, which often towered high over the horses. These huge stones were black and almost glassy, with many sharp, broken edges. They reminded Thelvyn of the obsidian and other volcanic stone he had seen at Torkyn Fall. He fancied that the stones had emerged through the sand, pushed up by unseen forces from far below, although he expected they only appeared that way because they were half-buried in the sand.

That led Thelvyn to a frightening thought. He could hardly imagine raw magical force in such concentration that it could burn miles of open land down to its very bedrock, fusing the stone. And yet this was what had occurred here, triggered by the magically charged smoke and dust cast from the explosion of an ancient Blackmoor device. Now he could understand how the wizardry of Blackmoor had almost destroyed the world. And if he was indeed descended from that ancient race, it was small wonder that the dragons, with their vast lives and long memories, would so hate his kind. To them, the events of twenty-five centuries past might seem like yesterday. He understood at last why it was dangerous for him to speak of his possible heritage to anyone, and so he resolved at that time never to mention it to anyone except his own companions.

At noon, Sir George had to ask the Yak Brothers to allow them a few minutes of rest, for the sake of the horses if nothing else. Their three remarkable companions had been setting a brutal pace. The three spirits turned to look back, then took the positions to stand guard while their companions rested. Sir George felt obliged, while the others were having a quick lunch, to offer their three guardians something as well, even if it was only some of the grain from their store of fodder for the horses. The Yak Brothers declined gallantly, even though they were obviously greatly tempted.

"They said we'll need all our fodder for our horses in the days ahead," he explained when he returned to join the others. "I suspect that, being what they are, they really have no need to eat."

"Are they always so aloof?" Perrantin asked softly, fearful of what they might think if they heard him.

"Actually, they are usually rather stupid and quarrelsome," Sir George told him. "They seem to find that behavior important, or perhaps even necessary, in their dealings with the Ethengar. I suppose that's because we are foreigners and more sophisticated in our knowledge of magic and magical beings, making such behavior irrelevant in dealing with us."

"What are they usually like?" Perrantin asked, his curiosity taking hold.

"When summoned to serve a shaman of the Ethengar, they will stop constantly to graze, especially when there are flowers to tempt them, and they have to be prodded along like animals or they tend to forget what they should be doing. I seem to recall that they also have an irresistible urge to pull wagons."

Solveig actually had to keep herself from laughing.

"You have to remember that the Ethengar live with a shamanistic view of magic, especially magical beings and environments," Sir George continued. "To them, everything in the world is representational. In their philosophies, simple, familiar items represent more complex situations in order to make them easier to understand. The spirits have adapted their own appearances and behaviors to make themselves more understandable and approachable to these people."

If the Yak Brothers were indeed only warriors in a hostile land, then they commanded power enough to impress their enemies. Their progress was being closely watched by something, Thelvyn was very sure of that. As they rode, he was often aware of some alien presence very close at hand, tense and ready to spring into attack, yet never daring to. The black clouds and lightning did not abate during the day but grew even darker and heavier as they came steadily nearer to World Mountain.

World Mountain was a peak of only modest size compared to the greater ranges to the north, rising perhaps no more than three or four thousand feet above the black plains below, although it seemed to tower over them as it stood alone above the evenness of the steppes. During the last couple of days, Thelvyn had been anticipating their approach, watching the mountain rise steadily before them. Now most of the mountain was completely hidden within the black clouds. Even many of the lower slopes were lost in the gloom and mist. They became aware that they were beginning to climb the mountain itself only when the land began to rise beneath them late that afternoon, becoming steep and even more rugged than before.

At that time, the Yak Brothers did something totally unexpected, turning their course sharply to the east and passing along the skirt if the mountain. Night began to fall, causing the darkness to descend quickly, but their guides kept pacing doggedly, even in the fading light. They were very determined, but they obviously knew their way. Just as darkness was almost complete, they came suddenly upon a small ledge in a pocket between towering cliffs, where a path led steeply into unseen heights. The Yak Brothers stopped on the ledge, spreading out along its edge as if taking position to stand guard against the night.

"We will go no farther this day," Hornhead announced. "This is where you will rest for the night. You may safely make a fire here, if you wish."

Thelvyn felt certain he had never spent a more uncomfortable night in his life, even during their journey to

Torkyn Fall. The sense of being watched that had been with him all day was even stronger now. He could hear the sounds of unseen creatures moving in the darkness, scattering the sand and rocks. The wind howled all through the night, and lightning flashed through the unseen clouds. He would have felt better about it if their only protection hadn't been three yaks in Ethengar armor, as capable as they obviously were. But the Yak Brother more than proved their worth, diligently standing guard the entire time. More than once they stalked off to one side of the ledge and made threatening gestures until they decided the unseen danger had passed.

The hard, stony ground made a far less comfortable bed than the soft grass of the steppes. But as fearful and uncomfortable as the night was, Thelvyn still did not wish for dawn. The new day only meant that they must begin the long ascent up World Mountain. Morning came all the same, as dark and gloomy as the day before. The black clouds hung just over their heads, and the branches of lightning continued to flash.

"This is very strange," Thelvyn said as they packed. "I've been able to see this mountain for the last three days on the trail, and I never saw a cloud in the sky. How long can this last?"

"I'm a bit surprised myself," Perrantin agreed. "This display is entirely for our benefit, but since it isn't stopping us or even slowing us down, I hardly see the point."

"It might make for some very nasty travel as we start up the mountain," Sir George said. "The spirits might be saving the worst for when we are well up in the heights. This could develop into a real storm yet."

The Yak Brothers approached and stood facing them. Some important pronouncement was obviously in order. Hornhead took a step forward. "This is the day that you must go up the mountain. We cannot go with you."

"No?" Sir George asked. "Why is that?"

"We are spirits tied to the steppes, and this place is alien to us," Hornhead answered. "But I can tell you what to do. The lesser spirits aren't going to make this easy for you. But there is one among you who bears the blessing of the

Immortals, and the spirits must respect him."

"Thelvyn?" Sir George asked quickly, much to the lad's surprise.

Hornhead nodded. "Go up the path until you come to a narrow pass. There you will see the great white palace far above you. That is where the ugly one will meet you, the guardian of the bridge, for he will not want you coming on up the path to his palace. You must talk to him. He will know why you are there, so do not allow him to mislead you, but you still must convince him to help you."

"Sir George is very good at that," Korinn remarked.

"That is known even among the spirits," Hornhead agreed, much to the old knight's embarrassment. "When you have completed your task, then you must return here, and we will lead you back again."

They would say no more on the subject. Clearly the spirits played by their own rules, and it was better not to question them but to accept the assistance that was offered. The travelers mounted their horses and began the long, slow climb along the path up the mountain. They elected to leave their packhorses behind in the care of their guardians, since there wouldn't likely be any need for their packs, and the extra horses would only be in the way. Thelvyn was filled with new misgivings. He had assumed that the Yak Brothers would be going with them to the top. Whatever he might think of their other qualities, he had seen that they were able to keep the dangers away. He felt extremely vulnerable.

The clouds closed in about them almost at once, encasing the side of the mountain like a dark mist. At least the clouds weren't black, as he had feared. The stray wisps that drifted like fog out of the darkness were as pale white as any cloud, but the blackness closed in so quickly that it couldn't be natural. The day was even darker within the canopy of clouds than below it, darker than the deepest, heaviest storm that Thelvyn had ever seen. They rode in a deep, gray gloom, briefly lit from time to time by flashes of lightning. Thelvyn began to grow fearful of each flash, suspicious that the lightning itself might be used against his group. He had no way of knowing how much power the evil spirits might be able to command against them.

The first attacks of the hostile spirits began about an hour into their ascent, and it caught them by surprise in spite of the fact that they had been warned. Thelvyn had been riding near the rear of the group, with only Korinn behind him. Suddenly the dwarf cried out and made some frantic move that Thelvyn saw only out of the corner of his eye. Everyone brought his or her horses to a sudden halt and turned to look back. That was when Thelvyn saw a pair of impossibly long arms emerge from the darkness to reach for Solveig. She drew her sword and swung it around in a single swift motion, and the arms vanished into the mist.

That was only the beginning. They tried riding on again, and for a time, the attacks were nothing more than disquieting annoyances—more hands reaching for them or terrible faces leering out of the darkness. The hands never actually grabbed and the faces only threatened, but the threat was effective. The constant attacks were unsettling to the riders, wearing at their patience and courage, but devastating to the horses. Even if the evil spirits couldn't attack them directly, they were in constant danger of one of the frightened horses making fatal misstep on the treacherous path,

After a time, an especially large, hideous face with horns and great fangs appeared out of the darkness directly in their path, and a pair of strong arms reached out for Sir George. He drew his sword and tried to make threatening gestures, but his horse was too frightened to approach the spirit. Frustrated, the former knight at last leapt down from his saddle and boldly approached the apparition. Only then did it at last give way.

"This is becoming impossible," he remarked when the others joined him.

"Well, the Yak Brothers said the spirits must respect one of us," Perrantin said, glancing at Thelvyn. "Lad, have the spirits been pestering you?"

Thelvyn almost jumped in his surprise. "No . . . now that you mention it, I don't believe they have."

"They have not," Korinn added. "I noticed that."

"Well, now, the thing to do is for Thelvyn to ride in the lead," Sir George said. "That should be enough to keep the path open for us. Just be very careful of your horses, all of you."

Thelvyn brought his horse up to the lead, although he found himself wishing he didn't have to do this. It was like that night outside Torkyn Fall, when he found himself wishing he might be excused from tasks like this because of his age or lack of experience. Hornhead had said the spirits would respect him, and Sir George seemed to trust him, but Thelvyn himself couldn't really believe the spirits would defer to him. There was no reason why they should, unless it was just another one of the mysteries concerning his unknown race.

He rode just far enough ahead of his companions to clear the path of threatening spirits before any of the horses behind became spooked, but near enough so the spirits didn't attempt to get between himself and the others. His doubts grew immediately into a deep, unrelenting fear. He felt cold and shaky in the cool wind, and the few short yards separating him from his companions left him with a sense of being utterly alone. The spirits continued to appear in the path ahead of him, but they kept their distance from the moment he took the lead, only half-emerging from the darkness. The spirits did indeed seem to recognize him. Whatever they saw, it was enough to make these strange beings keep their distance.

Somehow, Thelvyn found that inexplicably shameful, reminding him all the more of just how alone he was.

The climb seemed endless, riding in the darkness, constantly threatened by monstrous visions. Thelvyn looked back from time to time. Now that he was beginning to feel somewhat assured that the spirits did indeed respect him, he was becoming more concerned for his companions. Sir George was bearing up well, seemingly the least concerned of them all. Perrantin conveniently withdrew into his spellbook whenever he could spare the attention from his horse. Korinn and Solveig both looked as pale and shaken as Thelvyn felt, glancing about quickly and fearfully.

Thelvyn's greatest concern wasn't for his friends but for

their horses. They were all wide-eyed with fear, sweating and shaking, and a couple of the horses were foaming at their bits. Thelvyn hoped they didn't have much farther to go, for he could see that the horses were controlled only by the will of their riders, and he doubted the beasts could take much more of this bone-shaking fear. But the spirits seemed to become even more powerful as they neared the top and came closer to the gateway to their plane of origin. He reminded himself that spirits were strange and powerful beings, unlike anything of his own world. He certainly didn't want to make a mistake because he had become too sure of himself.

Time passed slowly, so slowly that he was certain the day had passed and night had fallen. The unending darkness made it easy to forget that the bright, warm sun was still shining somewhere above these cold, black clouds. Thelvyn began to long for a glimpse of the sun. So many apparitions of ugliness and fear had stared or grabbed at his companions out of the darkness that they were becoming numb to the sight of them.

The path grew steadily steeper as they ascended toward the summit. Thelvyn began to hope they might finally be reaching the top. At that moment the spirits retreated into the darkness and disappeared, and the moaning wind died away suddenly and without warning. The companions brought their horses to a stop there in the middle of the trail and stared into the black mists surrounding them. For a moment, they were uncertain whether they had reached their destination at last, or if they should prepare themselves for some new and even more deadly attack.

Then a figure emerged out of the darkness ahead of them. Slowly it became a woman, the last of all apparitions they might have expected. As she came nearer, they could see that she was dressed the elven manner, wearing a tunic and pants of soft leather and a cape of short, plush fur, but she was clearly not an elf. She was tall and black-haired, with pale brown skin that almost had the look of burnished gold. Her eyes were large and as black as night. Thelvyn was still wondering what this strange vision meant when Sir George rode up beside him. The old knight was staring in disbelief.

"Do . . . do you know her?" Thelvyn asked timorously.

"I do indeed, lad," Sir George said as he dropped down from his saddle. "It's your mother."

Thelvyn swallowed, feeling his heart give a sudden lurch. For the moment, he was too shocked to even know what to think, caught unprepared by this encounter. His mother had died years ago, long before he had been old enough to remember her, and he had never even entertained the fantasy that he would ever meet her. He dropped down from his own saddle, forgetting his horse as he walked over to stand beside Sir George.

The strange woman stopped a few short yards away and extended her hand to him. "Thelvyn?"

He swallowed and nodded, finding himself unable to speak.

"I wish I hadn't been forced to leave you so unprepared," she said softly, her voice rich and warm. "I regret that I haven't been there to protect you from the dragons."

"But you did save me from the dragons, before I was even born," Thelvyn insisted, distressed to witness her remorse.

"You must not fear the dragons so," his mother continued. "They are and will remain your mortal enemies for many years yet to come, and you must guard yourself well. Yet your fate is tied to theirs, and the day will come at last when you will make your peace with them."

"But . . . but who am I?" Thelvyn asked eagerly. "*What* am I? I want to go home."

"I know you do," she said, her voice soft and sad. "I cannot tell you how much I wish I could answer your questions and put your heart at ease. But I dare not, for the truth would be a danger to you if you were to learn it too soon. I can say only one thing to you: You can always trust Sir George, no matter what."

"I don't even know your name!" Thelvyn blurted desperately.

She smiled. "I am Arbendael."

She lifted her arms in a gesture Thelvyn didn't understand. He took a hesitant step toward her, but in the next moment, her form exploded violently outward, abruptly taking on the shape of a vast gold dragon. The horses screamed in terror and thrashed the air with their hooves as the dragon sat up on its haunches, lifting its arms and bending its long neck to stare down at them. Thelvyn responded instinctively, raising his own arms between the threatening dragon and his friends. Then a cold wind swept across the mountainside, shredding the vision of the dragon like tissue to fade into the darkness.

Thelvyn dropped his arms, his heart full of loneliness and regret. He would never know what else she might have said if the dragon spirit hadn't silenced her, although she seemed to have told him all that she could. He hardly noticed as Sir George struggled to calm their frightened horses. Thelvyn stirred at last, hurrying to take Cadence's reins and draw her head down until he could rub her nose to quiet her. At last he turned to the old knight.

"Was that really my mother, or merely a trick of the evil spirits?" he asked.

"I believe it was her," Sir George told him sincerely. "The spirits would have tried to mislead you. Most likely she was able to appear to you because this place is so near a gateway to other realms of existence."

"But my mother didn't speak any known language," Thelvyn protested.

"I don't believe that would be a problem for a ghost," Sir George said. "I know this must have been a shock to you."

"I just never expected . . ." Thelvyn began, staring at the ground. "I . . . I never thought about my mother. I suppose it was best that I never thought about her, since she couldn't be with me. I just never thought she cared."

"Are you all right, lad?" Sir George asked him gently.

"I don't know," he said, shaking his head slowly. "I . . . I just want to be done with this business and leave."

"All right, lad," sir George assured him. "I'll ride ahead with you now. There's no reason for you to be in front alone."

The companions all returned to their saddles, and they continued on their way up the slope. True to his word, Sir George remained at Thelvyn's side, and for a time, the old knight had to keep the horses on the trail. Thelvyn was distracted by his own thoughts. He felt as if he could sit down and cry for an hour, as if all his life was a big, empty hole, and all the things he had ever needed and wanted were things he could never have. He had never allowed himself to miss his mother or feel close to her in any way, and he realized now that he had kept that distance to protect himself from his own loneliness and uncertainty.

But his encounter with his mother had destroyed that barrier, allowing years of fear and loneliness to flood in. Now more than ever he wanted to know who he was, who his mother had been, and why the dragons were so opposed to them. At first he thought he hardly knew any more than he had before, but as he considered, he realized that his mother had told him something very important. The dragons weren't just his mother's enemies, but his own as well.

He eventually became aware that he had been lost in his own thoughts for quite some time. Only then did he realize that the spirits hadn't been harassing their party since the appearance of his mother's spirit, although the trail was steeper and more rugged and the darkness had drawn in about them closer than ever before.

They had come to one of those places he especially disliked, where the road followed a narrow ledge, with the dark stone of the mountain at their left and at their right an abyss of misty blackness illuminated by distant flashes of lightning. To make matters worse, the trail climbed particularly steeply here. Finally he was able to see the end of that section of the path, disappearing into a deep, narrow pass between towering cliffs of black rock.

Thelvyn warned the others to be ready for anything, and they proceeded more slowly. At that very moment, a wind as cold as ice rushed down the steep pass into their faces. The black clouds swirled, and a face larger and more terrifying than any they had yet seen appeared before them. The horses screamed and reared in terror. Thelvyn dared not even look at that monstrous face directly, for only the briefest glance was immensely unsettling, leaving him with confused visions of a gaping mouth filled with dripping fangs and surrounded by writhing tentacles, and great bulging eyes that slowly wept a sickly green fluid. Almost mercifully, it remained half-hidden in the darkness.

"I am the guardian of the palace and the bridge," the apparition declared in a voice that shook the very stone. "Why are you here? You are not even of the people of this land."

Sir George dropped down from his saddle and stepped forward. "Pardon our intrusion, but the Yak Brothers have brought us to this place, and they told us you would already know who we are and why we have come."

"That is so," the guardian agreed. Apparently being direct with a spirit of even this magnitude was permissible. "And who do you pretend to be? I see no one but five fools convinced that all their clever schemes will make them invincible against powers greater than themselves."

"Our world is in danger of an incredible war," the old knight said. "We must at least try."

"Then speak of your own motives," the guardian told him. "You have this boy, and you are convinced that he is the key to unlocking all your mysteries, even though you do not have the smallest clue why."

"He is my heir," Sir George insisted. "I regard him as almost a son."

"Then for the sake of the lad, I will consider your request," the guardian declared. "You desire to make a talisman of the forces of entropy. How is that to be done? Tell me, and then I will tell you if it is within my power to help you."

Now Perrantin came forward. He appeared to be too filled with professional interest to be frightened. "I have in my possession an object, the head of a staff made of a unique metal. If the head of the staff can be taken outside the influences of this world, into the void between the planes, then it will become a gateway of force in itself, to channel and focus the powers of entropy."

The guardian appeared doubtful. "A remarkable notion. How is this supposed to assist you?"

"In my research, I discovered that the elves use an artifact of much the same means to control monsters that stray into their land."

"You seem to be certain of its worth," the guardian said,

still sounding rather doubtful. "Show me this artifact."

Perrantin dropped down from his saddle and rummaged through the contents of his pack. He brought out a small wooden box and opened it with a brass key, then removed a bright red bag of heavy cloth. Then, taking a staff of wood tied to his saddle, he pushed one end into the object hidden inside the cloth bag, obviously reluctant to touch the thing itself. He tapped the other end of the staff against the stone of the path, wedging the head firmly into place. Only then did he remove the bag. Thelvyn saw it for the first time, a casting in dull gray metal of a dragon with glittering eyes of deep sapphire stones. It looked as if it were clinging to the head of the staff, its arms wrapped about the wood and its hands holding a large stone of dull red.

"Allow me to examine this thing," the guardian declared. Perrantin approached cautiously, holding the staff before him. The guardian regarded it only briefly. "The thing you wish can indeed be done. You may approach the bridge."

The guardian retreated into the black clouds, leaving the travelers alone in the dark pass. The mists drew back before them, revealing a broad ledge suspended above an expanse of empty blackness. A small stone fell from the point of the ledge, disappearing into the void.

"Is that all there is to it?" Perrantin asked as they hurried back to their horses. "After coming all this way and all the trouble we've been through, I would have expected a little more of an argument."

"Oh, Perry, do shut up," Sir George told him. He still seemed disgruntled over the hard questions that the guardian had put to him. Then he turned to look at the mage. "What do we do now?"

"I must step out onto the bridge," Perrantin said. "The idea is to hold the thing through the gateway into the realm between planes. All I have to do is hold it over the side of the bridge."

The path led them on through the pass, around one last steep turn, and then out onto a large rocky ledge, leaning well out from the side of the mountain. The path itself led around the back of the ledge and on into unseen heights in the mountain above. On the ledge, a simple stone bridge jutted out into the darkness, disappearing quickly in the clouds. Perrantin left his horse in the middle of the ledge and walked boldly forward to the end of the bridge, carrying the staff before him.

Thelvyn dropped down from his saddle to collect the reins of the mage's horse. When he turned back, he saw Solveig standing nearby, staring nervously into the night. She looked worn, even exhausted. Her eyes were dark with fatigue, and stray hairs were escaping from the loose braid she always wore when traveling.

"Are you all right?" he asked, concerned.

"Just tired of this," she said, then peered at him more closely. "I could ask the same question of you."

Thelvyn smiled uncertainly. "I'll survive. I just feel . . . rather empty just now. You learn how much you value your friends when you don't have anything else."

"We would have never come this far without you," Solveig told him. "The spirits would never have let us through otherwise."

"Do you think so?" he asked. "As frightening as they are, the spirits cannot actually harm anyone."

"Harm anyone?" she asked in disbelief. "The evil spirits that haunt this mountain have been known to tear men apart. The only reason we dared climb this mountain was that Perry believed there was already enough power in his artifact to keep them away. I can't imagine what power you possess that would cause such things to keep their distance."

"How do the Ethengar ever get up here?" Thelvyn asked. "As superstitious as they are, this should scare them to death."

"They trust their shamans," Solveig explained. "Sir George remembered that they never enter the Land of Black Sand without a shaman to guide them. He thinks Sirontai would have reminded us of that, but she probably assumed from the way we were acting that we knew what we were doing."

Perrantin stepped out onto the bridge after hastily consulting his spellbook and a list of last-minute instructions he had tucked inside the cloth bag. He leaned well out over the side of the bridge to stare into the mist. Responding at last to Sir George's urging, he held the staff aloft and recited the final incantation. The others couldn't hear his words, and even the sight of him was indistinct. Then he slowly lowered the staff, holding it as far out over the side of the stone bridge as he could reach.

Lightning flared from the clouds around them, scores of slender white branches snapping and crackling as they reached for the head of the staff. The others turned away, nearly blinded by the flash. Perrantin managed to keep hold of the staff somehow, although even he hadn't expected such a reaction. When he finally brought it back, the large red crystal held by the metal dragon head now glowed pale red in the darkness.

Perrantin was blinking and squinting so much that Sir George had to guide him back to where Thelvyn held his horse. He found the cloth bag and slipped it over the head of the staff without touching it, drawing the strings tight.

"I think that we should get down from this mountain as quickly as we can," Sir George told them. "I don't really want to talk to the guardian again. I suspect that after all of this, we're going to find the Yak Brothers considerably less strange. Thelvyn, you take the lead again."

Thelvyn climbed back into his saddle and moved his horse to the top of the pass, pausing a moment to wait for the others. Once everyone was ready, he led the way down through the long, deep cut of the pass. When Thelvyn looked back, he saw that the narrow pass had mysteriously closed, the two faces of sheer stone now joined together into a single unbroken wall as if it had never stood open. He was still hoping to sight, no matter how fleetingly, the palace of white marble said to stand at the summit of World Mountain.

Then he saw the vague form of a dragon crouching atop the cliff far above them, barely visible through the darkness and the mist. His companions noticed his reaction and stopped their horses. They turned to stare, waiting fearfully for the dragon to attack. Thelvyn realized that this must be a dragon spirit. Although it had been able to dispel the spirit of his mother, it most likely lacked the ability to threaten them as a real dragon could. Since they didn't seem to be in any immediate danger, Sir George urged his companions to continue on.

Thelvyn couldn't help looking back several times until finally they passed beyond the turn in the trail and the dragon disappeared behind them, hidden by the cliff. Surely this had some meaning, but Thelvyn didn't yet know enough about these matters to comprehend the answers. For the moment, he wondered what this spirit dragon had to do with himself and his friends, and whether it would tell the mortal dragons what they had been doing on World Mountain.

CHAPTER THIRTEEN

The companions stayed in the same camp as the
night before, on the bare stony ledge at the base of
the mountain. At least they rested somewhat more
comfortably than they had the previous night. The
black clouds had begun to lift as they came down from the
mountains, so that the sky was clear and the late-afternoon
sun was bright and warm by the time they reached the bottom of the trail. The entire character of the Land of Black
Sand seemed to have changed with the lifting of the clouds,
as if many evil things had gone back to sleep. But it
remained the same desolate, dangerous land, and they
didn't dare stray from the protection of the Yak Brothers.

Their three curious guides were still waiting the next
morning, ready to lead them away from that treacherous
land. But before they could leave, Sir George called a hasty
conference regarding their destination.

"Now that we have the artifact, we have only one task yet
ahead of us," Sir George pointed out. "We need to go find a
dragon. It seems the only question is whether we are ready

to do that at once, or we need to make other plans first."

Perrantin sighed loudly. "After what we've just been through, dealing with a dragon should be easy. What other plans could there be? As far as supplies go, we have enough food and equipment for at least three more weeks. And once we leave the Land of Black Sand, finding grazing for the horses should be easy."

"Then you think that we should go after a dragon immediately?"

"I don't see why not," the mage replied. "And I'm speaking as the fool who has to use the staff against this dragon."

"I agree with the fool," Solveig added. "We know what needs to be done. Let's do it."

Korinn nodded. "Remember also that time does not wait for us, nor will subduing a dragon mean we have won the war. All it means is that we will begin to know how to deal with the dragons. There is much yet to do."

"My thoughts exactly," Sir George agreed. "Thelvyn?"

"I'm still not sure whether it would be wise for me to show myself to a dragon," he admitted reluctantly. "But I suppose that we can decide that when the time comes."

"Then the next problem is deciding where we should look for this dragon," Sir George continued. "Or more specifically, where are we most likely to find a dragon in a situation that would be to our best advantage. I would suggest going back to Torkyn Fall. I suspect the city must have fallen to the dragons some time ago. If that is the case, then we are likely to find a dragon or two standing guard in the larger halls. If we can isolate a dragon underground in a tight space, then it can't fly, it can't move about quickly, and it probably won't dare to use its flames against us. At the same time, there are many smaller passages where we can run and hide if things turn out badly."

Solveig sighed heavily. "Well, I suppose it beats sitting on a hill waiting for a dragon to happen by, then waving our stick at it until it decides to attack. What's the range on that staff, anyway?"

"How should I know?" Perrantin asked. "Relatively short, I would suppose. No more than several yards. Under the circumstances, I agree Torkyn Fall would be best."

"Torkyn Fall lies some five days northwest of here," the old knight said. "Our quickest and easiest way would be to go back west through the northern steppes before swinging around north toward the Wendarian Range."

"We can go northwest of here," Hornhead announced, stepping closer to tower above them all. "With us to keep you safe, we can go around the mountain and travel north and west through the Black Sand, even if that is the longer way. If we leave now, you can camp this night in soft grass."

That was a reasonable suggestion, and one with a distinct advantage. It would save them a day of travel around the edge of the Land of Black Sand. Although it would mean a longer journey across the Black Sand, that wasn't a problem as long as they had the Yak Brothers to guide them and hold the evil creatures and spirits that lurked there at bay.

They had to move along smartly to cross a wide section of the Land of Black Sand in only one day. The Yak Brothers could keep a very quick pace for a long time when they needed to. Even Sir George wasn't certain where they meant to lead the travelers out of the sand, but he suspected they had twenty-five miles ahead of them after they looped around the base of the mountain. It would be a long, hard journey for the horses. The haze once again hung over the land, although the sense of danger was less.

Thelvyn was able to see the edge of the sand and the green grass of the steppes shortly after noon, although it was nearly evening and night was beginning to fall before they reached it. Once again they had to cross a band of pale, stunted grass for about a mile, but that soon gave way to the rich green grass of the steppes, dotted with a sea of small yellow flowers. These flowers were a particular delight to Wobblebelly, who plucked and ate all he could as he trudged on.

They camped that night on the edge of the steppe, tethering their horses to graze to their hearts' content after the short rations of the Land of Black Sand. The next morning, the companions prepared to make the long ride across the northern steppes to the mountains of the Wendarian

Range and Torkyn Fall. Sir George searched the packs for the totem of safe passage. Out of respect for the Ethengar, he had removed the standard from the pole and had put it away to keep it safe. That morning they needed to have a final talk with the Yak Brothers.

"There are no evil creatures in this land, nor along your path," Hornhead reported. "If you are threatened, then we will return. Now we must rest. Although it may not seem so, we have done great magic in your protection."

"We have some idea of what you have done for us," Sir George insisted. "We are indeed grateful."

"We cannot help you when you leave the steppes, for this is our land and the northern mountains are not," Hornhead continued. "But if things go badly and the dragons pursue you, then you must return to the steppes. The good spirits of this land will do what we can to help you."

They finished packing, and the Yak Brothers stood and watched quietly as they rode away. When the travelers looked back, they were gone.

Their ride across the northern steppes was uneventful. They saw riders of the Ethengar on a couple of occasions, once on each of the first two days of their journey, although the riders always respected the authority of their totem of safe conduct and kept their distance. Once they crossed the Streel River and came closer to the great mountains of the eastern Wendarian Range, they saw no one else. The inhabitants of that region appeared to have withdrawn completely.

As they approached the mountains, the steppes became more rugged, the hills rising and falling in great, rolling swells and troughs. In such places, they weren't able to see for any distance to search for dangers except when they came to the tops of hills. At least the hills weren't so high or steep that they had to go around them, and they continued to make good time. There was more than enough rich grazing for the horses, so they were able to save their limited supply of fodder for the journey ahead. There was also an abundance of water from the many cold, clear streams coming down from the heights.

As the mountains grew steadily closer each day, Thelvyn

began to think more and more about the confrontation that lay ahead. He was able to see dragons passing along the length of the Wendarian Range long before the others, even when they were still more than a day out in the steppes. He wasn't certain, since they were approaching from a different direction, but the mountains of the Three Fires and Torkyn Fall appeared to be a particularly busy area for dragons. After seeing a third dragon approach the area, he wondered if perhaps the city of the gnomes had not yet fallen after all. He also wondered if there might be too many dragons nearby for them to hope to be able to isolate one in order to subdue it.

Even so, the matter of subduing a dragon wasn't Thelvyn's only concern. He was anxious about what his own part in all of this would be. Also on his mind were his mother and her last battle with the red dragons, a battle she had won at the cost of her life. He was afraid the dragons of Torkyn Fall would recognize him. He couldn't forget the spirit dragon that had watched him at World Mountain. And he realized that the last thing he needed was to have the wrath of the dragons turned into a relentless hunt to destroy him. Although his mother might have been a sorceress powerful enough to fight an entire band of dragons, he knew that his own magical skills were still quite limited.

"Why are you looking so worried?" Solveig asked, bringing her horse close beside his. "Are you thinking about the dragons again?"

"I keep thinking about that spirit dragon on World Mountain and how it chased away my mother's spirit, then watched us go down the mountain. I'm sure it recognized me. I was wondering if the mortal dragons will recognize me as well."

"That's not exactly the same thing," Solveig told him. "Spirits have ways of knowing things. They ask other spirits, or they look into your thoughts. That's what I think the guardian did to you and Sir George. The dragons we'll meet now might be big and powerful, but they're still mortal beings.

"But these dragons have a reason to know me," he pointed out.

"I believe that you are correct in wanting to keep yourself hidden from the dragons," Solveig said. "There will be no reason for you to show yourself. Perry and Sir George will handle the task of subduing a dragon with the artifact. The rest of us will simply be there to keep watch."

Just when Thelvyn had come to the conclusion that his lost heritage might be something he would prefer not to know, his past suddenly seemed to be thrusting itself before him. He had decided that he wouldn't show himself to the dragons, but he couldn't escape the feeling that he would soon learn something he would rather not know.

He tried to put such thoughts out of his mind, suspecting he would only succeed in frightening himself. Surely Perrantin and Sir George would just have their little chat with a dragon and they would be on their way again. The dragon would never even know Thelvyn had been there. And just as surely, the mystery of his origins and his curious tie with the dragons had a simple, logical explanation. He reminded himself that he had never been very impressed with his obscure past when he had been younger, so there was hardly any reason to imagine all sorts of strange things now.

They headed almost due north toward the mountains now. Although they still rode the grass-covered hills of the steppes, the land was beginning to rise steadily, coming almost abruptly to the wooded foothills and lower slopes of the Wendarian Range. Sir George and Solveig, plotting the path between them, had brought the company almost exactly to the rugged road leading down from Torkyn Fall. They came to the woods just in time, for shortly thereafter a party of three red dragons flew slowly along the lower slopes of the mountains, as if scouting the southern boundaries of the Wendarian Range. If the travelers had still been out in the steppes, only a few miles away, they almost certainly would have been seen.

Sir George brought them to a stop only a couple of miles after the road began the climb into the foothills. They made their camp a little early that night, choosing a place among the trees and boulders that was sheltered from sight even from directly above. Then Sir George removed the totem of safe conduct from its pole and carefully put it away in one of the packs. They checked the condition of their gear and their mounts, making certain all the horses still had their shoes firmly in place now that they had left behind the soft grass of the steppes for the hard stone of the mountains. Finally Sir George called them all together to discuss their plan for approaching the city of the gnomes.

"We can't just ride up to the main gate," he reminded them. "That was dangerous enough the last time we were here, and then we had a late-winter storm to drive the dragons into shelter and conceal our approach."

Solveig considered that briefly. "Our only hope is to find some way into the city and back out again that the dragons don't know about. I've been thinking about this, and I believe that our only hope is to go back into Torkyn Fall the same way we came out the last time we were here. The hidden ravine allows us to stay under cover for the last few miles of our approach. It's a gate the dragons might not know about, and it's too small for them to use."

"That was the only thing I could think of," Sir George agreed.

"We can't very well enter there with all of our horses," she added. "They'd just slow us down through the ravine anyway. I suggest we make a hidden camp somewhere below and leave the horses and most of our gear behind, with one or two of us there to stand guard. The rest will go on up and enter the city. If we get into trouble and have to make a quick retreat, the ravine may save us once again."

"Won't the retreat be dangerous under any circumstances?" Thelvyn asked. "We might be safe enough as long as the dragon is subdued, but we have to leave quickly, and we can't take him with us. Will he honor the terms of his truce and keep his peace once we're no longer there to enforce it?"

"Draconic law is very tricky on that account," Sir George said. "A dragon who has been subdued will usually, when freed, withdraw peacefully, although he'll most likely bide his time until he can get his revenge. But keep in mind that we have a weapon with the power to subdue a dragon. By definition, that means it also has the power to kill a dragon. I expect the dragons are all going to respect that, and we can successfully fight our way out if we must. Does that suit you, Perry?"

Perrantin shrugged helplessly. "I have nothing to say. Just find me a dragon and get me close enough to do my job. I leave it to you to find a way to get me out again."

"Who stays behind to guard the horses?" Korinn asked.

"Perry has to go in, and I suppose that I should," Sir George said. "And I would prefer that Solveig goes with us, to help get us in and out through that ravine."

"I can stay behind to guard the camp," Thelvyn said. "I need to keep my distance from the dragons anyway."

"And I will stay," Korinn added. "I'm not built for climbing. And you may think me a fool, but I haven't the heart to look upon the destruction of Torkyn Fall."

"I understand," Sir George agreed. "I'm not looking forward to seeing it myself. But if you think you can watch the camp alone, I would prefer to take Thelvyn with us."

"I could be a danger to you," Thelvyn said.

"I don't believe you will put us in any more danger than we will find for ourselves," the old knight told him. "I agree that you shouldn't show yourself to any dragons we encounter, but I think you should be there just the same. Your past and possibly your future are irrevocably tied to the dragons, and this seems a good time to begin looking for some answers. But I leave that entirely to your judgment."

Thelvyn glanced down and sighed. "You're right. Caution tells me to stay behind, but I must know. Someday I want to be able to go home, no matter what my true home may be."

Perhaps if they had known Torkyn Fall better, they could have made better plans, but they were fairly satisfied with what they had. The most dangerous part of their journey would follow next, for they would need to follow the road for the better part of a day to reach the place where they would make their camp. The ride would be much as the one before, staying as much as they could near the shelter of the cliffs and boulders whenever a dragon approached. During their last visit, these heights had still been locked in the last days of winter. Now it was spring, even if it was still much cooler than it had been in the steppes below and occasional patches of snow remained in the deepest pockets between the rocks. The hardy grasses and mosses were green, bringing out tiny flowers of white, yellow, and delicate pink.

But the only dragons they saw now seemed to be on business of their own, moving either east or west along the Wendarian Range. Flying alone or in small groups, the dragons soared with long, slow sweeps of their broad wings just high enough to avoid the worst of the tricky winds that swept down from the heights. They certainly didn't appear to be on patrol, since they flew in a straight path and hardly ever looked down. Indeed, there didn't seem to be any scouts in the area of Torkyn Fall, either in the air or watching from some high peak or ledge. That seemed to suggest that the city of the gnomes had already fallen, perhaps some time ago. It was even possible the dragons had already abandoned Torkyn Fall, turning their attention to other concerns.

The travelers were able, without much difficulty, to find the trail leading down from the main road into the ravine. Thelvyn at least remembered the place well from their last visit. He could see the high ledge where the sleeping dragon had lain in ambush. He looked down and saw the narrow path at the base of the cliff where he had led the horses. They led their horses down to the same path, feeling somewhat better now that they were no longer out in the open. The best place to establish a camp where they could leave the packs and horses turned out to be right there, in the dense pine woods that filled the ravine at the path's lower end. The stream bubbled loudly over the well-worn boulders as it rushed through the middle of the stand of trees, the sound hiding most of the normal noises made by the horses.

The snow of a storm had still been deep in the bottom of the ravine when they had been here before, and Thelvyn was able to see the surface of the ravine better now. One thing he hadn't noticed before, which might prove especially useful now, was that the trail continued downward along the ravine. While it slanted away from the main road, it must lead somewhere. At least it was headed in the right direction to take them all the way down from the mountains. If they needed to stay under cover to make their retreat, he wondered if they might chance going that way.

They spent the night in camp, for it was already late. The next morning they made their final arrangements. All those who would be going on dressed in dark clothes to hide them in the poorly lit corridors of the gnomish city. They either left behind or concealed everything they were carrying that was made of metal so it wouldn't glint or make any sound. Then Sir George left his final instructions with Korinn. They would try to time their return to coincide with nightfall, so that they would be making their retreat from Torkyn Fall under the cover of darkness. The dwarf would saddle their horses and have everything ready to go by that time, sooner if the dragons were making a fuss.

The others started up the narrow valley to the hidden gate of Torkyn Fall. The distance wasn't great, not more than five miles, although it had seemed much farther the first time. Even though they tried not to hurry, they reached the gate by noon. There was no mistaking the place. They all remembered it well enough, a short cave in the back of an overhang of gray stone surrounded by large boulders. Sir George went in to look about. After a minute, he called for Thelvyn to bring him a magical light. They came back out again soon, looking perplexed.

"Now what? Has the gate been destroyed?" Solveig asked, already convinced there was trouble. There was no sign that the dragons had attacked or even discovered this gate. Then she realized what the problem must be. "Did you forget how to open the gate?"

"There *is* no way to open this gate from the outside," Sir George reported rather sourly. "This is an escape tunnel. The gnomes intended that there should be no way to open it from the outside, to discourage thieves who might discover their secrets. That's the part I forgot."

Solveig rolled her eyes. "Oh, for pity's sake! Among your many talents, you're supposed to be a skilled thief. Can't you find a latch?"

"What do you suppose I've been trying to do?" Sir George asked peevishly. "I know the gnomish designs. The trouble with a one-way door, at least from a thief's point of view, is that it can indeed be built with no way to open it from the outside."

"Then what do you suggest?" she asked. "Are we stuck?"

"No . . . we just need to go up to the main gate," he explained. "We shouldn't have any trouble there."

"Ho! Any trouble with the locks, you mean."

"Of course not, because I suspect that the dragons have long since broken open the gate. But I don't expect to find dragons there, if that's what you have in mind. They own this place now, and only an idiot would show himself at the main gate."

"Then by all means, that sounds like just the place for us," Solveig said dryly.

They began the long, slow climb up the steep slope of the narrow valley above the overhang. The way was difficult enough at first, since they had to make their way through a maze of massive boulders, stunted trees, and brush. The cliff became almost sheer near the top, and they had a difficult time pulling themselves up the rocky face. Sir George had to switch to one of his sturdier hooks, afraid that he might bend or even break the more delicate one he usually wore. The climb was even harder on Perrantin, who was more a scholar than an adventurer. But at last they reached the top, and they were surprised to find themselves on the wide landing before the main gate of Torkyn Fall. They knew they had walked for what seemed like a very great distance to reach the hidden gate from the inside, and therefore they expected the two gates to be at least a mile or two apart.

The main gate of Torkyn Fall had indeed been forced. The dragons had ripped apart the brittle stone of the cliff until they had been able to get at the frame of the massive sliding door of steel, and in a display of almost unbelievable strength, they had ripped the entire gate out of the side of the mountain and tossed it aside. That answered any questions they may have had about whether or not the city of the gnomes had fallen. The only question that remained was whether or not there were any dragons inside. They moved quickly to the ruined gate, fearful of staying out in the open.

Sir George stepped a few feet inside, then paused. "Does it smell strange in here, or is it just me?"

"It's just you, George," Solveig told him, putting on one of her most innocent faces.

They all stepped inside, having determined that there weren't any dragons lurking about just inside the door. There were a great many places to hide in the various storerooms and stalls within the massive chamber, which served as the underground stable for the city. None, however, could have hidden even a very small dragon. The animals were all gone, and there was nothing left behind except a couple of small carts. If Sir George had smelled something, it might well have been this place. But there was no sign of a battle to be seen, except for the wreckage at the main gate. Perhaps there had been no one left to defend the gate. Either the gnomes had been able to complete their evacuation, or else they had followed Sir George's advice and had barricaded themselves in the remote passages.

"I wonder if the dragons are here after all," Solveig said. "Some of the lighting globes are still working."

"I'm afraid that doesn't mean anything," Sir George told her. "The gnomes have machines to maintain the magic to operate many of their devices. The lights are still burning in most of their abandoned cities, and they will continue to do so for centuries."

If the dragons had been here, they hadn't ravaged the place as Thelvyn would have expected. Torkyn Fall was more than a series of great caverns, as were most of the cities of the gnomes and the dwarves. Many smaller chambers and passages had been excavated in the soft volcanic stone. For that reason, there weren't many places a creature the size of a dragon could have gone, even a small dragon. About the only part of the city open to them was the sequence of main chambers, a group of vast rooms and wide passages laid out in a straight line leading directly into the heart of the great plateau, the innermost being the

Chamber of the Fall. Perhaps the dragons looked through the few places open to them and then left. If there were even one dragon left, there weren't many places where it could be.

"Quiet now," Sir George warned the others. "If I were a dragon, I'd move all the way to the back. Not only is the Chamber of the Fall the most interesting place to take up residence, but the fall also keeps it fresh and cool there."

"Don't dragons like to be warm?" Thelvyn asked.

Sir George shook his head. "Dragons were born to ride the winds, which is usually quite a cold proposition. And such a large, active creature usually has no trouble retaining its own heat. You know from legends that all dragons spend much of their time in their lairs, some cool place underground, out of the sun. Not a word now."

As they moved deeper through the passages, Thelvyn was soon able to see that Torkyn Fall had suffered considerably from the attacks of the dragons. He was reminded of the last intense assault, which had begun even as they escaped into the morning, with dragons flying over the plateau to strike again and again with great, rumbling, lightninglike flashes. The fragile volcanic stone of the plateau hadn't been able to withstand such an attack; there had been deep cracks in the walls or cutting across the corridors even during their last visit.

Now, however, the damage was much worse. The sequence of main chambers seemed to have fared well enough, since those places had already been heavily braced with massive beams and columns to support the delicate native stone. But new cracks had opened in the stone between the beams, and small portions of the walls and ceiling had broken loose. The side passages, most of which had been thought too small to require extra support, had taken the worst damage. A few they passed had collapsed altogether. The lights remained in working order, but enough had been destroyed that the corridors were darker and gloomier than ever. Curiously the debris in the main passages had mostly been pushed or swept into piles in the dark corners, although the smaller corridors had been left as they were. That suggested the dragons had been coming in here often enough to want to clean up the place.

They weren't far from the end of the sequence of main chambers, and it seemed that if they were going to find dragons at all, it would be exactly where Sir George had predicted they would. As a precaution, he led his companions up into the gallery, approaching the Chamber of the Fall from above the lower level. The relatively high, massive stone rail that lined the gallery walkways would offer them some protection, both from sight during their approach and from attack if things went wrong.

At least the fall itself was still there. They could hear its dim thunder through the passages from some distance away. Thelvyn recalled his first visit to this place—Korinn's enthusiasm for the Chamber of the Fall, the dwarf teaching him to yodel in the ringing echoes of the hall. When he peered cautiously over the top of the rail, he could see that the Chamber of the Fall had fared well. There was only slight damage. The fall still held its course, its icy mountain water cascading in a narrow ribbon cloaked in its own cold mist, and the great pool below still held its proper level. The only real difference was that there were two red dragons sleeping on the tiled floor beyond the pool, a large male and a female.

Thelvyn fearfully drew back from the ledge, retreating into the deeper shadows of the passage behind him. He had never been so near to a living dragon in his life, and the sight of these two creatures aroused his instinctive fears. He was glad that for once it wouldn't be his responsibility to go in the lead.

Perrantin sat on the floor with his back against the stone rail. He removed the cloth bag covering the head of the staff. The red stone held by the dragon figure cast a dull, even baleful glow, and the sapphire eyes shone with a light of their own. "I suppose I might just as well get this over with before they wake up."

"Can we take them both on at once?" Sir George asked.

"I'm not sure it makes much difference," the mage insisted. "If we subdue the first, the second is going to be impressed. They don't have much room to fight. Besides, we don't have much choice, do we? If we wait to see if one might leave, we only run the risk of being discovered."

"True enough," Sir George agreed. "Thelvyn, be ready to get us out of here, since you're the only one who can see well in the dark. But don't show yourself to the dragons for anything."

Perrantin and Sir George made their way cautiously behind the rail to their left until they came to the wide stairs against the far wall of the chamber. They took each step cautiously, moving quietly but slowly, the mage holding the staff before him. Thelvyn and Solveig watched from their place of concealment on the ledge above, almost more frightened than if they were facing the dragons themselves. They could only wait, their hearts and stomachs fluttering with fear, knowing only too well that there was precious little they could do to help if things turned out badly.

The nearest of the two dragons, the large male, lay just beyond the bottom of the steps, its long neck stretched out so that its nose lay only a few yards from the lower end of the stairs. After a time, Perrantin paused long enough to gesture to Sir George to remain behind before he continued on alone. Thelvyn smiled to himself; the courage of the mage was boundless, and all the more surprising because he didn't look especially brave. But the dragon became aware of its visitors even while they were still on the steps, lifting its great head to stare at them.

"What do you want here?" it asked at last. "The gnomes have gone, and they took the better part of their treasure with them."

"We've come to ask you a few questions," Perrantin declared, trying to sound bold without being offensive. "I prefer that you simply tell us what we want to know, but I'm prepared to use this artifact of entropy against you. Then we'll be on our way."

The dragon rolled its eyes and sighed loudly, as if beseeching the dragon god for patience. "I'm afraid you will have to show me this artifact."

"Well, I tried to warn you," Perrantin declared.

With that, he took four quick steps forward and touched the dragon on the end of the nose with the head of the staff. There was a small flash of blue-white light, but it wasn't very impressive at all. The dragon drew back its head in alarm, twitched its nose a couple of times, then drew a deep breath and sneezed. Perrantin looked at his staff in dismay, realizing that it didn't have nearly enough power to defeat a dragon. Thelvyn's heart sank as he realized they were in terrible trouble. They could hardly hope to sneeze a dragon into submission.

"This is going to be one of those days," Perrantin said to himself as he handed the staff of Sir George. "Time for Plan Number Two."

While the dragon was still shaking its head, the mage reached into his pockets and removed a scrap of white cloth and a small bottle of brown glass. Thelvyn thought he recognized the bottle containing the potion that induced hypnotic control. When the dragon brought its head down to glare at its two adversaries, Perrantin tossed the rag directly into its face, hitting it once again on the end of the nose. The dragon straightened, got a very surprised expression on its face, then settled itself to the floor and lay perfectly still, staring aimlessly.

Mage Perrantin had actually managed to subdue a dragon, though not by the method he had expected to use. If they had known this would work, they might have tried it sooner. However, having a dragon and being able to hold it weren't the same thing. The other dragon roared a furious challenge and gathered itself to spring to the attack. Sir George and the mage had already turned to run for their lives.

"Quick, back to the main gate!" Sir George declared loudly just before he and Perrantin disappeared into the dark passages beneath the gallery.

Solveig and Thelvyn understood that the warning had been meant for them, and they began their own retreat into the darkened corridor behind the gallery, which ran directly above the passage their companions were in. The second dragon saw their movement and leapt into battle. Standing with its forelegs braced against the rail, which collapsed beneath its weight, it thrust its head down the passage after them. The corridor was wide enough to admit its head and most of its long neck. Fortunately they had already moved beyond reach. Thelvyn ran as fast as he could, suddenly terrified that the dragon was going to fill the tunnel with flame.

But the corridor proved to be too confining for it to draw a breath to bring its natural weapons to bear. It roared again, this time in fury and frustration, and its struggles brought the weakened ceiling down on its head. The brittle stone, already weakened by the attacks on the underground city, suddenly began to collapse in dusty rubble. The dragon escaped injury, but it would take several moments to get free.

Thelvyn and Solveig came to another length of open gallery and a flight of steps leading down, where they found the others waiting for them.

"I feared you were dead!" Sir George declared when he saw them.

"You wish!" Solveig answered as she and Thelvyn rushed down the steps. "Then you wouldn't have to pay me."

"You're not getting paid for this anyway," the old knight reminded her, which caused her to stop a moment and swear colorfully. He ignored her. "We have to find a passage leading to the hidden gate."

"You said to head for the main gate," Thelvyn reminded him.

"That was just what I wanted the dragon to think," he explained.

They ran desperately. The first dragon was going to be out of the fight for the next hour, and for the moment its rather unresponsive bulk was going to be in the way. But the second dragon would free itself soon enough, and it would be following them in full fury at any moment. They urgently needed to find a side corridor they recognized and disappear before it came up close enough behind them to observe where they had gone. What they hadn't counted upon was a third dragon coming at them from the other direction, catching them in the middle.

This dragon was even larger than the other two, so large that its folded wings only barely fit through the tight passage between chambers. It was right in the middle of that passage when they first saw it, and they had no hope of trying to get past it at the moment. It came on even quicker when it saw them, eager to reach an open area where it could fight. It came quickly into the large open chamber and rose to sit up on its haunches in the entrance of the passage, guarding the only way out of the chamber.

Then it paused, staring almost in disbelief. It brought its head forward until it was peering down at Thelvyn almost eye to eye, too close for either of them to see the other clearly. Thelvyn leapt back, so overwhelmed by his instinctive terror of dragons that he felt faint. The dragons had found him and recognized him as their enemy, and he didn't doubt his life could be measured in a few brief moments. Then the dragon drew back its head slightly and appeared startled, even profoundly surprised. It looked across at the dark corridor beyond.

"The Prophecy!" it cried. "The ordained one is alive! The Prophecy may yet be fulfilled!"

"Kill him!" the female dragon shouted from the distant corridor, and its form appeared suddenly out of the darkness. "Kill him now!"

"I have them trapped," the other dragon said, then looked down. This time its attention was directed at Sir George. "Traitor, what is your part in this? Do not pretend you are bringing him to us."

"I'm sure that I don't know what you mean, and that's the honest truth," Sir George insisted, sounding very sincere. "I've never heard of any Prophecy."

"Fool!" the dragon hissed at him, then it turned its gaze back to Thelvyn. "I will kill you now, and the Prophecy will die with you."

The large red dragon held its flame, knowing that to use it in such close quarters might prove disastrous for them all. Instead it darted its great head forward to crush its prey. At the same instant, Sir George suddenly changed shape in a rapid blurring, and in his place stood a drake, like a small tan dragon on powerful hind legs, clearly capable of speed afoot as well as in flight. But this drake would never fly again, for he was missing the end of his left wing. The drake drew himself together and then launched himself. His leap carried him over Thelvyn, to crash heavily into the dragon's long nose.

Sir George wasn't much larger as a dragon than he was as a man, so his attack was hardly devastating. A drake lacked the breath weapons of a true dragon, and his small fangs were incapable of piercing the red dragon's stout armor. The dragon shook its head violently, tossing Sir George forcefully aside against the stone wall of the chamber. But at that moment, Thelvyn attacked. No matter how surprised he was at the transformation, he knew that the old knight had attacked the dragon to save him. Reacting in fury, unaware of what he was doing, he raised his arms and stepped forward. The dragon swung around to face him, and their gazes locked, holding each other for a moment. Suddenly the red dragon froze, trapped by some hypnotic spell.

Thelvyn turned then to face the female dragon, but it hesitated and drew back into the shadows, unsure of the situation. That allowed the companions a moment to regroup. Solveig hurried to help Sir George pick himself up from the floor. He moved a little slowly at first, and then, regaining his senses, he suddenly returned to his usual form. Thelvyn could see from their reactions that the other members of their company had already known that Sir George was a secretly a mandrake. For a moment, Thelvyn felt suspicious of the old knight, who as a dragon-kin was closely related to his mortal enemies. But Thelvyn recalled that his mother had told him he could trust Sir George no matter what, and nothing had ever shown him otherwise.

Sir George was badly shaken, and for the moment, Thelvyn assumed command of their company, sending the others ahead to slip around the bulk of the stunned dragon into the corridor behind it. He stayed behind, never taking his eyes from the female dragon as it glared at him from the deep shadows of the opposite corridor. For the moment, his presence was all that kept the dragon from attacking. It recognized and feared him, even if he didn't know why.

Stepping backward, Thelvyn slipped into the tight space between the stunned dragon and the wall of the passage, then turned and ran after his companions. The immobile dragon made a very effective barrier to block the passage of the female, allowing them all time to retreat. Now that the moment of desperation had passed, Thelvyn began to realize what he had just done. What he couldn't begin to understand was how he could have done such things, for his command of magic didn't begin to give him such great powers. He was becoming very afraid, this time of himself.

After several moments, they reached the next large chamber, one that had previously served as a market square. There was a gallery on the second level, and both levels served as the intersection of several corridors. Now at least they knew where they were. The largest of the corridors to their right led to the inner chambers, and eventually to the secret gate. Thelvyn turned when they reached the center of the chamber, facing back toward the dark main passage they had just left, and again he raised his arms. A nearly invisible shield of force surrounded him, glowing slightly in the darkness, and a spear of lightning leapt out to strike the ceiling. The fragile stone crumbled and collapsed, filling the opening.

"That should hold them awhile, although not as long as I'd like," Sir George said. "The passage is so tight they won't have any way to clear it except to force their heads through the rubble."

"How long will they be under?" Solveig asked.

"The one Perrantin put down should stay under for the better part of an hour, the same as anyone," he replied. "The lad used a spell of holding against the other, a spell that isn't supposed to work against anything as large as a dragon in the first place. He might break it himself soon, or else the female will do it for him."

"Do we go out by the main gate now?" Perrantin asked. "We could be out of the city altogether before those brutes break loose."

"No, the secret gate is still our best bet," Sir George said. "We need to throw them off our trail, and we need the cover of the ravine to make our retreat."

He turned to Thelvyn, who seemed too stunned from all that had happened to know what else to do, at least until he had a chance to make some sense of it all. For a moment, the old knight looked very sad, knowing that he seemed to have betrayed a trust. He regretted it now far more than he would have ever anticipated when this had all begun more than seventeen years earlier.

"Come on, lad," he said. "We have to get the others out of this terrible place. Then we'll have a long talk about everything that just happened."

CHAPTER FOURTEEN

Sir George didn't realize why it might not be a good idea to seek the secret gate until it was too late to go back for fear the dragons had freed themselves. Torkyn Fall had taken quite a pounding during the siege, and a number of the passages had collapsed. He recalled how close the hidden door was to the main gate. If the long final corridor to the secret gate had been blocked, there was no other way around. They would have no choice but to go back and take their chances with the dragons.

The passage had indeed suffered some damage, and the lights were nearly out altogether. But the way remained open, and they found the inner chamber and the hidden gate at last. Sir George released the lock and the latches, checking a final time to be certain there were no outside latches he had missed. Then he pushed open the heavy door, which was shaped somewhat like a cork, with the narrower end inside so that it couldn't be rammed open from the outside if it were discovered. Solveig and Thelvyn went out first, watching and listening for any hint of the dragons, but the way was clear. If the dragons had freed themselves, perhaps they were searching the road for any sign of their prey.

Still, Thelvyn had to wonder where that third dragon had come from, whether it had come from outside when it heard the calls of the others or if it had been somewhere in the inner chambers and they had missed it in the dark. He wondered if they were indeed the only three dragons on guard at Torkyn Fall, or if more were hidden somewhere above, in the ridges and peaks. On second thought, that hardly seemed to matter much. He had seen dragons moving along the Wendarian Range for the last three days, so he knew more could be called to the hunt on short notice. Their only hope now was to get away as quickly as possible.

The best they could do was to follow the path along the bottom of the ravine until they reached their camp, five miles or more before they even rejoined Korinn and their horses. Thelvyn had remained calm through everything that had occurred, keeping his mind tightly focused on the matter at hand. He dared not even think yet of what had happened with the dragons, knowing he could be too easily distracted trying to figure it all out. At least one of the greatest questions of his life had been answered; the dragons did indeed know him, and they wouldn't hesitate to kill him on sight. But he still had no idea who he was, and now he had the new mystery of the Prophecy to occupy him.

Night was beginning to fall by the time they reached their camp, and it had been growing dark down in the depths of the ravine for some time. Korinn had saddled the horses and loaded the packs well in time for their return, in anticipation for the need of a quick retreat.

"What did you learn?" the dwarf asked.

"We learned never to try that again," Sir George said, glancing about. "I suppose we should return to the road and do the best we can to get down from the heights under cover of night. I don't much like our chances, I have to admit."

"Neither do I," Thelvyn added. "I noticed earlier that the trail continues on down the valley past the point where it joins the road. I suppose it must lead somewhere. I wonder if we'd do better to stay in the cover of the valley, even though it will be harder and take longer."

"That would probably be best," the old knight agreed. "Even if the trail leaves us somewhere in the wilderness, we would still be better off than trying to follow the road. Our previous assumption that the protection of the staff would be enough to see us down from the mountains seems to have been very much in error. Thelvyn, do you feel able to take the lead with Korinn and keep watch at night?"

"I'm not having any problems," he insisted.

They soon had reason to be glad they chose not to follow the road. Within an hour, just after darkness was complete, Thelvyn saw the dark shape of a dragon following the road behind them, making a quick sweep to check for any sign of their retreat. Half an hour later he saw two more dragons, this time making their way swiftly back up the road toward Torkyn Fall. Fortunately the narrow valley turned away somewhat to the west, while the road itself continued to follow the higher ground due south, for very soon after that they began to see distant flashes of flames. Thelvyn was reminded of how the old forester had told him of the deadly hunt of the dragons for his mother, and the flashes of fire in the mountains in an attempt to drive her from hiding. He realized that the dragons of Torkyn Fall were trying to do the same thing now.

Eventually they began to feel safer, for their path continued to lead them to the southwest, leaving the flashes of flame far behind them. As they had expected, this path was difficult to follow, often stony or steep, so that in places they were compelled to dismount and lead their horses through the worst of it. The valley widened out after several miles into a shallow trough.

The valley no longer offered the same degree of protection it had when they had been able to count upon the dark depths of the ravine to shelter them. There were occasional stands of trees where they could have taken the horses if danger had drawn near, but they were farther apart than they would have liked. They were still high up in the rocky, windswept heights, and trees grew here only in the more protected places. They relied upon Thelvyn to watch the night sky and warn them of approaching danger. After a time, Sir George came up to ride beside him.

"You seem to be taking it well," the old knight observed.

"It's all a bit confusing yet," Thelvyn admitted. "I knew from what my mother's ghost told me that I had some deep ties to the dragons. Perhaps because of that, I was a good deal better prepared than I would have been."

"You must be bursting with questions just the same."

He shrugged. "I suppose I am, but I thought they should wait for some better time. I realize now that the others already knew you were a drake, and that satisfied me. I hope you don't blame me for being more interested in my secrets than your own."

Sir George smiled. "This seems like a good enough time to talk about my secrets. I know the answers to mine. Your secrets will require a little more study."

"You've always been somewhat of a mystery to me, and I've accepted that," Thelvyn said. "But how much of what I know is true?"

"All of it, I expect," he said. "I'm older than I look—well past two hundred, in fact, although that's not old for a drake. And I really was a knight of Darokin. Twice, in fact, under different names."

"I remember the story you told Kalestraan about the knight who was secretly a mandrake," Thelvyn said. "I realized last night that you must have been talking about yourself."

"That's true," Sir George agreed. "And you might recall what I said about drakes, most of them being rather shy, unambitious sorts. I'm afraid I'm not at all typical of my kind. I began commonly enough as a drake, having trained to be a thief of considerable talent. That was what pointed me toward my present business as a trader in antiquities, for such things interested me. I'm not sure now just what started me in that direction, but I decided I wanted to be a knight. I changed my identity and managed to get myself taken on as a squire, and I was a real knight soon enough. It was a grand time, and the life suited me. I love traveling about and doing things."

"Why did you give it up?" Thelvyn asked.

"Well, I didn't want to," he admitted. "But I had been at it for forty years or so, and people began to wonder why I didn't appear to be getting older. I had to disappear for a while, so I went into the antiquities business for a time. That was when I began my study of dragons, since they were another of my special interests. I've even known a few dragons in my time. But I wasn't yet finished being a knight, so after a good many years, I went back to Darokin and established my new identity, the person you know me as now. I really did lose my hand in honorable combat, and that forced me to turn back to my business as a trader in antiquities. That was seventy years ago, by the way."

"But you said you used to know some dragons?" Thelvyn asked.

"That I did, more than a hundred years ago. They move around quite a lot. I wouldn't know where to begin looking for the ones I knew, and I expect that it wouldn't be safe to try. It was the dragons that first taught me magic, which isn't typical for a drake."

"You seem to think very highly of them," Thelvyn said. "You always have."

"I suppose," he admitted. "Dragons can be the grandest, most noble, most wonderful creatures in all the world, although I expect that you don't really want to meet them. It's really a shame that circumstances have made you enemies."

Thelvyn was becoming aware of the divided loyalties that haunted the old knight. Sir George was caught between his native devotion to dragons, who were his kin and whom he admired for the wisdom and nobility he saw in them, and his pledge as a knight to protect all innocent folk from danger—even dragons. Thelvyn realized that Sir George was motivated to find a way to turn them from their evil deeds, even to protect them from themselves. But he also knew, beyond all doubt, that there was still too much of the devoted knight in Sir George to allow his fancies to interfere with his duty. He would fight the dragons, if it came to that.

"You didn't want me to know just yet?" he asked.

"Actually, I had been thinking it was about time," Sir

George said. "I hadn't wished to keep such a secret from you. But dragons killed your mother, and they would just as willingly kill you, so I knew you have no reason to like anything about them."

"The dragon called you a traitor," Thelvyn observed. "Have you betrayed your duty to the Nation of Dragons?"

"No, not according to the letter of draconic law," Sir George replied. "But I suppose the red dragons assume I should have turned you over to them long ago, befitting my station as a humble drake. Well, how was I supposed to know? That spares me any guilt in the matter."

"I wouldn't want you getting into trouble with the dragons on my account," Thelvyn told him.

Sir George laughed to himself. "I can get into quite enough trouble with the dragons on my own account."

They came farther that night than they had expected, for after midnight the trail turned toward the south to lead them quickly down toward the wooded lower slopes, where they would be safe. It had been a long day and night for them all. For the last two or three hours, Korinn had been entirely dependent upon Thelvyn to find their way in the darkness, for it was all the dwarf could do to stay in his saddle. Thelvyn was holding up very well.

Dawn was about to break when they at last came down into the heavier pine forests, where they were reasonably safe at last. Much to their surprise, they suddenly came upon shelter, a hut tucked in among the trees, complete with crude stables for the horses. They realized it must be a way station built by the gnomes, located a long day's ride from the gate of Torkyn Fall.

Once he had helped to tend the horses, Thelvyn ate for the first time since the morning before, and then he slept for the first time since the night before that. He dreamt that night of dragons, of running through the mountains while flames leapt around him. When he awoke that evening, he found that most of his companions shared his disgruntled mood. Perrantin looked especially annoyed; he was sitting on the stones beside the fireplace, staring at his beloved staff of entropy. Solveig looked as if she had been drinking too much and was trying to deal with the effects. Sir

George wasn't even in the cabin, and Korinn was his usual quiet self. He hadn't been inside Torkyn Fall.

Sir George came in after a moment, closing the simple wooden door behind him. "The world is full of dragons. Our three friends are hard at work, and they seem to have called in the troops. I wouldn't be surprised if there were three dozen dragons out there."

"That's my fault," Thelvyn said sourly.

"Actually, you're probably right," Sir George agreed. "Well, it hardly matters if there are three dragons or three hundred since they're looking for us east of here. We can go on again if we're careful, and I certainly recommend getting away from this area while we can, but I think we should wait another hour until full darkness. Perry, what's your problem?"

"This staff of entropy," the mage said. "I can't imagine what went wrong. You know, I'm beginning to think that the Wizards of the Flaem don't know their heads from a hedgehog."

"You may recall that you weren't entirely impressed with this artifact of entropy at first yourself," Sir George reminded him. "The only reason you agreed to it is that the elves appeared to use something similar against their own monsters. Even the spirit guardian of World Mountain was rather doubtful."

"But the books said it would work," Perrantin insisted. "I found the references myself, so I know they were accurate."

"Yes, I saw those references. The elves were using an artifact of entropy against the strange hybrid monsters that sometimes appear in their places of dark magic. But these monsters have been shaped by magic, and so are especially vulnerable to the forces that brought them into being. Dragons are creatures of our own world and enormously secure in their own magic."

"But we found references to circumstances when it did work."

"The Highland wizards found and translated references for you," Sir George reminded him. "They set us up. They were so afraid of losing prestige if someone else made peace with the dragons that they filled us full of false information and sent us with a worthless artifact to meet our deaths trying to confront dragons. The only things that saved us were several bits of luck that even we had not had reason to expect."

"The dwarvish ambassador said the wizards fear a loss of their prestige and power more than anything, even the dragons themselves," Korinn added. "For the hundred years they've been in the Highlands, they've been trying to wrest power away from the dukes to keep for themselves."

Perrantin sighed heavily. "I see it now. All that business about not wanting anyone to annoy the dragons for fear of retaliation was nothing more than Kalestraan's ploy to keep us from succeeding. But sending us out with a worthless artifact seems like an overly complicated way of getting rid of us. He could have just had the archduke imprison us."

"I suspect even that was meant to serve their purpose," Sir George said. "When the wizards point out that we failed even after all our preparations, they'll be able to demand more power from the dukes in the name of the archduke and get it. Fools! They seem likely to receive the power they want just in time for the dragons to destroy them all."

"Oh, fine," Solveig complained bitterly, poking at the small fire they had lit in the fireplace. "Now we can't even go home, at least not back to the Highlands. Our return would be an embarrassment to the wizards."

"Who said we're ready to go home?" Sir George asked. "We might not know what we came to find out, but we know something at least as valuable. The dragons are scared to death about this Prophecy, and we have the object of the Prophecy right here with us."

Thelvyn looked up in surprise. "But you always knew about the Prophecy, didn't you?"

The old knight shook his head. "Yesterday was the first I had ever heard about it. I never even suspected such a thing. I just always believed there must be something special about you, considering the circumstances prior to your birth. Being in a position to know a thing or two about dragons, I just thought I should keep you safe and see what came of it. I still can't tell you who you really are, why you should be the object of such an important Prophecy, or what that Prophecy might be. I hope you don't think I've manipulated you or that I only kept you around in the hope of profiting from you."

"I've known better than that for a long time," Thelvyn said. "I've been aware for years that the mystery of my origin first brought me to your attention, and I decided a long time ago that your interest was less a matter of forcing me toward my destiny than helping me there."

"I'm glad you can appreciate the distinction," Sir George remarked dryly. "I hope you're not too upset."

"No, I can't say that I am," Thelvyn admitted. "Even though I expect I really should be upset, considering what's happened. But I've always felt up in the air, caught between my past and my future, with the feeling that something inevitable would happen someday. It's almost a relief not have to have to wonder about it anymore."

"It looks to me as if our adventure is not yet at an end," Solveig remarked as she began carefully selecting pieces of dry wood and setting them on the fire. "Korinn, it might be time to occupy ourselves with preparing what might be our last hot meal in some time."

"That remains to be seen," Sir George remarked cautiously. "Lad, I won't ask you to be a part of any attempt to discover the meaning of this Prophecy until we've discussed it and you have some idea of what it involves."

"We could always ask a dragon," Solveig commented, still in a rather dour mood. "At least we've proven that we can subdue a dragon or two, as long as we don't employ artifacts made for that task."

"By the beard of Denwarf, what are you talking about?" Korinn asked. "You've never spoken of what happened in there. Were you actually able to subdue a dragon?"

"Our good wizard was able to put one under with that potion of his," Sir George said. "Thelvyn caught a second with a spell of holding. I would say we won, but there was a third dragon staying just out of range to argue the point."

"A spell of holding?" Solveig asked. "I never knew for certain just what happened then, after Sir George turned himself into a drake and jumped on the dragon's nose. I know that the lad has been trained in magic, but I would have thought a spell of holding powerful enough to repress a dragon would be far beyond his skill."

"Exactly," Perrantin agreed. "He couldn't have cast such a spell. It's not listed in his book of spells; I can attest to that, since I've been supplying him with his spells recently. Therefore he couldn't have learned the spell in the first place. What he used was a clerical spell, a low-level one to be sure, but with power enough to hold a dragon."

Thelvyn was the most surprised of any of them. "But how can I use a clerical spell? I'm not a cleric."

"You're not a typical cleric," Sir George said, having already figured out that much for himself. "By definition, a cleric is devoted to the service of one of the Immortals, or at least to a great cause. You therefore assume that you cannot be a cleric if you haven't declared yourself to the service of one of the Immortals. But there are very rare circumstances, in time of great need, when one of the Immortals will designate his own champion."

"Is that what happened to me?" Thelvyn asked.

"It would explain a good many things," Sir George said. "We know that one of the Immortals has chosen you to serve him, since he was required to save you by granting you the powers of a cleric and guiding you in the use of that spell of holding. But we don't know which Immortal is involved. We also know that you are the object of a Prophecy that frightens the dragons. But we don't know the Prophecy. If we put the two together, we can make a few good guesses about the parts we don't know. If an Immortal opposed to the strategies of the dragons has designated you his cleric and champion to put an end to the dragons' schemes, then they in turn might have been warned of it by way of the Prophecy. Needless to say, they would want to put an end to you before you have a chance to interfere."

In other words, Thelvyn thought, they would kill him on sight, just as they had killed his mother in the attempt to prevent his birth. Obviously they had assumed that he had died, or had never been born, although the Prophecy had obviously concerned them enough that they hadn't forgotten it in all that time. He suddenly understood many of the events of his life much better, if not perfectly.

"But how could Thelvyn be a cleric?" Solveig asked. "He doesn't follow the commands of a cleric. Quite aside from not knowing his patron, he also uses edged weapons. I've trained him myself to use his sword. I always understood that clerics were forbidden the use of edged weapons."

"In most cases," Sir George agreed. "However, there are exceptions. The followers of Odin in the Northern Reaches use swords and axes, the favored weapons of the Northland gods. Those people might be called shamans rather than clerics, but it's much the same thing. But that does bring up one very interesting question."

Thelvyn glanced up. "What's that?"

"I was thinking of the clerical spells you employed, back in Torkyn Fall. For one, you used a spell of holding. Perry, correct me if I'm wrong, but isn't it true that a common spell of holding doesn't work on a creature much larger than the one casting the spell? Then you used lightning strikes to bring down the ceiling of the passage to trap the dragons. Those are not normal clerical spells, quite aside from the remarkable fact that you didn't have to receive them through meditation. Clerics just don't function that way."

"Those were unusual circumstance," Perrantin reminded him. "I was under the impression his patron was simply giving him the powers he needed to save himself. He uses edged weapons because he has never had any reason to expect that he shouldn't, and so his patron has allowed it. We should wait to see whether he continues to display extraordinary talents before we assume anything."

"Should I start behaving like a cleric?" Thelvyn asked. He was generally unfamiliar with clerics, since they tended to avoid magic-oriented places like the Highlands. In all he had ever heard or read about clerics, they had always seemed like a lot of self-satisfied boors.

"I should think not," Sir George told him. "If your patron had intended for you to behave like a cleric, he would have found a way to make you do so from the first. However this doesn't answer one unsettling question about you. Who gave you your spellbook?"

Thelvyn looked surprised. "I always assumed that you did."

"Indeed not," the knight insisted. "I had been waiting for Perry to attend to that matter. That's the scary part, you see. Your patron grants you the powers of a cleric, but he also gives you a spellbook to make an accomplished magic-user out of you. That not only isn't normal, but it's also rather dangerous for a person to attempt to be both. You come from a very remarkable race indeed. Now I know how your mother was able to defend herself against a band of dragons. If she could command both types of spells, she may also have had the power of an Immortal backing her up."

Thelvyn frowned, marveling how his life had gotten so complicated so fast. He had always wondered about the vast power and authority he assumed his race must possess, based upon what his mother was said to have done, but he had assumed that he'd never find it until he could discover who he was and return to his own people. Now that power seemed to be his, but it also brought with it much responsibility and danger. He didn't regret what he had been given, at least not yet, but he would have to work at it, and he had reason to be fearful.

"This was what you wanted me to know before I made any decisions?" he asked. "I really don't see that I have any choice. Now that the dragons know about me, they won't leave me alone. My best hope is to discover the meaning of this Prophecy and be done with it."

"Unfortunately, you seem to be stuck with it," Sir George agreed. "But we can hide you, if you prefer. I can take you into a distant land where you can live quietly. But if one of the Immortals has indeed chosen you to serve him, I suspect he will contrive a way to involve you in the Prophecy whether you want to be or not. That's the way these things work."

Thelvyn shook his head. "I think we should try to find out what this Prophecy demands of me first. I feel a lot better as far as the dragons are concerned now that I know that I have an Immortal behind me. It's very reassuring company, don't you think?"

Sir George laughed. "That's looking at the bright side. Well, I suppose that we have to begin somewhere. That brings us back to the question of just who can tell us about this Prophecy. The dragons know, obviously, but I don't recommend going back to them. Their fear of this Prophecy seems to be so great that they would do anything to defeat it. I know dragons well, and I know when they can be safely approached, and that's something you don't attempt when they are behaving unpredictably."

"What alternatives do we have?" Solveig asked.

""As far as I can tell, only the Immortals and the dragons know about the Prophecy. The Immortals started this whole business, you might say, and under the circumstances, we might find it easier to get one of them to talk to us. Perry, is there any way Thelvyn can speak with his Immortal patron?"

"It's more likely to be the other way around," the mage answered. "An Immortal can commune with his favored clerics whenever he wants to. Thelvyn's patron apparently either will not or cannot speak with him just yet. You have to keep in mind that the Immortals must abide by some very strict rules, which limit their interference in mortal affairs. Thelvyn's patron has already pushed the limits of those rules by designating a champion who wasn't already one of his clerics. Possibly he cannot yet acknowledge his ties to his champion through communion."

"Then what's the good of having a champion?" Sir George asked. "He has to have left us some way of finding out what he requires so we can act upon it. Can you try to help Thelvyn to commune with his patron?"

"No, not very well," Perrantin admitted. "That would best be left to another cleric, preferably one of his own order. But that might not be our only choice under the circumstances. We do have certain alternatives. We can try to find a senior cleric of an order loyal to one of the Immortals allied to his patron. That cleric can then commune with his patron, and we can get the information we seek second-hand. That's the way these things usually work in such cases."

"But if we don't know Thelvyn's patron, how can we know which Immortals are his allies?" Solveig asked.

"Ah, but we can guess," Perrantin reminded them. "Alliances between the Immortals are only temporary, for the sake of common needs or goals. We must ask ourselves which of the Immortals would be most actively opposed to the aggressions of the dragons, particularly which of the Immortals is the patron of a race or nation due to suffer most from the attacks of the dragons. They seem to be hitting the Highlands especially hard, but the Flaem are new to this world, and they have no Immortal patrons. And the great spirits of the Ethengar have already denied knowledge in this matter when the Yak Brothers insisted that they can't tell Thelvyn who he is."

"Kagyar," Korinn said. "Kagyar is the immortal patron of the dwarves, and renegade dragons have always been the enemies of the dwarves. Kagyar would certainly be opposed to their plans."

"Perhaps," Sir George said cautiously. "I have thoughts of my own on that matter. But first I think Thelvyn should try to commune with his patron. We could solve this problem without having to go out of our way to do it, although I doubt that it will be that easy."

Although neither of them were entirely happy about the situation, Perrantin took Thelvyn out into a quiet place in the woods near the cabin and tried his best to help the lad commune. The trouble was that Perrantin was a wizard; he was really in no position to teach someone else to commune with a higher being when he himself had no idea how to do it. Since neither one of them expected to succeed, they weren't disappointed. Thelvyn sat beneath a tree and tried hard to meditate, which he took to be a focus of negative concentration. He wasn't entirely on the wrong track; after an hour, the intense negative concentration had brought him five of the lower-level clerical spells, which was impressive for a rank beginner. But he didn't succeed in communing with anyone or anything except his stomach, since he was getting hungry.

The others were packing to leave by the time they returned. Although they didn't know yet where they were going, they all agreed that they needed to get far away from the dragons as quickly as they could. At least Solveig had kept their dinner warm for them. Night had fallen, and they could be on their way any time now in reasonable safety.

"No luck?" Sir George asked.

"I wouldn't exactly say that," Perrantin remarked sourly. "The lad can now cure lesser wounds, resist cold, detect and protect himself against evil, and summon light."

"I could already summon light with a magic spell," Thelvyn said. He felt vaguely cheated at knowing redundant spells.

"I suppose you can keep trying," Sir George said. "You might get it yet with practice. But just in case, I recommend that we begin taking steps to learn what we need by other means. I suggest we seek the help of a senior cleric who would be sympathetic to our need."

"I still recommend Kagyar," Korinn declared. "There has been ancient animosity between the dwarves and the dragons. Kagyar is highly protective of the welfare of the dwarves. Even though Rockhome hasn't yet been threatened by dragons, that will eventually follow. I believe that Kagyar would, like the spirits of the Ethengar, see the need to take steps to protect his people. I believe he will help us."

"I'm not so sure," Sir George said. "Like the dwarves, Kagyar tends to prefer isolation. He might not be willing to give assistance to foreigners if he believes the strongholds of the dwarves will be enough to frustrate the dragons. I was in and out of Rockhome nearly two hundred years before you were born, and I know something about this."

"Then you have a suggestion?" Korinn asked.

"Yes, I expect I do," he said. "I happen to know a cleric of senior standing, a follower of the woodland order devoted to Terra, living in one of Terra's sacred places in the forests of Alfheim."

"An elf?" Korinn asked, displeased. That in itself was enough to convince him that his plan was the better one.

"I had no idea there were elven clerics," Solveig observed.

"There is an ungainly number of elven clerics," Sir George told her. "Most are devoted to their own Immortals, Ilsundal and Maeliden, although the elder Immortal Terra is also revered as the senior patron of the natural world, especially the woodlands and the deep forests. Terra is perfect for our purposes because she's always been fond of dragons. She sponsored the only dragon Immortal, known only as the Great One."

"If she's so fond of dragons, is she going to want to help us?" Perrantin asked. "She could just as likely send the dragons after us."

"No, I don't believe that," the old knight insisted. "She'd never approve of any schemes the dragons might have to seize power, and she certainly wouldn't sanction their attacks against other folks. If nothing else, she would assist a plan opposed to the attacks of the dragons just to get them back under control once again."

"But that would mean going into Alfheim," Korinn complained.

Sir George smiled. "If it suits you better, you might keep in mind that Rockhome is directly between us and Alfheim. I mean to stop in Dengar under any circumstances, to renew our supplies."

"The Great One," Perrantin said suddenly, as if speaking to himself. "What about it, George? If you want to know what's going on, then why not go right to the source? Is there any way to get the Great One to talk to us? I mean, you should know all about that."

"I'm not a cleric, you know," he said, looking uncomfortable. "Nor am I a dragon. I'm just a drake, a dragonkin. By law I belong to the greater Nation of Dragons, and as such I do enjoy certain rights. But the drakes generally don't feel comfortable in the company of our greater brethren. We tend to go our own way, and there are many secrets of the dragons that we don't know. I know more than most because I am one of the few who has sought the company of dragons."

"Meaning that you really don't know how to go about it?"

"That's pretty much it."

"Well, what about the Great One?" Perrantin asked. "Is he behind all of this, or would he be opposed to it?"

"The attacks of the dragons, you mean?" Sir George asked. "I believe that he must be opposed to it, for whatever my opinion is worth. The Great One has generally been peaceful and benevolent, being at one time a disciple of Terra, and I've always understood that his main interest as their patron was to protect the dragons. I've wondered since this all began why the Great One hasn't tried to put an end to it himself, unless he has tried and the dragons have refused his authority."

That obviously surprised the mage. "Refused his authority? Would the dragons dare to refuse their own Immortal?"

"They could and would, if it suited them. A mature dragon at the height of his power, especially one of the dragon clerics, is only a step or two away from being an Immortal. I've often wondered why there aren't more dragon Immortals than just the Great One. Among dragons, a cleric is usually more powerful than a mere magic-user, because a cleric will be an accomplished magic-user as well. As far as I know, that's a situation unique among dragons."

"I'm apparently both a cleric and a magic-user," Thelvyn reminded him. "But whatever else I may be, I'm obviously not a dragon."

"That's true enough," Sir George agreed. "The fact that you were born and not hatched proves that. A dragon may be enchanted into human form, and some can even take that form at will, but he has to have been born a dragon. You can rest assured that you were not hatched. Mayor Aalsten would have told you if you had been."

"Mayor Aalsten would have pitched me back into the wild if I had come out of a dragon's egg," Thelvyn remarked.

"And I would have known it, because a dragon can always recognize another dragon, or a dragon-kin, on sight, no matter what form he might take. That was why the dragon in Torkyn Fall called me a traitor even before I assumed my true form."

"I suppose that means I'm back to being some distant kin to the elves," Thelvyn said.

That had to be the end of the matter for now. Sir George couldn't allow them to sit and discuss the possibilities any more, for night had long since fallen, and they needed to be on their way. They would be much safer this night than they had been the night before, now that they had come down from the lower slopes to the forest where the dragons couldn't easily find them. Sir George wanted to be down from the mountains altogether and well out into the steppes by dawn, or else they would be required to stop early and wait for the following night before they dared to leave the safety of the forest.

The dragons were still searching well to the east, following the main road leading down from Torkyn Fall. Thelvyn could see them across the miles even in the dark, and he watched them nervously, fearful that they might expand their desperate search into the surrounding mountains at any time. For the first time, he finally understood why they feared and hated him so much.

CHAPTER FIFTEEN

Thelvyn had no idea how sick he was of the flat, grassy, featureless steppes until he had to return there. His only consolation was that he had never been there in winter, when the windswept plains were even colder than the snowbound heights, nor in the fierce summer heat. But they intended to pass through as quickly as they could, five days of hard riding from north to south across the Steppes of Ethengar.

After some debate with himself, Sir George brought out the totem of safe conduct and returned it to the top of the long, slender pole. Although they weren't on the same quest anymore, they were still on business that, if successful, would be for the good of the Ethengar. In George's estimation, that certainly seemed to count. As long as they carried the totem, the clans would allow them to ride in peace.

Time was short, and they had many riddles to solve. If the number of dragons moving along the Wendarian Range was any indication, the northern Highlands was already under a fierce siege. Quite possibly other lands were suffering from the attacks of the dragons as well, and none of it was likely to end until they were able to understand and act upon the Prophecy. More immediate to their concerns, they were running short of supplies. They grazed their sturdy horses upon the fresh spring grass of the steppes to save fodder for the journey through the mountains of Rockhome.

Thelvyn had a great deal to occupy his thoughts during that long ride. He was at a loss to figure out just how he was supposed to have any part in a Prophecy that seemed to suggest he had the power to defeat the plans of the dragons. He seemed to keep coming back to the matter of his unknown race, which took on new relevance now that he knew he had the remarkable ability to act as both a magic-user and a cleric. Perhaps his mother had possessed much the same powers.

He recalled that the few people who had known her, Mayor Aalsten and the old forester and especially Sir George, had all described his mother as being a lady. They had always insisted that something about her, even if they never understood a word she said, had proven her someone of great authority, dignity, and nobility. He wondered if what they had sensed in her instead had been the stately demeanor of a senior cleric, one who had been touched by the presence of her patron.

There were two problems with the assumption that he might have inherited such power. For one thing, he would need many years of experience to become either a formidable wizard or a powerful senior cleric, much less both. And he would have to be even more powerful than his mother, who had not been able to survive her own battle with dragons.

Obviously there had to be still more to learn about the Prophecy, and about himself as well. He even realized that it might not be his part in the Prophecy to actually fight dragons. His role could involve something altogether different. Sir George believed that the dragons wanted something; perhaps he was to find it for them.

He eventually had to admit that he would just have to

wait to find out more about this business before he could guess what he was expected to do. He also realized that he might not like what was expected of him, and he wondered if he had the right to refuse. A cleric had to make the decision that he wanted to serve, but after that, his duty required him to do what was expected of him beyond any personal considerations, including his own life. Thelvyn's greatest fear was that his duty as a cleric had already been decided for him in some way, leaving him no choice in the matter.

He thought he was the perfect addition to their company of misfits—a towering barbarian woman who had been raised among the first families of Thyatis, a young dwarf, a middle-aged wizard who traded in antiques, and a one-handed mandrake who fancied himself a knight. Added to that odd mix was one Thelvyn, an orphan of unknown race, neither mage nor cleric but parts of both, and the chosen champion of an Immortal who would not declare himself. Small wonder that the Wizards of the Flaem had filled them full of false information and sent them on their way, glad to be rid of such a band of eccentrics.

"Do you suppose that the fire wizards knew more about us then we knew ourselves?" he asked Sir George as they rode together.

"Eh?" the old knight asked, stirring from his own thoughts. "No, I don't think so. For one thing, if they had known about the Prophecy, they would have kept you safe for their own uses."

"Unless the conclusion of the Prophecy is something they don't want." Thelvyn suddenly looked surprised. "You know, it hadn't occurred to me until just now, but I might yet be about to find out who and what I am. My patron would be able to tell me that, even if the Prophecy does not."

"That may well be," Sir George agreed guardedly. "That's why we have to stick together, you and me. I'm not exactly human and, I don't necessarily want to be, but I'll never be a dragon either. And you don't even know what you are. We have something in common, you see."

All the same, thoughts of actually going home were on

Thelvyn's mind.

In time, he could see the distant outline of the mountains rising above the steppes before them, the high, rugged peaks of northwestern Rockhome that were known as the Altan Tepes. The companions turned east once more, staying just below the harsh, treeless foothills until they approached the banks of the Styrdal River, which flowed out of the steppes through a deep pass between the mountains and finally emptied into the cold depths of Lake Stahl, one of the two great lakes in the land of the dwarves. Here it was that they came at last upon a trail that appeared slowly out of the steppes, at first seeming to be nothing more than some track laid down by a wandering herd or passing tribe.

This simple track was called the Styrdal Road, and it led the travelers southward around a wide bend in the barren foothills and then toward the deep pass of the river between the mountains. That night, soon after they had come upon the road, they camped for one final time on the edge of the steppes. The next morning they crossed a narrow band of hills and passed into the deep, still forest above the pass. Just after midday, they crossed the river over a great stone bridge that had been built by the dwarves. Although trade between the dwarves and the Ethengar was limited, because there wasn't much the dwarves wanted from the steppes, the industrious dwarves encouraged such trade as there was all the same. They maintained some of the best roads and bridges in all the world.

Dwarves were highly dependent upon trade, more so than most of them would have wanted to admit. Not farmers nor herdsmen, having neither the land or temperament for it, they were required to trade for much of what they ate. As a nation of smiths, metalworkers, and jewelers, they desperately needed an outlet for the products of their labor, or their caverns would have soon been filled to overflowing with finished goods. The Ethengar didn't have the means for refining and working metals, due to their nomadic way of life, and so they were largely dependent upon the dwarves for such objects.

They rode the rest of the day though the hilly, deeply

forested land that led into the pass between the northern arm of the Altan Tepes and the Denwarf Spur on the eastern side of the river. After a time, when they came to small clearings in the woods, Thelvyn could look ahead and see a great fort of dark stone sitting solidly on the highest point of land in the most narrow part of the pass. The Denwarf Pass was too wide for the dwarves to build a fortress that closed off the entire pass, which was never less than five miles wide. Still, Fort Denwarf was as large as any of the forts guarding the three major passes into Rockhome. The garrison there was as large as that kept in Karrak Castle to the south, which watched over the single road leading into the wild, dangerous desert lands of Ylaruam, although that place was more easily defended.

"That would be Fort Denwarf," Sir George told him. "Rak Denwarf, in the language of the dwarves. The fort guards the only pass into the steppes. The Ethengar themselves are of little concern, having learned the lesson long ago that their tactics are of little effect against the dwarves. But there are orcs and hobgoblins in great numbers in the foothills and the steppes just beyond the fort. If need be, they'll come right over the mountains to raid the mining settlements and the farms around Lake Stahl."

"What are the lands here like?" Thelvyn asked.

"Very much like the lands where you were born, but less cold and slightly less wild. There are great mountains with small villages not unlike your own to serve the many small mines in the mountains, swift rivers leading down from the heights, and deep forests between the small bands of farmlands."

"I never knew the dwarves farmed," Thelvyn said.

"The farming is done by the clanless ones," Korinn explained. He had been riding in the lead so the dwarven sentries would see him and not contest their passage. "These people are outcasts, often criminals and traitors, or folk expelled by their own clans for cowardice or sloth or being disruptive. Most outcasts leave Rockhome and never return. Those who refuse to leave, or those who return, must take the work that other folk will not do. Among dwarves, that most often means farming."

"Every people has its rogues and misfits," Sir George told him. "Even the Immortals."

Korinn smiled, but only briefly. "The lad has never been in this land before. He should be told something of what to expect, and what is expected of him, to get along. Do you want to tell him?"

"You know best what to expect, unless you'd rather not speak of it."

"Then I shall attempt to speak candidly." He glanced over his shoulder at his young companion. "You shouldn't expect dwarves in their own land to behave like dwarves you have known in other places, even me. Dwarves you do not know will be cold and unfriendly. Speak with them fairly, confidently, and politely to get along best. You may speak of matters of business, or even of things touching their professions, but don't ever even seem to pry. Remember that you will have no friends in this land, for friends here are hard to find. A dwarf must know and respect even another dwarf for a long time, months or even years, before he would dare consider him his friend. And though it pains me to say it to you, most dwarves disdain folk of other races. We are much like the elves in that regard."

"Not quite like elves," Sir George interjected. "Elves measure by their disdain, judging one race to be better or worse than another, but always with themselves on top. Dwarves are not judgmental in their disdain. They simply don't care to associate with foreigners. I suspect it must be a matter of instinct with them."

"That is true," Korinn agreed. "But dwarves now are less suspicious and closed to the world than we have been in the past. We are in an age of expansion, of establishment of dwarven settlements in other lands. At this time the Syrklist Clan is supreme. Daroban the Fifth is a Syrklist king. The Syrklist are a clan of traders, with great interest in the outer world. Not for the sake of curiosity, but because of the seemingly unlimited potential of the outer world for trade. There is much demand in the outer world for our vast surplus of goods, and there are jewels and metals in other lands that are rare at home."

Evening was approaching rapidly. The sun was already

going down behind the mountains to the west when they came upon a small fortified outpost. It was situated at the top of a long, slow rise where watchers at their posts could see the road for nearly a mile, long enough for them to identify travelers well in advance and respond as needed. Thelvyn believed the outpost existed soley to keep watch over the pass, for there was no way through the pass that could not be seen from the outpost. It lacked the size or garrison to contest any invasion. The responsibility of the guard was to send word to the main fortress four miles farther south. Several soldiers, wearing their sturdy dwarven armor, stepped outside the gate to watch as the company passed.

As darkness began to fall, they could see lights in the windows of the great fortress just ahead of them. Thelvyn knew he'd be glad for a meal and some rest.

"We'll spend the night in a real bed for the first time since we left Braejr," Korinn said.

"Is there an inn," Thelvyn asked, "or will they take us in at the fortress?"

"There is no inn," the dwarf said. "When the commander of Fort Denwarf knows we are on a quest of great importance, he will not deny us."

"Should we tell him about it?" Thelvyn asked.

"I do not intend to tell him anything," Korinn insisted. "Perhaps it is more accurate to say that he will not deny me. You know my name?"

Thelvyn nodded. "You are Korinn Bear Slayer, Son of Doric."

The dwarf turned to face him. "I am the second son of Doric, and Doric, Son of Kuric, is known as King Daroban the Fifth. Although I do not speak of it when I travel abroad, I am the younger son of the king of Rockhome. The others know of this, although they have kept my secret."

"Why am I always the last to know a secret?" Thelvyn asked.

"Because this is your first journey with us," Sir George told him. "Every two weeks in the saddle earns you a new secret."

Korinn smiled. "Perhaps you should know everything, for you will be going with me into the court of my father. You see, my older brother, Dorinn, should succeed my father, who is now an old man. But Dorinn was gravely wounded in a battle two years ago in the Broken Lands. He has not fully recovered yet, and perhaps he may always remain too weak to win the support he would need to be king. In the event he does not recover, my father has begun my training for that role so that I will be ready if I am needed."

"Riding about in the company of a mandrake who trades in antiquities and a pale barbarian woman is proper training for the next king of the dwarves?" Thelvyn asked incredulously.

Korinn had to laugh at that. "Not specifically, no. But it is felt that traveling unknown for a time in the role of an adventurer would help me to gain an insider's familiarity with other lands and races. Since trade is a primary concern of the Syrklist dwarves, this is important to us. I knew Sir George and Solveig from their visits to Dengar in the past, and I thought it best to spend my time traveling with them. They are hardly common adventurers, and I have learned much in their company. I informed them of my need, and they agreed to keep my secret."

Thelvyn could appreciate the advantage of traveling in the land of the dwarves with the son of the king. When the commander of Fort Denwarf came down to the yard to meet them, Korinn discreetly showed him a secret token of his authority and requested to be boarded for the night. No further questions were asked. Their horses were led away to be tended, and the travelers were immediately taken to warm baths, a hot meal, and soft beds. Of course, there were only a limited number of accommodations in a border fort, although none of the companions had cause to complain. Korinn and Thelvyn were given a room together, granting Solveig a rare measure of privacy, and the knight and the mage also shared a room.

"This is beginning to worry me," Thelvyn commented later. "We have with us the son of a king, the daughter of one of the first families of Thyatis, a knight, and a wizard.

I'm beginning to wonder if I'm worthy of such company."

"You are indeed," Korinn told him. "But I should warn you of one thing. There has always been animosity between dwarves and wizards of other lands, and magic-users are not particularly welcome here. It would be best not to mention that you are a student of magic. You would be in no danger because of it, but you would be held in some suspicion if it were known."

"What about Perrantin?"

"He is known here and welcomed as a scholar," Korinn explained. "Mind you, the fact that you are a cleric is to your advantage, especially since your patron is opposed to the aggressions of the dragons."

"Then the clerics of Kagyar might still help?" Thelvyn asked.

"I believe that they will do their very best for you."

Thelvyn had never known Korinn to speak so much or so openly. If dwarves were slow to make friends, then the sharing of secrets seemed to expedite the process. Of course, Thelvyn realized that Korinn wouldn't have shared his secret with anyone he wasn't prepared to consider his friend. Thelvyn was appalled to remember their first meeting, when he had mistaken Korinn and Solveig for thieves in Sir George's home and had given the dwarf a blow to the head that had knocked Korinn unconscious for the better part of ten minutes. Curiously, defeating them in battle had earned him grudging respect from both the barbarian woman and the dwarf.

They traveled south again the next morning, crossing the river by a stone bridge just beyond Fort Denwarf. The road led into the fringes of the mountains. Thelvyn wasn't sure why the road cut so far inland from the river, as much as eight miles, except perhaps that it brought the road closer to some of the small mountain villages and mines, and also the many small outposts and garrisons bordering the heights. He recalled being told that this was an especially dangerous area of the Altan Tepes, overrun with orcs and goblins, and he realized it was probably all the dwarves could do to keep their northwestern border secure.

The road wound back down from the heights after only

ten miles or so, descending into a gentler land of light woods and glades. After another half an hour's ride, the Styrdal Road ended abruptly as it came to a wooded crossroads and joined with the Stahl Road. This took them east for several miles before they crossed the Styrdal River for the final time. The Stahl Road joined the two largest cities in Rockhome, running along the northeast shore of the great Stahl Lake from the city of Stahl in the north down to Dengar. The only other city along the way was Evemur, far to the south, although there were many small villages.

They rode as long as they could into the night, hoping to get far enough to ride on to Dengar the next day. They spent that night in a small, clean inn in a village along the way. The wide, flat land to the east of the lake was one of the best of the few farming regions in all of Rockhome. From Korinn's statement that farmers were the outcasts and criminals of the dwarven nation, Thelvyn expected to find a wild, ill-kept, and possibly dangerous land. Instead, he found small, homey villages and farmhouses amidst precisely laid fields between fences of weathered stone or timbers, separated by narrow stands of pleasant woods. Apparently even the dregs of dwarven society couldn't deny their impulses for neatness and efficiency, and they even worked hard at what were to them most degrading tasks.

They reached Evemur by midday, stopping there for an hour to have lunch and rest the horses. This was Thelvyn's first look at one of the dwarvish cities. Evermur was little more than a small farming town, and he was almost disappointed to find that, except for some storage rooms, the entire town was built aboveground. He was surprised to discover that, more often than legend had led him to believe, dwarves lived on the surface of the land like other folk.

After they left Evemur, the Stahl Road led northeast across the last fields and pastures before reaching the mountains. Thelvyn was excited about their arrival at Dengar, since Korinn had told them they would be going down into the lower city at once. He could see the upper city from nearly five miles away, even though the afternoon light was already failing in the shadow of the mountains. Upper Dengar, as the aboveground portion of the city was called, was built atop a low plateau, nestled back against one of the most steep, majestic peaks Thelvyn had ever seen. The only approach was up a long, winding ramp.

"That's Point Everast," Korinn told him as they rode together. "In the ancient days following the Rain of Fire, Kagyar awoke the first dwarves there on the high slopes of Point Everast. There they met Denwarf, who was sent by Kagyar to be their first teacher and guardian. He served as the first king of our people for four hundred years."

"That was a long time even for a dwarf," Thelvyn observed.

"Denwarf was not like other dwarves. The power and wisdom of Kagyar was within him, and he remained with us until our race was strong and we were ready to care for ourselves."

All three of the great trade roads of Rockhome, the Stahl Road from the west, the Sardal Road from the south, and the Evekarr Road from the east, joined together just below the ramp leading to the only gate of Dengar, which was why it was called the Three Roads Gate. The gate fort seemed unnecessarily large to Thelvyn, but Korinn explained that the interior of the fort served as an immense trap for any enemies who got past the outer gate. Korinn presented himself to the gate wardens, identifying himself with a token of his clan, and arrangements were made for the stabling of their horses. Three young, strong soldiers were sent to carry their extra packs, and they began their descent into the lower city.

They were taken to the far rear of the upper city, to a place called the Grand Plaza, which served as the final defense to the entrance of the caverns. A long, winding tunnel, more than half a mile long, brought them from the upper city to the mouth of the upper cavern. This was the first main cavern of the city, the Dwarfheart, a vast natural chamber well over a mile and half long. It was the principal residence of the lower city.

He followed the others through a long, straight lane down the center of the cavern to the rear, past lines of dwarven buildings with their odd shapes and low doorways. This place wasn't at all like the tidy chambers and passages of Torkyn Fall, but an underground city of streets and houses filling the floor of a great cave, as in the stories Thelvyn had read and heard in his younger days. Many of the residents stood watching as they passed. Thelvyn noticed that there seemed to be no one in the lower city who wasn't a dwarf other than themselves, and he fancied that they must be a remarkable sight to people who rarely saw foreigners.

They came at last to the king's palace, another strange, solid structure, with its yard between the outer and inner walls filled by a sprawling stone garden, complete with streams and small bridges and extraordinary fungus growths. Korinn was recognized even before he could make himself known. He spoke with the chamberlain briefly in the dwarven language, and then servants descended upon them and took them to their rooms.

No one had told Thelvyn what was expected of him, or what was likely to happen next. He anticipated that he might be called down to dinner soon, or perhaps sumoned to meet Korinn's family. He washed as quickly as he could, although he thought he'd never get the dust of the road out of his hair, then dressed in the shirt and pants he kept in the bottom of his pack for special occasions. A servant appeared shortly afterward to take him down to dinner.

Dinner that night was served in the king's private chamber, for Korinn had already sent word to his father that he needed to speak with him in private. Sir George and Solveig were already there, although Perrantin had yet to appear. King Daroban was seated at the head of the one long table in the room, an elderly dwarf who was nearly bald on top, with a beard as white as snow. Korinn was seated at his left.

Across from Korinn sat a dwarf who must surely be his brother. Dorinn was slightly older than his brother, a dwarf who had just come into the solid, responsible years of adulthood. Before his injury he had been a strong, tall dwarf, in contrast to Korinn, who was rather average in appearance for one of his race. Yet now Dorinn's back was bent uncomfortably even when he sat, and he hardly seemed able to use his left arm at all. He had grown thin and weak from his long infirmity.

"So this is the lad who is feared by dragons," King Daroban said as Thelvyn entered. His voice was neither mocking nor unfriendly. "As you say, he is not of any race I recognize."

"I have no idea myself," Thelvyn admitted, taking the place that was offered to him. "I have a vague suspicion that I might be distantly related to the elves."

"Do you have any qualities in common with the elves?" Daroban asked in a slightly guarded tone.

"Aside from my keen vision, only some vague similarities of appearance," he explained. "I don't believe I possess any elven qualities that dwarves would find disquieting."

The dwarves all laughed, Daroban most of all. "Well said. I confess that I do find something of an elven air about you, but only those elven qualities that are most noble. Elves do have their virtues; I will not blind myself to that, no matter what their faults. But back to this matter of a Prophecy that my son has mentioned. What do you think about it?"

"Well, I really don't know what to think," Thelvyn had to confess. He was trying not to look uncomfortable, although his chair was too small for him and the table was too low. "I might have a better idea when I learn what this Prophecy is about, beyond the fact that it upsets dragons. I expect that I really don't have much choice in the matter."

"Are you afraid?" the king asked.

"I'm afraid of dragons, which I suppose is normal enough. But I'm not really afraid of the Prophecy, because it might tell me who I am or where I came from. I would very much like to go home someday, if only to know where home is."

Daroban sat back in his chair for a moment, weighing the possibilities. "I appreciate your position. I can see you feel you must do your best, if you alone have the ability to stop the attacks of the dragons. Yet how can you commit yourself fully to this goal, or know how to plan for the future set before you until you learn of this Prophecy and what it asks of you?"

"That is very much the case," Thelvyn said. "I appreciate your concern for my dilemma."

"Yes, well, as the king of the dwarves, I must consider the needs of my own people in this," Daroban said thoughtfully. "If you are indeed the object of a Prophecy that will spare my kingdom the attacks of the dragons, then your interests are my interests. As your companion and friend, my son has sworn to your virtues, and I am satisfied. Therefore I will commit myself and my realm to your quest to discover the meaning of this Prophecy."

"We appreciate this," Sir George said, speaking for the first time. "We are very much in need of help. To get directly to the point, you do not object to our journey to Alfheim to consult the cleric who may assist us?"

The king tried not to frown. "If it is necessary, I do not object. As I have said, I will not blind myself to the virtues of the elves. It is said that the duties of a cleric may transcend duties to race or nation in pursuit of an even greater good. I should tell you that red dragons have been seen patrolling our lands every few days, watching our cities and our roads. Do you have any idea when the first attacks are likely to come?"

Sir George shook his head. "I honestly cannot say. The greatest attention of the dragons seems to be focused upon the northern Highlands. Now that they know about Thelvyn and sense that the Prophecy they fear is still valid, they may care for nothing else but finding him. If so, they may resume their search in the last place they saw his mother, far to the west of here."

"So someone else's misfortune works to our advantage?" the king asked. "Of all the lands in this part of the world, Rockhome would be best able to resist the attacks of the dragons. But from your report of the siege of Torkyn Fall, I am not so certain. From time to time, we have had to deal with a renegade or two lured by rumors of our treasure, but we have found it easy enough to defend ourselves. I suspect we have misled ourselves into believing that we are the equals of the dragons. That mistake could be costly."

"The dragons have more than enough strength to devastate every nation in the world," Sir George said. "If they wanted to, they could sweep through Rockhome or Thyatis in a week, leaving the cities and armies of an entire nation in ruins. That is why I contend that the dragons are not yet at war with us, if indeed that is their intention."

"Then what can we do?" Daroban asked.

"Exactly what you are doing," the knight told him. "Prepare yourself as best you can, and put your faith in the Prophecy. Only the Immortals can stand against the wrath of the dragons, and you can rest assured that Kagyar and the patrons of all the other races aren't going to just stand aside and allow the dragons to destroy the world. The Prophecy is their response of the Immortals. I suspect it's our only chance to make peace with the dragons before there is war."

"So much of their attention is focused upon the Highlands," Perrantin said, entering at last and taking his seat. He joined in the conversation as if he had been there all along. "I'm becoming more and more convinced that it's not a coincidence. The Flaem are new to this world, and they have brought their own magic with them. When we were in Braejr, I became aware of enough hints to suspect that their fire wizards are up to something with their magic, something powerful and possibly more dangerous than they realize. This might have set the dragons against them."

The conversation paused for a moment while servants brought dinner. Thelvyn looked at his suspiciously. He was an adventurous sort and always ready to try new things, but he was glad he wasn't being served the strange fungus that dwarves seemed to enjoy.

After dinner, Thelvyn elected to take a walk in the palace grounds. He was having a hard time getting used to the smaller size of everything in the dwarven city, especially the ceilings, which were only slightly higher than his head, and the doorways, which were so low he had to bend. He knew Solveig must be having an even harder time, since she was unable to stand upright anywhere except in the larger chambers.

The caverns of Dengar were neither night nor day, but a perpetual twilight from the glow of lanterns and magical lamps. Others may have found it dusky, even gloomy and oppressive. But Thelvyn's ability to see in the dark was at least equal to that of the dwarves, and therefore it gave him no problem.

"Thelvyn!"

He heard Korinn's voice call. He looked up to see the two sons of Doric together in a portion of the garden that was partially enclosed by abstract shapes of carved stone. Korinn stood, while his brother Dorinn was seated on a stone bench.

"I see you have survived your first meeting our father," Korinn said. "What do you think?"

"I found the king to be an open-minded and remarkably considerate man," Thelvyn replied. "I confess that I have heard certain unflattering things about dwarves, that they can be cold and suspicious of strangers, but I have not found it so."

"Our father is well disposed toward you," Dorinn said. "And I might add, my brother swore to him that you have been a true friend and brave companion, the two qualities that dwarves admire most. That was all that needed to be said for my father to accept you."

"I'm honored," Thelvyn said.

"If so, then you have earned it," Korinn insisted. "I will accompany the party once again when we leave. My father has consented to that."

"I hadn't considered the possibility that you might stay with us," Thelvyn admitted, surprised.

"Nor had I," Korinn said. "It was one thing for me to go out into other lands as a simple adventurer. It was a means of traveling about and seeing other lands and other folk for myself. Apparently it is quite another thing to undertake a quest to discover and fulfill a Prophecy of such great importance. As the son of the king, I have a duty to my realm and my people. At this time, my duty is best served with you."

"I am honored," Thelvyn said, and he meant it.

"My brother, could you bring us a drink from the cellars?" Dorinn asked.

"Certainly," Korinn said with a bow, then grinned at Thelvyn. "But I fear we have no cherry liqueur."

Dorinn waited until his brother had disappeared into the palace, then turned back to face Thelvyn. "I fear that my brother may find me rather transparent in my motives, but no matter. There are things you should know about Korinn that he cannot easily tell you himself. You have seen that our father is very old. Although his health has remained good so far, he must remain fit enough to be a strong king for another nine years. You see, I am not the eldest son of Doric. I once had an older brother, who of course would have been the next king. When he died in battle more than forty years ago, I became the heir. But my father desired yet another child, in case something should happen to me also. The life of the son of a king of Rockhome is a dangerous one."

"I am beginning to get that impression," Thelvyn said.

"Our parents were already old, and they despaired of ever having another child," Dorinn continued. "But when Korinn was born, everything seemed fine. Then I was wounded in battle in the Broken Lands, and we had to face the possibility that I will never be fit to be king. I could not be king at this time, for a king of Rockhome must be fit to serve. But he must also be mature. Korinn is only forty-one, and a dwarf does not come of age until his fiftieth year. Until that time, he would not be considered seriously should it become necessary to choose a new king."

"Is that likely to be a problem?" Thelvyn asked. "You still have time to recover."

"That is far from a certainty. I am told privately that my chances of recovering enough to become king are about even. We must be prepared. If neither of the sons of Doric are found suitable, the kingship will most likely pass to another clan. We have enjoyed a time of great expansion and prosperity, largely because the Syrklist Clan is devoted to trade. That may end if the Everast Clan reclaims the kingship."

"I understand your concern," Thelvyn admitted. "Is there nothing that could help? Have you consulted the healers of other lands?"

Dorinn frowned. "We do not speak of this to strangers, but dwarves are resistant to magic, including magical healing. Mages cannot help me. Our clerics have been doing their best, and by the will of Kagyar, I will recover. But Kagyar might have other plans. That is why Korinn must return to us safely. I beg you as his friend to watch out for him."

"I will," Thelvyn promised, "if he will allow it."

CHAPTER SIXTEEN

Sir George declared that they would spend an extra day of rest in Dengar, although his concern was more for the horses than their riders. The horses had been from Braejr to World Mountain, up to the ruins of Torkyn Fall, and down again across the steppes to the center of Rockhome. They were a sturdy breed, but it was still remarkable that there had been no trouble with any of the horses so far. Orders were given by the king himself that the horses were to be tended with the best of care.

Korinn's plan was to spend their day of rest showing his younger companions the lower city of Dengar. Sir George, Solveig, and Perrantin had been there before, on business of their own, when they had first met Korinn. Because she was so much taller than dwarves, Solveig hadn't gotten along well with them until she had met him. Korinn hadn't returned home in the two years since he had joined their company.

"Solveig has always fascinated Korinn," Sir George explained at breakfast while they were making plans to see the city. "He has always been amazed that she has legs as long as he is tall."

"That's neither accurate nor fair," Perrantin commented. "He stands just over four feet tall. That brings him up to just below her breasts."

"Where he can admire the view," Sir George added, this being the tactic he and Perrantin used to get themselves uninvited. It worked.

Korinn began their tour just outside the palace. He explained that five of the six different clans held portions of Dengar, sometimes in the sense of armed camps. The chief opposition to the king's policies came from the senate, and the senate compound was located directly to the west of the king's palace. All the clans had their representative in the Senate, voting upon new laws to be recommended to the king and reviewing the laws originating with the king. While the kings were hardly fond of the senate, they recognized the fact that allowing the clans to have a voice of authority in the senate was perhaps the only thing that spared Rockhome from civil war. Left to their own policies, each of the clans would prefer to be a small nation unto itself.

The most immediate concern to King Daroban and his heirs was the powerful Everast Clan. As Korinn explained, they more or less owned Dengar, both above and below the ground. The first king of Rockhome after the legendary Denwarf had been an Everast dwarf, and their clan had provided most of the kings ever since. For this reason, the entire northern end of the main cavern had been the Everast stronghold for centuries. The great mansions and estates of the wealthiest Everast families stood together just south of the palace itself, very much like the lines of an enemy encampment. The Everast-owned pumping station and the compound of the King's Guard were located beside the palace, and by both tradition and law the King's Guard was composed entirely of younger Everast dwarves.

In all, it left the king and his family feeling much like an island in a sea of hostility. The Clans of the Everast and the Syrklist were not commonly in opposition to each other, for they were both wealthy trading clans primarily interested in commerce and the prosperity of their nation. Indeed, because of their shared interests and goals, they were often aligned politically with the Skarrad Clan against the other clans. But the Everasts couldn't forget that one of their own had occupied the throne more often than not since the beginning of dwarven history, and they wanted it back. Daroban I had taken the crown by senate vote when there had been no Everast contender for the throne capable of inspiring confidence, a matter of great shame to the Everast Clan ever since.

The militaristic Torkrest Clan, which dominated the armies of Rockhome, had their stronghold in upper Dengar and were generally out of the way, but they were on reasonably good terms with the other clans anyway. The small Buhrodar clan, mostly devoted to Kagyar as clerics, occupied an area just beyond the center of the main cavern. The Hurwarf Clan occupied the Riverrun Cavern just east of the main cavern of Dwarfheart. They were on the whole a band of traditionalists, mostly miners and engineers. They were also adamantly opposed to contact with other races and the outside world, and they were very much against the ruling Syrklist Clan and their policies of expansion and trade. The Skarrad Clan didn't have a stronghold of its own in Dengar. They were the smiths of the dwarven nation, very much fascinated with the sciences and especially architecture and machines. Because they valued trade with the outside world as a market for both their goods and their hired skills, they were supportive of the king.

"So you can appreciate why there is much concern that either my brother or I assume the throne after our father," Korinn said. "Because our clan's reign has been relatively short, we do not have the weight of tradition to support us. I daresay that the Everasts have been grooming an entire stable of contenders since the day Dorinn was wounded."

"Daroban seems respected, even liked," Solveig observed. "That should count for something."

"Not a great deal," Korinn replied. "It's true that Rockhome has prospered under my father's long rule, and this has been a time of peace. But the possibility of war with the dragons has damaged our family's prestige. Trouble with the dragons would have various ramifications, all of which could spell political disaster for us. The Torkrests would demand a military king, no doubt one of their own, to face the threats of a hostile world. The Hurwarfs would want to expel all foreigners, close the gates of our cities, and hunker down below the ground. And they would say the policies of our clan have been the cause of the unrest."

"Unless a Syrklist heir happened to play a part in a Prophecy that promises to oppose the wrath of the dragons," Solveig observed shrewdly. "I understand politics well enough. I was raised as the daughter of one of the first families of Thyatis, where politics is both an art and a religion."

"What you say is true," Korinn agreed. "If our quest succeeds, then the honor I gain from my part will assure my right as heir, or my brother's right by virtue of my support. A Prophecy involves the Immortals, which means that our quest gains the unquestioned support of the clerics, and the entire Clan of the Buhrodars in the bargain. And the wishes of the clerics have great bearing upon the policies of the other clans, especially the Torkrests and the Hurwarfs, who would otherwise prefer an Everast King."

"Then what you're saying is that the next king of Rockhome could be decided by the success or failure of our quest," Thelvyn said, appalled at the idea.

"The quest is our secret," Korinn said. "It is best for our company if our purposes are not known, either to our enemies or to our allies. My father will respect our secret. Besides him, only the king's family and the senior clerics of Kagyar will know."

Thelvyn was learning a good deal about politics, although he was rather dismayed by what he had learned. He had grown to dislike politics when he lived with the Flaem. Their prejudices and their endless schemes convinced him that as a nation they were the most sly and petty people in the world. The clans of the dwarves and their bids for power almost made the Flaem seem inconsequential by comparison. He had always thought of dwarves as being solid and practical, too occupied with their personal affairs to give much thought to political schemes.

He was beginning to think that there was no place in the world where honest folk treated each other with fairness and justice and were free to go about their lives in peace and security. The dwarves had let him down. He had heard Solveig speak often enough of the ruthless politics of the first families of Thyatis, and Sir George said much the same thing about Darokin, and he knew that the elves were almost obsessed with their need to be judgmental. Even the tribes and clans of the Ethengar were constantly at war with one another, over nearly identical pieces of the steppes. He was almost beginning to admire the dragons, who were at least honest.

Korinn continued his explanation of the political factions and alignments of the clans and how they helped to shape Dengar and even Rockhome itself. After he finished, his tour of the city became more conventional, which is what Thelvyn had expected in the first place. The tour continued with the Syrklist stronghold in the Singing Chambers. Thelvyn was misled by the name at first, for it brought to mind the dwarvish fondness for yodeling. He could imagine whole choruses of dwarves holding forth with all the volume they could muster.

The actual reason for its unusual name was quite different. The cavern was located next to the mountain wall, and long, narrow shafts had been cut through the rock. The strong winds of the upper slopes swept down these tunnels, creating a dim, eerie wailing that the dwarves rather imaginatively referred to as singing. For that same reason, the Singing Chambers were often the coldest part of the city, but the Syrklist dwarves did not mind either the cold or the noise, for their cavern was next to to the entrance of the lower city, providing an easy exit to transport their trade goods to Upper Dengar.

Korinn's tour was cut short in a couple of places. He knew better than to take his companions very far into the Riverrun Cavern, for the Hurwarf Clan did not care to have foreigners near their stronghold. The Black Lake Cavern on the west side of the city was closed to visitors altogether. This small cavern was dominated by a large lake fed by an underground stream. The entire cavern was owned by the Everast Clan, which took advantage of the dampness to grow the giant fungus. The fungus was extremely fast-growing; Korinn insisted that, if necessary, the dwarves could close their gates and live belowground for years.

One of the problems with Dengar, at least as far as Thelvyn and Solveig were concerned, was that all the shops were located in the upper city. There was only so much to see wandering from cavern to cavern watching dwarves hard at work, no matter how much delight a dwarf might find in it. The dwarves dressed plainly in simple, dark clothes, and both Solveig and Korinn had dressed much the same way, hoping to avoid standing out any more than they could help. It was a futile effort. The constant stares they attracted made them feel like exotic animals in a zoo.

They returned to the palace at lunchtime. Korinn promised that the northern caverns of Dengar, the old city and Crystal Lake, were much more interesting. But when lunch was nearly over and he still hadn't returned, they began to think that he must have had business to attend to.

Thelvyn had lunch with Solveig on a covered terrace on the north side of the palace. Watching from the terrace, he soon discovered why the dwarves had roofs on their underground buildings. The roof of the cavern was always wet from the water that condensed there, only to drip steadily on the house below. This part of Dwarfheart Cavern had a high roof like a vast dome, and he was surprised to see that there were houses perched on the ledges high above them.

"Look at that!" he exclaimed. "Dwarves live up there."

Solveig came over to the rail of the terrace to look up. "I suppose they learn to be careful. It certainly gives new meaning to the idea of having neighbors drop in."

Sir George sauntered in at that moment, looking generally at peace with the world. "Korinn sends his regrets. He says he'll take you through the back caverns later, if he can get away in time. By the way, is there a good reason why neither of you are wearing shoes?"

"It was Thelvyn's idea," Solveig said. "It helps with the problem with the ceilings. Boots make you at least an inch taller."

"An inch seems rather like a drop in the bucket for the two of you. Does it really help?" Sir George asked as he took a seat at the table.

"It's easier to walk bent over without boots." Solveig replied. "I don't hit my head on doors nearly as often,"

"What happened to Korinn?" Thelvyn asked, changing the subject. "Has something come up?"

"I suspect so," Sir George replied. "I get the impression the king has consulted with the clerics of Kagyar on the matter of the Prophecy. Korinn has probably been called to testify on the matter."

"Is that bad for us?" Solveig asked.

"No, I had expected it. And if Kagyar should see fit to tell his clerics what the Prophecy is all about, it might spare us a ride all the way to Alfheim."

Thelvyn was unfamiliar with anything to do with clerics. He had never dealt with clerics of any type, since they had little business in the Highlands, and the Flaem didn't want them about anyway. In the few stories he had ever heard about them, they had always been domineering and cold, entirely too eager to sacrifice the lives and fortunes of others to serve their own ends. In his own imagination, they had always seemed to be everything he disliked about wizards but worse, and he had never yet met a wizard he liked other than Perrantin. At the same time, he reminded himself, his mother may have been a cleric, and it seemed quite likely that he was one as well.

He found himself hoping the dwarven clerics could tell him about the Prophecy so he wouldn't have to become involved in the process. He hoped it wasn't cowardly to think such thoughts. He needed the company of clerics who had the knowledge and experience he lacked if he were to ever be any good at it himself.

Korinn didn't return before dinner, so they missed their chance to see the rest of the city. It seemed unlikely they would see it this visit, since Sir George wanted to leave early the next morning. When he finally returned, Korinn was apologetic, since dwarves disliked having to break a promise, but Thelvyn and Solveig both assured him that their quest and the threat of the dragons had to come first.

They felt themselves more than compensated, however, for King Daroban entertained his guests that night in the true dwarvish manner, together with members of his household and his clan. There was much singing and dancing, which dwarves aren't particularly good at, and also some drinking, which dwarves did very well. Thelvyn did far more feasting than drinking, but Korinn was able to cajole him into showing what he had learned of dwarvish yodeling. Thelvyn was getting fairly good at it for a beginner, in spite of his lack of opportunity to practice, and the dwarves were both impressed and flattered. The feast ended fairly early, for the travelers had to be on their way at dawn.

Thelvyn looked forward to enjoying his last night in a real bed, even if it was a bit too short, since he had no way of knowing when he might get another chance. However, it seemed as if he had only just fallen asleep when he heard a soft knock at the door of his chamber. Thinking that it must already be dawn, he pulled on his shirt and went to answer it, expecting to find Sir George or Solveig waiting for him. To his surprise, he found that it was Korinn, in the company of a dwarf woman he had never met.

"It's more discreet than Solveig's white robe," Korinn told him, amused. Thelvyn's shirts had been made with unrealistically optimistic expectations about how much he was likely to grow. "May we come in? It's important."

"Yes . . . certainly," Thelvyn said, still sleepy. "Please excuse me a moment."

He hurried to a dark corner of the room to slip into his pants. When he returned, his two visitors had uncovered the magical lamp on the room's small table, which cast just enough light for them to see each other plainly. The dwarf woman had seated herself beside the table, while Korinn remained standing. Thelvyn felt obliged to sit in the remaining chair so he didn't tower over them. The woman was rather slender for a dwarf, with straight black hair worn in a single loose braid, much the way Solveig wore her hair. Her eyes were dark, and she wore a robe of deep rust with the hood pulled back.

"Thelvyn Fox Eyes, this is Kari," Korinn said. The fact

that he didn't give her full name seemed significant.

"I am a cleric of the Immortal Kagyar," she explained. "When we act in the service of our order, we do not use our full names. As a measure of trust, you may know me as Kari, Daughter of Gilas, of the Clan Buhrodar."

"I can't tell you my real name," Thelvyn said. "I don't know it myself."

"I understand," she assured him. "We came to ask something of you, but only to ask. You may refuse at any time, and without fear of insult to us. But I do ask that this visit must remain a secret, even to your companions."

"Sir George knows the essence of what we plan to propose," Korinn added.

"I will keep your secret," Thelvyn said. If Sir George had not objected then Thelvyn saw no reason to object. "In fact, I suspect I know why you are here. You have some reason to believe Kagyar may be able to help solve the mystery of my Prophecy."

"That is true," Kari agreed. "Your Prophecy touches upon the security of Rockhome, as well as dwarves in other lands. That makes it Kagyar's concern. He may be able to answer your questions. Are you willing to try?"

"Of course," he said quickly. "They tell me I am a cleric, but I know nothing about it. I should like to meet other clerics and see what they do, although I know you don't want me prying into your secrets."

Kari wasn't offended. "I do not know your patron, but he is opposed to destruction, and that makes him an ally of Kagyar, at least in this matter. We will help you in whatever way we can, if you are willing to help us. You may not know that all clerics are warriors. Few will ever need to take up weapons against their enemies, yet we are all protectors nevertheless. Granted, I speak only for the lawful orders, for there are also Immortals devoted to evil and conquest, and their clerics act as warlords. Yet if I am able to judge you at all, I would swear that you belong to a lawful order. You have the sense of a protector about you, even a champion. Are you afraid of this Prophecy? It may ask a fearful duty of you."

"I have no choice in the matter," Thelvyn said. "The

dragons know of me now. I doubt I can avoid them forever. However fearful it may be, the Prophecy is my best protection."

"I fear you may be correct," Kari agreed. "You must understand that I cannot promise success, but we will do our best for you. By your leave, we will go now to a place that is holy to Kagyar and where his presence is strong. It is a long journey, and we will be gone most of the night. When it is done, then we will place a spell of restfulness upon you so that you will feel as refreshed in the morning as if you had slept all the night."

"Then let's be on our way," Thelvyn said. "Will I need anything?"

"Come as you are," she told him. "Do not bring any weapon or any artifact of magic or any artifact that may be the symbol of an Immortal other than Kagyar. I am told that you are also a magician. Do not, I beg of you, bring your spellbook. There would be no danger in it, but its presence may be disruptive to our efforts."

They left the palace as quietly as they could. Although they couldn't escape the notice of the guards, Korinn's presence was enough to insure that they weren't challenged.

Lower Dengar was never entirely asleep. The lights were dimmed somewhat, and distant hammering and other sounds of industry still drifted through the great cavern. Kari led the way once they were beyond the palace grounds, leading them to the second of the two great caverns of the Lower City, the Cavern of the Crystal Lake. This was the larger of the two main caverns by far. The ceiling was easily three times as high as the ceiling in Dwarfheart Cavern.

But this cavern was not as heavily settled as the other, for most of its floor was dominated by the a vast lake of icy mountain water, the Crystal Lake, fed by a river emerging from a dark passage at the far end of the chamber. An "island" stood in the center of the lake, although it was in fact a great column of natural stone that supported the roof of the cavern. A line of foundries lay to their left, where ore from the mines was processed into various metals. Thelvyn would have liked to inspect them, recalling his own work at the foundry in his village, for there was work being done here even in the middle of the night. But Kari hurried them along the edge of the lake in the opposite direction, anxious to get past the inhabited regions as quickly and inconspicuously as possible. In a city of dwarves, Thelvyn was anything but inconspicuous.

Beyond this lay only portions of the Old Town, great, dark buildings tucked into corners of the cavern, long since converted into warehouses. The main part of the Old Town lay on the opposite shore of the lake, a maze of narrow passages and crude chambers dating from the days of the first kings, now used only for the convenience of the miners, whose tunnels led north and west beneath the mountain. The entire cavern was cold and damp from the icy waters of the lake. Kari led them into a long arm of the cavern, which gradually became narrower as they went along, until at last she brought them to a place where the river feeding Crystal Lake emerged into a dark passage.

Kari stopped and turned to face her companions. "As far as most of the inhabitants of this city are concerned, the Cavern of the Crystal Lake ends here. But there is a way that leads onward to the north, beneath the mountains. Only the senior clerics know of this route, and we are committed to keep it secret, for it leads to a cavern that is the most sacred place of the Immortal Kagyar. We believe that Denwarf himself may have gone this way when he departed, although we cannot be certain."

"We will keep your secret," Korinn promised her. "Is it far now?"

"The cavern is another three miles," she said, then turned to Thelvyn. "It is not lighted, although I have brought a small lamp."

"Thelvyn can see in the dark as well as any dwarf," Korinn said. "My concern is that he may not be built for the natural passages."

"That is not a concern," Kari told them. "It does require some climbing, however."

Kari had warned him of this before they left the palace, which was why Thelvyn hadn't worn his heavy riding boots. He was young, and he had gone barefoot most of his life. Kari led them on to the very mouth of the river tunnel, where they climbed down the steep embankment that bordered much of the lake and made their way farther along the river until they were just inside the dark river tunnel. Kari told the others to wait for a moment while she went on. After a moment, the dim glow of her lamp appeared from behind a great stone just ahead.

Thelvyn had a hard time slipping around the narrow space between the stone and the river, but then he found himself in a smaller tunnel that led away from the river tunnel for a short distance before turning to parallel it. The bottom of this smaller passage was flooded, but flat stepping stones had been laid along one side. The stones had been placed just far enough apart for a dwarf's short stride, and Thelvyn found the footing rather awkward. Fortunately the tunnel began to rise slightly after a couple hundred yards, becoming dry stone worn smooth by the passage of water.

"This way is under water when the river is high," Kari explained. "For that reason, it is worn smooth by the river, with all the gravel and sand swept away. You will find it easy walking even without shoes, although there are some steep places."

"The clerics haven't improved the passage?" Korinn asked, hurrying behind her.

"A place sacred to Kagyar should be left as he created it."

That seemed to surprise Korinn more than Thelvyn. One of the basic dwarvish philosophies was that almost anything could be improved, especially the gifts of Kagyar. And the first gift of Kagyar to the dwarves had been the caverns of Rockhome.

There were indeed some steep places. At the first one, the passage rose suddenly over three large, rounded boulders, each one higher than Thelvyn was tall. Later they came to a place where the tunnel twisted and circled tightly, at the same time making its way over another series of sharp rises. The rock had smooth, rounded surfaces, with no protrusions to help them pull themselves up. The

dwarves had the native ability to scamper up stones like
lizards, although Thelvyn would have never suspected their
stocky builds would allow them to climb so easily. He had
enough problems of his own. He realized he never could
have come this way in his riding boots.

The passage opened suddenly upon a broad ledge that
ran beside the icy waters of the underground river that fed
Crystal Lake. A few yards beyond where the two passages
came together, the tunnel widened out into a small cavern,
a round chamber perhaps thirty yards across and less than
half again as long. Magical globes cast a soft light, forming
many deep shadows among piles of rounded boulders and
fallen blocks of stone. The river itself ran just to one side of
the cavern, so that there was something of a rounded
pocket or alcove on the near side. Fallen stones made a
crude natural bridge over the river.

Thelvyn knew that this must be the sanctuary of Kagyar,
for there was no denying the sense of some mystic presence. As they stepped into the chamber, five older dwarves
came forth to greet them, all of them in robes of deep rust
like the one Kari wore, although a border of some odd
design graced the hoods of their robes, skillfully embroi-
dered in threads of silver. Thelvyn guessed they were senior
clerics of their order. Kari approached the oldest of the
dwarves, a woman who looked thin and frail but whose
dark eyes shone brightly.

"It was good of you to come, Fila," Kari said, honestly
grateful. "I know the journey here must have been difficult."

"The need was great," Fila replied. She looked up at
Thelvyn and smiled warmly. "So you are the cleric who
does not know the one he serves. An awkward position, I
am sure. You seem to bear no resentment for having so
great a responsibility thrust upon you."

"Resentment would be of no help to me," Thelvyn said.

"Your wisdom makes you worthy of your trust," Fila told
him. "I understand you have tried to commune with your
patron. You have received no message or hint of any type,
not even in your dreams?"

"Not that I'm aware of," he admitted. "I fear that the
time has not yet come for me to know, and that your own

efforts, however much I appreciate them, will be in vain."

"We will see."

Fila led them over to the small alcove, where they could sit on the various boulders scattered about. Dwarves had a great affinity for stone, and it seemed perfectly natural for them to use it for furniture. Fila pushed back the hood of her robe and made herself comfortable. Even though Thelvyn was new at this business, he was convinced that she was preparing to meditate.

"You may indeed be correct," she said. "Perhaps you have not yet received the information you need because it is not yet time for you to know. If that proves to be the case, we cannot help you. Yet you must also consider that there are times when the Immortals must be circumspect, when all their actions must be subtle and indirect or they would not be free to act at all."

"I wouldn't know about such things," Thelvyn admitted. "I've lived my entire life as an orphan among the Flaem of the Highlands. They are quite new to this world and rely on wizards rather than clerics. They don't know much about the Immortals, and they don't seem to want to know. Such things are never spoken of there."

"No one really understands the Immortals or their motives," Fila said. "Still, there is cause to hope. Politics being what they are even among the gods, your patron may not be able to speak with you directly. If that is so, then perhaps an Immortal friendly to his cause could tell you what you need to know."

"That's what we hoped," Thelvyn agreed.

"Then perhaps we should begin," Fila said, settling herself even more comfortably with her legs crossed. "I will attempt to commune with Kagyar, although in such an unusual situation, I cannot promise success. If I am indeed successful, then we will be allowed at least three questions, which must be answered either yes or no. On rare occasions, I am allowed six questions, but we must not expect that. If Kagyar can tell you the meaning of your Prophecy, then he will either speak through me or appear himself in incorporeal form before us. Kari, are you prepared to assist me?"

"Of course."

Kari brought Thelvyn a couple of yards in front of the old cleric. For a long time, Fila sat in silence with her eyes closed as Thelvyn watched carefully, hoping to learn some trick that might help him to do this himself. He had always suspected that his difficulties with clerical spells were largely because there had never been anyone to teach him. After several minutes, he became aware of a presence in the cave.

Kari glanced at him and made a gesture to remain silent, then looked back at the older cleric. "We seek the meaning of a Prophecy that involves Thelvyn Fox Eyes and the dragons. Is there such a Prophecy?"

Fila sat in silence for a moment longer, then took a deep breath. "Yes."

Thelvyn fought to keep himself from shouting out loud. As much as he had felt sure there was a Prophecy, he still had had no way of being certain. Now he finally knew.

"Can you tell us the meaning of the Prophecy?" Kari asked.

Again Fila remained silent for a long moment before she stirred. "No."

This time, Thelvyn was not certain whether or not he should feel relieved. He wasn't sure he was ready to know. Kari turned to him.

"If the answer had been yes, I would have asked if the time had come for you to be told," she said softly. "Now I wonder if it would be better to ask if the clerics of one of the other Immortals might tell you."

Thelvyn smiled. "What do you advise?"

"I am not yet certain," she confessed. "If I ask if the time has come and the answer is no, then you will know that you must wait until the time is right. If the answer is yes, then you must keep searching, but you will not know whom to ask."

"Let's think about the problem," Thelvyn said. "The part we cannot determine for ourselves is whether or not we should keep looking for the answer or waiting. It seems to me that the answer to either question tells me pretty much the same thing, since Kagyar can't actually tell me where to look. I could simply ask if we should go on to Alfheim, but an answer of no wouldn't be specific enough."

"I defer to your logic," Kari said, then turned back to face the older cleric. "Has the time come for Thelvyn to be told the meaning of the Prophecy?"

"Yes," Fila said. Then she started and opened her eyes. "Well, that seems to be the end of it. I'm sorry it was not enough."

Thelvyn rose to his feet, and Korinn appeared beside him.

"What will you do now?" Kari asked Thelvyn. "Will you seek the help of this cleric of the elves?"

"I think so," Thelvyn said. "Sir George believes we should, and he knows more about dragons than anyone. According to him, Terra was the Great One's patron a long time ago, and she wouldn't be pleased by the way the dragons have been behaving lately."

"That seems to be your best hope now. If you must go into Alfheim, then you must," Fila agreed resignedly, as if she thought he was going to the worst of all possible fates. Thelvyn had known all along that one of the principal reasons the dwarves had been willing to help was to spare him the need of getting involved with elves.

"Then if you must leave in the morning, I should get you both back to your beds," Kari said. "As I promised, I will give you a spell for restfulness. I am sorry that we couldn't be of more help to you."

"It was still worth it," Thelvyn assured her. "I know some things now that I could only assume before."

CHAPTER SEVENTEEN

Thelvyn's morning began with another long walk, all the way across Dwarfheart Cavern and then up the long, twisting tunnel that led back to Upper Dengar. Kari's spell of restoration had worked well. Although he had slept less than half the night, he felt completely rested. His feet hurt from walking so far on hard stone, but the spell couldn't do anything about that. Korinn also looked rested, but he said nothing about the journey they had made together during the night, and Thelvyn wasn't about to betray that secret himself.

The horses also seemed refreshed after their extra day of rest. Cadence nipped at him playfully as Thelvyn tried to saddle her. He hadn't seen the sun for two days now, and he was surprised to emerge from the tunnel into a cool, pleasant, sunny morning. The caverns of the dwarves had always felt to him like being indoors during a cold, heavy autumn rain.

They were able to ride their horses through the streets of the city, since it was still early and few people were about yet. Soon they passed through the Three Roads Gate and descended the long, steep road leading down the escarpment from the city. Only when they reached the crossroads and turned southwest upon the Stahl Road did they pause briefly to consider their plans.

"You're planning to take the Darokin Tunnel, aren't you?" Korinn asked Sir George before anyone could speak.

"Our destination is just inside the forest of northeastern Alfheim," the knight explained. "It's probably a five-day ride if we take the most direct route. The alternatives are going back north to the steppes, then east into the Highlands and around the Broken Lands through Darokin, a journey of some four weeks. Or we could go south on the Sardal Road into Ylaruam, a matter of two weeks."

"Enough!" Korinn declared. "I have no objection to taking you through the Darokin Tunnel—that is, if I can find it myself. I've never been through it."

"No?" Sir George asked. "You mean to say that you never used the Darokin Tunnel to raid and harass the elves during your misspent youth?"

"I'm still in my misspent youth," the dwarf said. "And, no, I have never been to Alfheim. My clan believes in trading with the elves, even if we don't like them. Think of the embarrassment to our nation if the son of the king had been slain or captured raiding elven villages."

They took the road south from the city of Stahl. Although it wasn't one of the major roads, leading only to villages and mines in the far south of the Stahl Valley, it was still maintained meticulously, with stone bridges over all the rivers and major streams. Within two days, they had passed through the lowlands of Stahl and entered a narrow wooded valley that led deep into the mountains. From time to time, Korinn stood in his stirrups to watch for the trail south, but it was Thelvyn who saw it first. By nightfall, they had come to the top of the valley at the very edge of the mountains, where they made their camp for the night.

The next morning they followed the trail into the mountains, the southern reach of the Altan Tepes. In spite of its name, the Darokin Tunnel wasn't an underground passage but a trail that ran a remarkably straight, level course through a series of valleys and hidden passes. Korinn laughed when Thelvyn was surprised to find it wasn't an actual tunnel. It was forty miles across the mountains, a long day's ride, and the dwarves would never have dug a forty-mile tunnel merely for the sake of harassing the elves. Thelvyn enjoyed the ride through the mountains, which reminded him very much of home.

The companions came through the mountains late that same day, but Sir George had them make their camp for the night there in the woods bordering the mountains. Although they were now in Darokin, in the narrow band between the mountains that closed the circle around the forests of Alfheim, this was a wild and empty area, often overrun by bands of goblins. The elves and the army of Darokin did their best to keep evil creatures driven out of these lands, but bands of goblins and orcs were always wandering eastward along the mountains from the Broken Lands, searching for villages and travelers to rob.

When they rode on again in the morning, they stayed in the light woods and hills near the mountains rather than the open lands beyond. This was Sir George's idea, and his reason was simple. If they rode out in the open, then they would be visible to bands of goblins or the elves of Alfheim for miles. And while he knew he could handle the elves, even with a dwarf in their company, he would rather not have to. His plan was to stay out of the open as much as possible until they were directly opposite their destination, then ride straight in. That would would keep the time they had to spend in the Canolbarth Forest, and their chances of meeting elves, to a minimum.

"We're making for the woods just this side of the region known as the Shadowdown," he explained to the others when they asked. "The place we seek is called Silvermist, which is fortunately only a few miles from the edge of the forest."

"Shadowdown," Korinn muttered derisively. "Silvermist. Silly elven names."

"Is Silvermist a village?" Solveig asked, ignoring the dwarf.

"No. It's a large home standing alone in the woods," Sir

George said. "It's a sanctuary of Terra, and elven clerics of Terra dwell there."

"I get the impression you've been there before," Solveig said.

"I go there when I can," he admitted. "The last time was years ago, when you were still a child. I have old friends there."

Whenever they came to the top of a hill, Thelvyn could see the dark forest of Canolbarth on the horizon across perhaps twenty miles of empty, hilly land. He had seen elves before, but only rarely and briefly. They had always been strangers among the Flaem.

He had never thought much about it before, but he found he was becoming quite interested in meeting the elves. He had always wondered if his own people were distantly related to elves. He wanted to see elves at ease in their own element, so that he could watch them and listen to them and perhaps learn if they were in any way like him.

Around noon of the second day since they had emerged from the tunnel, they came to a large region of rugged woods south of the mountains. Sir George and Thelvyn climbed to the top of the highest nearby hill. After they had stared at the distant forest for some time, Sir George declared that they were directly north of the forest path that would take them to Silvermist. Thelvyn wasn't sure he liked the looks of the land, for he could see a large area of darkness that lay like a deep, dense fog over that part of the Canolbarth. At this point, the edge of the forest was no more than ten miles away. Sir George allowed them to stop for lunch only briefly, declaring that it would be best to reach their destination before they were required to stop for the night.

"This part of the Canolbarth Forest is called the Shadowdown," he explained during their hasty meal. "Some strange, permanent enchantment has been laid upon this part of the forest. The region is blighted by darkness, which causes even the brightest days to be dim and dusky and the nights to be deep and dark. Elves who thrive upon the night prefer to live in this place."

"Is this where you are taking us?" Korinn asked nervously.

"We'll only be going through the very edge of it," Sir George answered. "The part of the forest where we will be going is unpopulated and seldom visited out of respect for the special magic of that place and for the clerics who dwell there."

"The elves aren't fond of strangers coming into their forests, or so I have always heard," Solveig said. "Are the clerics going to be pleased to have us turn up?"

"The clerics of Terra differ from any of the elves you will meet elsewhere in Alfheim," Sir George replied. "They exist to serve their Immortal, and few others seek the service of Terra. Even the elves have nearly forgotten Terra in their fascination for their younger patron Immortals, Ilsundal and Maeliden."

They rode on again as soon as the horses had had a short rest. Sir George met no objections when he encouraged his companions to hurry. They had all heard stories about the mysterious forest of Alfheim, and no one wanted to be caught there at night. Thelvyn was sent to ride in the lead, using his sharp eyes to watch for the trail leading into the woods. But when they came into the open lands just beyond the forest, Thelvyn began to feel as if they were being watched. Turning in his saddle, saw distant figures moving through the sparse woods far behind them.

"Trouble," he warned. "We're being followed. Maybe dozen goblins riding wolves some three miles behind us."

"They probably won't follow us into the forest," Sir George said, staring at the dark woods ahead. "How far would you say we have to go?"

"Eight to ten miles, I'd guess," Thelvyn answered. "That region of darkness makes it hard to say for certain."

"They could make up three miles in that time," Sir George admitted frankly. "It depends on how far they've come already. Wolves are faster than horses, but horses have greater endurance. Well, this is yet another inducement to hurry. I suggest we do."

They urged their horses on, setting the best pace they could hope to maintain over the next ten miles. These were the same horses that had been with them all the way from Braejr; they were a swift, hearty stock, and they should be used to anything by now. Thelvyn hoped he wasn't getting too sure of himself, but he wasn't overly concerned about a dozen goblins. He had held his own against dragons, and he had some formidable companions as well. If they had to, they could fight.

"Will they follow us into the forest?" he asked Sir George quietly as they rode alongside each other.

"I think not," the old knight said. "I certainly hope not. Wolves are better in the forest than horses."

Thelvyn had to stay in the lead to try to spot the path. He wasn't certain he could. The shadows of the forest hampered his ability to penetrate the darkness while he was still riding in the sun. He would have to rely entirely upon his distance vision. He could only hope that Sir George had chosen well, since he doubted he would actually see the path until they came quite close. At the worst, they could simply try to lose themselves somewhere in the deep forest. The only trouble was that goblins could see well in the dark.

He couldn't help turning around again to see if the goblins were gaining on them. They had emerged from the rough, scattered woods and were riding through the rolling, grassy hills. He could see them plainly, which meant the goblins could see their party as well. By the time they were about three miles from the forest, the goblins were no more than a mile behind. Sensing success, they were urging the panting wolves to give everything they had left. Thelvyn noticed that they weren't common wolves such as he had seen in the north, but massive animals, almost the size of ponies.

At last they entered the fringes of the region of darkness. The sun grew dim and distant, and the light of the bright afternoon faded to nearly dusk. Thelvyn could see the edge of the forest more clearly now, for the shadows that had distorted his vision resolved themselves into the shapes of trees and brush. The outer edge of the Canolbarth was dense with saplings and small trees and other low forest growth, which helped him to spot the opening of the wooded path. Sir George's choice had been fortunate, or else his memory for a place he hadn't been in twenty years had been uncannily accurate. By the time Thelvyn saw it, the path lay no more than a quarter of a mile ahead and some two hundred yards to their right.

"Quickly now," Sir George shouted to the others. "If the horses have anything left to give, this is the time to give it."

Since they had packhorses with them, they couldn't easily urge the horses to a full run, so they settled into a long, loping gallop. Fortunately it was enough to keep them ahead of the goblins. The Canolbarth Forest rose quickly before them. They passed the first few saplings and smaller trees, then disappeared among the deep shadows of the forest. Sir George had them slow the horses to a trot almost at once, for the forest trail was too rough and narrow to try to lead the packhorses at a run.

Sir George knew what he was doing well enough. The deep underbrush began to thin rapidly after the first couple of hundred yards, for too little light penetrated the thick forest canopy to support much low growth. The trees here were towering giants with dense, dark canopies. The land about their massive trunks became hilly, broken by small cliffs and ridges of stone and great, moss-covered boulders. Even so, the relatively clear path meant they could once again encourage the horses to greater speed. Although it was still only the middle of the afternoon, the day was as dark as dusk.

Thelvyn dropped to the back of the line to watch the trail behind them. When he saw that the goblins had followed them into the forest, he shouted a warning to the others. Sir George called for them to stop.

"We'll never outrun them now," he said, drawing his sword. "We'll have to provide additional discouragement."

They formed a line across the trail, with Solveig and Sir George in the center, while Thelvyn and Korinn took the outside, near the edge of the forest where they could see better in the dim light. Perrantin took his place behind them, where he could be protected from attack while he prepared his magic. Thelvyn drew his sword, realizing he had never used it before. He had been in some dangerous places, but his only previous fight had been with magic when he had used his unexpected clerical abilities against the dragons of Torkyn Fall.

Their enemy was upon them even sooner than the goblins had expected. Their great wolves suddenly leapt out of the shadows of the forest into their midst. Solveig and Sir George charged into battle without a moment's hesitation. Korinn came at the goblins with gusto, taking advantage of the height provided by his horse to use his heavy battle-axe against their round iron helmets. Thelvyn responded mostly by instinct, urging Cadence forward to close with the goblins before they could organize a counterattack. He seemed suddenly possessed of a cold, calculating fury, immune to fear, moving with a precise skill he hadn't known he possessed. His calm reaction seemed to prove that he was indeed the child of a race of warriors.

The goblins shouted and their wolves howled, but they were unable to recover from the surprise attack to organize themselves. The wolves were nearly spent after the long chase, but nevertheless they leapt and snapped with almost insane fury. Thelvyn soon realized that the wolves remained formidable opponents even after their rider had gone down. Perrantin did his own part to help. One after another, small shafts of white light like daggers or magic arrows would dart from him, each one unerringly striking one of the swift wolves as it snapped at the horses.

After several minutes of savage fighting, the surviving goblins drew back a short distance up the trail, then turned and brought out their short, curved bows. Thelvyn decided that matters had gone far enough. Making his first conscious effort to command his powers, he lifted his arms toward the goblins. He was surrounded by an indistinct sphere of magical force, and then blinding spears of lightning leapt out from his fingertips to rip across the ground in the center of the enemy line. Goblins and wolves were scattered by the blast, and the air was filled with the stench of burnt fur. The few survivors decided that they had had enough and retreated as quickly as they could.

"You could have done that sooner," Solveig told him.

"I wasn't sure I could," Thelvyn admitted reluctantly.

They took stock of themselves, eager to move on. As fierce as the battle had been, it had also been brief, and things had gone very much in their favor. Solveig had been bitten on the arm, hardly more than a scratch, and a couple of the horses had also taken minor bites. Sir George reminded Thelvyn that he probably possessed a cleric's talent for healing minor injuries. Solveig made him practice on the horses first, but he proved himself an adept healer. They tended their weapons, then returned to their saddles and were on their way again in minutes.

Once Thelvyn began to feel certain the goblins hadn't dared to follow, he began to look about. His ability to see in the dark had been with him all his life, so he really had no idea what the shadows and the night looked like to other folk. He could only guess from what they said and from how they acted. He had never understood how people could go bumbling into walls or doors or furniture in a dark room when he could see perfectly well. The deep shadows of the forest, even in the enchanted darkness of Shadowdown, were completely invisible to him. The colors were deeper, the green of leaves darkened almost to black, but every small detail was readily discernible.

And so he watched the forest, or perhaps it was more accurate to say that he tried to leave himself open to the feel of the forest. All he knew for certain about the elves, except of course for their disagreeable manners, was that they loved the woods. They had come from a forested land in the ancient days, long before the fall of Blackmoor, and their age of exile had brought them back at last to the forest where they felt most at home. Thelvyn had always supposed that his own race might share some distant ancestry with the elves, based on certain facets of his appearance. His ears were slightly pointed and his dark eyes were large. His features were fine and distinct if not actually delicate.

And so he wondered if he might feel some affinity for this forest, if a place such as this might awaken some ancient memory or satisfy some need that he had never felt before. The mountains had always felt like home to him, and he loved the heights and the northern forests. But he had always assumed that that was simply because he had been born and raised there. He noticed after a short time that he felt something in this forest, unlike anything he had ever known. It felt like a very ancient place, and there was a sense of presence here, in some way related to the presence he had felt in the sanctuary of Kagyar, a sense of the power of the Immortals. He sensed some inexplicable delight, even excitement, although he couldn't say why. Nevertheless, he felt somehow that the mountains and the deep pine forests were his home.

Night was at last beginning to fall when the winding forest path brought them suddenly to their destination. Silvermist was a large rustic house, built of mortared stone and timbers, with a roof of brown tiles shaped like leaves. It sat back from the trail, in the shadows beneath the dark, dense forest. There was a small clearing in front of the house, although sunlight probably could only penetrate the small opening in the forest canopy above during the middle hours of the day. There was a round wooden structure of some sort in the middle of the yard, apparently a small covered alcove where people could sit, although Thelvyn admitted that it might have been nothing more than a covered well. A wide path beyond the house led to the stables, a long structure also constructed of heavy timbers.

It was a welcome, comfortable sight after a long journey in the wilds. Soft golden lights shone from many of the windows, and the smell of fresh bread baking and other things cooking for dinner tantalized their nostrils. Elves came out to meet them as they brought their horses into the yard. They looked like the few elves Thelvyn had seen in the Highlands, small, slender people, mostly a head or more shorter than he, with pointed ears and large eyes. Most of them had brown skin and woody brown hair with black eyes, also much like himself, although any similarity ended at that point. Their ears were much larger than his own, their faces narrower, with delicate, pointed chins and small noses. A few elves were closer to his own height, with slightly heavier, sharper features.

He reminded himself that this wasn't a village, but a small, isolated order of clerics. Certainly they seemed unafraid to have a band of visitors descend upon them out of a dark evening. Thelvyn suspected there were perhaps two dozen elves in all. They were dressed in the elven manner, wearing white shirts with long, flowing sleeves and vests and pants of dark, supple leather. Some wore soft forest boots, although most were barefoot. Since they all dressed much the same, Thelvyn dedcided it must be the attire of their order.

The elves recognized Sir George before he could introduce himself. It was obvious they were pleased to have him return. Eager hands took charge of their horses even as the riders dismounted. One of the taller elves came forward to greet Sir George.

"It's been a long time, even as an elf counts the years."

"My travels don't bring me this way often," the old knight said. "Things look just the same, Derrion. How have you been?"

"Busier than ever," the elf admitted. "Alfheim is changing in subtle ways. Other folk believe the Canolbarth is just settling into her maturity, but we believe that the forest is preparing itself for a new age of the world. By what little we have heard, we seem to have been right."

"Perhaps a new age is beginning," Sir George said thoughtfully. "And we're stuck smack in the middle of it all. But more of that later. How is Ferial?"

"Ferial departed for a sanctuary in the eastern forest five years ago," Derrion replied. "Sellianda is our leader now. She is young—very young indeed—but wise and strong."

"I don't recall that I've ever met Sellianda," Sir George remarked. "Can you take me to her right away? This is more urgent than I can easily describe."

"She will see you at once, I am sure, if this cannot wait until after the evening meal," Derrion said, looked concerned. "Do you recall the way to the study?"

"I do," Sir George said, then turned to his companions. "Thelvyn, you come with me. The rest of you get settled in. Go on to dinner without us if we don't return in time."

Thelvyn stepped away from his horse to join Sir George, and the elves saw him clearly for the first time. Several of them drew back in surprise, and then they all began to stare at him and speak among themselves quietly. He thought he could guess the reason for their surprise, and he was rather embarrassed. They probably supposed, from his height and his general larger size, that he was a half-breed, yet they didn't seem offended or angry. Just very interested.

He followed Sir George into the house, feeling anxious. Somehow he had the feeling that something in his life was about to change. On the inside, the great house of Silvermist looked much as it did outside, a comfortable rustic home, simply but attractively, built with many exposed timbers and planks of dark wood, although some of the walls had been plastered and painted creamy white. The ceiling was supported by wooden beams. The chairs were made of leather stretched over curious-looking frames, which he was to find more comfortable than he had expected.

They came at last to a large room on the lower floor where books lined shelves along the walls nearly to the ceiling. Framed glass doors looked out upon a porch set in a corner, formed by the main part of the house and a short wing behind it. An elf maiden stood before one set of shelves, an open book in her hands. She was taller and had less delicate features than most, although Thelvyn found her more beautiful because of it. Indeed, he was quite taken with her, although he wouldn't have dared to let her know it. But if she was the leader of this group, there was nothing about her to show that. She was dressed very much like the others, in a flowing shirt of white and soft leather pants and vest.

She turned sharply as they entered, perhaps surprised to see foreigners in her house. By the look she gave them, Thelvyn was convinced that she was the leader here. Her gaze was neither hostile nor disapproving, but it conveyed at once that she was mistress here, no matter what business had brought them. When she saw Thelvyn, she reacted much as the others had. Her eyes widened, and it seemed for a moment that she could not, or dared not, speak. She closed the book quickly and placed it back on the shelf.

"Do you know me?" Thelvyn asked at last, overcome by curiosity.

"No, I do not know you," she said. "I think I must have been shown a vision of you, in a dream I still cannot recall. That is often how the Immortals speak with us. I have been waiting for you, although I didn't know it until this moment. Come, you must tell me all about why you are here."

She sat them both down in chairs near the glass doors, while she brought over a chair for herself and sat facing them. Although she sat casually, with her long legs folded beneath her, she seemed somehow to convey great dignity and nobility. Thelvyn was distracted by Sir George's rather uncharacteristic discomfort. He paid her more honest respect than he had the king of Rockhome.

Sellianda wanted to know every detail of Thelvyn's life, particularly the circumstances surrounding his birth and his mother's escape from the dragons and recent events on his travels. Sir George seemed embarrassed to explain the part he had played at the time of Thelvyn's birth. Perhaps he was beginning to think he had rather overstepped himself. Interfering in the affairs of dragons was one thing, but interfering in the affairs of the Immortals was quite another matter. But while he might have been embarrassed, it didn't stop him from responding to her question. Sellianda became especially interested when she heard of the events at Torkyn Fall.

"That was when I became aware that something very strange was happening," Sir George explained. "You see, the dragon wasn't about to let us escape, but Thelvyn was able to save the day with a quite unexpected display of clerical powers. He was able to cast a spell of holding on the dragon."

"That is impressive," Sellianda said. "Only a dragon cleric should have been capable of that."

"He also was able to block a passage with lightning," the knight added. "His newly discovered powers, however, have led to considerable confusion. He is unquestionably a cleric, for he is able to use clerical spells, although he continues to be a magic-user as well."

"It does not necessarily follow that he is a cleric," Sellianda told them. "His patron Immortal might simply have been acting through him, granting him temporarily all the powers he needed to save himself. However, the fact that he continues to use clerical powers argues strongly that he probably is. I could judge this matter best if you will tell me which of the Immortals is his patron."

"That's the part we were hoping you could help us with," Sir George said. "Despite being a powerful cleric, he doesn't know the identity of his patron and is not allowed to commune with him. The only clue we have is a Prophecy we don't know anything about except that it scares the willies out of dragons."

Sellianda sighed loudly. "Discovering his patron may not be an easy task. Have you tried?"

"I was taken before the clerics of Kagyar," Thelvyn explained sheepishly. He hadn't told this to Sir George, but he thought he should reveal it now. "They discovered very little, but Kagyar confirmed that there is a Prophecy and that the time has come for me to know about it."

"I thought perhaps a cleric of Terra could help us," Sir George told her. "Your order is devoted to Terra, and she was always sympathetic to the causes of the dragons. I don't think she would approve of their present behavior."

"My patron might be able to tell me something," Sellianda agreed, although she still sounded uncertain. "I cannot say how long I might need. Perhaps tonight, if the time has indeed come that you are to be told. You are welcome to stay here for as long as it requires."

They had been talking together for so long that dinnertime had come and gone, although the elves had saved something for them. Sellianda didn't join them at the table, much to Thelvyn's disappointment, but chose to remain in the study. It was probably just as well, Thelvyn decided. She hardly looked any older than he, but that could be deceptive with elves. But the matter of years wasn't the principal problem. She was a lady, wise and learned and the proud and capable mistress of her order, while he was just a lad with a Prophecy he didn't understand.

Silvermist had been built to accommodate more residents than it had presently, so there were guest rooms available for each of the travelers in the back wing on the second floor. In the evening the elves gathered on the wide patio behind the house, talking and singing and playing musical instruments. They invited their visitors to join them, but Thelvyn felt uncomfortable. He remembered all too well their reaction when they first saw him. He felt embarrassed to think they might take him for a half-breed or some distant barbaric kin. He was also somewhat self-conscious about the fact that these were real clerics, while he felt as if he were only a make-believe one.

As it happened, he didn't have a chance to join the others anyway. He had been watching the elves through a set of framed glass doors at the end of a short hall leading out onto the patio, wondering if he should join them or return to his room. Then Sellianda approached him from behind.

"I am going to the pool, the sacred place of our sanctuary," she told him. "Come with me."

She led him out the main door of the house and across the yard. He could see that the small round structure he had noticed earler was indeed a shelter with places to sit. Beyond that, they came to the forest itself, where they followed a path leading into the woods. The forest seemed dark and vast, but also ancient and very much alive, threatening only to those who did not come as friends. The path was narrow, a well-worn dirt trail that weaved slowly between the stones and the trunks and spreading roots of the trees.

Sellianda led them several hundred yards through the forest, until the lights of the house were far behind them. Suddenly the path opened up on the edge of a forest pool. The pool was in the shape of a broad oval, the water cold, deep and clear. The far side of the pool was surrounded by a bank cut from a low cliff of gray stone. The pool was fed by a small stream that trickled gently from the cliff above. The near side of the pool was encircled by a bank that was covered with what Thelvyn took to be grass, although it was in fact soft, thick moss dotted with tiny white flowers. Sellianda removed her slippers, signaling Thelvyn to do likewise, so that they would not trample the moss.

"This feels like the most ancient place in the world," Thelvyn said.

"It does, although you are deceived," Sellianda told him as she seated herself on one of the rounded boulders near the back of the bank. "What you sense is the presence of one of the most ancient and elemental forces in our world. Alfheim itself was magically created by the elves out of a desolate land a thousand years ago, which is not a long time in the age of the world."

"There used to be elves in the land where I grew up," Thelvyn said. "They didn't care for the Flaemish settlers, and they went away."

"Do you dislike elves for some reason?" Sellianda asked suddenly.

"No, I like elves well enough," he insisted. "I'm just embarrassed about myself, to tell the truth. You see, I don't even know what race I belong to. Sir George knew my mother, and he's always said she looked just like me, which suggests that neither she nor I am a half-breed. But I have no way to be certain of that. Except for my size, I look quite a bit like an elf."

"You are not an elf," she told him decisively. "I cannot say what you are, but you could not belong to any breed of elf, unless there was some tie between your people and the elves a very long time ago. I haven't failed to notice that your eyes are blue where the eyes of all other folk are white. Is it so important that you know your race?"

"No, not really. But I saw the way your people reacted to me. I saw the way you reacted to me. To tell the truth, I was afraid of being treated like an outcast."

"No, quite the opposite," Sellianda insisted. "Thelvyn, there is a myth among our people of the half-elf, a remarkable being who possesses the best qualities of both men and elves with none of the faults. In all things, in your appearance, in your abilities, you seem to be exactly what the half-elf is said to be. Is it surprising the elves wonder if that is what you are? But the half-elf is only a myth. The product of the union of human and elf is always either one or the other, depending on the mother. But you have other concerns, I suspect."

Thelvyn nodded. "The dwarves tried to help me, but they couldn't. Am I a cleric? You said earlier I might be able to use clerical spells because one of the Immortals is granting me enough power to take care of myself. I've always wondered how I can be a cleric when I don't even know my patron."

"There are clerical orders that serve a cause rather than one of the Immortals. Yet Immortals sympathetic to their cause will often grant them powers. Or did you not know that?"

"Yes, I had heard that," Thelvyn said thoughtfully. "Then it's possible that I don't know my patron because I don't have one."

"Yes, that is entirely possible," Sellianda agreed. "But speculation is useless. I might be able to answer your questions in the morning, assuming you are allowed to know everything you desire."

Thelvyn nodded slowly. "I don't know have the faintest idea how to act like a cleric."

Sellianda laughed. "My young friend, there is no such thing as acting like a cleric. Clerics behave according to the dictates of their order, and those dictates vary widely. We tend to be very informal here, because nothing is expected of us except that we be more open-minded than most elves. Races other than elves belong to our order, and in other lands. You should behave according to the dictates of your duty. Since you do not yet know what your duty is, I would say that you are doing fine just as you are."

"I hope so," Thelvyn said, sounding somewhat doubtful.

"Are you concerned with the reputation of clerics?" she asked, and laughed again at his surprise. "Being one myself, don't you suppose I know what reputation clerics have? I have found you to be neither cold nor self-serving. I hope that you have not found me to be too much of a bore myself."

"Hardly," he said. "I must admit, you scared me a bit at first. But that's your job, I suppose."

"And I still frighten you a bit, I suspect," Sellianda added, to his great discomfort.

"You are very perceptive," he said.

"Perceptive enough to know when someone is developing an infatuation with a certain elf maiden?"

Thelvyn thought he would fall off the rock he was sitting on. "I'm sorry about that. I know you must be years older than I."

"I am one hundred and sixty-eight years old, which is not at all old for one of my race," she told him. "But I will say this. We will meet again, you and I. When you have learned to command the life that lies before you, you will become a very remarkable person indeed. For now, at least, I must ask that you leave me. I feel my patron is willing to speak with me, and I must be alone with him."

Thelvyn bowed awkwardly, then withdrew quietly. As he followed the path back to the clearing, he became aware of the growing sense of some great mystical presence, and he felt that he was intruding. Yet he also felt that his whole life was about to change suddenly once again, and for the first time, he was beginning to look forward eagerly to his future. Sellianda had made him aware of something he would have never realized for himself—the person he might become because of the Prophecy. Until now, he had simply assumed he would remain very much the same, a confused and inept young man who would muddle through as best he could.

CHAPTER EIGHTEEN

The next morning, Thelvyn found his companions sitting on the benches on the porch behind the house. They were finishing a light breakfast and entertaining themselves by comparing strange names of people they had known. Solveig seemed to have the advantage at that point, since she had once known a Traladaran merchant named Borrick Bottuck. That had led to a listing of the names of every halfling any of them had ever known, which had put an end to the game. Thelvyn was inclined to think that none of them were in a position to make fun of anyone's name.

"So what do you want on this fine morning?" Sir George inquired, referring to breakfast.

"Blithe company and stimulating conversation," Thelvyn remarked as he seated himself on the bench beside Solveig.

"I'm not entirely certain, but I suspect I detect a faint note of criticism," the knight remarked, taking note of Thelvyn's bare feet. "Have you once again foresworn the use of boots?"

"No, but I can't for the life of me recall where I left them," he answered. "Would the elves have taken away my boots during the night for some reason?"

"I suspect your boots would be too large for them, if you are implying theft. As for cleaning or repair, I'm rather sure they would have asked first," Sir George replied. "I haven't seen Sellianda this morning. I wonder if she had any luck in her chat with her patron."

"For someone who has business with the Immortals, you don't worry much how you speak about them," Perrantin observed.

"I don't believe you have much cause to worry," he said. "I'm not a cleric. I'm just a business associate."

He paused, seeing Sellianda approach. He decided he'd really rather not have her hear what he was saying. She was carrying a pair of boots, which she handed to Thelvyn. "You left these on the bank of the pool last night."

"I wondered what happened to them," Thelvyn said innocently as he took the boots from her. He took no notice of the surprised looks of his companions.

Sir George was at a rare loss for words. He finally recovered and turned to Sellianda. "Did you by any chance find time to commune with your patron?"

Sellianda brought over a wooden chair so she could sit facing them. "To come directly to the point, I cannot tell you what you wish to know. I learned nothing about the Prophecy. I am afraid you have come to the wrong place. This matter began with the dragons, and only the dragons can tell you what you need to know."

"The dragons?" Korinn repeated incredulously. "We've seen enough dragons to last a lifetime. Somehow, they never seemed to be in a mood to be helpful."

Sellianda smiled. "What I should have said is that you need to talk to the *right* dragons. The good news I have for you is that the dragons are not at war with the world. The attacks are limited to rogues, mostly young red and green dragons, resulting from a very unsettled state of affairs among the dragons but hardly a state of war. As indeed Sir George has already guessed, the Great One, the Immortal patron of all dragons, is in no way responsible for this state of affairs and wishes to see it brought to a peaceful conclusion. Needless to say, his primary concern is for the welfare of all dragons."

"Then is he willing to assist us?" Sir George asked.

"That is more complicated. I cannot easily explain, and for the moment, I am not permitted to. The reason is that there is someone who is better suited to tell you what you must know. My own part is limited to explaining what you must do next. You must return to the mountains of the far north. There you will be met by one of the dragon clerics, who will lead you to your final destination."

"A dragon cleric?" Thelvyn asked. "A cleric of the order loyal to the Great One?"

"That is so," Sellianda agreed. "Do you have any problems with having a dragon join your company?"

"It does sound a little intimidating," Thelvyn admitted, "Considering that the dragons hate me."

"You will have no reason to fear the cleric who joins you," she told him. "You will both be serving a common cause. Where you must go to meet this cleric of the dragons is quite another matter, however. Now you must journey to the other kingdom of the elves, the Sylvan Realm, on the far side of the Hyborean Reaches."

"Oh, that's a simple matter!" Sir George declared. "We should be there by the middle of summer."

Sellianda smiled. "I am also instructed to assist you on that account. I know a way to get you there by tomorrow night, although I fear it will betray one of the greatest secrets of the elves. You must ask no questions about our destination."

"We've had practice keeping other people's secrets," Thelvyn said.

"I'm sure you have. If you are ready, we will depart within the hour."

Thelvyn had heard of the Sylvan Realm, the oldest of the elven settlements in that part of the world. He also knew that it was very far away, beyond the mountains of the Hyborean Reach, which were far to the northwest of the Wendarian Range. From Alfheim, they would need nearly two weeks just to return to the frontier village where he had grown up, and it would still be a long journey to the Sylvan Realm. If Sellianda had some means to get them there by the next night, it must be magical.

He was also excited about the thought that Sellianda herself would be going with them for a time, although he didn't fool himself into thinking it was because of him. He was pleased that she seemed to like him, which came as a total surprise. But he also sensed that she wanted to wait to get to know him better until after his affair with the dragons was settled. Her words had seemed a polite way of telling him that he was very young and inexperienced, but she expected him to grow up quickly.

Thelvyn had spent his entire life among humans, either Flaemish settlers or people like Sir George and his friends and associates. Of course, Sir George wasn't any more human than he was, but the old knight had seemed very human in character and habits. Thelvyn was beginning to think that he was doing himself a disservice by thinking of himself as human. By doing so, he may well be limiting himself. Sellianda was an elf, and he felt close and comfortable with her even if he wasn't an elf. Whatever Thelvyn was, she had shown him how to see what a strange yet unique and remarkable person he really was.

Sellianda led the party out of the clearing onto one of the dark forest trails. She was riding one of the small, curious elven horses, too tall for a pony but lean and graceful, almost frail in appearance. Thelvyn couldn't tell where she was leading them, and, true to their promise, no one ever asked. At first they were challenged frequently by elven warriors, but Sellianda's quiet explanations were enough to insure that they were allowed to continue.

These challenges soon turned to stares of curiosity, for word had preceded them that a half-elf was in their party. Whether it was true or not, the elves wanted to see for themselves. Thelvyn was beginning to feel that he was some kind of oddity; he didn't care for it. He supposed that much of his discomfort was due to his childhood among the Flaem, who considered anything different to be undesirable. But it was Korinn who was most ill at ease. In his mind, a dwarf traveling in Alfheim was asking for trouble.

The first day of travel brought them out of the region of darkness. Thelvyn knew only that they were going southeast, through lower Shadowdown into the heart of Alfheim. Since he knew so little about the land, he had no idea where they could be going. The trail they traveled was intersected at frequent intervals by crosstrails, which reminded Thelvyn of a spider's web. The great forests and sunlit glades of Alfheim were beautiful and peaceful, but they all seemed the same to Thelvyn. He had no idea how Sellianda was finding their way.

They camped that night in the deep woods. There were many small villages where they might have spent the night, but Sellianda seemed to be purposely avoiding any towns or settlements. That probably was best, considering how most elves felt about having foreigners in their lands. Sellianda insisted upon standing watch, explaining that there were dangers in the elven woods that were to be faced nowhere else. Thelvyn decided to sit up with her for a while. He didn't expect to have another chance to speak with her for a long time to come.

"Aren't you tired?" he asked.

"Elves do not need to sleep as regularly as other folk," she told him. "If we must, we can stay awake for a long time. Simply by sitting and relaxing, we can be as refreshed in the morning as if we had actually slept. Perhaps you will find the same is true of your race."

He wondered if it could be true. He knew he could go for a long time without sleep and not feel the worse for it; he generally went to bed at a certain time out of habit. He felt both excited and a little annoyed with himself that he was still discovering things about himself. "You were up all last night as well, were you not?"

"Not at all," Sellianda insisted. "I concluded my business with my patron very soon after you left."

Thelvyn poked for a moment at a piece of wood in their small campfire. There had been few times during their long journey when they had dared have one. "You spoke last night of the legend of the half-elf. Could there have been a union of men and elves in the distant past, perhaps assisted by magic, from which a new race was created?"

"Perhaps," Sellianda agreed. "Magic, or even the intervention of the Immortals, could have made possible the selection of only the desired traits of both races. But I still do not believe you are a half-elf. You seem to be much more."

Thelvyn frowned uncertainly. "I suspect that I've been complimented."

"I was speaking honestly and objectively," she said. "I do not mean to disappoint you, but you should not concern yourself with the mystery of who and what you are just yet. You have a long, difficult task ahead of you."

They rode on through the next day, finally coming to a land of many small lakes and streams. They had passed out of the deep forest into a broad, shallow valley scattered with small bodies of water, which glittered like silver in the afternoon sun. Dense stands of tremendously tall trees stood majestically between glades of green, windswept grass. There was much evidence that elves lived in this land. From time to time, they would see a cluster of small houses set back amid the trees, or even up in the trees themselves. None of these were large enough to be considered a village. Indeed, the entire valley seemed like a great city that was so widely scattered that the land hardly seemed inhabited.

Far ahead, in the middle of the valley, they saw the first buildings of stone they had seen in all of Alfheim. There were three of them, all built of brownish stone, and by their odd shapes, it was difficult to say whether they were castles or fortresses or something else altogether.

As always, news of their arrival had preceded them. A small band of soldiers, mounted on slender elven horses, waited beside the road to join them. They seemed more like an escort of honor than a guard as they led the travelers down the trail.

"Is our destination the Path of the Rainbow?" Perrantin asked.

Sellianda glanced at him. "I should have known you would guess. You should know that the function of the path is quite different from stories you might have heard."

Thelvyn looked confused. "I'm afraid I haven't heard

any stories about such a path."

"In ages past, an unknown Immortal created the Path of the Rainbow," Perrantin explained. "If you locate one end of the enchanted rainbow, and if you can find the proper stream of color, it will take you anywhere you want to go in the world. At least that's the popular lore."

"It is true," Sellianda agreed. "Sometimes the path occurs naturally, without being summoned. To use the Path of the Rainbow when it appears naturally, you must know how to predict the place of its appearance. You must also be prepared to deal with the apparitions that infest it. But the elves have learned how to control the enchanted rainbow. They have the ability to command it to appear when and where they want, and to send travelers precisely to their destination, without concern for the monsters."

"I have heard there is a pot of gold at the end of the rainbow," Korinn remarked.

"An avaricious dwarvish fancy," Perrantin remarked. "Everyone knows that there are affectionate nymphs at the end of the rainbow."

"Then no wonder no one has ever found the end of the rainbow," Solveig said dryly. "No woman has ever looked for it. Only adolescent boys."

Sellianda smiled. "The elves also say that the rainbow brings babies when it isn't transporting elves."

"I've seen plenty of rainbows," Thelvyn said. "How do you know if you've found the enchanted one?"

"Because it won't be raining," Sellianda told him. "The Path of the Rainbow is a complex and powerful variation of a common dimensional door spell. What appears to be the rainbow is only the manifestation of the link between the two ends of the gate."

By late afternoon, they had reached the center of the valley and were nearing the three stone structures. They were passing through the middle of an actual elven town. The houses were much like the ones they had seen in the outer valley, some high in the trees, others on the ground. Standing by the doors of their homes or leaning out windows, elves stared as they passed. Thelvyn was certain they were all staring at him. He felt glad he would be leaving Alfheim soon. Korinn, of course, was equally certain that the elves were staring at him.

Two of the great stone buildings stood close together, in what appeared to be the center of town. The third was on a small wooded island a short distance away. The purpose of these buildings remained obscure, although they seemed to be palaces, mansions, or ever great schools or temples. They were large, with deep windows and heavy doors of dark timbers. Sellianda led the travelers through the elven town to a bridge of dark stone, which leapfrogged in a series of short arches to the island. The hooves of the horses rang on the stone with a dense metallic sound.

As they approached the island, Thelvyn saw that the third of the great stone structures was indeed a fortress guarding the only approach to the island. The last section of the bridge was a wooden-planked drawbridge. Doors of wood and iron secured the gatehouse. Their escort stayed behind at this point, but Sellianda led the travelers through the gate and on, beyond a dense, dark ring of woods to a grassy meadow. The most remarkable tree Thelvyn had ever seen stood in the center of the glade, taller than any other tree in Alfheim. Its dark green leaves had a silvery tint. He recognized this as one of the Trees of Life, the heart of each of the clans of the elves and the source of their magic.

"You will be traveling to Elvenhome, otherwise known as the Sylvan Realm," Sellianda explained as they rode across the glade. "When the way is open, you must pass through at once. Do not delay. The elves here can summon and direct the Path of the Rainbow, but they cannot hold it beyond a few moments after it appears. They must begin their work at once, even as we approach. We have been delayed, and night is at hand."

"It doesn't function at night?" Perrantin asked.

"I do not know," she admitted. "I was told only to have you here before nightfall. You will be passing many hundreds of miles into the western lands, where the sun might not yet have set."

"What do we do when we get there?" Thelvyn asked.

"You will see the mountains of the Hyborean Reaches

immediately to the northeast. Ride eastward to the mountains, then north. Within two or three days, one of the dragon clerics will meet you. Then you will be told what you must know."

She paused, as if considering her next words carefully. "Unfortunately you will find yourselves in the very heart of Elvenhome, and the elves there may not have been warned of your coming. They will not seem at all like the elves of Alfheim. They are an older, sterner, and more learned folk. The Alfheim elves have chosen to become a primitive woodland people. Perhaps too primitive, as odd as that might seem for me to say. The elves of Elvenhome are a race of warriors, wizards, and clerics. They belong to an older time. Your appearance on the Path of the Rainbow will have to be explained quickly."

"Then we should send Sir George through first," Solveig said.

Sellianda brought her horse next to Thelvyn's. "Like the elves here, the elves of Elvenhome are likely to wonder if you are one of the legendary half-elves. It might be to your advantage to allow them to believe that. Keep in mind that these elves live in a remote place, and they are not familiar with other races. They dislike dwarves no more than any other race."

Korinn looked undecided as to whether he was relieved or insulted.

Elven clerics waited at the edge of the great canopy of the Tree of Life. They appeared more like typical clerics than the simple, informal order to which Sellianda belonged. He was reminded of the clerics of Kagyar, imposing figures in dark robes decorated with elaborate symbols. The clerics were performing some complex spell or ceremony. They stood in a half-circle facing an elder of their order, who was turned toward the great tree, holding out a staff before him. These were not the followers of Terra but of the elven patron Ilsundal, who seemed to be taking his own hand in this matter.

"Wait here. Be ready," Sellianda told them.

They brought their horses to a stop several yards from the clerics. They made one last check of the leads of the packhorses, which would follow them through. Sellianda brought her horse up beside Thelvyn's, then reached out suddenly and took his hand.

"We will meet again," she told him, just as she had that night beside the pool.

"Is that a prophecy?" Thelvyn asked.

"No, but I expect it will be inevitable anyway," Sellianda replied. "Perhaps not for a long time, even several years, but we will meet again. When we do, we will have cause to discuss just how much we have in common."

Then, to his even greater surprise, she leaned forward and kissed him right on the mouth. He was so unprepared that he didn't even have the time to make a mess of it. He had been kissed before, but only by young girls of his village who had thought it extremely daring. This was different.

Then he thought about what she had said. She was an elf, and years meant little to her. But to Thelvyn, a few years could seem like forever.

In the next moment, a shaft of pale light seemed to leap down from the sky, becoming a translucent rainbow. The nearest end touched lightly to the ground before the Tree of Life, just beyond the clerics, while the other end of the rainbow disappeared beyond the horizon to the northwest. Sir George urged his horse forward without waiting to be told. He entered the shaft of the rainbow and appeared to be sucked inside. Then his form vanished up the length of the rainbow in a blur. Solveig followed next, leading one of the packhorses.

Remembering Sellianda's warning of the reception they were likely to receive on the other side, Thelvyn thought he should go through as soon as possible. Releasing Sellianda's hand, he gripped the lead of his packhorse firmly and nudged Cadence forward into the rainbow. For an instant, a maze of colored lights seemed to wash over him, and he felt a vague sense of being pulled forward. In the next instant, he felt himself gently dropped, although Cadence's stride continued unbroken and the packhorse was still behind them. But they were no longer on a grassy hill in the light of a fading day. Suddenly they were in a small forest clearing. The end of the rainbow reached down through tall, dark trees, and sunlight danced in widely scattered patches as a cool breeze stirred the leaves.

Realizing that his last two companions were still to follow, he urged Cadence forward to make room for them. Sir George and Solveig were already there, trying to look unthreatening and innocent as elves rushed out to confront them. They were so unprepared that their swords were not yet drawn and their bows unstrung. When Thelvyn peered into the shadows, he could see that a second Tree of Life stood just beside them, half hidden in the surrounding forest. Many buildings of dark stone were scattered in the forest around them, joined by paths of the same dark flagstones, which seemed to be locked in a hopeless battle with the spreading roots of the trees.

The elves appeared to be of a different breed than the frail, delicate elves of Alfheim. They were small, but heartier of build, almost stocky by elven standards, brown-skinned and black-haired. The gear of the soldiers was rather fanciful, in a way that appeared primitive. He was almost ready to question Sellianda's assertion that the elves of Alfheim were in fact a simpler and more primitive folk. But as she had predicted, the elves stopped short when they saw him, pointing and talking among themselves. They approached more slowly.

Thelvyn rode forward to join Sir George. "I wonder if I should talk to them. Sellianda warned me that, because of my appearance, they might believe I'm one of their legendary half-elves."

"There is no such thing," the old knight said, but he wasn't about to argue with their good fortune. "But it would be convenient for us if they do."

Not all the elves who hurried out to meet them were soldiers. Several were clerics. After a moment, an elf who appeared old even for one of his long-lived race approached, a tall, wizened cleric with a shaved head and peculiarly decorated robes. The other elves made way for him almost fearfully. Even though he was lean and frail-looking, he still had the appearance of someone who could be dangerous to refuse, as commanding as an elf lord and as cold as a powerful wizard, the very embodiment of all the frightening stories Thelvyn had ever heard about clerics. Despite the cleric's appearance, Thelvyn felt it was his part to face him, and it was important that he hold his own without any show of fear. The old cleric paused a moment when Perrantin and then Korinn appeared at the end of the rainbow. Then the rainbow faded.

"Father, do you understand my language?" Thelvyn asked. He wondered whether anyone here knew any eastern tongues, as isolated as these folk were.

"I understand you," the old cleric replied, his accent heavy and his wording uncertain. "I spent some time in the east when I was young. Are you by any chance a half-elf? I have always understood that half-elves were beings of legend."

"Some say that I am a half-elf," Thelvyn agreed, sensing a challenge. He spoke slowly and simply in order to be understood. "I have also been told that half-elves are only beings of legend. I cannot tell you the truth, for I don't know it myself."

"Then you are not of elven ancestry?"

Thelvyn dropped down from his saddle and stood tall above the old elf. "I don't know, although I seem to possess many elven traits. I was raised as an orphan. My mother came out of the wilderness of the mountains beyond Wendar, pursued by dragons. But she died when I was born, mortally wounded in her last battle, and I was raised among strangers."

"Perhaps legends are meant to remain legends," the cleric said, seemingly to himself. "I am Pardein, tender of the Tree of Life. You must be trusted by the elves of Alfheim, since only they could have commanded the Path of the Rainbow to appear for you. Even so, I must ask why you have come."

"We are on a quest," Thelvyn said. "The clerics of Alfheim have helped us to come into this land to seek the meaning of a Prophecy."

"And the nature of this Prophecy?" Pardein asked, interested in spite of his efforts to seem aloof.

"Have you heard of the dragon attacks in the eastern

lands?" Thelvyn asked. "Recently we discovered that I am
the object of a Prophecy that the rogue dragons fear. The
clerics of Alfheim helped me to discover that I can somehow divert the hostilities of the dragons. I came here to the
Hyborean Reaches to meet the dragon clerics, who can tell
me the meaning of the Prophecy and what I must do to fulfill it."

"There are a number of dragons in these mountains,"
Pardein said. "Most are gold dragons, who are wise and
gentle. I have been warned of your coming in a dream, and
I was instructed to assist you. What do you know of the
Immortals, lad?"

Thelvyn shook his head hopelessly. "I know nothing of
the Immortals beyond what is commonly known. For some
reason, they have chosen me, but I don't even know what
they want of me. I certainly don't know why."

The cleric seemed displeased, or at least disappointed.
"So the Immortals now hide themselves from their most
loyal servants to consort with bastard boys," he muttered
bitterly.

He turned abruptly, for the captain of the King's Guard
had arrived. A tense minute followed while the captain and
the older cleric argued in their own language. The captain
seemed to be making many loud demands, while Pardein
calmly refused him. Thelvyn realized that he and his companions were in a great deal of trouble if the animosity of the
elves for foreigners was so great that they would even consider disobeying the commands of their Immortals. The
cleric put an end to the discussion at last by pronouncing
some stern order. The captain was still unhappy with the
matter, but he was at least willing to discuss it reasonably.

At last Pardein returned to Thelvyn. "You will be taken
to the place where you will spend the night. In the morning, guides will take you into the mountains. My own
people will not lead you beyond our woods, but others will
be waiting for you."

Obviously the only thing that suited the elves was to put
their visitors somewhere where no one had to look at them,
then ignore them as much as possible. Since that seemed to
be the only available alternative, the companions didn't feel

inclined to complain. They were led to a single large room next to the stables, apparently an unused barracks with rough cots along the walls and a drafty fireplace. Their dinner was brought to them, and a troop of elven soldiers stood guard outside the door all that night. The only difference between this and being prisoners, Thelvyn suspected, was that they would be allowed to leave in the morning. At least he hoped they would.

"Are these people actually your relatives?" Korinn asked once they were shut inside the barracks.

Thelvyn frowned. "I certainly hope not."

"It seems to me the solution is to get one of the locals to fall in love with one of you," Sir George remarked as he began poking at his bed. "Now, if that captain were to go off into the woods with Solveig and come back without his boots, I might be able to get a good night's sleep."

Thelvyn was so embarrassed that he felt like hiding somewhere, but of course the elves would never have let him out the door. Until now, he hadn't considered what the others had inferred from the incident with the boots.

"You did well with that sour old elf today, lad," Sir George told him.

"Did I?" Thelvyn asked, quietly relieved. "I didn't mean to interfere in your business, but I sensed I had an advantage over him."

"Two or three advantages, I should say," Sir George replied. "First of all, that business about the half-elf left him uncertain. Also, his own patron had told him to treat you nicely whether he liked it or not. And like all senior clerics whose heads have grown too big for their hats, he wants to be invited along the path of Immortality himself. Did you hear that crack about how the Immortals are willing to play with you when they won't play with him?"

"I thought that was what he had in mind," Perrantin observed.

"He's probably been begging Ilsundal to sponsor him for the past four hundred years. I'm sometimes surprised the Immortals don't simply send a lightning bolt to strike down these boors, except that the stern and dogged types like him are useful at everyday business. Holding down the fort and all of that. When you have a special job needing to be done, then you contact a hero. Someone flexible, like Thelvyn here."

"The bastard boy," Thelvyn said bitterly.

"That was highly presumptuous of him," Sir George insisted. "Even the most noble of young princes can be an orphan. Why, between you, Solveig, and myself, most of us here are of uncertain origin. I don't know about Perry."

The mage looked up from a book he had pulled from his pack. "I had a perfectly ordinary, even happy childhood, thank you."

"Oh, you poor thing! You seem to have overcome it nicely," Sir George teased.

The elves knocked on the door at first light to bring them some breakfast and to tell them to prepare to leave. By the time they emerged from their room with their packs, their horses had been saddled and brought around for them. Not surprisingly, Pardein wasn't there to see them off, although the promised guide was waiting for them. As it turned out, their guide was a young centaur. From the very first, the centaur proved to be much more friendly and pleasant company than the elves.

"These forests belonged to us long before the elves came," explained Cerran, a strong stallion with white coat and hair, as they followed the trails through the deep woods. "At least the elves don't forget their gratitude. I suppose that we're their friends, as far as anyone is allowed to be. It's hard for anyone to be their friends when they don't even like themselves."

"It was good of you to agree to guide us," Thelvyn said.

"They didn't ask us. We are children of Terra. It was she who asked this of us, and we are happy to serve."

Sir George looked at him in surprise. "Are you a true centaur, or are you a chevall?"

Their guide seemed alarmed at the mention of that word, and he turned to face the old knight. "What do you know about chevalls?"

"I happen to be a mandrake myself," Sir George said, as if it were of no real importance. "I assumed that you knew. You must have smelled it on me."

"Our sense of smell is not as keen as usual in this form," Cerran said, still somewhat defensively, although his mood was improving rapidly. "By my reaction, you must have guessed my answer."

"Please don't be offended," Thelvyn began cautiously, "But what exactly is a chevall?"

"We are the guardians of the wild woods and of the horse-kin. We have been granted the ability to change form, either horse or centaur as the need arises. As children of Terra, we are defenders, like yourselves, chosen by our patron to serve a need."

Although their guide was indeed a chevall, there were tribes of real centaurs in the woods. Thelvyn would have liked to see these graceful and remarkable creatures. He had heard that young centaur fillies, like the males, didn't wear clothes. But legend has a way of being more interesting than truth. Cerran spoke of the centaurs when they camped that night. He explained that centaurs usually wore clothes on their human portions. The skin of their upper parts was as soft as any human's, and so they found it necessary to protect themselves from the cold and the sharp branches of trees.

They left the deep woods of the Sylvan Realm behind that first day, moving quickly into the foothills of the tall, rugged mountains beyond. There were no proper roads or paths leading into the mountains, for this was wild, uninhabited land. Only elves lived in this part of the world, and they journeyed into the mountains only rarely. But there were game trails, which often ran as straight and true as any path, and Cerran knew these well. The Hyborean Reach was a line of coastal mountains, towering peaks of gray stone, and deep, sheer valleys cut by rivers of ice. This was also a northern land. Spring was still early in this frigid land, even though it was approaching summer in the lands they had recently left behind. The higher places were still cold, especially at night.

They rode that first day among the low ridges and hills, camping that night in a shallow depression between a jumble of great boulders. The next morning Cerran led them northward. They learned from him that he had no specific destination. Instead, his instructions were to lead them in a certain direction. It was up to the dragon cleric to find them.

They traveled northward all that day and well into the next. Whenever they came to a high, open place, Thelvyn was able to see the Sylvan Realm far behind them and the glittering expanse of the sea westward beyond the mountains. On one particularly towering summit on the third day, he caught a glimpse of the coastal region, a narrow fringe of green between the skirt of the mountains and the sea. The great peaks ahead were becoming even higher and more rugged, cold and forbidding and snow-covered. Later that same afternoon, just as they were making their way slowly up a rising path, Thelvyn observed a dark winged form approaching steadily from far behind them, soaring back and forth between the ridges and valleys as if casting about for something.

"Company," he warned the others.

They all stopped and looked back, watching apprehensively as the dragon came slowly nearer. They were expecting a dragon, but they wanted to be sure it was the right one. Otherwise they needed to find a place to hide.

"Can you see it, lad?" Sir George asked.

"It's not like any dragon I've ever seen," Thelvyn said. "This one is leaner and more graceful than the red dragons. From what I can make out from here, the face is more slender and noble in appearance. The color is burnished gold, darker along the crest."

"That's a gold dragon, all right," the old knight said. "I guess we're about to be found. He should spot us any moment if you can see him that clearly."

Indeed the dragon did seem to see them almost at that precise moment. Leaving off his gliding search, he flew directly toward them with long, powerful sweeps of his wings. He was nearly upon them within a minute.

"Did I say 'him'?" Sir George asked. "That lovely lady is a female gold dragon."

CHAPTER NINETEEN

The gold dragon circled them twice, once making a wide sweep to take a good look at their company. They could see her clearly as she turned her head slowly to stare down at them. Then she made a tight circle, although she veered away abruptly when she saw that she was unsettling the horses. Now that she was satisfied that she had found the ones she had been searching for, she withdrew a short distance. Circling wide one last time, she came around to land lightly at the top of the rise before them, on the crest of a steep hill carpeted with pale, dry grass that rippled in waves under the powerful strokes of her wings. She turned so that she faced the travelers, then folded her wings and sat back on her powerful haunches.

Thelvyn could see her clearly now, and he felt there could never be a more noble or magnificent creature in all the world. Her face, neck, and body were reminiscent of a horse, a sleek and powerful thoroughbred. Her wings were hinged before her forelegs, giving her breast the appearance of being thrust forward proudly, and her chest was especially deep and full. Her back was long and her waist narrow, but her haunches were wide. Her hind legs were particularly long and powerful, to help thrust her into the sky, and her tail was a long, sinuous whip that she held aloft when she walked.

Her most striking feature was her face. She held her neck in a graceful S-shaped curve above her deep, full chest. Her slender muzzle dipped slightly so that she could peer regally at them above it. Her large eyes were as blue as a clear winter sky, almond shaped and accented by an expressive brow that gave her a very intense, intelligent countenance. A long, full crest of backswept armor plates or frills rose like a stiff mane along the back of her head and neck, beginning between her two slender horns.

"I'll stay with your horses," Cerran offered. "They won't willingly approach a dragon."

That reminded Thelvyn of his duty. This was his Prophecy, and the time had come for him to take charge of their quest. The dragon had come to speak with him. He dropped down from his saddle and released the reins, knowing both Cadence and the packhorse he had been leading would stay with the chevall. Then he followed the path up the steep slope.

As he approached, the dragon lowered herself until she was lying full-length upon the grassy hilltop. With her neck bent back, she looked down at him as he stood several yards before her. Thelvyn had always heard dragons described as great reptiles, yet her appearance was more feral than saurian. Her mouth wasn't split all the way back to the ears as a snake's or lizard's mouth. Instead, she had rounded equine cheeks and lips well formed for speaking. She also had long, mobile ears just behind her horns, which tracked around to face him when he moved.

"You are the one they call Thelvyn Fox Eyes?" she asked. Her voice had an almost hollow sound to it, but it was definitely female and not especially deep.

"I am," he answered, drawing back. He had never before been so close to a dragon, and he found it daunting.

"I have been sent to you," she said. "I am Kharendaen,

senior cleric of the Great One, Lord of Dragons."

"Can you tell me what I must know?" Thelvyn asked.

"I will," she said. "But I would prefer to speak of it tonight. Time is short, for soon the rogue dragons will begin to press their attacks deep into the inhabited lands. Every day, indeed every hour, is precious now. We must continue on while there is still daylight."

His own part done, the chevall bade them farewell and left them. The last they saw of him, he had taken the full form of a horse and was running back down the trail toward home. One at a time, Thelvyn's companions led their horses up the rise, and Kharendaen inspected them, being careful to keep some distance away from them. When they were ready to travel on again, she took to the sky, soaring and circling above them or along the trail just ahead, scouting the best way to proceed.

Thelvyn watched her admiringly. He wondered what it would like to be a dragon. She made flight seem so effortless and delightful, riding the winds with slow, stately grace through the ridges and valleys. He had been enamored of dragons since the first time he had seen them moving boldly through the sky above the Highlands, but this graceful lady was an aristocrat compared to the red dragons, with their harsh features and heavy armor.

They rode another two hours before nightfall. Kharendaen found them a camp deep among the rocks where they could have some shelter from the cold night wind, then disappeared into the gathering darkness. They had only just settled the horses for the night and were preparing their camp when she returned, bearing the body of a small deer. She had brought her own dinner to be dressed and cooked. She rose into the night once again and returned soon with enough wood for a large fire.

Kharendaen explained that she had had a long flight from a distant land to meet them here, and she was quite hungry. Thelvyn was afraid he wouldn't get her to speak until after dinner, but Solveig and Korinn offered to prepare the fire and cook dinner.

The dragon settled herself in an open area off to one side of the camp.

"You have many questions, and you seek answers," she began. "Yet I cannot answer you unless I speak first about the dragons, for there is much you must first understand. Since the fall of ancient Blackmoor, the Great One has sought to give the dragons a nation of their own, one founded not in territory but in unity. For if the dragons are unified, then they can defend themselves against others while controlling their own rogues, thereby establishing peace and respect with other races.

"But the Nation of Dragons remains fragmented. Others look upon dragons as a single race of many variations. From the point of view of the dragons, they are a collection of many races, the gold dragons as different from red or green dragons as elves from orcs. But orcs and elves do not try to live together, while the dragons are bound together by the commonality of their ancient origins. The only element of unity for many centuries has been the Parliament of Dragons, under the guidance of the Great One."

"And that is the source of the unrest among the dragons?" Sir George asked. "We were told that the attacks are being made by rogue dragons, young red and greens, which we have observed for ourselves. What we could never figure out is why they have been attacking. That is to say, whether they expected to profit by their attacks or if we've simply been witnessing the outward effects of some greater conflict between dragons."

"And you reasoned that if you could discover that, you might be able to bring the attacks to an end," Kharendaen concluded. "Commendable, but misguided. The dragons cannot restore order among themselves. An outsider could hardly manage it for them."

"But the situation can't be hopeless, or there would be no Prophecy," Thelvyn said.

"The Prophecy is part of the problem," she told him. "On the surface, the Prophecy seems redundant. It exists to solve a problem that was created by its very existence. It all began nearly twenty years ago, when the Great One withdrew from the world without warning and has not returned. Since that time, the Parliament has been struggling to maintain unity in the Great One's absence. The dragons have no way of knowing if he is gone forever, or if he means to return. Uncertain whether the Great One will ever return to guide them, the dragons must now be responsible for their own fate, and there is much debate over what part they wish to play. All dragons think fondly of their legendary past, when they were masters of the world, before and even extending beyond the coming of men. Many dragons, especially the chaotic ones, believe they should reassert their position as masters of the world."

"The rogues?" Thelvyn asked.

"The rogue dragons are like children, play-acting to promote policies they wish their elders to adopt," Kharendaen said scornfully. "You have doubtless noticed that only young dragons have taken part in these attacks."

"In fact, I had," Sir George agreed.

"And yet their actions may make true war inevitable," she admitted. "As I have said, this situation has been complicated more by the Prophecy of the return of the Dragonlord, the most feared figure in dragon lore. Long ago, the men of Blackmoor employed their most powerful arcane skills to create armor and weapons capable of turning any physical or magical attack the dragons could muster. It could only be used by the Dragonlord, a wizard-warrior of almost Immortal status. The Dragonlord led the men of Blackmoor in a great war that subdued and almost destroyed the dragons. Needless to say, the dragons fear the return of the Dragonlord. The Prophecy states that the time is now at hand."

"Oh, my," Sir George said. "And I think I can guess who that happens to be."

Thelvyn swallowed, wondering why he wasn't more dismayed. He had suspected it had to come to something like this. There had to be some reason for dragons to fear him. He was only just beginning to discover why.

"There is much that I cannot explain to you even yet, for I am forbidden to answer all but certain questions," Kharendaen continued. "The dragon clerics have learned that the Great One has only withdrawn for a time, but we are sworn to secrecy. Even we do not know why. But we have been instructed to watch for the Dragonlord and to assist him in preventing the dragons from going to war. Even we clerics are not entirely pleased with the matter; we certainly do not want to see the Dragonlord turn on the dragons as before. Only our trust in the Great One forces many of us to obey. I have been sent to you because I accept the logic of this. If the dragons allow themselves to go to war, another age of the world may pass before they can ever again hope to be trusted."

"You should have no fear," Thelvyn told Kharendaen. "I am more interested in protecting the dragons than destroying them, even if I must use the power of the Dragonlord to accomplish this goal."

"I have never feared that," she told him. "I know who you are. In that knowledge, I understand and trust your motives."

"Then you can tell me who I am," Thelvyn said with growing excitement. "Or is that something you are forbidden to say?"

"I fear that it is," Kharendaen said sadly, seeming to honestly regret she could not help him. "You must not know the secret of your past until your duty as Dragonlord is at an end, for knowledge of your race and its long history would influence your decisions. The actions you take must be decided entirely upon the needs of the present, in the pursuit of the greatest peace and fairness you can achieve, uninfluenced by the ghosts of the past."

Thelvyn frowned. "I suppose there is some logic in that. But what can you tell me? Do you know which of the Immortals I serve as a cleric?"

"No, I cannot say," she insisted. "The Immortals are jealous of how much information they impart, for fear that their enemies might learn their secrets and their plans. I know more of this matter than anyone alive, but there is much that even I do not know."

"Then can you at least tell me where we are going?" he asked, no longer able to hide his impatience and frustration. "I doubt that we have been brought so far just to be able to have this little talk."

Kharendaen sighed and extended her neck to bring her head closer to him. "It is not my wish that our time together should begin this way. I do not desire to seem to be conspiring against you, to make you a mere tool of the Immortals. But there are certain things that I am sworn not to reveal by my duty to my order, and there are many more things that I do not know myself."

Thelvyn nodded, realizing that he shouldn' turn his frustration against her when they were both merely clerics acting out their assigned parts. "I understand."

"I am to lead you into the far north," she explained. "In perhaps another day, we will come to the Citadel of the Ancients, which is also known as Dragonwatch Keep. This is where the armor and weapons of the Dragonlord have awaited your coming for nearly four thousand years. Dragonwatch Keep is the last of the hidden fortresses of Blackmoor."

It seemed to Thelvyn a curious irony that the name of Blackmoor had come back to haunt him once again. He had always suspected that he might be a descendant of the race of ancient Blackmoor, and now he wondered if this was proof of his suspicions. There would be no one better suited to become the new Dragonlord than a descendant of that line, someone who possessed the same abilities. Kharendaen had said that the first Dragonlord had been a wizard-warrior of almost Immortal status. Thelvyn in no way considered himself worthy of such a claim, but he was both a magic-user and a cleric, a combination that seemed unprecedented among any of the modern races.

Once such a revelation would have been a matter of great delight to him. But he had since seen the results of the great destruction of the Blackmoor devices, and he understood how the Rain of Fire had nearly destroyed the entire world. All the races of the world had seen the lives of their people changed as a result of that terrible event. Being a descendant of Blackmoor was no longer a matter of pride to him, but disquiet and shame. He was resolved never again to speak of that matter, certainly not beyond his own trusted companions, and now he silently resolved to do his best to restore what honor he could to the name of Blackmoor.

When he heard of their destination, Perrantin was delighted almost beyond words. The artifacts of Blackmoor had been a special interest of his for a long time, and he prided himself upon being one of the few people in possession of an actual Blackmoor device. Now he was to be granted the rare privilege of seeing Dragonwatch Keep, the only known edifice of the Blackmoor era known to survive, and known only to the dragons at that. Thelvyn suspected that Sir George was also pleased with the way things were turning out, but the old knight seemed perfectly happy now to follow quietly, letting Thelvyn and the dragon take the lead. Solveig and Korinn looked as if things had gotten entirely too complicated for their comfort.

Kharendaen took to the sky early the next morning while the others were still packing, casting about quickly for the best route. Thelvyn watched her as she took to the air, and he had to revise his earlier opinion about flying being so graceful and effortless. The gold dragon used her strong hind legs to launch herself as high as she could, then she struggled with long, powerful sweeps of her wings until she gained speed. Only then did her flight begin to look graceful and effortless.

Now that he had time to consider it, he began to appreciate Kharendaen's own rather awkward position. He realized how ironic it was for a dragon to help restore the Dragonlord, the most ancient and hated enemy of dragons. However things turned out, she couldn't help but look like a traitor to her own kind. Her duty to her patron must surely be a lonely one just now, for it might not be able to protect her from the wrath of her own kind. In a curious way, Kherandaen had much in common with Thelvyn, both of them outcasts for the sake of a duty neither of them had asked for. The final irony was that Thelvyn had been hiding from dragons all his life, only to discover how much he had in common with Kharendaen.

She returned as they were nearly ready to leave, settling onto the rocks above them. She folded her wings and sighed heavily. "I have been to the Citadel of the Ancients and back again, but I fear that you will not arrive there before tomorrow morning."

"At least we know for certain where it is," Thelvyn said. "It will help greatly to have you to lead us."

"I can show you the quickest way there," Kharendaen offered.

Thelvyn had never thought of dragons as being built for walking. Their stance had always seemed to him rather awkward. What he soon discovered was that Kharendaen's long legs and catlike movements served her quite well on the ground. The dragon was also a good deal larger than the horses, so that the best pace the riders could set was rather leisurely for her. Certainly having a gold dragon prowling behind them was an incentive that kept the horses moving at a brisk pace.

Thelvyn was rather surprised at how well he was getting along with his new companion, recalling that dragons had been responsible for the death of his mother. Kharendaen was such a personable sort that he couldn't help liking her. Whatever personal consequences she might face with her own kind, she took her duty seriously, and her devotion to their quest was absolute. Sir George had always insisted that dragons were intelligent beings and not savage beasts, but Thelvyn hadn't completely accepted that until now. Perhaps he had been given a dragon companion deliberately, to teach him compassion.

Thelvyn had been hoping that Kharendaen had overestimated how long they would need to reach Dragonwatch Keep. After all, she had no familiarity with traveling such distances on the ground. But as they traveled on, he realized her estimate had been quite accurate. They turned eastward that morning to push deeper into the mountains, and the way became even steeper and more rugged. There was no hope of going anywhere in a straight line, so that they were constantly making their way into and out of valleys and along treacherous slopes. When they came to a high place, Kharendaen was able to point out their destination, a large, sturdy fortress clinging to a ledge on a distant peak. Besides the dragon, only Thelvyn was able to see it clearly, but he knew she was right. They wouldn't get there until the next day.

They camped that night at the edge of a wooded valley below the peak of Dragonwatch Keep, then began the ascent early the next morning. Kharendaen returned to the air at once, casting about to search for the easiest route for their horses. The peak was steep and rugged, and the climb was difficult. There were no roads, if there ever had been, not after thirty centuries. Only dragons had known about this place for all that time, and they had never needed a road. She soon despaired of searching for a way and began to suspect that she would simply have to take some of the members of their company up to the fortress herself, while others stayed below with the horses.

Still, simple logic argued that there must be some way up to the keep, since the ancients had included a stableyard off to one side of the castle. She spent some time searching along a rocky ledge just beyond the gate, and at last she discovered the opening of a tunnel in the deep shadows behind a great slab of rock at the back of the ledge. Although it was large enough to permit the passage of the horses, she didn't dare to force her way into that dark passage for fear of becoming trapped.

Her solution was to fly Thelvyn up to the ledge, riding at the base of her powerful neck where the plates of her crest were small enough for their sharp edges to be covered with blankets. He wasn't especially frightened of the prospect of flying, but forcing himself to come into such close contact with a dragon awakened in him a vague, nameless terror. He concealed his fear the best he could, not wishing to seem rude to one who was trying so hard to prove herself his trusted friend.

Once Thelvyn had been deposited on the ledge, he used a magical spell to command a light, slipped behind the stone, and began following the passage. He knew beyond question that this wasn't a natural passage, for the sides of the tunnel were smooth and the tunnel turned back on itself in precise steps, making for a smoother climb than any natural passage. Although he hurried, he didn't emerge on the lower slopes of the peak until nearly an hour later.

Kharendaen was the first to see him when he emerged from a great pile of massive boulders. She was able to lead the others to him by midday. They had to lead their horses through the passage, since the ceiling was too low for them to ride. Thelvyn led, while Perrantin took position near the middle of the group, both of them casting magical lights so the others could see. The climb up was more difficult than coming down, despite the gradualness of the slope. They reached the ledge outside the keep early that afternoon, only to find that Kharendaen had already opened the gate for them from the inside. They fed and tended their horses in the long-abandoned stables, then took time for a quick lunch before entering the fortress. Perrantin was so eager to get inside that he could hardly sit down for lunch, although Thelvyn was glad to have a brief time to prepare himself for whatever fate awaited him.

At first glance, Dragonwatch Keep seemed to be a large but fairly ordinary fortress, with the walls and high, slender towers rather elegantly constructed of large blocks of polished blue-white stone. While there were some facilities such as the stables for the convenience of visitors, it seemed clear that it had never been intended to house an actual garrison. In spite of the keep's tremendous age, and its vulnerability to the storms and winds and bitter cold of the northern mountains, it seemed relatively untouched by time.

"You say that the dragons have always known of this place," Perrantin said, turning to Kharendaen. "Do they know what it used to be?"

Kharendaen shook her head slowly. "The original name and purpose of the Citadel of the Ancients is unknown, but it seems to have been built by the wizards of Blackmoor to serve as a safe, remote place to keep some of their most powerful creations, things they probably did not dare to keep in inhabited regions. Since everything except the armor of the Dragonlord was removed, it is possible one was the very device that destroyed Blackmoor."

"But how could this place have survived the destruction of Blackmoor and the Rain of Fire, when nothing else in the world did?" the mage asked, insatiable in his curiosity.

"We do know something of that secret," she told him. "This citadel was originally protected by very powerful magic, the exact means long since forgotten. Perhaps it was magically shielded with impenetrable barriers."

When they were ready at last, they approached the great

main doors of the citadel cautiously, fearful not so much of danger but of the secrets hidden there. The two great halves of the double door were made of massive planks of wood, which amazingly showed no sign of decay after so much time. Kharendaen was able to open the doors easily enough, for the citadel had belonged to the clerics of the Great One for a very long time and they kept the key.

A wide foyer lay beyond the doors, and a flight of wide steps led into a central chamber in the shape of a vast octagon, rising by degrees to several levels above the foyer. Each level was ringed with a broad walkway or balcony bordered by a high stone rail, and each of the eight walls on each level of the octagon bore a door. Many of these doors stood open, revealing plain, windowless rooms beyond. Once the greatest devices and magical artifacts of ancient Blackmoor, the most valuable and the most deadly, had been safely sealed within these chambers, but each cell now stood empty, for the arsenals of the wizards of Blackmoor had been emptied for a war that had changed the shape of the world.

The companions were still staring in wonder when Kharendaen entered behind them. As large as the main doors of the citadel were, she was still forced to crouch low to pull herself inside, folding her great wings as tightly as she could and crawling on her belly to clear the top of the doorway.

"The chamber of the Dragonlord is the innermost room," she told them. "It's there on the lowest level, beyond the short passage at the very back. I won't be able to accompany you there, for only my head and neck will fit through the passage."

"Are there any traps?" Sir George asked her.

"I do not know," she admitted. "You must be careful."

"I suspected as much. Dragons would never have been able to get into that final chamber to find out," he said. "There is some virtue, I suppose, in being an experienced thief."

"Perhaps you'd better allow Thelvyn to go first," Kharendaen said. "The ancient traps would most likely be magical in nature, and he is expected."

Thelvyn wasn't entirely certain he was happy with that logic, but it seemed prudent. They descended the steps to the lower level and approached the passageway. Whatever means the ancients had employed to light their citadel still remained in effect. The blue-white stone itself seemed to cast a pale light, but the corridor to the inner chamber remained dark. Still, he could see well enough in the deep shadows to be aware of the massive wooden door that stood closed at the end of the corridor, although when he tried the latch, he discovered it was locked. He laid both hands on the center of the door to push, when suddenly the latch clicked and the door swung open. He was expected indeed.

The chamber beyond was merely a larger version of the others, a plain cell of stone, softly lit. Here at least were the first signs of decay, for tapestries that had once covered the stone of the walls and other objects that may have once been decorations or tokens lay in crumbled ruins on the floor. In the center of the room was a low circular wall of smooth, white stone, like the rim of a fountain or pool. This served as the foundation for a pillar of translucent crystal, which rose all the way to the ceiling of the chamber, the top held by an identical rim of stone. A dark form, like a tall man, stood in the center of the column, although the crystal was too opaque for them to see any true detail. Thelvyn approached the crystal slowly. The others remained just inside the door.

"The armor of the Dragonlord," Kharendaen said, her head filling the doorway. "You are meant to have it, although I cannot tell you how you are to get at it."

Thelvyn considered the problem for a brief moment, then turned back to the crystal column and stepped close enough to lay both his hands on its smooth, cold surface. The same trick had worked on the door, as if his touch made him known to the ancient spells laid upon this place. Again it was enough, and he drew back his hands when the crystal suddenly grew warm and began to glow with a soft light of pure white. In a matter of moments, the crystal melted away, evaporating into the very air without a trace.

The armor of the Dragonlord stood revealed before

them. The various sections were arranged on an upright rack so that, through the translucent crystal, it had seemed to take on a shape larger than life. The armor was massive plate of black metal, resistant to scratches and dents. Plate armor usually consisted of many small pieces that must be individually strapped on to the body of the wearer, but the armor of the Dragonlord was cleverly designed so that all the pieces were joined together into four large sections. The chestplate and both arms and shoulders were all permanently joined together into a single piece, while the entire lower section was also one piece, like a pair of trousers. These were worn with a full-sleeved jacket and trousers of silver metal mesh, too light and delicate to be considered mail. Even the boots were armored, the ankle pieces hinged to allow mobility.

The helmet seemed to stare down at them expectantly. It was constructed in the simple, stylized shape of a dragon's head with crystal eyeplates. A sword unlike any Thelvyn had ever seen stood in a separate rack in front of the armor. The blade wasn't especially long, but it was very wide, with a rounded hilt guard that would nearly enclose the hand of its bearer.

Thelvyn turned to Kharendaen. "What am I supposed to do now?"

"You must put it on," she replied.

They removed the pieces of armor from the rack and brought it out into central chamber, so that Kharendaen could get close enough to assist them. Thelvyn had to remove everything except his shirt and pants, since he could not wear anything too tight beneath the armor. He began by putting on the full-sleeved jacket and trousers of silver mesh, which proved to be deceptively light and supple, but tremendously strong.

The plate armor was also very light, even though it was rather thick. He suspected that similar armor of iron or steel would have weighed nearly as much as he did. Remembering the mail vest he had been given by the wizards in Braejr, he expected Dragonlord's armor to be cumbersome and restrictive, but that wasn't the case at all. He didn't have the absolute freedom of movement he would have had in regular clothes, but he could still move quite quickly and freely. The armor had been designed for someone his height but with a slightly larger frame. He expected he would fill out to fit the armor as he matured over the next couple of years. The boots of the armor had never been intended to wear over other shoes, and he was left to wonder what the first Dragonlord had done about that.

His first great surprise came when he put on the helmet. He had been afraid he wouldn't be able to breathe, since the helmet had a collar that closed over an inner collar attached to the chestplate. But once the helmet was set in place, he found that it supplied him with all the fresh, cool air he needed. Indeed, the entire suit kept him quite comfortable, whereas the leather and steel of most armor was rather stifling. He could also hear and be heard perfectly. Perrantin asked to look inside the helmet and concluded that magical devices set into the short, stylized muzzle of the dragon face provided fresh air.

"It's all quite marvelous," Thelvyn said. "I suppose I must look rather ridiculous with my head sticking out of this armor, but if you will excuse me for sounding like a pessimist, I'm still not sure how this makes me every dragon's worst fear. I get the impression that there must be something more it than meets the eye."

"Just so," Kharendaen agreed. "If the lore of the dragon clerics is accurate, then I can tell you about your armor. Needless to say, it is an absolute maze of special enchantments. First, once the armor is on, it does not have to be removed but, at the will of the wearer, may be teleported off and on again as needed. For the sake of your safety, you should never remove the armor unless you are certain you are safe from unexpected danger. I suspect you mustn't wear anything that won't fit beneath the armor if you suddenly decide to teleport into it. You will have to keep your sword and your knife in straps on your saddle. And you certainly cannot wear those boots."

Sir George smiled wickedly. "You should have given your boots to the elf lady after all."

"But what am I supposed to do about shoes?" Thelvyn asked, confused.

"We will have to see about getting you a pair of those light, soft forest shoes like the elves wear," the knight replied. "Of course, we'll have to get some made to your size."

"Until then you'd best remain barefoot," Kharendaen added. "You can still wear your boots, but if you are in danger, you have to remove them. You should practice using the suit. Imagine that you want to teleport it off. I suspect that the enchantment functions something like a clerical spell."

Thelvyn held out his arms slightly and closed his eyes. The suit was gone almost at once. It happened much easier than he expected possible, and without any sudden flashes of light or other effects. It just simply disappeared. He willed it to return with the same ease, although he was surprised to discover that it came back with the helmet in place and the sword at the belt clip, when both had previously been lying on the floor beside him. It was all amazingly convenient.

"The defenses of the suit are built into the armor in the form of a series of invisible shields," the dragon continued. "These shields have the power to turn physical attacks, flames, or magical spells. The main shield is projected at will by holding up either arm as if you were holding a shield. The size of the invisible shield is controlled at will."

They experimented with that next. Thelvyn held up his arm and willed the shield into place. There was no indication of anything, although he thought he could sense the shield was in place. Korinn drew his battle-axe and made a poke at him, only to have even his light blow deflected forcefully aside. The shield not only blocked the blow but also absorbed most of the impact, so that Thelvyn hardly felt a thing, even when the dwarf swung at the shield as hard as he could.

"The shield is capable of deflecting a blow from a dragon, even the whip of his tail," Kharendaen explained. "The armor is also said to possess a body shield, responding either to the will of the wearer or acting of its own accord in response to a threat. This projects a shield of large size in the direction of danger, or even fully encases the wearer and anything he holds. Like the main shield, the body shield provides counterforce, and a rebound effect can then be used to push heavy objects away. In that way, the body shield can be used to greatly enhance the wearer's strength. You cannot actually lift a massive object such as a boulder, but you might be able to get beneath the object and use the shield to push it away."

Since the lore of the dragon clerics had been accurate so far, Thelvyn didn't question Kharendaen's words. Still, he wanted to test all the enchanted effects until he could instinctively trust the armor to do what it should. For the first time, he was beginning to feel encouraged about his ability to face the task he had been given.

"What about the sword?" he asked. "No matter how good my defenses, I cannot imagine an ordinary sword being very effective against a dragon."

"In the books of dragon lore, many colorful words were devoted to describe the bite of that sword," Kharendaen said. "The blade possesses many powerful enchantments of its own. It can be used normally or enhanced with a cutting force. The cutting force is either cold or hot, depending on the object to be cut. By aiming the blade at an object, the cold force can be projected at will in a sharp blast of striking force, as strong as the strike from a catapult. The hot force may also be projected, either as a brief strike of blistering heat or a sustained beam of less intensity, and with little or no striking force."

"Well, the wizards of Blackmoor certainly knew their business," Thelvyn said as he tried returning the sword to its clip. "We always knew that they could build some powerful devices. This one seems easy to control."

"That depends on the judgment of the Dragonlord," Kharendaen told him. "But that is why the Immortals chose you. They trust you."

CHAPTER TWENTY

Thelvyn awoke early the next morning at first light.
The realization that he was indeed the Dragonlord
seemed to have settled over him during the night,
accompanied by troubling dreams that he could
only half recall. He could remember only an overwhelming
sense of desperation, the pressing, life-or-death need to do
too much at once until the flood of trials and duties overwhelmed him. He remembered also the fear of failure, the
sense that his companions were not only watching him, but
also relying upon him to succeed.

He knew what it all meant. He was the Dragonlord, and
the time had come for him to do his duty.

He found his sword and slipped out of the large room off
the stables where they had spent the night. He stepped out
into the yard, where Kharendaen was curled up like an
immense cat in a corner to keep out of the wind. The great
bulk of Dragonwatch Keep loomed above him, the pale
stone of the upper turrets only now beginning to catch the
first pink glow of morning. He watched the dragon for a

moment while she slept, recalling that she had promised to help him work with the armor and learn its secrets.

He wondered where the armor was now. He hadn't been in the armor since the previous evening, and he was afraid he might have lost it during the night. He set aside his sword. Then, holding his breath, he willed himself into the armor. It failed to appear as it should have, and he tried to contain his panic while he struggled to will it to return. After several moments it was obvious that something was very wrong. Then he saw that Kharendaen had lifted her head to watch him.

"I suspect that the enchantments of the armor prevent it from appearing while you are wearing anything that will not fit inside," she told him. "If your boots were compressed within the boots of the suit, you might find yourself unable to walk."

"I guess I'll have to learn to be more careful," Thelvyn said.

He sat on the steps before the door of the citadel to remove his boots. The paving stones felt like ice after a cold night in the high mountains, but he had gone barefoot most of his life and he was used to it. When he tried to summon the armor again, it worked exactly as it should have. To prevent the same thing from happening again, he returned the boots to Solveig that same morning. He found himself wishing the first Dragonlord had left behind a book about all the problems that went with the job. As far as he knew, he was only the second person ever to wear the armor, and it had waited empty for a very long time.

He walked over to join Kharendaen. She extended her head unexpectedly and pushed her nose gently against his chest. Thelvyn leapt back instinctively, suddenly overtaken by a great and terrible fear. After the panic subsided, he was ashamed of himself, but Kharendaen seemed to understand.

"You have had reason to fear dragons all your life," she told him gently, withdrawing her head a short distance. "It is reasonable that you should have such a reaction. I will be more careful."

"I must learn to be more tolerant," he insisted, reaching

out to stroke her muzzle. She had been sent to serve him, but her devotion and affection were her own. He had never expected it from a dragon.

"I suspect no one ever asked you if you wanted to be the Dragonlord," she said.

"Do I have a choice? I thought that this was a matter of Prophecy."

"No. There was never any Prophecy," she told him. "You were chosen because you possess the necessary qualities. The rogue dragons discovered that even before you were born, and they sought to destroy you to prevent you from interfering. But there is no true Prophecy in the sense that your destiny is inevitable."

"But why was I chosen for someting that didn't occur for nearly seventeen years?" he asked. "Did the Immortals know the rogue dragons would begin attacking?"

"When the Great One withdrew from the world and left the dragons to fend for themselves, such events became almost certain. The dragons are trying to determine their role in the world, now that they are no longer content to keep themselves in hiding. Some wish to be conquerors and masters of other folk. Your task is to see that they do not prevail."

"Then there are dragons who desire a more lawful role?"

"Most do," she said. "The gold dragons and their allies believe that our best place is as a nation among many nations, and that our greatest power and security will come with honest respect. We are tired of being treated as beasts. Many of the wiser and more powerful reds and blacks agree. But violence and anarchy will likely prevail without the intervention of the Dragonlord. Those are the matters that you must face when you return to the east and assume the resonsibility of the new Dragonlord. Are you willing to accept that task?"

He considered only briefly. "I must. The matter is too important, and I feel that time is short. Who will do it if I don't?"

"I do not know," Kharendaen admitted. "But I will always be with you, as long as you wish and my duty allows."

"But what about you?" Thelvyn asked. "Won't the other dragons see you as a traitor for taking sides with the Dragonlord?"

"Perhaps at first, until the will of the Great One is seen," she said. "As you said yourself, the matter is too important. We are committed to a long and lonely task, and we have only each other."

"Then where do we begin? I need a great deal more practice before I'll feel ready to face a dragon."

"Just the same, we must start back to the Highlands this very morning," Kharendaen said. "Spring is advancing toward summer, and soon the rogue dragons will be turning their attention toward an all-out invasion of the Highlands. We must stop them. Even if we leave at once, we cannot expect to be there any sooner than two weeks from now. We must practice on the way."

Perrantin would have preferred at least another day to explore the keep, in spite of Kharendaen's assurance that the chambers were all empty. As he explained, the Citadel of the Ancients was an invaluable artifact of the age of Blackmoor. He was rather annoyed at being sworn to secrecy about its existence and location, but that secret belonged to the dragons, and he wasn't about to cross them. Sir George was undoubtedly of the same opinion as Perrantin, but he recognized the need for haste and didn't complain.

Their first day of travel brought them back down from the mountains of the Hyborean Reach to the very edge of the seemingly endless wilderness that lay beyond. The horses were better off here, for the constant climbing up and down steep slopes and walking on hard stone was beginning to take its toll on them. Sir George thought it best to stop a little early that evening. Kharendaen was pleased because it gave her some time to help Thelvyn experiment with the armor. She decided to get one of the most frightening tests out of the way at once. After she had had him make a final check of the fit of his gauntlets and helmet, she abruptly drew a deep breath and thrust forward her great head, bathing him in a blast of flames.

The image of Kharendaen, jaws agape and fangs the size

of small daggers coming at him, awakened a lifetime of terrified dreams. For a long time, he wouldn't tell her how close he had come to drawing upon the powerful weapons of the Dragonlord and attacking her. Aside from the fright, however, Thelvyn was unharmed and the armor wasn't even singed.

The next day led them into the wilderness itself, a great sea of forests and plains extending for hundreds of miles across the northlands. None of them knew quite what to expect. They had all heard vague rumors that this was a land of primitive folk, men and elves who lived mostly by hunting, but also of many strange, deadly monsters that haunted the dark woods. No one from the civilized lands ever came here, for there was simply no reason. There were no cities or towns, no trade nor any other lure. Even Kharendaen could tell them little of this land. The dragons seldom came here, and when they did, they remained aloft on their west to the Hyborean Reaches or the Endline Mountains farther south.

What Kharendaen did know was that this land wasn't safe for travelers, and trouble was certain to follow if they didn't take some very careful precautions. She knew Thelvyn could take care of himself, but there was too much danger of losing a horse, or one of the other members of the party being hurt in an attack. And so she stayed on the ground for almost the entire journey, following just behind the company unless she needed to scout ahead from the air. The very presence of a gold dragon was quite enough to convince most other creatures to keep their distance, and they weren't threatened during the entire trip. But the woods were still dark and hostile, and they all sensed that danger always lurked nearby. If Perrantin harbored any thoughts of returning to the Citadel of the Ancients, he was learning just how difficult that would be.

As seldom as he was allowed a chance to practice his command of the armor, Thelvyn still had some time to become used to it. Actually learning how to manipulate the various enchantments of the armor was simple enough, since so much of it took care of itself. The rest was only an extension of what Solveig had already taught him about fighting. He had never learned to fight with shields before, relying entirely upon his own speed, strength, and dexterity, so he had some trouble learning to block an attack rather than simply evading it. He also had trouble mastering the striking force of the sword, partly because the sword was large and heavy enough to give him trouble aiming steadily at a target.

His companions learned to keep their distance when he was using the enchantments of the sword. The striking force discharged with a great flash and snap of power, shrieking through the air until it exploded against the target. Even the cutting force was frightening, for the blade would generate enough heat to cut its way into solid stone. At such a time, Thelvyn needed the armor to protect him from the deadly heat.

But perhaps more than anything, he needed time to become used to being the Dragonlord. He had begun the initial journey to Torkyn Fall in the first cool days of spring, only slightly more than three months ago. At that time, he had been an apprentice adventurer making his first journey with his master, riding a horse for the first time and learning how to use a sword. Now he was the master of an ancient heritage, setting forth to tame an army of rogue dragons. He was glad he had never heard of the Dragonlord until he had met Kharendaen. No matter what a dread figure the Dragonlord was in draconic lore, he could face this matter without feeling the weight of history and legend. That helped to make it all less frightening, more a challenge to be faced for the sake of the excitement of the accomplishment.

Just the same, he knew he was running out of time.

His lessons continued to progress until Kharendaen was eventually making determined attacks against him as if she were doing all she could to actually hurt him. The armor protected him completely, but he wasn't able to press a counterattack for fear of hurting her. She insisted that he needn't worry about hurting her as long as he employed only a light charge of the sword's striking force, but he disliked using even that against her. The fact that he actually had to be careful not to harm a gold dragon seemed encouraging.

"As strange as it may seem, we need to have something very nasty attack us," Kharendaen observed one evening after they had made camp. "That seems to be the only way you will get proper fighting experience before you have to face a dragon."

"This land is full of nasty things, but they seem to be very careful about keeping their distance," Solveig said. "I can think of lots of times in my career when I would have been delighted to have the Dragonlord along to bash a few heads."

"Aren't we being a bit presumptuous?" Thelvyn asked. "It seems to me that my objective is to subdue dragons, not slay them. I would rather force the rogue dragons to listen to reason than beat them into submission."

"That is true," Kharendaen agreed. "The dragons will never be truly at peace unless they are content with their situation."

"Well, it seems to me that I can do that."

She glanced at Thelvyn fondly. "If you were to strike me between the eyes with the full force of that sword, I assure you that I would submit. It has the power to leave me half dizzy as it is."

Eventually they could see the mountains of the great Wendarian Range in the distance. Thelvyn had lived in the shadows of these mountains all his life, but he was seeing them from the north side for the first time. His eyes were sharp enough that he could also see dragons soaring and circling in the winds over the mountains. Kharendaen's sight was even sharper than his own, and for the rest of the day, she dared not take to the sky for fear of being seen. They were coming into the deep northern forests of western Wendar now, forests that were said to be inhabited by tribes of wild elves. The trees were taller and denser than in the wilderness beyond.

They decided not to try to cross over the width of the Wendarian Range from the north, where the mountains were many long, difficult miles across. The northwestern corner of the Highland was fenced on three sides by the Wendarian Range to the north and a long, narrow spur of the mountains that reached southward, then curved east yet again to divide the northern Highlands from the south. They elected to turn due south before they came to the mountains, staying on the western side of the narrow spur, within the woods and out of sight of ranging dragons. Then they planned to cross the relatively narrow band of mountains and approach the small village of Graez from the west. By following that plan, they would be in the heights for less than a day, and they were less likely to be seen.

Thelvyn watched the mountains closely during the two days they skirted the mountain spur. This was where the history of his life had begun, in those final hours before he had been born when his mother had fought dragons in the same pass they would soon be following. He wondered if she had in fact followed this very same path, staying in the cover of the forest before she had finally dared to make a hurried and ill-fated dash through the pass. He was relieved that he no longer saw dragons in the sky. If the dragons stayed to the north, then their chances of making a rush through the pass undiscovered would improve greatly.

When they camped that night in the woods below the pass, Kharendaen approached while the others were having their meal. She seemed unhappy, even apologetic. "I fear that I must leave you in the morning. My presence may betray you to the dragons. Nor can I be with you when you confront the dragons, for I need to protect my trust as a cleric of the Great One. I would surely be recognized. If I am seen taking your side before a truce can be arranged, the dragons may conclude that the Great One has betrayed them."

"I understand," Thelvyn assured her. "This matter isn't as simple as knocking a few heads together until they submit. But I have seen the fear that they have of the Dragonlord. Will they submit to me, or will their fear and fury drive them to fight to the death?"

"It is possible they will fight," she said. "You must approach this carefully. When you first meet a dragon, put on the armor of the Dragonlord and tell him that you wish to challenge their leader in combat, that you will fight him to submission but that you do not expect the same. That will be regarded as a gesture of trust on your part, and their leader will almost certainly accept and fight you according to draconic law.

"When their leader comes, you must fight him until he submits. Although I am not certain, I suspect that their leader is Jherdar, one of the speakers for the red dragons in Parliament. You must be sure that you do not kill him. If he submits, then you can dictate the terms by which all dragons must abide. If you kill him, it is possible that the others will abandon draconic law and attack you themselves, possibly all at once. Then you will have no choice but to keep slaying dragons until they are defeated."

"I will do as you say," Thelvyn agreed, swallowing nervously. The talk was reawakening old fears.

"Remember also that a dragon who has submitted to another in battle will regard that dragon as his liege," Kharendaen added. "If the battle is fought according to draconic law, then that right will also extend to you. This is important. Be prepared to remind him of that, in order to prove that you understand the rules."

"But why would I want to have the loyalty of a dragon who hates the sight of me?" Thelvyn asked.

"You don't, but it will be an important bargaining point in establishing a truce with the dragons. I will explain later, depending on how things turn out. Once your battle is done and he submits, I will be free to return to you."

"What if we're attacked first?"

"Then you will have to issue your challenge at once," Kharendaen explained. "It would be best if you confront the dragons in the time and place of your own choosing, which is why you should keep yourselves hidden until you are ready."

Kharendaen arose early and departed at first light, hoping to get well away from the area before she was seen. The red and green rogue dragons would find her presence here curious if not downright suspicious. The golds weren't the enemies of the rogues, for the dragons were not fighting among themselves, whatever their disagreement on matters of policy. Still, she thought it best not to complicate the situation by allowing herself to be seen. Thelvyn stood for a time to watch her as she flew away into the fading darkness, feeling curiously sad that she wouldn't be with him. A dragon made for a very reassuring friend. Such thoughts not only surprised him, but they also disturbed him deeply.

They had a little trouble finding their way up to the pass, for this was a rugged land, with no roads or trails to follow. By noon, they had reached the top of the pass and could see the familiar forests of the Highland frontier spread out before them. Thelvyn knew he could walk home by nightfall from this point. The old forester had brought him here from time to time, and he knew the place well. Now he needed to find a way to get the horses down through the boulders to the path only a couple of miles below.

That took some time, and they were forced to lead the horses almost the entire distance. Thelvyn had expected this, recalling that the slopes below the pass were steep and littered with loose stones and great piles of boulders that had crashed down from the heights. He regretted not having boots, but the risk that danger might suddenly be upon them was too great. Once he found the winding path leading down from the mines, they were able to ride the rest of the way.

He wished he had paid more attention when they were in the heights above the valley, for now he saw that the dragons had been here in force. Many of the sturdy farmhouses and barns and sheds had been shattered and burned. As they approached along the main road, they saw that the village itself had been ravaged. At least half the houses and shops were destroyed, reduced to burnt ruins and snapped timbers. Even the old log stockade around the village had been set to flames. Some of the damage looked quite recent. It had certainly occurred since the last rain, although none of it was still smoking.

Thelvyn stared at the ruins as they rode slowly past, looking to see which of the houses and shops had been destroyed. The goldsmith shop where he had once been apprenticed was gone, although Dal Ferstaan's foundry was still standing. The task of rebuilding or even clearing the wreckage had not yet begun, for there was no guarantee the attacks were at an end. The people of the village were too concerned with saving what they still had left, setting aside supplies in safe places, preparing troughs of water for any new fires, or removing fences, piles of firewood, or anything else that might spread the flames. Thelvyn didn't even dare to look ahead for fear that Sir George's comfortable home was gone.

As it happened, Sir George's house was still very much intact, although Mayor Aalsten and his wife had moved in after their own home had burned two weeks earlier. They offered to move out at once, but the old knight insisted that there was room enough for them all. Indeed, they would most likely be on their way again the next morning, or certainly by the day after. As much as Thelvyn dreaded his confrontation with the dragons, he was filled with a growing sense of urgency to fulfill his duty and put a stop to this destruction. He meant to continue on in the morning no matter what.

"The attacks have been getting particularly fierce," the mayor reported that night over dinner. "The word this morning is that dragons have been seen gathering in the heights around Nordeen and Linden. No one doubts that an actual invasion will come any day now. The archduke has seized command of the Highlands because the dukes refused to act together. They say he's leading the Highland armies and the wizards into the frontier even now."

"Does he have any hope of turning them back?" Sir George asked.

"Probably not," Aalsten admitted dejectedly. "They also say the wizards have spent the last year rummaging about for some way to fight the dragons with magic, but they don't seem to have found anything useful."

Perrantin and Korinn both made derisive noises at the mention of the fire wizards, who seemed likely to get exactly what they had coming.

"I'm surprised you came back just now, if you don't mind my saying so," the mayor continued. "When your business took you south, I expected you'd stay there until the trouble was over."

"As a matter of fact, we've been right in the middle of all the trouble," Sir George said. "Have the archduke's men or the wizards been poking about my place or asking about me?"

"No . . . I haven't noticed a thing," Aalsten replied, looking a little worried.

"I just wondered if they might want to check my credentials," he explained. "You see, we've been all over the place lately, and we've come back with a way to force the dragons to agree to a truce."

Of course, Sir George wasn't about to explain matters any more than he already had, and the mayor and his wife weren't inclined to ask. After they were gone, Thelvyn went to the bar and brought everyone his or her favorite drink, recalling what each preferred without needing to ask. It was almost like the old days . . . to everyone but Thelvyn. He was no longer the young man sitting at the edge listening to the seasoned adventurers.

"I suppose there's really no reason for any of you to go with me," he said, finding it difficult to speak so boldly even yet. "I'm grateful that you've been with me this far, but you can't help me fight the dragons, and none of you are getting paid for this."

"I was never in it for the pay," Korinn objected.

"And you need me along to help you with the politics," Sir George added. "Once you subdue a dragon, you still have to work out a truce. Do you really want to leave that to the archduke?"

Solveig glanced at the ceiling and sighed. "You'll need me to watch your back. I'd just lie awake nights worrying about you otherwise."

"Actually, my inclination is to go home," Perrantin added. "But I very much want to see the look on the faces of those sly wizards when we ride into the archduke's camp and show them the armor of the Dragonlord."

"Well, I must admit I want to have you all there," Thelvyn told them. "Especially since Kharendaen won't be there to help me understand the dragons."

"Keep in mind that she herself is a dragon," Solveig remarked. "I'm not saying you shouldn't trust her, but you must remember that she's a servant of the Great One, and neither she nor her master wants you to bring harm to their dragons. Perhaps you should worry more about your own safety and less about the safety of the dragon you'll be fighting."

"I found her advice to be excellent," Thelvyn insisted. "She only told me what I would have done myself. Sir George, did you think her advice made sense?"

"Actually I did, and I would follow it to the letter."

Solveig shrugged helplessly. "She just made me a little nervous. There were times when I thought that she was being a little too friendly."

"Dragons tend to be very affectionate with their friends," Sir George said. "No one knows that because no one has a dragon for a friend."

"You had your chance to be affectionate," Korinn remarked to Solveig in wicked innocence. "You just never learned how."

"I know the value of all of my friends," Thelvyn said, forestalling any arguments. "I know that we've come a long way, but I feel compelled to go on again in the morning. Is that possible?"

"I don't see any point in delaying," Sir George agreed. "If the dragons are about to move against the Highlands, we need to intercept them."

They all enjoyed their one night in a real bed . . . all except for Thelvyn, that is. The mayor and his wife were in one of the guest rooms, so Solveig had ended up in Thelvyn's bed and he in turn ended up on the sofa in the den. He might have been the Dragonlord, but he was still the youngest member of their party. They all awoke early the next morning and packed up to leave. At least their brief visit home had allowed them to replenish their stocks of certain essential supplies, mainly food for themselves and fodder for the horses. Thelvyn also packed a quick change of new clothes, keeping in mind that he would soon be keeping important company, and he wanted to look the part he was to play. Allthough he tried, he was unable to find shoes that would fit inside his armor.

Two days brought them at last to the north-central Highlands. All during their journey, they had seen signs of devastation similar to the destruction in Graez. Aalbansford had suffered even more. Fires had gotten out of hand there and taken out half the town, and the duke's castle was mostly in ruins. The farmholds in the surrounding lands had also suffered greatly and some of the livestock had escaped, but the spring crops were still in the ground. At least the Highlands wouldn't have to face the grim possibility of starvation in the year ahead.

Thelvyn hated to see the destruction, and he blamed himself. There had been too many delays along the way, too many days wasted in efforts that hadn't mattered. He knew his companions would have insisted that he had done all he could, and that so much of the time lost had been due to the secretiveness of the Immortals. But he couldn't help but think that if he had only been smarter about certain things, perhaps they could have prevented much of the damage they were now seeing.

When the company came over the top of a hill and saw the Flaemish army camped in a valley about a mile ahead of them, Thelvyn's first thought was to admire the archduke's courage in taking to the field with such a weak and pitiful force. He recalled from his time in Braejr that Jherridan Maarsten had impressed him as a devoted and reasonably honest man, possibly ruthless in the pursuit of what he believed was right and patriotic even to a fault. From the archduke's point of view, his duty required this of him. No matter how hopeless the situation, he had to defend his land the best he could.

The army had made its camp at the very edge of the high, steep hills at the point of the spur of mountains leading to the Eastern Reach. Thelvyn suspected that there could be no more than three or four thousand soldiers in all. That led him to wonder if the archduke's bid for power had been very effective. It could well be that the dukes were sending him only a portion of the forces he needed and holding the rest for themselves. They seemed a sad and rather impoverished lot, with only a few colorless tents and larger pavilions and a small string of supply wagons pulled off to one side. But they had drawn their battle line just below the hills, and the dragons had responded. Thelvyn could see at least forty dragons either sitting atop the high, steep hills above the camp or circling in the sky overhead.

Archduke Maarsten had chosen for his battleground a mile or so of open land between the forest and the hills. Catapults and giant crossbows had been brought into position at the edge of the woods, where the tall trees at their backs offered some protection against attacks from the sky. Soldiers had taken positions about the catapults. Their main weapons were longbows to use against flying dragons and long, sharp pikes, which would be most effective on the ground. The fire wizards had taken up positions where they could work whatever magic they possessed.

The intent of the archduke's army was to drive the dragons from the Highlands, but their first battle had immediately become a matter of desperate defense. The dragons seemed to be having sport with them, coming at them in small bands of two or three but never more than half a dozen. At intermittent intervals, the dragons would descend upon the defenders from above, diving in swiftly and then darting away again. Their strikes kept the army in a constant state of terror and disarray, and many of the catapults were smoldering in flames. Generally the dragons were doing little real damage, especially if this battle had been in progress since morning. Even so, it seemed doubtful that the archduke's army would survive the day.

"I would say the archduke's forces aren't in any position to turn down any help that might be offered to them," Sir George observed.

They stopped for a few minutes in the woods above the valley to prepare for their own part in this battle. Solveig and Korinn donned their armor and strapped on their weapons, while Sir George removed the hook from his left cuff to replace it with one of his more deadly attachments. Perrantin wasn't about to be left behind; he knew a spell or two even a dragon could respect. But Thelvyn knew deep down that the responsibility for fighting this battle would be his own. He delayed teleporting himself into the armor of the Dragonlord, wanting the dragons to have a chance to see who he was. He wore only his shirt and pants, leaving his weapons on his saddle, so that he could get himself into the armor instantly.

"Are you ready, lad?" Sir George asked.

"I'd better be," Thelvyn replied, trying not to sound as nervous as he felt. "The longer they fight, the harder it will be to bring them to terms."

"I didn't think the dragons were going to be left with much choice," Korinn observed.

"I wasn't thinking so much of the dragons," Thelvyn admitted. "There are harder heads involved."

They rode their horses directly across the glades and stands of light woods to the field of battle. The horses were already tired after a brisk morning on the road, and their riders were obliged kept them to an easy canter when they would rather have charged forth into battle. Dragons darted across the sky, making low, swift runs over the Highland army. For the first time, after many long weeks of furtive travel, the companions took no great notice of them. All except Thelvyn. Once again he was finding it difficult to deny his instinctive fear of dragons, a deep, unsettling terror that kept insisting he hide himself from his oldest enemies.

Soon they skirted the edge of the camp, which stood nearly deserted and oddly intact, as if the dragons were politely refraining from causing damage to the empty tents and the wagons of supplies. Only a handful of boys remained to stare at them as they rode past. They descended a long wooded slope to come up behind the ranks of the Highland army. Thelvyn released the clips on the hilt of his sword and replaced his helmet, expecting to ride directly through the archduke's lines into the open fields beyond. He thought it best to continue on to his confrontation with the dragons while he still commanded his courage and resolve.

They emerged from the woods to find themselves suddenly upon the very back of the ranks of Highland defenders. Soldiers and elven archers turned to stare in amazement at their unexpected arrival. Thelvyn didn't hesitate as he led the way, directing Cadence on through the lines of fighters into the open field beyond. His companions followed closely behind him, although he knew they couldn't remain with him for long. They lacked his enchanted protections and soon would have to retreat to safety, leaving him to face the dragons alone.

The Highland soldiers watched with great curiosity as the companions rode forth. They had no idea what was about to happen. The appearance of the remarkable band of foreigners was enough to tell them that something unexpected was at hand, and they paused to wait in expectant silence. The dragons stopped their own attacks, circling cautiously to watch or retreating to the steep hills beyond the field to the north. When the riders reached the center of the field, they stopped and Thelvyn dropped down from his saddle. He handed Cadence's reins to Solveig.

"Are you going to be all right, lad?" Sir George asked, looking concerned.

"Kharendaen said that if I don't let them get on top of me, I should be safe enough," Thelvyn replied.

"I suppose so," the old knight agreed dubiously. "I just don't like leaving you now, after I've brought you to this."

"Someone might have brought me to this, but I don't believe it was you," Thelvyn said. "I just want to be done with it. I think you should take everyone back now. I might be able to hold my own with the dragons, but I don't know if I can protect the rest of you."

Sir George looked back over his shoulder. "I suppose I should find the archduke and explain things before he does something stupid."

Sir George led the others back across the field to where the Highland defenders waited. Thelvyn looked back for a moment, watching the lines of soldiers and elven archers. He realized they had no idea what to expect, whether he was a young wizard who foolishly presumed he could fight dragons, or an omen to the dragons, or even a sacrifice. He hadn't realized until Sir George said it that Archduke Maarsten might attempt some action of his own, perhaps even a rescue, in response to Thelvyn's unexpected appearance. The last thing Thelvyn needed now would be for the archduke's forces to charge into the field of battle.

In a strange way, he knew that the dragons were fierce but relatively predictable; they would play the game according to their rules. The Flaem were likely to be the most difficult element to control. They were otherwise a quiet and practical folk, but matters of glory and conquest had a tendency to set them off. He would have to watch them to be certain they didn't get out of hand.

Of course, the dragons had also been watching very closely. More had gathered in the hills to the north, at least a hundred in all, staring and talking quietly among themselves. Thelvyn walked slowly out toward them, forcing them to recognize him. Kharendaen had assured him that he could count on their curiosity, but he thought they were taking a long time to make up their minds what to do. Soon a single dragon was dispatched to discover what this strange, solitary figure was up to.

Thelvyn waited as the young red dragon flew down from the hills, circled once, then descended sharply in a manner calculated to be intimidating. The hardest thing Thelvyn had ever done in his life was to stand there unflinching, barefoot, and weaponless, without the armor of the Dragonlord to protect him. Yet he knew that proving to the dragons that he possessed not only the power but the authority to deal with them was as important as anything he could accomplish that day. All he could hope was that he didn't show outward signs of fear.

The dragon slowed himself with powerful sweeps of his broad wings, the cool wind rushing outward in waves through the grass. He landed in the field less than two hundred yards away. When he took a close look at Thelvyn, he stopped short and stared, lifting his head in his surprise and terror.

"You!" he declared.

"I am called Thelvyn Fox Eyes," he declared boldly, trying hard to sound stern and wise. "Many years ago, the red dragons hounded my mother to her death. Now I have come to challenge the leader of your band. I charge you to tell him that I wish to face him in private combat, according to the terms of draconic law."

"You are a fool!" the dragon hissed.

"I think not," Thelvyn replied. "I know the meaning of your Prophecy. I have been to Dragonwatch Keep, and I am the new Dragonlord."

He lifted his arms and teleported his armor into place. He could have wished for a flash of light or a crack of thunder to emphasize the sudden transformation, but he hardly needed it. The dragon drew back fearfully, then turned and launched himself into the sky, hurrying back into the hills. The soldiers of the Highland army shouted their approval, encouraged to see a dragon retreat in fright even if they didn't understand why.

Thelvyn waited in the field for what seemed like a very long, lonely time. He had teleported back out of the armor so that the leader of the dragons would also be able to know him for who and what he was. The dragons could see him as clearly as he saw them, and he could tell that the news of who it was that confronted them had shaken them badly. Their fearsome attitude had weakened considerably in only a moment's time, and he wondered if their leader would even dare to face him. The irony of the situation didn't escape him, for the first and perhaps the most desperate battle to be fought that day was one of courage. The greatest irony of all was that Thelvyn didn't think he could have survived that test if he hadn't seen how much the dragons feared him in turn.

CHAPTER TWENTY-ONE

The dragons could see Thelvyn as clearly as he saw them, and he knew that the news of who confronted them had shaken them badly. They had been disheartened in only a moment's time, and he wondered whether their leader would answer his challenge or withdraw rather than face submission. Either one suited his own purposes, for Sir George insisted that their leader had to accept the challenge or the others would lose their will to fight. But Kharendaen had told him that the return of the Dragonlord made all such things unpredictable. They might decide to render him ineffective by ignoring him altogether, passing him by to continue their attacks on the army of the Highlands.

After several minutes, the largest of the red dragons flew slowly down from the hills, flanked by two other dragons. They circled the field and the army of the Highlands twice before they landed, facing Thelvyn from perhaps a hundred yards away. They were vast and threatening, their shoulders arched and their heads held low in threatening attitudes. Thelvyn had to swallow a rising sense of panic at finding three angry dragons facing him.

"I am Jherdar, lord of the red dragons," the leader declared. "You claim to be the Dragonlord, returned to this world after thousands of years. The dragons can accept no such claim unless it is proven in combat."

"I have given you my challenge," Thelvyn replied, forcing himself to answer boldly. "I will fight you and your two companions together, so that there can be no question of my claim. For my own part, this fight will not be to the death. I do not have to slay you to prove that I can defeat you, although I do not expect the same courtesy."

"And I cannot give it," Jherdar replied. "The Dragonlord is the greatest bane to all dragons there ever was, and I must slay you if I can."

"I'm not here to destroy or conquer the Nation of Dragons," Thelvyn said evenly. "I know I cannot expect you simply to accept my word. Therefore I must prove what I say by my deeds."

Jherdar lifted his head, almost in surprise. "What is it you want?"

"Only peace."

Thelvyn teleported into his armor while Jherdar was in a good position to see it. Then he drew the massive sword of the Dragonlord and saluted his adversaries. The enchanted armor of the Dragonlord eased his sense of vulnerability, making him more a match for the dragons confronting him. Jherdar seemed undecided for a moment as to whether some gesture of honor was now required on his own part. As desperate as Thelvyn felt, he could see that everything was going according to plan. If he was indeed in some way responsible for the fate of dragons, then he had to count on more than just their fear. He needed their respect and trust.

Jherdar spread his wings and launched himself into the sky, his two companions close behind him. Quickly Thelvyn weighed his strategy. Watching them, he became aware that dragons had an instinct for hunting in packs like wolves, circling their prey to wear it down, darting in to harass one at a time while the others held back, being careful not to tire themselves while never granting their enemy a moment of rest. And so they began their attack by circling him, not all together but separately, each of the three dragons moving in a different orbit and constantly varying their patterns.

With his vision restricted by the eyeplates of the helmet, Thelvyn couldn't keep track of them all. Suddenly he understood why Jherdar had wanted Thelvyn to fight him and his cohorts at the same time. They knew only too well his weakness, that the helmet greatly restricted his vision. Although the collar was hinged, enabling it to turn with his head, he still had to be looking almost straight at something to see it. The dragons would try to get behind him and dive at him while his attention was focused elsewhere. And while the armor of the Dragonlord was indeed invincible, Thelvyn was not. He could still be knocked around inside the suit soundly enough to be hurt badly, which was what the dragons were counting on.

Kharendaen had been able to tell him a good deal about his armor and sword, and now he wished he had thought to ask her if every dragon knew as much. The best he could do now was to keep the dragons from drawing their circles so tightly about him, giving himself more time if one of them made a run at him. He lifted the sword and began discharging bolts of force at the dragons, a moderately strong striking force with just enough heat to be uncomfortable against a dragon's armor. As before, holding the sword by the handle, even with both hands, was awkward, especially against a distant moving target.

His first shots missed entirely, although the dragons could both see and hear the bolts of force shriek past, and that alone was enough to keep them a little more cautious. Then he managed to catch one of the dragons in the wing, which he knew from past experience was the most likely place to hit a flying dragon and also the most painful. He was giving the bolts more power than he ever had in his practice with Kharendaen, so that the dragon yelped loudly in pain and nearly lost his balance.

But in concentrating on using the sword, Thelvyn had momentarily forgotten to watch his back, and he realized his mistake only when he felt a dragon's tail snap him squarely in the back. He was picked up by the blow and sent flying more than thirty yards over the grassy hills. It seemed to him that he was in the air an unbelievably long time, long enough to realize in a sudden flood of terror that people generally didn't survive the kind of fall he was about to take. In fact, he was just beginning to wonder why the strike of the dragon's tail hadn't killed him outright when he hit the ground and was sent tumbling end over end.

He finally came to a stop lying on his back, staring up at the sky. The first thing he realized was that he wasn't dead, in spite of all his expectations. In fact, he didn't even hurt all that much. Moving slowly and stiffly at first, he rolled over and began to pick himself up, his movement restricted more by the armor than from any pain. He had just learned something about the armor of the Dragonlord that he had not been able to test before. It had indeed taken care of him, in some way protecting him and making him nearly as invincible as the armor itself.

Then he saw that the dragon that had hit him was already on the ground, moving quickly toward him to finish him off. The young red dragon was surprised to see Thelvyn pick himself up. He paused a moment to appraise the situation before he lowered his head and renewed his charge. They were both aware that Thelvyn was suddenly without a weapon, which left the Dragonlord at a huge disadvantage. Thelvyn glanced about frantically, seeking the lost weapon. He finally saw it buried in the grass only a few yards away from where he stood.

A frantic race began, with the dragon desperate to get to him before he could reach the sword. His armor, for all its remarkable enchantments, didn't enhance his strength or speed. He moved at an awkward half-run under the weight of the suit, all the while able to see the dragon hurtling toward him at a swift, leaping gait like an immense cat. Thelvyn threw himself forward in desperation, diving at the sword. He felt the handle in his grasp and rolled over and came up on his knees, aiming the length of the blade directly at the head of the charging dragon.

The discharge, more powerful than he had intended, struck the dragon like a bolt of lightning squarely in the top of the head. At this range, he couldn't have missed. The dragon recoiled slightly, as if knocked physically backward by the force of the blow, then went limp in midstride and collapsed heavily to the ground. Thelvyn had to leap aside to avoid its great bulk, tripping in the process. He picked himself up quickly, having learned the lesson not to be caught off guard even for an instant.

The second young dragon was on the ground a short distance away, torn between the desire to press his attack and the urge to escape. Thelvyn realized that he had the advantage for the moment, and he decided to make best use of it. When the dragon spread his wings and gathered himself to spring into the sky, Thelvyn struck him once very hard in the haunch, then hit the dragon in his massive chest muscles to discourage him from taking flight. Afraid now and growing desperate, the dragon turned in a hopeless attempt to carry the attack to his enemy.

That was just what Thelvyn needed. When the dragon turned to face him, he took it out neatly with one sharp bolt to the middle of the head. He had remembered Kharendaen telling him that even a modest discharge right between her eyes left her feeling dizzy, so this was the trick he needed to take a dragon down in a hurry. The second dragon collapsed very heavily to lie limp and lifeless beside his fallen companion.

Thelvyn lowered the sword and took a deep breath, a gesture of relief. Defeating two dragons in battle in such short order had done much for his confidence, but he didn't forget that the largest and no doubt the most crafty of his opponents still remained. Once he caught his breath, he moved away into the open field as quickly as he could, not wanting the bodies of the two unconscious dragons to get in his way if he needed to move about in a hurry.

He stepped cautiously, careful to know where Jherdar was at all times. The older dragon was taking stock of the situation, circling slowly well out of the reach of the magic sword. He was watching and waiting, determined not to make the mistake of moving too hastily. Thelvyn knew he must be searching his long memory for a way to fight the power of the Dragonlord. Thelvyn remained concerned that the dragons might attack in force, recognizing that their best strategy against his sword lay in the brute force of overwhelming numbers. The scores of dragons in the hills to the north were still watching intently, but they seemed disinclined to take part in the battle themselves.

Jherdar continued his wide, slow circle, watching his enemy with a cold, calculating gaze. Thelvyn's sharp eyes could see him clearly. As each long moment went by, Thelvyn began to feel more and more afraid. They both faced with the same problem—how to meet an unapproachable enemy—but Thelvyn had to admit that the advantage was now with the dragon. As long as Jherdar remained out of his reach, he lacked the mobility to do anything about it. All he could do now was wait for the dragon to decide upon his own course of action and make the first move, and Thelvyn had to hope that he would be able to counter it.

Jherdar was a clever dragon, and he didn't need long to assess the situation. As remarkable as it seemed to a dragon, his ability to fly was an advantage now. If he came within range of Thelvyn's weapon flight, he made a very large and inviting target. Even his great size was against him in that respect. When Jherdar finally did make his move, Thelvyn had no idea what he had in mind. The red dragon widened his circle, climbing steadily higher and higher until he seemed distant even to Thelvyn's sharp eyes. He seemed almost to be soaring lazily, no longer concerned with the field of battle nearly two miles below.

Thelvyn hurried at once to the highest ground he could find, determined to watch the dragon's every move. Then he realized that he had made the mistake of assuming that the battle would remain a physical one, the natural weapons of the dragon against the sword and armor of the Dragonlord. But Jherdar was an older dragon, wise and learned, and also highly skilled in magic. Unable to find any other advantages, he turned now to his reserve of powerful spells. Suddenly the full, white clouds of the spring day began to expand visibly, reaching out to join into the vast, dark mass of a storm. The bright morning sun disappeared, and a cold, damp wind rushed through the grass.

Thelvyn realized his disadvantage immediately. He couldn't fight something he couldn't see. Jherdar would be able to rush under the cover of the clouds. The great storm continued to grow, expanding in a few brief minutes to fill nearly the entire sky, while lightning flashed deep within the dark clouds or leapt and raced along the underside of its seething mass. Then the storm began to descend, slowly settling until it lay almost upon the land. Thelvyn lost sight first of the dragons waiting in the hills to the north and then the Highland army behind him. Suddenly he began to feel very alone and frightened as darkness closed about him like his own growing sense of terror.

Then the first attack came, different and far more deadly than anything Thelvyn had expected. A searing white spear of lightning raked the hilltop about him until the bolt caught him directly in its deadly grip. The armor of the Dragonlord protected him even from that, but not completely against such a terrible destructive force. He was blinded by the flash, and the shock of some vague pain ripped through his body, while a vast weight was pressing him down. For a long moment, it was all he could do to remain standing and retain his hold on the sword while he struggled against his own rising panic.

Then the lightning passed, freeing him at last. He straightened stiffly and lifted the sword in both hands, certain he knew what to expect next. He turned rapidly, watching the black clouds that hung heavy and threatening just over his head. Suddenly he saw movement, a dark form hurtling through the mist of the clouds, and he desperately brought the sword around to discharge a bolt of power. Jherdar roared, more in fury than in pain, for the bolt was a fairly minor one. Even so, the dragon's scales deflected the worst of the attack, and the shields of

Thelvyn's armor protected him as the whiplike end of the dragon's tail snapped him across the shoulders, forcing him to his knees.

Thelvyn leapt up, turning quickly to watch the dark clouds, suspecting that Jherdar might double back, hoping to take him by surprise. The clouds were so thick overhead that the dragon could easily be upon him only moments after emerging from the darkness. What he didn't understand was how Jherdar was able to find his own way through that blinding mass. Jherdar couldn't be seeing him any sooner than he saw the dragon, and the black armor of the Dragonlord made him even more difficult to find.

Obviously Jherdar was employing magic to locate him in some way Thelvyn did not understand, but he knew of no way to track the dragon. The list of spells available to him was a distressingly short one, and he wasn't yet familiar enough with his unusual clerical powers to know whether they would do him any good. At the moment, he couldn't spare the time to test his clerical abilities, and his patron didn't seem inclined to help him anyway. He thought he was very much on his own, and for all he knew, the enchantments of his armor were so powerful that he didn't need to be concerned. Just the same, he was worried that if Jherdar was able to get him down, the dragon would be able to pull him out of his armor.

After a long moment, he saw movement, and he brought up the sword to loose a rapid scattering of bolts. Although he hadn't actually seen the dragon, the wind of his passage was swirling apart the clouds. One of the bolts flashed in the darkness, and the dragon roared again. Jherdar required no more encouragement to break off his attack and disappear back into the storm.

Again Thelvyn could only wait and watch. His fear and desperation was beginning to grow, slowly but insidiously, for he had no way of knowing whether his defense was truly effective or if he was just delaying the inevitable. He needed more time to learn to be the Dragonlord, time to use the enchantments of the armor more instinctively. And time to learn to command formidable magic, and to explore the tremendous powers of a cleric. It was suicide to be pitted against such a crafty old dragon in his first true battle, yet he had no choice.

As the time passed from long moments into endless minutes, he realized that Jherdar had broken off the attack to reevaluate his tactics. Thelvyn knew that when the battle resumed, it would begin again in some totally unexpected manner. At that moment, the lightning struck again, the weight of it forcing him down while the vague, tingling pain coursed through him. He struggled against it, knowing it wouldn't last, but fearful that Jherdar would be upon him before he could recover, moving through the dark clouds while he was blinded by the flash.

Then the lightning was gone, and Thelvyn fought against the pain coursing through his back and neck, knowing he couldn't take much more. He could see Jherdar moving beneath the clouds, circling rather than rushing directly toward him, and for a moment, that confused him. Then a tremendous impact struck him from behind, hurtling him to the ground with such force that his vision went momentarily dark and he had to struggle for breath. Even so, he recognized his mistake. He turned his head to see that one of Jherdar's cohorts looming over him, crushing him to the ground beneath one vast foreleg so forcefully that he wasn't able to recover his breath. The young dragon had awakened during the battle and crept up behind him in the darkness while Jherdar kept him distracted.

Thelvyn's desperation went beyond fear, and he acted without thought. The sword had been knocked from his hand and lay just beyond his reach. Almost by instinct, he willed himself to rise, putting the full strength of his back against the weight of the dragon. It was a hopeless task, except that the armor of the Dragonlord responded to his will. The tremendous force of its powerful enchantments came to bear even against the tremendous bulk of the red dragon, thrusting him suddenly backward. Sitting back on his haunches, the young dragon was nearly tossed onto his back and had to struggle for his balance.

That gave Thelvyn just enough time to fumble weakly

for the hilt of his sword. He forced himself to his knees, then lifted the heavy sword in a two-handed grip as he climbed hesitantly to his feet. The long blade glowed briefly, then discharged its bolt of power, striking the unlucky dragon between his eyes. The young dragon gasped and shook his head feebly. Then his strength failed, and he collapsed limply on top of Thelvyn, bearing him facedown to the ground.

Thelvyn struggled to free himself, but he couldn't get the repelling shields of his armor to bear while the dragon's massive breast lay across his legs and hips. He forced himself up slightly with his arms, then paused in renewed fear when he saw that Jherdar was now on the ground and bounding straight toward him. In a moment more, Jherdar would be upon him and the battle would be done. Thelvyn forgot his efforts to free himself and reached as far as he could with his left hand to take up the sword, still supporting himself awkwardly with his right arm. He could hardly steady the quivering blade in the difficult one-handed grip, and the muscles in his upper arm burned with fatigue as he held the weapon out before him.

Again the blade glowed and discharged, bolts of raw power shrieking through the damp air. The first two shots missed entirely, but the third caught Jherdar squarely in the chest. He drew himself up sharply, dazed by the pain, then roared a desperate challenge and gathered himself for a final leap. Thelvyn struck him again in the chest, just at the base of the neck. The blow robbed him of his breath. Jherdar closed his eyes and shook his head, obviously in pain and at the end of his strength, yet he remained standing by sheer force of will. Then Thelvyn hit him again, this time between the eyes with just enough force to bring him to the very edge of unconsciousness. Jherdar collapsed, too dazed and weak to continue the battle.

Satisfied that the red dragon would be down for at least a few moments, Thelvyn turned his attention to freeing himself. He could find no way to bring the power of the armor's repelling shields to bear against the young dragon's great bulk. By turning his boots well to one side, he was finally able to draw out first one leg, then the other. He rose slowly and painfully, feeling dizzy with exhaustion, but he collected his sword and walked over to where Jherdar lay. The dragon was still struggling to get his legs beneath him when Thelvyn arrived to stand before him, the sword aimed directly at his head.

Jherdar ceased his struggles to glare furiously, although he was shaking violently. Thelvyn thought at first that it must be from pain or perhaps rage, but then he realized that the dragon was terrified. The deep fear his race held for the Dragonlord possessed him now, face-to-face and helpless before the greatest and most terrible of all the rogue dragons there had ever been. That realization came as a shock to Thelvyn. The largest and most powerful of all the rogue dragons feared him as much as he feared dragons. He knew how it felt to shake with fear in the sight of an enemy he couldn't fight, and that awakened within him unexpected compassion. He lowered his sword.

Jherdar was taken by surprise. He had been certain the Dragonlord would slay him. He lowered his head and sighed. "I submit. Tell me what it is you wish of me."

"I wish to negotiate peace with the dragons," Thelvyn said. "I want an end to the attacks, not a surrender but a truce that both sides can trust."

Now that Jherdar was no longer able to control his spells, the storm was rapidly beginning to break up and drift away. The oppressive darkness began to lighten as the heavy clouds rose in the cool wind. Thelvyn returned his sword to its place at his belt and removed his helmet.

Jherdar had recovered enough to sit up on his haunches. "I can promise you only that I and those who obey my word will not continue our attacks. I cannot speak for all dragons."

"I have not asked that of you," Thelvyn answered. "What I do ask of you is that you should speak for me before the Parliament and ask them to send representatives who will negotiate with me."

"I cannot promise they will come," Jherdar told him. "The Nation of Dragons has not been at war, nor have they condoned our attacks. Therefore they may not see any need to negotiate with you."

"I think they will, when you tell them what it is I wish to negotiate. The dragons fear my return. I am prepared to make promises that I will never use the powers of the Dragonlord against the dragons without just cause, as long as the dragons are willing to make certain promises about their own conduct."

Jherdar considered that. "Perhaps they will be interested in talking to you after all. I confess that we did not want the Dragonlord to return, and we were prepared to prevent it at any cost. But you are here now, and it would be better to speak to you of truce than to fight you."

"The dragons will find that they do not have to find me as frightening as they believe," Thelvyn said. "Whatever may have happened long ago, I am not here to kill or conquer dragons."

"Then you trust me to deliver your message?" the dragon asked.

"If you give me your word, that is enough. A dragon's honor is said to be beyond question."

Jherdar was still rather displeased with his lot, and Thelvyn could appreciate his uncomfortable position. He wasn't one of the young rogues, but a mature dragon and a member of the Parliament of Dragons himself, and he had been leading the young red dragons in attacks upon other lands and races in defiance of the Parliament's own position. He was in trouble enough, and now he had to face the added embarrassment of having his schemes fall apart, being conquered in battle, and sent home as an errand boy for his new master. The only honor he had left was in his promise to the Dragonlord. He didn't like to be reminded of that, but he would keep his word.

Jherdar bore it all with reasonably good grace. As soon as he went to tend to the nearest of his fallen companions, the younger dragon began to stir, and he lifted his head, furrowing his brow in a way that suggested he had awakened to a nasty headache. Thelvyn was relieved to see that he hadn't killed the two young dragons. He hadn't been certain just how much damage he had done to them.

Thelvyn turned to join his own companions. The storm that the dragon had summoned was passing away over the fields and woods to the east, accompanied sheets of rain on distant hills and occasional cracks of distant thunder. As soon as he began to walk away, he teleported out of his armor, taking somewhat of a chance that Jherdar would fail to honor the truce and attack him from behind. His shirt was creased from being pressed inside the armor, and he had managed to work up a sweat in spite of the armor's best efforts to keep him cool. He didn't seem too much the worse for having been flipped across a field by a dragon's tail. All in all, his first day as Dragonlord had gone very well.

His companions had joined the army at the edge of the woods to clear the field for the battle, but now they returned. They hadn't allowed their fear or uncertainty to show before, but now they were obviously delighted and relieved to see him unharmed. Although Sir George never spoke of it, Thelvyn knew that the old knight, in his love and awe of dragons, was especially grateful that he had spared both the lives and the dignities of his adversaries.

"I wasn't sure what happened to you once that storm descended," Solveig declared. "We couldn't see a thing until the clouds began to lift."

"That big fellow was a fairly crafty old wizard in his own right," Perrantin said. "His magic shield seemed to have limited effect, although your shots managed to batter their way through. He tried to use a spell to dispel magic against you to no effect at all, but we knew beforehand that the enchantments of the armor are immune to most magic."

"I don't want to seem critical, lad, but why did you agree to take on all three of them at once?" Sir George asked. "Draconic law would have been on your side if you had refused to fight more than one at a time."

"I thought it was important to show that I could do it," Thelvyn explained. "The dragons wanted to find out whether or not I commanded the full powers of the Dragonlord. Kharendaen told me that dragons have to feel satisfied with something before they'll leave it alone. By taking out a senior red dragon and his bodyguards, I proved myself beyond question to all dragons."

"Oh, I'll agree that it was a clever move politically," Sir

George said. "It just worried me to see you try something like that."

Archduke Maarsten and his captains were approaching. Thelvyn teleported back into the armor of the Dragonlord to present himself in a more formal manner. He took Cadence's reins from Solveig and climbed into the saddle, although the horse complained of the added weight. If he were going to ride in armor much, he'd need a larger, stronger horse.

As the companions started back toward the Highland army, the ranks of soldiers gave a loud cheer. Although they still didn't comprehend what had happened, they could see that the dragons had been fought and defeated and that the threat of battle seemed to be over.

The archduke halted his horse and waited to welcome them. He wore the armor preferred by his people, a tight-fitting suit of sturdy leather, to which had been fixed a covering of small metal plates like the scales of a fish, golden in color and worn with a surcoat of red. With him, dressed in similar armor, stood the Knights of the Order of the Flame, the only order of knighthood in all the Highlands. Their thirty-six members represented the entire company.

"Your companions have told me as much of this matter as I need to know for now," Maarsten said. "I admit that I must defer to your leadership in this matter. I harbor no delusions that I would have won this day without you."

"The matter is settled as far as the Highlands are concerned," Thelvyn told him. "Jherdar has already given me his promise that the rogue dragons will stop their attacks. He will also summon representatives of the Parliament of Dragons to negotiate a formal truce with the Nation of Dragons. My recommendation is that we leave such matters to Sir George, since he knows them best."

"That will be satisfactory, I am sure," the archduke agreed. For the moment, he was pleased just to know that he would be going home alive.

Thelvyn paused a moment to look back, concerned for the two younger dragons he had defeated. Others had come down from the hills to assist them, and they were both sitting up at last, looking like two very unhappy lizards. They were all talking among themselves and looking toward the Highlands army. Thelvyn would have liked very much to be able to hear what they were saying.

"They don't much like it, do they?" Maarsten asked him privately, standing close at his side.

"They hadn't expected it," Thelvyn explained. "They knew I was out there somewhere, but they must have been hoping I wouldn't interfere in their plans. They thought today's battle would be nothing more than sport. They still need time to accept what's happened."

"Then you expect that they'll be in a better mood to talk to us in a day or two?" the archduke asked.

"They need time to accept the blow to their honor," Sir George interjected. "The only thing in the world a dragon values more than his honor is his life. As odd as it may seem, the ancient ties the dragons have to the Immortal Terra lead them to hold life sacred. A dragon's own life is the most sacred, the life of another dragon nearly as sacred, and the rest of us fall somewhere below that."

"Then by this truce, you mean a truce between the Dragonlord and the dragons. By inference, our own truce with the dragons would be redundant."

"You might put the matter of a formal truce to them if you want," Thelvyn said. "You can remain here or return to Braejr as you see fit. But I do ask that your army remain. I'd like to have the weight of an army behind me, if only for the sake of appearance."

*   *   *   *   *

The dragons remained in the hills and mountains to the north like an army gathered to strike, although they were scrupulous to stay out of the inhabited lower regions of the frontier. The only exception was that one or two would occasionally fly down slowly over the field of battle, watching the Flaemish army. They were careful not to fly over the camp itself. Their gestures weren't threatening. Thelvyn recalled that these rogues were younger dragons. He reasoned that they were only curious, mostly about him. He hadn't asked that the dragons remove themselves, thinking that they would be more inclined to accept the truce if he allowed them some concessions from the outset.

The representatives of the dragons arrived the next morning. Thelvyn suspected Kharendaen had something to do with their prompt arrival. Jherdar returned to the field beyond the Highland camp, true to his word, bringing with him a pair of gold dragons. Thelvyn went out to greet them, together with his companions and the archduke. Thelvyn teleported into the armor of the Dragonlord and waved so that the dragons could recognize him. The dragons had been making very slow, wide circles over the encampment, waiting for some sign. They saw him at once and began to drop down, making a final circle before they landed. As they approached, Thelvyn saw that the smaller of the two gold dragons was Kharendaen herself.

The largest of the gold dragons landed first, standing off to one side with his neck arched proudly as he stared down at the Dragonlord, waiting patiently for his companions to join him. Jherdar approached next, then Kharendaen. They all folded away their wings and sat back on their haunches, looking noble and calm. They had come to negotiate, not to submit.

"I am Marthaen, First Speaker of the Parliament of Dragons," the larger gold said, introducing himself. "This is my younger sister, Kharendaen, who is a cleric. You already know Jherdar, Speaker of the Red Dragons."

Thelvyn took a step forward. He would have preferred to leave all the talking to Sir George, but he knew that he must speak for himself. "I am Thelvyn Fox Eyes, and by the will of the Immortals, I am the new Dragonlord. My companions are Sir George Kirbey, formerly a knight of Darokin; Solveig White-Gold of the north; Korinn Bear Slayer; and Mage Perrantin of Darokin. And this is Archduke Jherridan Maarsten of the Highlands."

"Jherdar has chosen to take part in the unrest of the young red dragons and lead them in their raids upon your folk and others," Marthaen began at once. "That matter is entirely his own responsibility, and it seems to have been settled between you. They might have seemed to be acting on the part of the Nation of Dragons, but that was not so."

"I understand that," Thelvyn agreed. "I haven't asked you here to discuss the past, but the future. I'm willing to set aside all matters of the past if you will speak with me now."

Marthaen lowered his head, bringing it closer. "Jherdar has told us of your insistence that you are not here to kill or conquer dragons, and that you are willing to pledge peace to us if we will give a pledge of peace to you in turn."

"That is so." Thelvyn removed himself from the armor of the Dragonlord so that he would appear less threatening. "I've been told that there is unrest among the dragons, the cause being an uncertainty about the direction of the future for reasons that I will not divulge before strangers. The dragons must be free to shape their future as they see fit, but the Immortals have ordained that they shall not be conquerors. The return of the Dragonlord is not for the purpose of fighting or subduing dragons, but to insure that they will not pursue a violent path in the future."

"You know much of the wishes of the Immortals," Marthaen observed.

"I am a cleric as well as a wizard and a warrior," Thelvyn replied.

They spoke for some time, continuing on after the sun had set and night had fallen. Servants came from the camp to set out lamps and bring them food and drink. Whole elk had been spitted and cooked for the dragons. Sir George did most of the actual negotiation. Thelvyn and the archduke were both satisfied to leave that matter to him, since he was obviously a master of the art. Kharendaen and Jherdar had little to say. Marthaen was wise and cunning, as well as stern and commanding. Thelvyn suspected that was mostly a matter of his duty to his own kind, and that he was in truth a fair, even goodhearted dragon. The golds were said to be as kind as they could be fierce.

Despite the lengthy negotiations, the terms of the truce were in fact quite simple. The dragons swore not to make war as long as the Dragonlord did not make war against them. Both sides would abide by the terms but go their own separate ways. The War of the Dragonlord had been the most frightening and terrible event in all the entire history of the dragons, and they feared him almost beyond reason. The only promise that the dragons demanded was that the Dragonlord should stay completely out of their lives, their affairs, and their territories. At the same time, they also wanted the assurance of knowing where the Dragonlord was and what he was doing at all times. Thelvyn perceived that the dragons were too afraid of him to allow the matter to rest otherwise.

Marthaen's proposal to solve that problem was a simple one. Thelvyn had subdued Jherdar, and the red dragon was now his to command. If Thelvyn was willing, Kharendaen would remain in Jherdar's place to serve the Dragonlord. That suited both sides, since she would be able to represent the dragons as an informal ambassador, advisor, and observer, while Thelvyn would have a representative of the dragons he could trust.

"Then so be it," Marthaen concluded. "By the terms of the treaty, you may confront, subdue, or even destroy any rogue or renegade dragons, for they have foresworn draconic law and are not protected by the truce. But if you should ever make an unjust attack upon any dragon or dragon-kin, then Kharendaen's term of service to you is broken and she must report the transgression to her own kind. You must subsequently answer to the Parliament of Dragons and explain yourself, or we must hold that the terms of our truce have been broken."

"I agree," Thelvyn said.

"In accordance with the terms of truce, we will do our best to insure that any dragon who attacks those of other nations or races will be accountable to the Parliament. And unless that dragon had just cause, he will be punished. Know also that we are not responsible for the actions of renegade dragons, and we will not be held accountable for their transgressions, although we will help discourage the renegades. As First Speaker, I am empowered to agree to these terms on behalf of the Parliament of Dragons."

Thelvyn nodded. "I am satisfied."

Marthaen rose to leave. "Now I must consult with my

companions. We will speak again in the morning. At that time, Kharendaen will return to you to stay."

Marthaen left first, striding rapidly into the night before he spread his wings and launched into the sky. Kharendaen followed next. At the last moment, Jherdar hesitated and turned back to Thelvyn, dropping his head close so that they could speak privately. Thelvyn had to steady himself against an impulse to leap back.

"I want you to know one more thing," Jherdar said. "I did not have any part in the death of your mother. It was not done with my approval or knowledge. I do not know who was responsible."

"I understand," Thelvyn assured him. "I have said I am willing to set aside all matters of the past, including that."

He knew that Jherdar had spoken the truth, and he appreciated the fact that a dragon would trust him that much.

Early the next morning, Marthaen and Kharendaen came down to the woods near the encampment to speak with the Dragonlord alone. Thelvyn was privately amused to see the two together, since he had never expected that a brother and sister dragon could be so much alike. Marthaen was quite young for a dragon, especially for one of such authority, although he was two hundred years older than his sister. He was a scholar and a powerful wizard, much respected for his wisdom, and a very capable arbitrator, with an uncanny ability to make even the most fierce and hardheaded dragon listen to reason. Although he wasn't a cleric, he possessed the calm, patient wisdom and dedication of one.

"I am not afraid of you," Marthaen told him. "That is not the same as saying I believe that I could defeat you. I know better. But you are honest and fair, even quite wise, in spite of your lack of experience. You are charged with guarding what is best for all concerned, and I want what is best for the dragons. I know you have not come to destroy us, as did the first Dragonlord."

"I thought the first Dragonlord was created to defend other races against draconic aggression," Thelvyn said. "Legend has it that the dragons had decided to wage a war of conquest upon the world."

"In truth, I believe that the first War of the Dragonlord was mostly a matter of misunderstanding," Marthaen said. "The men of Blackmoor were arrogant; history agrees on that point. They believed that the world would be best served if all nations and races were gathered together into a single large nation, and they naturally believed that nation should be their own. The dragons wanted no part of such plans. They fought back and quite possibly found that they were stronger than they had expected.

"Thus the men of Blackmoor, frightened to discover that they couldn't defeat the dragons, created the Dragonlord. When the Dragonlord began defeating the dragons, they fought back even harder and more desperately than ever, fearing that the Dragonlord meant to destroy them utterly."

"But obviously the Dragonlord didn't destroy the dragons after all."

"No. The men of Blackmoor finally made peace with them," Marthaen said. "As a token of their goodwill, they gave the dragons their greatest treasure, the Collar of the Dragons, an artifact of tremendous magic and wondrous beauty. Perhaps the misunderstandings of the first War of the Dragonlord should serve as a lesson to both of us, so that we do not find ourselves having misunderstandings of our own."

He lifted his head, gazing for a moment toward the mountains to the north and the young dragons waiting there. "The dragons fear you terribly, and as First Speaker, I must give much thought to their fears. That is why our pledges of trust have been so important. I do not want to see the dragons, in their fear, decide that they must make war upon you before you make war on them. Such misunderstandings can only lead to disaster."

"Will the dragons believe my pledges of trust?" Thelvyn asked.

"They will, in time. Have you ever heard the saying that only a mad dragon knows how to lie? Dragons put a great deal of faith in the spoken word. I have accepted your pledge of trust, and that will mean a great deal to most dragons. They will also know that I have agreed to allow my own sister to remain in your service, a matter of great trust. You must be aware that Kharendaen is one of the most senior of all the clerics of the Great One. The dragons love her dearly."

"I will not betray your trust," Thelvyn insisted.

"I know that she was with you on the last part of your quest," Marthaen said. "She is very fond of you. If matters of political expediency allowed, I might also be tempted to call you my friend. If the Immortals have determined that there must be a Dragonlord, their choice was a good one."

Thelvyn hesitated in his reply, uncertain how to answer.

"A time of great change has come upon the race of dragons," Marthaen added. "I believe that matters have not ended with this event. We will meet again, and I can only hope that it will not be in war. Conflicts and misunderstandings may yet be unavoidable, in spite of our best efforts."

With those final words, Marthaen spread his wings and leapt into the morning sky. He veered north, heading into the mountains, where the dragons waited for him. Thelvyn was still watching him when Kharendaen bent her head around to rub her nose against his chest. He drew back in spite of himself.

"So that was why you wanted me to remind Jherdar of his debt to me," Thelvyn said. "So that you could take his place in my service."

"You are the Dragonlord," she told him. "You need a dragon, and I assumed that you would prefer one who is already your friend. It seemed a good way for me to remain in your company."

"So now I have my very own dragon," Thelvyn remarked. "I suppose now I'll have to get a job so I can afford to feed you."

In his heart, Thelvyn knew that he needed Kharandaen. She could provide him with both insight about the dragons and a quick means of communication with the Parliament of Dragons. Furthermore, she was a cleric, a link to the Immortals who had chosen him for his strange fate. She was his only guide in such matters.

But more than that, even though it was her duty to her Immortal that had brought her to him, she had proved her devotion as his friend and companion, and she did not hesitate to promise that she would stay at his side always. Thelvyn had his own companions, and they had been beside him all through his quest, but they had lives of their own. Soon they would be going their own separate ways. But in Kharendaen, he had a friend whose service to the Immortals was tied to his own, and he found that immensely reassuring.

Of course, Thelvyn could never forget his old friends. With that thought in mind, he decided to look for Sir George. The old knight was never hard to find. The companions had of course been sharing the same pavilion with him, since other accommodations were scarce. Thelvyn never went far without noticing Sir George or Korinn and Solveig keeping a watchful eye for his safety. As soon as Thelvyn started back to camp, he found Sir George waiting discreetly at the edge of the woods.

"I wasn't eavesdropping on you, lad," he said.

"I know better than to think so," Thelvyn assured him. "Frankly, since you are dragon-kin yourself, I was wondering what you think of how things turned out."

"You mean are the dragons being honest with you?" Sir George asked. "It's as Marthaen told you, only a mad dragon knows how to lie. I must admit I've wondered why Kharendaen seems to be trying so hard to be your friend, but the fact is that she's treating you as a dragon treats a friend. Most people don't know it, but dragons are a very affectionate lot. You might say that they tend to be boundless in all things, and that's especially true of their feelings. I think the reason you were chosen to be Dragonlord is that dragons seem to respect you. You've even won Jherdar's respect."

"I respect the rare gesture of trust he made last night," Thelvyn agreed. "However, what I was wondering is whether or not you might like to go home."

"Now?" Sir George asked. "No, I don't think so. After all we've been through, we want to see how things turn out for you. I know none of us went into this expecting to be paid. But the archduke seems to be in an enormously grateful mood, and I'm curious to see how far his gratitude might extend."

"Oh, really?" Thelvyn asked innocently. "I hadn't noticed."

"That's yet another reason you need me to stay."

The dragons left that morning. Marthaen himself led them away, a single gold dragon, larger than any of the others, flying in the lead. The others followed behind him in a broad column, nearly two hundred young red dragons in all. They came straight down from the hills to the north, then turned as they passed over the Highland encampment, gliding on vast wings as they circled back to head northeast toward the Eastern Reach. The sight of so many dragons passing overhead was indescribably majestic and beautiful. Everyone in camp stopped to stare in awe.

Now that truce had been declared and the dragons were gone from the Highlands, the army prepared to depart. The elves were eager to return to their woods in the south, and the Flaem needed to help repair the damage left by the dragons. The archduke was also anxious to return to Braejr, and he made plans to leave the army in the care of his captains while he rode south at once with members of his personal guard and, of course, the Dragonlord and his remarkable companions.

Although Thelvyn had never expected such a conclusion to his own affairs, he suddenly found that he was on his way to Braejr to become the archduke's captain and advisor. He got the impression that the archduke wanted him on hand as insurance against the dragons. The archduke's own fortunes had changed considerably in the past few weeks. The authority of the wizards had been considerably reduced because of their inability to do anything about the dragons, and the archduke had been able to gain full command of the realm after the dukes had been unable to work together to protect the Highlands. Maarsten needed to return to Braejr to consolidate his new power.

Thelvyn was to be given a fine home in Braejr, one with a large enclosed courtyard and a building where Kharendaen could stay, an abandoned mansion of a foreign merchant who had fled the Highlands when the dragons came. Thelvyn expected that Sir George would find some reason to move in with him.

All in all, things were happening a little too quickly for Thelvyn to digest. He hadn't had any time to consider his future beyond his confrontation with the dragons. He found it strange to think that, as recently as the end of winter, he had been a mere orphan lad in a remote Northland village, uncertain of his future and not entirely wanted by the people who had felt required to raise him. Since then he had become both a wizard and a cleric, not to mention a warrior of legend.

But through it all, he had never had the time to ask himself how he felt about it. Now that he did, he realized that he had faced the challenges he had been given and he had managed to bring everything to a successful conclusion. In addition, he had avoided having to hurt anyone too seriously in the process.

When he considered that, he decided that he felt good about how everything had turned out. That came as something of a surprise to him. He had always been a misfit, unwanted, hardly able to do anything right. Life had never before given him much opportunity to feel good about who or even what he was. Being a hero really didn't mean all that much to him. What he valued far more was the respect he was shown by his friends and companions.

Still, he wasn't entirely satisfied. He had met the spirit of his mother, but he still had no idea who she had been. His race remained a mystery to him, and he realized now how much he had been hoping that his quest would lead him to his true home. He was a powerful cleric belonging to no order but his own, serving a patron who protected him and guided him but denied him even the most basic reassurance. There was so much he wanted desperately to know, and he wondered if he ever would.

The morning after the dragons had departed, Kharendaen had a surprise waiting for Thelvyn. When he came out into the field beside the camp to join her, he saw that she was wearing a dragon saddle strapped to the base of her neck.

"Now you can ride me without fear of falling off or being poked by my crest plates," she explained. "I can take you anywhere in the Highlands in hours, or anywhere in this part of the world in a couple of days."

Thelvyn hesitated, recalling only too well the terror he had felt on his first ride. His fear wasn't so much of flying itself but of trusting himself so completely to a dragon. He felt ashamed for his inability to shed such an unreasonable fear, especially when he saw that Kharendaen was watching him closely.

"It is never easy to part with a deep fear," she told him. "Dragons have been the greatest single danger to you all your life. I understand."

"I don't like to admit that such an instinctive fear can rule my will and reason," he told her bitterly. "I have the power to command dragons, but I must learn how to command myself. So let's go for a ride."

Kharendaen crouched low to the ground, allowing Thelvyn to climb up into the saddle using one of the stirrups. The saddle rested over the short plates of her crest at the base of her neck, just above her wings. A wide skirt of hardened leather kept the plates of her armor completely covered. The seat was larger than that of a horse's saddle, complete with a curved backrest and straps to hold him in even if Kharendaen turned upside down.

"Would you feel more secure wearing your armor?" she asked. He was dressed, as always, in shirt and pants, barefoot and weaponless so that he could teleport into the armor in an instant if necessary. Sir George had warned him about assassins, and not necessarily dragons.

"I don't think so," Thelvyn replied. "I want to prove to myself that I can trust you. I can't hide behind the Dragonlord. You've never been afraid of me."

"Indeed I was, the first time you put on that armor," she told him, bending her head around to watch him with one huge eye.

Kharendaen spread her broad wings, then crouched low to launch herself into the air with her powerful hind legs. With a mighty leap, she rose into the bright morning sky.

She beat her wings in long, powerful sweeps to gain speed. Then, responding to a playful impulse, she made a slow, complete circle over the encampment. Many of the men of the Highlands below stopped in the middle of their morning chores to cheer and wave. Then she turned, banking sharply, and soared skyward.